# *The* KING'S TRAITOR

THE KINGFOUNTAIN SERIES

# BOOKS BY JEFF WHEELER

## The Kingfountain Series

*The Queen's Poisoner*
*The Thief's Daughter*
*The King's Traitor*

## The Covenant of Muirwood Trilogy

*The Lost Abbey* (novella)
*The Banished of Muirwood*
*The Ciphers of Muirwood*
*The Void of Muirwood*

## The Legends of Muirwood Trilogy

*The Wretched of Muirwood*
*The Blight of Muirwood*
*The Scourge of Muirwood*

## Whispers from Mirrowen Trilogy

*Fireblood*
*Dryad-Born*
*Poisonwell*

## Landmoor Series

*Landmoor*
*Silverkin*

# *The*
# KING'S
# TRAITOR

THE KINGFOUNTAIN SERIES

# JEFF WHEELER

Text copyright © 2016 Jeff Wheeler

Published by 47North, Seattle

www.apub.com

Amazon, the Amazon logo, and 47North are trademarks of Amazon.com, Inc., or its affiliates.

ISBN-13: 9781503937727
ISBN-10: 1503937720

Cover design by Shasti O'Leary-Soudant/SOS CREATIVE LLC

Printed in the United States of America

*In memory of Brigette Dawn*

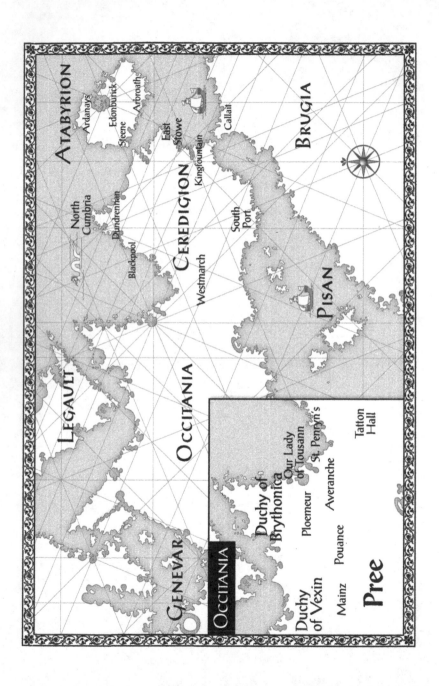

# REALMS & CHARACTERS

## MONARCHIES

**Ceredigion:** Severn (House of Argentine): usurped throne from his brother's sons and has defeated all attempts to break his grip on power. He is now the most powerful ruler of any realm.

**Brythonica:** Sinia (House of Montfort): succeeded her father as Duchess of Brythonica at age fifteen, and Lord Marshal Roux was named protector during her minority. At age twenty-one, she began ruling the duchy under her own authority. She is never seen outside her realm for risk of abduction and a forced marriage by power-hungry nobles throughout every realm. Allied with Ceredigion.

**Occitania:** Chatriyon VIII (House of Vertus): Occitania has been financially jeopardized following the battle of Averanche, after which, many of the noble families were ransomed. Further aggressions by Ceredigion and Brugia have forced the king to surrender major portions of the kingdom. In a state of enmity with Ceredigion for his marriage to Elyse Argentine, Severn's niece. They have three children, a son and two daughters.

**Atabyrion:** Iago IV (House of Llewellyn): Atabyrion is the chief ally of Ceredigion through a marriage alliance between Iago and Elysabeth Victoria Mortimer. The couple has two children, and the kingdom has prospered due to increased trade.

# LORDS OF CEREDIGION

**Owen Kiskaddon:** Duke of Westmarch, master of the Espion

**Stiev Horwath:** ailing Duke of North Cumbria

**Jack Paulen:** Duke of East Stowe

**Thomas Lovel:** Duke of Southport

**Lord Catsby:** chancellor of Ceredigion, king's new confidant

◆  ◆  ◆

Dear Owen,

*Thank you most ardently for news of my grandfather's seizure. The latest letter I had from him held no reference to any complaints, mild or serious. When I received word from you that he was dying, I persuaded my husband to come with me at once to Dundrennan. It grieves me that my children have not known their great-grandfather as I knew him. A visit home is long overdue. I pray it will not be awkward between us. I still consider you a dear friend and long for you to find happiness as well. Dear Owen, I hope you will come to Dundrennan. My grandfather looked to you as his own son.*

*Yours with loyalty,*
*Elysabeth Victoria Mortimer Llewellyn*
*Queen of Atabyrion*

◆  ◆  ◆

# CHAPTER ONE

## *The Winter of the North*

The mountain road leading north was coated in ice, and Owen Kiskaddon was cold and saddle-weary as he made his way to Dundrennan. He was used to the feeling. Stiev Horwath had finally begun to show his mortality over the previous few years, and Owen had inherited most of the unpleasant tasks that had once fallen on the grizzled duke of the North. More often than not, he was traveling—riding from one end of the kingdom to the other on behalf of his master, Severn Argentine, King of Ceredigion. But Owen was grateful for any excuse to stay away from court. Watching the king's degradation had soured his outlook on life and the world. More than once he had regretted his decision to support a king who eventually turned into the creature his enemies had once only feared him to be. Years before, he could have allied himself with Severn's enemies and deposed him. If he was going to do that now, he would have to do it himself.

Though Owen was twenty-four years old, he felt like an old man. His cares and responsibilities were an unshakable burden. He was sick at heart, sick in his soul, and the only force that kept him going was the slender hope of escaping the daily misery his life had become.

The thought of seeing Evie again—no, seeing *Elysabeth* again—both worried him and rekindled sparks of warmth inside his cold iron heart. He had not spoken to her once since the day they had said good-bye at the cistern in the king's palace seven years ago. He occasionally received letters from her, flowery prose talking about the wonders of Atabyrion and the antics of her two children. He never answered—he could not bring himself to—but he had finally written to tell her of her grandfather's failing health. He owed her that much, a chance to see her grandfather before he passed. Besides, Owen felt a debt of duty and gratitude to Duke Horwath, enough for him to summon the courage to face the girl he had loved and lost. That she was happy in her marriage to Iago made it worse somehow.

The trees opened up to the grand vista of Dundrennan, and Owen reined in his horse so he could take in the view. The mountain valley was thick with snow-capped peaks and gigantic avalanching waterfalls that roared off the jagged faces of cliffs. The scene never failed to fill him with wonder, but this time it was bittersweet. *She* would be there, and he could not look at nature's incredible display without summoning memories of walking along those cliffs as a boy when he was a ward of the old duke, hand in hand with his former love, the duke's granddaughter.

"Impressive, my lord," said one of the knights who was part of Owen's escort.

He kept his expression neutral and only nodded in agreement. Within the hour, they were dislodging chunks of ice and snow on the bridge to the city, watching the banners of the proud Pierced Lion, the sigil of the Horwath line, flutter in the gentle breeze. The courtyard teemed with visitors who had come to pay homage to the beloved duke of the North.

After dismounting, Owen handed the reins to a servant and took a deep breath, preparing for the whirlwind of emotions about to be unleashed inside him. More than anything else, he wanted to curl up on a pallet in the stables and hide from everyone. But he had made this pilgrimage for many reasons that he could no longer avoid. He was a little surprised that Elysabeth had not met him in the bailey in a rush of words and enthusiasm. Of course, her *husband* would not have approved of that.

As he entered the vast castle, hand on the hilt of his sword, he thought briefly of the scabbard belted to his waist and how he had discovered it in the palace cistern at Kingfountain. The treasures hidden in the cistern waters could only be seen or touched by the Fountain-blessed. It was as if they existed in another realm until claimed by those who had been bequeathed that right by the magic of the realm—the Fountain. He had taken other items from the cistern over the years. A brooch that he always wore fastened to his cloak. A dagger he had fancied, with the symbol of the drowned kingdom of Leoneyis on the guard. There was even a chain hauberk, completely rust free, which he'd found in a chest that had been submerged for centuries. He wiped his mouth, feeling the bristles across his chin. He rarely shaved now, finding it more bother than it was worth. He wasn't trying to impress anyone anyway, least of all the Mortimer girl.

He was greeted by the duke's steward, the son of the man who had served Horwath for so many years. His name was Johns. "Lord Owen, I bid you welcome in your return to Dundrennan," the man said, falling into stride with Owen. "It has been many months since we have seen you here."

"How is the duke?" Owen asked, following Johns as he led the way to the duke's bedchamber. That surprised Owen, for he had expected to find his old mentor in the solar.

"He's old, my lord. His strength is failing." The steward's eyes shined with emotion. "He'll be grateful you came."

Owen frowned, trying to steel himself.

"I thought you should know that his granddaughter has come from Atabyrion." The steward looked pained as he said this. It was no secret to anyone living in the castle that the duke himself had longed for a match between Owen and his granddaughter. Only the king had dissented. Owen kicked aside the memory as if it were a piece of clutter.

"Yes, I was aware of that. Would you make sure my men are given something to eat? We had to stop by Kingfountain on the way here, and they deserve a rest."

"Of course, my lord. I have your room ready as well."

Owen gave the steward a dark look. "It's not my room, Johns. I am a guest here. Like any other."

The gloomy hall was lit by a few mounted torches that hissed ominously in Owen's ears. When they reached the door at the end, Johns tapped twice respectfully before opening it. He glanced inside, took in a breath, and then opened it for Owen to enter first, giving him a look of compassion that Owen didn't feel he deserved.

And there she was.

It felt like someone had struck Owen's shield with a lance and knocked him violently off his horse. That rarely happened to him, in fact—it *hadn't* happened to him in years. But the memory of the pain and the sudden lack of air perfectly fit this moment. She was beautiful still, her long dark hair braided and bundled into various intricate designs. She was a woman now, a mother of two. There was a glow about her, a radiance that struck him forcefully and made him ache inside.

Elysabeth was sitting in a chair at Horwath's bedside, holding his hands. The duke's hair was as white as the snow of his mountains, his breath coming in fitful gasps. The duke's eyes were closed in sleep. It hurt to see him so still, a mighty tree fallen to the earth. Owen's eyes returned to Elysabeth as she turned to see who had entered.

"Owen," she breathed. The smile that lit her face tortured him.

"Hello, Elysabeth," he said thickly, trying to master himself. Failing.

She rose from the chair and gave him a look of warmth, tinged with pity. In the years that had separated them, he could see that she had progressed. She had learned to love again, to live a full life, while he had not even tried.

"I hadn't imagined you with so much stubble," she said, smiling kindly as she approached him. "But that spot in your hair hasn't changed. I'd know you anywhere, Owen Kiskaddon. I am so grateful you came. Did you get my letter?"

He nodded, unsure what to say, how to bridge the chasm yawning between them.

Her eyes crinkled with sadness. "Is it to be like this between us now?" she asked him softly. "Strangers instead of friends? It pains me to see you this way. You look awful, Owen."

What to say to that? The retort came easy enough. "At least you're not wearing one of those silly Atabyrion headdresses. I'd feared the worst."

He'd meant it as a barb. Being with Severn so much, he couldn't stop them now. They came to him as naturally as breathing.

She flinched at his tone, his disrespect. "I had hoped our reunion wouldn't be this painful. But I see now that it must be. I am sorry, Owen."

"For what?" He chuckled, not understanding. "It wasn't your fault. We both know who is to blame." He sighed deeply, stepping around her and approaching the bedside. He looked down at the duke's sunken cheeks, his gray pallor. "Sometimes I wonder how he endured it for so long. The sniping. The invectives. I tried to let it all go. But I'm a man. I bleed. He never seemed to."

He felt Elysabeth sidle up next to him, and it made him cringe inside. "Why didn't you answer my letters?" she asked him. "I tried to prevent this . . . distance from developing."

He shook his head. "You could not be loyal to me without being unfaithful to your husband," he said bluntly. "Nor did I want to tempt myself—or you. It was best that we stayed apart for so long. And the king has kept me busy," he added dryly.

Elysabeth laughed. "That is true. You have expanded the domains of Ceredigion extensively. I've heard about your exploits, you know. I follow each one. First, you captured several more towns in Occitania and seized their castles. Then you subjugated Legault and made it a vassal state. The king sent you to Brugia to help Maxwell unite the land under his power, but you betrayed him to keep him from getting too powerful."

Owen smirked. "That was the king's idea, of course," he said bitterly. "He doesn't want any of his allies getting too powerful." He looked at her. "Including Atabyrion."

She blinked at him in surprise. "What do you mean?" Her eyes had always seemed to change color like the weather. Today they were green, but they were a lighter shade than the dark green gown she wore. He could barely see the tiny scar at the corner of her full eyebrow. An injury from falling off a horse during a riot.

"When your grandfather dies," he said in a quiet voice, a *warning* voice, "you will not inherit Dundrennan. I think the king plans to give it to Catsby."

Her eyes went suddenly gray with anger. "But I am the heiress," she stammered, her cheeks turning a shade of crimson.

"Welcome to the court of Kingfountain," Owen said, giving her a mocking bow. "As I said, don't be surprised. No one is secure, Elysabeth. Not even me." Owen shook his head and started to pace. "He does this, you know. Frequently. He pushes his lords, promises one something they want and another the same thing. Then he lets them squabble and rip at each other. And in the end, he'll give it to a third man instead. There is no allegiance anymore. People obey because they fear him. He is paranoid about anyone getting too much power. He hasn't forgotten your husband *invaded* Ceredigion. Nor has he forgiven it."

She looked at him in horror. "This is news I hadn't even considered possible. Owen, how it must pain you to serve him!"

He shook his head. "You don't know. There is so much you don't know." He stepped away from her, scraping his fingers through his hair.

He felt her hand on his shoulder. "Tell me. Who do you confide in now? There must be someone you trust."

Owen nodded, but he felt dejected. "I trust Etayne."

"The poisoner?"

"The very one. She's loyal to me. She helps me deceive the king. Trick him." He shook his head again, wondering why he was opening up to her. Secrets were always trying to get out. He carried so many he felt he would burst. It was as if they had all been building up inside him until he saw her next. He clenched his jaw.

She came and stood in front of him, her eyes imploring him to trust her. She was still his friend, still cared about his well-being. He had almost forgotten what that felt like. "How are you deceiving the king?" she whispered.

Owen pursed his lips. "I'm disgusted with myself sometimes. When I defeated the king's nephew's attempt to claim the throne, Eyric claimed to have been Piers Urbick, a pretender, all along. It was a lie, Ev—Elysabeth. It was a lie, but the king has been wooing Lady Kathryn ever since. According to the laws and rites of marriage, their union is null and void if they were married under false circumstances. They have not *lived* as man and wife since St. Penryn. Eyric is still a prisoner in the palace, like Dunsdworth. The two of them are conspiring, looking for ways to escape. I have to keep the Espion watching them constantly. Eyric wants to be with his wife . . . and so does Severn."

Elysabeth's face twisted with revulsion. "I've heard she still wears a widow's garb. That she's always dressed in black?"

"It's true. The king is always making her new gowns. He's fixated on her. He wants to marry her, but she insists she is still married to Eyric. He's tried to use his Fountain magic to persuade her otherwise."

"That is abhorrent!" she said, her emotions totally riled.

He nodded feverishly. "His determination sickens me. And so I've used Etayne to deceive him. She is Fountain-blessed herself, and has the power to look like anyone else. When the king is in one of his *moods* to persuade Kathryn to relent, Etayne stands proxy and resists him. I help her as often as I can because the king's magic won't work on Kathryn when I am near. The poor woman is still faithful to her husband, but this constant pressure to yield is wearing her down. The king knows he's not getting any younger, that he needs an heir. The privy council is practically bullying her to accept him." He threw up his hands. "I don't know how much longer we can hold it off. I want Eyric to escape. But no other kingdom would risk the wrath of Severn by abducting him."

The look Elysabeth gave him was full of respect. She was silent a moment, staring at him. "I'm proud of you, Owen. It takes courage to do the right thing, especially when no one around you is helping."

Owen sighed, grateful for her words but hating the way they made him feel. "If I had courage, I would depose him," he said frankly. "I know the measure of the man now, and I don't respect him. I'm probably the only one who has enough power to defeat him. Yet your grandfather never did." He glanced down as he said the bitter-tasting words. "He set the example of loyalty that we *both* follow. I'm torn in so many ways! If I'd known then what I know now, I would have helped Eyric become king. Even though I knew he wasn't the Dreadful Deadman."

Her eyes narrowed at the words. "You mean that old prophecy is true? The one about the great king Andrew returning someday to save Ceredigion?"

He realized he had said too much. He shook his head and tried to turn away, but she caught his wrist and pulled him back.

"You tell me, Owen Kiskaddon. What do you know of the prophecy? I thought it was just a legend."

He blinked at her in misery. "I know it's true. He's here in the castle," Owen whispered.

Her eyes widened with shock. "The . . . the little boy in the kitchen? The one my grandfather has been raising? Little Drew?"

Owen shuddered at the word. "He is Eyric and Kathryn's son. *He* is the reason Eyric lied about being the king's nephew. He wanted to protect his wife, his son. The boy is only seven. About the age we were when we first met. He's the Argentine heir. The Dreadful Deadman."

Elysabeth blinked with astonishment. Then her voice fell to a whisper. "My daughter Genevieve is playing with him in the kitchen right now."

Owen nodded and looked at her seriously. "Can you imagine me writing *that* in a letter to you? Are you willing to keep it a secret from your husband? Etayne and the Deconeus of St. Penryn are the only others who know the truth. But do you think that little boy can defeat a grown man? In ten more years, Severn may be too powerful for anyone to stop."

# CHAPTER TWO

## *The King's Command*

Being back at Dundrennan was both a balm and a torture. The castle was steeped in memories that followed Owen as ghosts. Occasionally, he would turn a corner and see Genevieve tug Drew down the hall ahead of him, trailing giggles, and he would see himself and Evie doing the same. It hurt to be there, to be reminded of those memories, but at the same time, he found them soothing.

Watching Stiev Horwath die was especially agonizing, and Owen spent as much time as he could sitting beside the old duke's bed, watching the irregular rise and fall of his chest, hearing the rattled sound of his breathing. Horwath's death would usher in the end of an era. The days of the Sun and Rose of Eredur, of battles fought and won, fought and lost, glory fading like a sunset. Owen feared that when the duke finally stopped breathing, the last glimmer of daylight would be gone and night would descend. Owen would not be surprised if the duke's life was the last bulwark standing against Severn's fullest depravity. He stared at the man's sunken cheeks, wishing he would heal and knowing he would not.

He took the old duke's gnarled hand and sighed with despair. "You're leaving me, old friend," he murmured. "You're leaving me alone to fight for a future worth saving."

Horwath's eyelids fluttered. His eyes opened, and a look of pain crumpled his brow. "Still alive," he said darkly. His head turned and he looked at Owen. "You're still here, lad," he said, a fragile smile on his bearded mouth. "I'm glad you came in time. Wasn't sure you would."

"How could I not?" Owen answered, grateful to have a moment alone with the duke. Evie's children had been in and out of the room, but the stale confinement of a deathbed was not an enticing environment to the young. "How are you feeling?"

Horwath grunted. "Old." He shuddered beneath the blanket.

Owen smiled. "As old as the yews on the road to Castle Beestone," he jested.

"Not that old," Horwath said gruffly. His sharp gaze turned to Owen. "Would you heed some advice from one with more wisdom?"

Owen already knew what he would say, but he patted Horwath's hand and nodded.

"Get you a wife," the old duke panted.

The touch of the old man's hand was growing colder. His skin was like ice. "That is counsel I receive constantly," Owen said with a tug of bitterness in his throat. "Every month I get an offer of marriage from the father of some lass or other in realms as far as Genevar. If I stay at Tatton Hall longer than a fortnight, they start lining up their carriages." He shook his head. "The *best* wives are already taken," he said thickly.

Horwath's eyes crinkled. "I'm sorry I failed you in that, lad."

"You didn't fail me," Owen answered, shaking his head. One of the duke's nurses peeked into the room—summoned by the sound of voices, no doubt—and Owen surreptitiously gestured for her to fetch the rest of the family. The duke's moments of lucidity were growing increasingly rare. No one knew when the last would be. "We all followed our duty, did we not? I can't imagine your journey has been any less fraught with heartache."

Horwath gave him a weary smile. "Loyalty binds me. Only death . . ." He stiffened with increasing pain. ". . . will release me from its bondage." His eyes blinked rapidly and he stared up at the ceiling beams, his breath coming in little bursts.

Bondage. What an interesting word to describe it at such a moment.

"Do you ever . . . regret?" Owen asked in a low voice.

The duke suddenly clenched his hand. The pulse was strong, but then Owen felt the grip slacken. "Aye, lad. I have many regrets. Too many. But I don't regret befriending a frightened boy. I don't regret bringing my granddaughter to meet him. And I cannot regret having ambition for my duchy." His teeth clenched together as another wave of pain struck him. "I did what I thought was best. I led men. I was fair."

"You served with integrity," Owen said hoarsely. "Even if it wasn't always deserved."

"I did," Horwath grunted. "I've asked . . . the king . . . if he will let my granddaughter inherit Dundrennan." He licked his chapped lips. "I don't know . . . if he will. He never promised." He sighed deeply, uttering a small groan.

Owen glanced at the door, willing Iago and Elysabeth to come quickly.

The duke started shuddering. "Duty is a heavy burden, lad. My knees ache from the load. It is time I set it down." He turned his head again, his eyes full of pain and suffering. He pierced Owen with his gaze. "It's yours now. I . . . bequeath it . . . to you."

A shard of torment dug into Owen's heart. He didn't want the burden. He loathed it. But he could see Horwath would not die in peace without handing off his duty to someone else. He felt tears prick the corner of his eyes.

"I will take it," Owen said miserably. "Be at peace, Grandfather. You've carried it long enough."

Stiev Horwath closed his eyes and sighed deeply. Owen thought it was his last breath, but the wave of pain had passed and he was breathing easier. His hand was limp against Owen's.

"The duty I give you," the duke whispered softly, "is found in the ice caves."

Owen stared at the old man in shock. The duke had a tranquil look on his face now, an expression of calm. Owen heard the susurrus of the Fountain coming into the room.

"What did you say?" Owen asked, leaning closer. His heart started to burn.

"The Maid's sword," the duke murmured. "I know where it is. One of my people . . . a Fountain-blessed lad by the name of Carrick, can lead you to it. He's one of the castle hunters. So is his father. He found the Maid's sword in the ice. The sword of King Andrew. I have forbidden my people to wander the ice caves. To keep the secret safe."

Owen stared in surprise. "Why have you not spoken of it before?"

The duke blinked. "Because we already have a king," he said in a hoarse whisper. "But Severn has no heir. No child. It is the sword of kings. Do not . . . tell . . . the Occitanians. If they get it, they will conquer our kingdom. They want revenge for the past. This duty, I lay on you. Be true."

Iago and Elysabeth came rushing into the room, each shepherding along one of their children. Iago seemed quite comfortable in the role of father. Owen had seen him interacting with his children—sweeping them high into the air and making them laugh and squeal. He was especially close to Genevieve, very patient and indulging, even when she had interrupted one of Iago and Owen's conversations about trade and their dealings with Brugia's ambitious ruler. Owen could not deny a certain grudging respect for Iago, both the ruler and the man. It was as unexpected as it was unwelcome.

Now, though, the entire family looked disconsolate—even little Genevieve, who was constantly prattling, seemed at a loss for words as she stared at her great-grandfather's wheezing body.

"Thank you for telling us," Elysabeth said, squeezing Owen's arm as she rushed past him to her grandfather. "Grandpapa! The king is here! He just rode into the bailey and is coming shortly. The king is here!"

Owen felt a wriggle of doom at the words. Horwath blinked at her, then smiled.

"He came," Horwath said in surprise.

Iago scooped up Genevieve in his arms and nudged past Owen to get nearer. He gave Owen a look that was difficult to interpret. Was it smugness? Exultation? Or did he simply pity Owen for losing the woman they both loved, for not having a family of his own?

Elysabeth and Iago's younger child was only two, too young to understand matters of death, and he was tugging on his mother's skirts, pleading for something to eat.

Owen left the chair and retreated back to the door, allowing the family to crowd in around the duke. He saw the nurses dabbing tears from their eyes. The people of the North loved Duke Horwath. He was treated with the honor and deference that was owed to a man who had proven his integrity throughout his life. Owen wrestled with the dilemma seething inside his chest. Could Owen make a mockery of that memory by deposing the king?

As he leaned back against the door, he spied Drew standing on the other side of the awning, peeking into the room, his boyish face full of pain as he watched his guardian gasping for air and murmuring words to his relations that the two of them couldn't hear from so far away. Owen stared at the boy, struck again by the memories of being that age. For a moment, he was back at Beestone castle, lying on his bed as Ankarette Tryneowy, the woman who had saved Owen's life more than once, lay dying at his bedside, bleeding to death from stab wounds inflicted by the Espion.

The boy didn't even know his true identity or importance. Drew was tall for a boy his age. All the Argentines were tall. The hint of red in his blond hair came from his mother. He was a handsome boy disguised in the garb of a servant. The lad believed he was destined to become a knight, and he loved practicing in the training yard with wooden swords. But he also had a fondness for watching games of Wizr. Whenever he spied Owen playing, he would slip up unnoticed and stare at the pieces as if they were the most fascinating thing.

He looked so much like an Argentine that Owen did not want the king to see him. "Go play in the kitchen," he said to the boy, wanting to get him out of sight quickly.

Drew looked instantly crestfallen. Owen could see he longed to be at the duke's bedside, grieving the loss of the great man who had watched over him. His face frowned with potential rebellion, but he obeyed and skulked down the corridor. Owen felt guilty, but he had to conceal the boy from notice for as long as he could.

His mind was still whirling with the news Horwath had given him about the sword. Evie had always mentioned the ice caves in the mountains, and they had both longed to explore them. Now he understood why it had been forbidden. Had the sword been trapped in the ice for decades, waiting for someone who was Fountain-blessed to retrieve it? Owen had found another powerful relic in the sanctuary of Our Lady of Kingfountain, a Wizr set with mysterious powers, and he had hidden it for safekeeping in the fountain of St. Penryn, sequestered at the very edge of his land. The waters would help keep it hidden from all but the Fountain-blessed.

The sound of Elysabeth's weeping captured his attention, and he watched as she pressed her face into Iago's shoulder for comfort. A twisting sensation unleashed inside Owen's gut as he watched Iago hug her. They were each other's comfort now. The only person Owen had to confide in and offer him comfort was Etayne, who loved him and despaired that he would never return her feelings. With Etayne's magic, she could look like anyone, deceiving anyone except for Owen. He had kept their relationship limited to friendship, though he knew she longed to be his mistress. He cared about her, but he didn't love anyone. He wasn't even sure if he could anymore. Nor was the King's Poisoner a suitable marriage partner for a duke. No, Etayne's job was to keep Owen from falling in love with anyone else. He had tasked her with that assignment years ago, for his heart was still loyal to one woman. A woman who grieved at her grandfather's passing. A woman whom he could not comfort.

From the corridor came the shuffling gait of the king. Owen would have recognized his approach blindfolded. He knew the king's walk, especially when Severn was weary or saddle sore. Owen tried to compose himself, to keep his face from revealing the true depth of his bitterness and resentment.

Elysabeth lifted her head, hearing the sound, and looked to Owen for confirmation. His expression said the words for him.

"The king is here," she whispered to her husband. Iago scowled instinctively. There was no love between the two sovereigns. There was only grudging dependency.

Owen turned to face the king, and his heart quickened with panic. Severn was holding Drew's hand and leading him back into the room. The flow of the Fountain emanated from the king, who relied on touch to fully transmit his power of persuasion.

As they approached, the king's power began to wane and subside. He glanced at Owen in annoyance. "The lad tells me you banished him to the kitchen," he said curtly. "He's grieving over his fallen master. I thought you'd have more compassion than that."

Owen accepted the barb without even pursing his lips. He had gotten quite adept at masking his expressions when the king was around.

Suddenly Genevieve came rushing up and took Drew's hand. "Do you want to see him?" she asked, tugging the boy toward the bed. He's very still now. He's gone to the Deep Fathoms. It's nothing to be scared of, Drew. You'll see. Don't be scared."

"I'm not scared," Drew countered, affronted. But he followed her into the room, giving only halfhearted resistance to her pulls.

The king sidled up next to Owen in the doorway, watching the two children as they approached the bedside. "Those two remind me of breakfast in the great hall," he murmured. "I remember . . . she wanted to build a fish pond! Now look at her. So poised and motherly." His voice was just above a whisper, pitched for Owen alone. "She saved Iago's life. I hope he's grateful to her. But they won't be pleased when I give the North to another. Someone who has fully earned the right of being a duke."

"Catsby?" Owen said blandly.

"Indeed," the king said with relish, and then sighed. "They'll be bitter. Aren't the disappointed always bitter? But you see the wisdom in my decision, don't you? I can't give Iago *that* much power."

"I see the wisdom," Owen replied. "But no man likes to be kept on the ground with a boot on his neck."

The king stiffened and frowned, giving Owen a sharp look. "Well, my outspoken young friend, it is easier to kick a man while he's *down* than slog through a battlefield against him. Or perhaps you *want* him to invade Ceredigion? So you can have the pleasure of killing him." It was a brutal thing to say and it was said deliberately. Owen had long endured such provoking comments. Although it rankled him, he didn't let it show.

He found sarcasm to be an adequate defense in such moments. "I could have him killed at any time, my lord," he said knowingly, his eyes bright. "But it would grieve me to make Elysabeth suffer. So I patiently wait for the man to get the pox."

Severn chuckled at the dark humor and clapped Owen's back, which was especially annoying. Then he heaved another sigh and stared at Horwath's lifeless body. Despite his posturing, he almost looked relieved that he had arrived too late. "Well, Catsby will be content, and I'll get a moment of peace. If you'd fancy a remembrance of the duke, you'd best take it now. Catsby counts the coins, you know. He won't give up a florin without a fight. Not that you are in need of *coin*. I've rewarded you amply and am about to reward you further."

Owen crinkled his eyebrows. "How so?"

"You're going to start another war," Severn said with a grin of enjoyment. He looked positively devilish when he schemed. His black hair was riddled with streaks of gray, each one a testament to the troubles he'd endured since seizing the throne of Ceredigion. His slight deformities were draped in the costliest of court attire, all black with jewels, and he still wore a chain vest beneath his tunic as an extra layer of defense.

"With whom this time?" Owen said, controlling his tone so he didn't sound as exasperated as he felt. The king was always tweaking the noses of the other realms, putting them in fear of an invasion. His dominion had expanded relentlessly over the last seven years, with more and more cities and areas allying themselves to the badge of the white boar. Years before, Ankarette had helped fool the king into believing Owen had the gift of precognition. Although he *did* have powers from the Fountain, reading the future was not one of them. Still, Owen sometimes interfered with the king's riskier plans by claiming to have had a dream from the Fountain. As the years passed, his visions seemed to convince the king less and less—almost as if the king were losing his belief in the guiding force of the Fountain, something Owen did not understand since the Fountain was the source of the king's own preternatural abilities. Owen had become more judicious in his use of the dreams, especially when common sense said the risk was too great.

"Brythonica," the king said.

Owen turned to look at the king. "They've been our ally for seven years. What would we gain?"

Severn chuffed. "They've enjoyed immunity long enough. Besides, I need their land to wage war on Occitania. Chatriyon has been fortifying the borderlands each year, making it more and more difficult to conquer new cities. But he's exposed on his flank, Brythonica. We take that duchy and Chatriyon will cave like those tiles you used to play with." Owen's childhood pastime of stacking tiles had always helped him focus, and it also replenished his natural supply of Fountain magic.

Now that he was older, he found the same benefits by playing Wizr, reading history, and plotting strategies with the Espion. The king gave him a smug look. "You're the one who has taught me to be devious, lad. You're blessed with a cunning mind."

The thought of betraying the duchess disgusted Owen, and he was not eager to face Lord Marshal Roux, her advisor and protector, on the battlefield. Owen and Roux were allies, but uncomfortable ones, and had danced around each other for years. The lord marshal had an uncanny knack for showing up places unexpectedly—a trait that set Owen on edge.

"My lord," Owen said. "Brythonica is full of valleys and woods. I've explored the borders between Averanche and Cann, but no farther. They also have a strong fleet."

"Not as strong as ours," Severn said reprovingly. "It's not your place to question my commands, Lord Kiskaddon. It's your place to fulfill them." It was a tone of voice he had started using with more regularity. "With Stiev dead, I must count on you more than I ever have. Now, I've made this conquest simple for you."

Owen wanted to vomit. He knew something else was coming. He could see it in the gleam of Severn's eyes. His mouth went dry.

"You are to go to the capital of Brythonica—Ploemeur, I believe, is the name. And you will finally meet this elusive duchess that Marshal Roux has been shielding for so long. The most eligible heiress of all the realms. Her name is Sinia—after that breed of butterfly, or so Polidoro tells me. She's a pawn. Roux's been using her to hold on to power himself. Well, you tell that scheming Lord Roux that I insist the duchess and you should marry at once. When they refuse, and I *know* they will, that gives us the pretext we need to invade and open up a new front against Occitania."

He clapped Owen on the back again. Then he looked back at the view of the room, his mood becoming more somber. "Brythonica used to be our duchy. And I mean to make it ours once again. I want it all, lad. Every town, every village."

# CHAPTER THREE

## Deep Fathoms

It would have been a more fitting send-off for the duke if clouds had come and threatened rain or snow. But the sky was a blindingly bright shade of blue. The jagged mountains capped in snow stood out so starkly against it, it felt as if it were a vivid dream. Even with the sun blazing down, the air was sharp enough to cut, and everyone assembled on the bridge was bundled up in fur cloaks and hats. The stone bridge overlooked the falls in the canyon past Dundrennan, and the waters were roaring so loudly it was difficult to hear the shrill notes of the pipers and the steady boom of the drummers. Waterfalls had always fascinated Owen, and he had been at this location many times in the past, had stared at the endless flood of waters rushing through the rocks and boulders, building into a snowy white churn before leaping off the cliff into the valley below.

Turning his neck, Owen saw Evie sidled up next to Iago, his arm wrapped tight around her shoulders. Their two children were straining against the bridge, staring down at the rapids rushing beneath them, their eyes full of wonder. Owen had been to the falls at Edonburick in

Atabyrion, which were impressive, but they paled in comparison to the size and force of the waterfalls in North Cumbria. This was Evie's true home. This was the place where he had hoped to kiss her for the first time, years ago. Almost in defiance of this thought, Iago brushed his lips against her hair in a comforting way. Owen forced his eyes to look away.

The bridge was full of spectators awaiting the launch of Duke Horwath's body back to the Deep Fathoms. In the distance, farther upstream, Owen could see the black-garbed knights preparing the body. The smoke from the torches they carried mixed with the mist coming up from the waters, and Owen could smell a hint of it in the air. The knights were saying their final respects as the music played on.

Owen felt the king's shoulder butt against his. It would be difficult to hear over the tumult of the falls, so Owen leaned closer to him.

"Who is that lad?" Severn asked, motioning surreptitiously to Drew.

Owen pretended not to know. "Who do you mean? There are many children on the bridge."

"The boy with the flax and reddish hair," he said. "Bless me if he doesn't look a little like my nephews who died." He sniffed, his eyes narrowing warily. "He told me his father died at Averanche. His mother could not care for him. I asked him who his mother was, but he doesn't know." He smirked. "I even used my magic on him, but he wasn't concealing anything."

Owen grew more and more uncomfortable. "You should stop using your magic like that, my lord. It makes people even more wary about you. But why the interest in the lad?"

Severn shrugged. "He reminds me of you. Though he's not as timid as you were. I miss having children at the palace." He gave Owen a look of suspicion. "Assign an Espion to find out who his parents were. I assume you're stopping through Kingfountain on your way to Brythonica?"

"Naturally," Owen said. "I don't plan on going there without some protection. Marshal Roux has always made me wary."

The king smiled shrewdly and nodded. "I was going to ride back with you, but I may linger here a few days more." He sniffed, his gaze going back to the boy. "Something about him. Find out who he is, Owen. Have your man report directly to me."

"I will, my lord," Owen said with a neutral voice, though he squirmed with guilt.

A raven squawked from atop a nearby evergreen and took to the air, flapping its wings as it swooped toward them. The king started with surprise, his mouth suddenly a rictus of disgust and fear, and waved his arm to ward it away.

As the bird flapped off into the distance, the sound of the shrill pipes became louder and the drumbeat increased in pace and volume. Owen was surprised by the king's involuntary reaction—Severn loathed losing control, especially around others—but he soon forgot it, for Severn's gaze had once again settled on the boy. He only watched him for a moment, though, before turning his attention on the musicians.

The body of the duke had been tied into a canoe, and the knights were assembled in two rows, each pair holding the staves upon which the canoe rested. Elysabeth dabbed a tear from her cheek and kept one hand on her youngest, who was still peering over the far side of the railing for a better view at the waters.

The knights marched to the edge of the river, the sound of their boots lost amidst the noise of the crowd. Then they stamped to a halt and angled the staves so that the canoe slid forward and landed in the river with a splash.

Everyone in the crowd stopped breathing as the canoe was snatched up in the current and hurtled forward. Owen was fixated by the dark shape as it knifed through the ripples in the river and rushed toward the bridge at breakneck speed. It was a matter of heartbeats before the canoe approached their gathering. All was silent except for the clamor of the falls, so there was nothing to mask the collective gasp as the little boat came up. Owen could see the gray cheeks of the duke, his closed eyes, and his sword fastened to his hands by straps. A deep sadness pierced Owen's heart as he gazed at the face of Stiev Horwath one last time.

And then the canoe tipped over the edge, plummeting into the snowstorm mist of water vapor below. A shared gasp and sigh came from those assembled as he disappeared.

To the Deep Fathoms. Wherever that was.

The king clapped Owen's shoulder, his face full of respect for the fallen soldier who had given his entire life for the Argentine family. He had left behind a legacy of faithfulness and honor that was about to be pillaged and sullied by the new duke of the North. It grated on Owen to see the undeserving rewarded, while Elysabeth, who had sacrificed her own wishes to do her duty to the king, was forced to give up the lands and rights that were her due. It was cruel and it was wrong. Yes, it was pragmatic. Yes, it was clever. But punishing Elysabeth for her husband's previous treachery was disrespectful to the loyalty that *she* had shown.

"I've given this some thought. I share your distrust of Lord Marshal Roux," King Severn said in her ear as everyone turned and moved to the other side of the bridge. There was always a feeling of hopefulness after a boat was sent down the falls, people lingering around to see if it would survive the fall and continue on downstream. The river wound all the way to Kingfountain and, ultimately, the sea.

"He won't be pleased with me, you can be sure," Owen said, chuckling darkly. "A demand for marriage won't be met with good feelings, not when we protected her from the Occitanian king's demands seven years ago."

"Which is why we're doing it." Severn chuckled maliciously. "It's just a pretext, Owen. An excuse to invade. But when you go, bring Etayne with you." His eyes narrowed coldly. "Just in case."

Owen wrestled with the conflict in his heart. He wanted Etayne to stay in Kingfountain and help shield Kathryn from Severn while he was gone. "My lord," he started to hedge, but the look in Severn's eyes was enough to silence him.

"I insist," the king said. "If Roux gets in the way, then get him *out* of the way."

As they stood by the bridge overlooking the massive falls, Owen had the unbidden urge to shove the king over the rail.

"Yes, my lord," Owen said with a weary sigh.

◆　◆　◆

He wanted to be gone, far away from the ill feelings that had descended on Dundrennan like an evil shroud. Lord Catsby was only too eager to assume his new title. He did not have the grace or wisdom to recognize the offense his new position would cause to Elysabeth and her relations. Her mother, Lady Mortimer, was told in the rudest of terms that she would need to either return to her own estates or follow her daughter back to Atabyrion. Catsby did not care which she chose. She was no longer welcome in the castle that had belonged to her father, a venerated and loyal servant to the king.

Outspoken as always, Elysabeth rebuked the new duke for his insensitivity, but he condescendingly informed her that while she might be the queen of a backwater kingdom, she had no authority in *his* estate. Iago looked ready to draw a blade, so Owen tried to calm the hostilities by pulling Lord Catsby aside and reminding him that he was being a jack.

Catsby might not care about giving offense to Iago and Elysabeth, but he dared not rile the Duke of Westmarch, who was the king's general and the leader of the Espion. Catsby was cowed, for a while, but ill will made Owen eager to depart. The place that had always been his sanctuary was no longer welcoming.

The next day, he was inspecting the girth straps of his horse in the bailey, preparing to leave, when Elysabeth called to him from the castle doors. He left the horse with a groom and strode back to see what she wanted.

Her lip was quivering, her eyes full of tears.

"What's wrong?" he demanded, concerned.

She swallowed, clearly trying to master her emotions. "Owen," she gasped, shaking her head. "I'm . . . I'm so frightened! I don't know how I can do this!" Her eyes skittered wildly, and her hands grasped at his tunic.

He looked at her with increasing alarm. "What's happened?"

They were alone in the doorway, no one within earshot.

"The king has asked . . . well, more like *ordered*, that we leave one of our children behind. He . . . he said he misses the days of old when you and I used to run around the palace together. But we both know—Iago and I—we know he's doing this to ensure we don't do anything rash now that Catsby commands the North. My husband is furious, as you may well imagine. He wants to force the king to accept my rights to Dundrennan, but I think that would be foolish. Not now, not when he's so powerful. I must pick one of my children." Tears coursed down her cheeks. She let out a breath. "I'm sorry, Owen . . . but my heart feels ripped asunder. I think of your own mother. How did she endure it? It feels unbearable . . ." She started to sob, and Owen yearned to comfort her.

He closed his eyes, trying vainly to shut out the memories of leaving his mother as a young boy, the fear and the aching realization that he would never live with his parents again. He had been sent to Kingfountain in a similar manner, so he knew firsthand what Genevieve was about to experience. He had no doubt that the daughter would be chosen instead of the son. He shook his head slowly. "Even I can still be stunned at his cruelty."

Elysabeth nodded, hiccupping as she tried to stifle her tears. "My son, Iago, must return to Atabyrion. He's the heir and he's so little. The king knows I will have to send Genevieve." She clenched her fists against her chest, trying to quell more tears. "And it's worse knowing that you're going to Brythonica. I would feel so much better if I knew you were there with her. Watching over her. Would you ask Etayne . . . ?" she implored.

Owen grimaced. "I can't. The king ordered me to take her with me in case Roux causes trouble." He rubbed his forehead, anguished by her ordeal. By this newest sign of the king's wickedness. "I will ask Lady Kathryn to watch over her. She's a fellow native of Atabyrion, which should be comforting to your lass. And Liona as well. She won't be gone for long, Evie, I promise." He realized he had used her pet name and flushed deeply. "I beg your pardon, Elysabeth. I will do what I can to make sure your daughter is protected. You have my word on that. I don't think that I will be in Brythonica for very long," he added wryly. "When I get back, I'll persuade the king to send her home."

Gratitude shone through her misery. "You are so dear to me," she said softly, blinking away tears. "Thank you. You can still . . . call me Evie. That name is only for you. Iago has another pet name for me."

Owen did not want to know what it was. "Where is he?"

She pursed her lips. "Arguing with the king. He's a passionate man. You can be sure he's not making this easy for Severn."

Owen sighed. "As long as he doesn't do anything rash. He chose well in you." He shook his head, feeling hopeless and wretched. "Your daughter is beautiful and curious," he said, the words rushing out in spite of himself. "Just like you were. I'm going to make sure the window to the cistern is nailed shut."

Elysabeth smiled, a genuine warm one. "Do that," she said emphatically. "I'm sorry to keep you, Owen. The king thought you were already gone, which is why he announced it when he did. Safe travels." She stood awkwardly for a moment and then impulsively wrapped her arm around his neck and hugged him. Before she pulled away, she brushed a small kiss on his cheek. Her eyes were very green.

"I want you to find love, Owen," she blurted earnestly. "I don't care if she's a duchess or a waif. I want you to be *happy*. Promise me you will try."

He stared at her, caught off guard by the hug and tender kiss, very aware of the surging emotions that raged in his dilapidated heart. He had resisted the allurements of other women for seven years, clinging to the dwindling and perverse hope that Evie's husband would somehow manage to die. It had happened to Severn with his wife. But each year had diminished the hope and convinced Owen that waiting for her would be foolish. Sourly, he wondered if he'd waited too long. Perhaps Severn would force him to act. If not with the Duchess of Brythonica, another woman.

As Owen mused on these dark thoughts, he decided he was glad he'd come back to the North after all. He was grateful that he and Evie had reconciled at long last. They would be friends again, if only friends apart. He was a better man for having her in his life. The sun warmed all that it touched.

He gave her a courtly bow. "I must do as my king commands me," he said with a mocking tone. "I must order a powerful woman to marry me. What could possibly go wrong?"

With a wry smile, he turned away and walked back to his horse and slung up into the saddle. He looked back at the castle, Dundrennan, and wondered when he would next return. It would have to be soon. There was a sword in an ice cave that he needed to find.

Suddenly, the first stirrings of a plan began to shape in his mind. The plan required a boy and a sword.

◆ ◆ ◆

My lord Kiskaddon,

We have apprehended a plot to smuggle the pretender Piers
Urbick and the wretch Dunsdworth out of Holistern Tower,
where they are presently confined. We intercepted a communi-
cation from Duke Maxwell of Brugia offering a sizable sum
for the capture of these two men. There have been two attempts
in the last fortnight to bribe the guards for access. The second
attempt was intercepted by the Espion, and we're now holding the man who instigated the plot in the city. Guard over
Holistern has been increased. We await word from our spies
in Brugia as to the motives behind Maxwell's interference.

 Sent with all haste,
 Kevan Amrein
 Kingfountain Palace

◆ ◆ ◆

# CHAPTER FOUR

## *Prisoners in the Tower*

While Owen was still weary from the ride south to Kingfountain, he had little time to rest. He had received a note from an Espion courier about a Brugian plot to free Eyric and Dunsdworth, so he immediately met with his second in command—the Espion he always put in charge during his absences from the palace. Kevan Amrein was a capable man, adept at reading both court subtleties and the people around him, and he had proven his loyalty to Owen again and again despite being twenty years his senior.

Owen and Kevan walked through the Espion tunnels honeycombing the palace, heading toward the entrance to Holistern Tower. They moved with haste, for Owen knew the king expected him to leave for Brythonica as soon as possible.

"That's a sizable sum," he told Kevan, watching the bob of the lantern illuminate the tunnels they passed. They had a dank smell that made Owen wrinkle his nose. "No wonder they were tempted. What's the name of the man you captured?"

"His name is Dragan," Kevan said. "It's not an uncommon name in Ceredigion, but there are records of a man with that name in Mancini's books. A sanctuary man before the king cleared them all out. He skulks in the city now, trying to stay out of the way of the sheriff."

"And his motive was purely greed?" Owen asked.

"Seems to be the case. I don't think he has any loyalty to any man. He's loyal to gold. The sum offered was hefty enough to entice him to risk his neck."

"And no doubt it will entice others as well," Owen reported. "Well, if Duke Maxwell wants to stir up trouble in our domain, we can easily accommodate him. While I'm gone, I want you to have someone consider how we can pay Maxwell back in kind. I'm sure there is a nobleman or two in his country who would love to see him fall."

Kevan smiled cynically. "I imagine there are, my lord." His gaze narrowed. "You have read the reports about Duke Maxwell, though. He seems a bit strange. An odd fellow obsessed with the legends of the Fountain-blessed. He claims to be Fountain-blessed himself."

Owen chuckled. "Oh yes. Their equivalent of the Espion is called the Secret Instruction. The head of it is a poisoner named Disant. According to our friends in Brugia, Disant calls Maxwell by a different name—Time. They say his special gift with the Fountain is the ability to travel through time itself." Owen chuckled with disgust. "The man is daft and overly ambitious. I didn't think he would be fool enough to poke at Severn, but if he wants another war, he's welcome to one. We still control Callait and can bring in an army quite easily."

Kevan's smile stretched wider. "I do enjoy working for you, my lord. And I'm not trying to wipe my snot on your boots either. You're unpretentious."

"I'm a bone-weary soldier," Owen said, brushing off the compliment. "And I grow wearier by the day. Ah, here we are."

They arrived at the locked door of the tower. There were three men guarding it at all times. They recognized Kevan and Owen immediately and snapped to attention. One of them fumbled with a key ring and hastily unlocked the door.

"Anything to report?" Kevan demanded, folding his arms and projecting an impatient air.

"Nothing new, my lord," one of the guards said, tipping his cap to Owen as well. "We changed their schedule as you instructed."

"Good man," Kevan said, nodding to him.

The door opened and Owen began to ascend the tower steps. As the sound of their boots echoed up and down the shaft, he thought about the misery of these two prisoners' existence. It was the king's will that Eyric and Dunsdworth be thrown together as companions of misfortune. Owen still remembered the day when Severn had humiliated Eyric in front of his wife, Lady Kathryn. It was a dark memory that made Owen squirm with antipathy.

Kathryn had been persuaded to leave the sanctuary of St. Penryn with the promise that she would be able to see her husband again, but their reunion had been a form of torture for both of them. Owen recalled how Kathryn had sobbed at the sight of Eyric in chains, his princely garb exchanged for that of a commoner. The king had provided her with an assortment of widow's attire, a cruel jest on his part, and she had worn nothing but black since that fateful day. Seven years had passed since they had been together as man and wife. Seven years since the birth of their son. They only knew that Owen had taken the child somewhere to be raised as a knight. Neither parent knew where Drew was or who was raising him.

Such dark thoughts reminded Owen of his own parents, whom he had not seen in sixteen years. They had been exiled from Ceredigion for their role in an attempted coup at Ambion Hill. Rumor had it they had taken refuge in Occitania, where they lived in a small manor on a meager stipend. He had tried to make arrangements for them, to contact them, but his messages had always been returned unopened, the couriers unsuccessful in tracking their location. Perhaps they had changed the spelling and pronunciation of their last name so they could disappear into obscurity. He thought about them on occasion, yearning to know what they were doing, how they had fared. His sisters would be married by now in all likelihood. Were his parents still living? He imagined so. They were getting older, but there was no reason to think they weren't alive somewhere. Did they still think about him? The son they had sent away to live as the king's ward?

He was out of breath by the time they reached the top of the tower. Two more guards stood at attention in front of the door, both of whom Owen recognized, though not by name. They greeted him formally and then unlocked the door.

Owen turned to Kevan, holding up his hand. "Fetch Etayne. I need to speak with her. Wait for me outside Dragan's cell. I'll only be a moment with these two."

Kevan looked a little taken aback, especially since Owen had waited until they were at the top of the spiral staircase to convey his message. But he sighed and nodded and started back down the steps.

Owen nodded to the soldiers and they pulled open the door.

The stench inside was almost unbearable.

Owen gritted his teeth and stepped into the stink. He saw Dunsdworth lounging on a chair, his eyes bloodshot and full of enmity. There were a few books in the room—some on a shelf, some on the small table. The pallet was just wide enough for two, but Owen saw a blanket in a heap on the floor, and he imagined that Eyric had chosen to sleep elsewhere.

Eyric was sitting at the desk, a book in his hands, and his eyes lit with a desperate hunger when he saw Owen. His jaw started to tremble. His eyes were haunted with despair.

"Hello *Kisky*," Dunsdworth drawled, using the old pet name like a bludgeon.

Owen barely gave the man a look, for what he saw made him depressed. This was a man who had grown so complacent and lazy, they had to cut his rations. He had a beard, pocks on his cheeks, and soulless blue eyes full of hate.

Eyric leaped out of his chair. "What's happened, Lord Owen?" he demanded, his voice a little feverish. "We're only allowed to walk the grounds once a week now. No exercise. Is the king trying to kill us with boredom?" His cheeks grew flushed as he spoke.

"My father was permitted to drink himself to death," Dunsdworth said irreverently. He rocked the heels of his boot back and forth. "I would gladly accept that fate. Can our dungeon be moved to the wine cellars, please?"

Eyric gave Dunsdworth a look of pure annoyance, but he had learned long ago not to spar with him. He turned back to Owen imploringly. "My lord, what have we done to deserve such punishment?"

"Nothing," Owen said flatly. "It's not your fault at all. Someone tried bribing the guard to rescue you."

Dunsdworth let out a spluttering laugh followed by some unspecific grunted syllables.

Eyric's eyes widened with hope. "Truly?"

"I would not get my hopes up," Owen said, shaking his head. "It will come to naught."

"Then why are you here?" Eyric asked. He started to pace anxiously.

"I wanted to see you with my own eyes," Owen said with a smirk. "To be sure no one had tricked me. And I brought you another book." He pulled out the small book wedged into his belt. "I see you've been through this collection. This is a book of legends of King Andrew and Myrddin. I read it as a boy."

Dunsdworth hawked and spat on the floor, the glob landing dangerously close to Owen's boot. "You didn't bring me a bottle of wine, did you?"

Owen seethed internally, but he remained calm. He tossed the book onto the table. "What were you reading?"

Eyric glanced surreptitiously. "That one."

Owen shrugged and sauntered to the table. The room reeked of filth. He picked up the book and thumbed through some pages. "I haven't read this one in a while. Did you like it?"

"I enjoyed it very much," Eyric said meaningfully. "Thank you."

Owen nodded his indifference and folded the book under his arm. "I'm leaving the kingdom for a fortnight or so. If the risk of escape shrinks, I'll authorize more time in the training yard."

"Thank you," Eyric said with relief.

Dunsdworth looked at Owen with utter loathing, his lazy eye twitching. "You never bring me any gifts," he grumbled.

"He does," Eyric answered flatly. "You just don't take advantage of reading them."

Dunsdworth rolled his head and then gazed up at the timbers propping up the tower. "This was the cell that Tunmore jumped from to his death. I can see why he did it. Take away those bars and I would try flapping my wings as well."

"Farewell," Owen said, nodding brusquely.

Eyric stepped forward earnestly. "How much longer, my lord?" he said with agitation bordering on hopelessness.

He gazed hard at Eyric. "We all make choices. And we live with the consequences." Then he turned and rapped on the door with the book spine. As the soldiers opened it, he heard Dunsdworth spit again. Then he felt the wad strike his back. The soldiers' faces turned red with rage, and they looked ready to barge in to pummel Dunsdworth for his insolence and disrespect.

Owen held up his hand in warning. He left the tower and motioned for them to lock the door.

"How dare he!" one of the soldiers snarled.

Owen shook his head. "He wanted a beating," he said softly. "He was trying to earn one. He can't feel anymore. Even pain is something he misses. Have pity on them, but do not hurt them. They endure enough torture."

Owen hurried down the tower to meet Kevan and Etayne by the cells where more common prisoners were detained. Etayne gave him a curious look as he came into view. It was unusual for him to summon her to the dungeon for a meeting. The dankness was slightly offset by the prettiness of her stylish and formfitting gown. The corridors smelled of rot and filth, and the air shivered with groans and wet coughs.

Kevan brought them to a cell and inserted a key into the lock. "My lord, meet our latest guest," he introduced.

Owen ducked through the opening and took the lantern from Kevan, who waited outside. The man in the dank cell shielded his face from the light and flinched, backing away from the glare. He was an oily man with a hawk nose and a handsome, squarish, pocked face with long sideburns that matched the color of his dark hair. His clothes looked like they had been worn by a nobleman and then discarded after too much use. There were splits at the seams and some of the stitching threads were loose.

A surge of Fountain magic filled the cell, startling Owen because it was so unexpected. He dropped the book cradled in his arm and reached for his dagger. He felt Etayne's hand touch his shoulder, and when he jerked his neck around to face her, he saw she was in a disguise. Her face had been distorted to look like Evie's maid, and her blond hair had gone long and dark.

"Who is that?" Dragan grunted and growled. He was still shielding his face. Owen had never seen him before, but his expression did look somewhat familiar.

"It's not him," Etayne said in Justine's voice, shaking her head vigorously. She turned and left.

Owen stared after her and then turned back to face Dragan. He slowly crouched and picked up the fallen book.

"What do she mean I'm not him?" Dragan said with a croaking voice. "Who was that lass? Do I know her?"

It came together in Owen's mind like a puzzle. He gave Dragan a sharp look. "Who hired you to abduct the prisoners?"

"I'm not saying nuffin," the man said firmly. "What's a man to do, I ask ye, now that the king thrust us out of sanctuary. I tell you. I ask you!" He huffed. "I don' mean nuffin, my lord. Just want a few coins in my sack, eh? Can you blame a man for tryin'? Eh, my lord? Can you blame me? I can't blame myself. You would have done the same in my place. Sure as milk, you would have."

The man's shabby clothes were proof enough of his ill-kempt condition. "You knew what you were doing when you went against the king," he scolded. "You're the kind of man who'd steal coins from the fountains at the sanctuary."

The man grinned sheepishly. One of his teeth was missing. "You can't blame me, eh?"

Owen shook his head and left. He felt the churning of the Fountain magic dwindle in the cell. Kevan shut and locked the door.

"Do you want him tortured, whipped, drowned, or set loose, my lord?" Kevan asked with a chuckle.

Owen glanced at Etayne, who looked like herself again despite her pale cheeks. She wasn't looking at either of them. Her face was composed, but he could see she was reeling inside. "No. Let him stew a few more days, then release him with a threat and have him followed. See where he leads you."

"Aye, my lord. Is there anyone else you wanted to see before leaving? Anything I can fetch for you before your trip?"

Owen shook his head no. "I'm leaving you in charge while we're gone." He glanced at Etayne.

"While *we're* gone?" Etayne asked with sudden interest, her eyebrows lifting.

Kevan bowed. "Understood. Let me know if you need anything further." Then he started away, leaving Owen and Etayne alone together in the corridor.

They walked in silence until they reached the Espion's secret Star Chamber. Owen slid the bolt in the door, trying to shake the ominous feelings that were making him ill. When he turned, Etayne was pacing and wringing her hands. She was agitated.

"So that was your father," Owen said softly. "Dragan."

Her head shot up and she nodded.

"You startled me," Owen laughed, shaking his head. "When you summoned your magic like that, I thought we were being ambushed. You chose Justine? Of all your disguises, her?"

Etayne gave him a wry smile. "She was on my mind at the moment and I needed something quickly before my father saw me."

"Do you think he did?"

"I don't know. He wouldn't have been expecting to see me . . . especially not dressed like this." She looked disturbed. "Why did you bring me to see him?"

"I knew you grew up in the sanctuary," Owen said. "I wanted you there in case you recognized the man. As it turns out, you did."

"There was something in his eye. A glimmer of knowing. I know he thinks I'm dead, and I make it a point *not* to visit the sanctuary because I don't want to be recognized. When I do, I always use a disguise."

Owen saw she was trembling. "Bad memories?"

She looked at him again in surprise. Her mouth twisted into a scowl. "There is no love lost between us, my lord." She looked even paler than before, and he could only imagine what childhood trauma she had endured.

"Is he dangerous? Should I keep him jailed?" Owen came up to her and put his hand on her shoulder.

The trembling melted away at his touch. "He's a thief and I'm a thief's daughter. I wasn't prepared. It startled me, that's all." She looked at him boldly, her courage returning. "I'm not that girl any longer. I'm not defenseless." She changed her expression, looking more at ease. "So where are *we* going, my lord? Who does the king wish killed this time?"

"There are many he wishes were dead," Owen said with a snide laugh. "No, we have a unique assignment, you and I. He's ordered me to go to Brythonica."

Etayne looked interested. "Indeed. For what purpose?"

Owen dropped his hand and shook his head. "To start another war."

# CHAPTER FIVE

## *The Prince's Widow*

Severn had spared no expense in indulging Eyric's disenfranchised bride. Lady Kathryn had her own private rooms in the palace, furnished with the best couches, sitting room chairs, and tapestries that the king's prodigious coffers could bestow. She had handmaidens, although she regularly dismissed them to attend to more important things. She also spent as little time as possible in the private rooms, always seeking opportunities to minister to the lowlier castes. The people had taken to calling her the Prince's Widow for her persistent widow's weeds.

Owen arranged the meeting for her sitting room, and had Etayne join them. The poisoner quickly opened and inspected the secret doors and spy holes where the king could covertly watch the meeting. That was another reason Lady Kathryn did not enjoy spending time in the rooms. Although she knew about his penchant for watching her secretly, she had to pretend otherwise.

After Etayne nodded that the room was secure from eavesdroppers, Lady Kathryn's expression wilted with anxiousness.

"How is he?" she whispered nervously. He wasn't sure who she was referring to—her husband or her son.

"Your husband is enduring as bravely as he can," Owen said dejectedly. Being with her always made him uneasy. He was the one who had deceived Eyric into leaving sanctuary and had arrested him. Lady Kathryn had never forgotten that, and while she appreciated his intercessions, her look was always wary and distrustful. "I brought this for you."

He dropped the book on the table. It was the one he had taken from Holistern Tower. Eyric left her little messages scribbled in the margins of the book. To someone picking it up, the words were crafted in a way to make it look like he was making notes or commenting on passages that were meaningful to him. But when he underlined words about love and affection, they were the jailed man's only way of expressing his feelings for his wife.

Kathryn's eyes filled with emotion, and she reverently lifted the book and pressed it to her breast. "Thank you, Owen," she said sincerely. "I know you risk a great deal helping us."

He shrugged and sighed, watching Etayne as she examined one of the globes on the table against the far wall. "I do what I can. I've also come from North Cumbria. The boy is healthy. He's a strapping lad. Very guarded and serious. He has your eyes."

She blinked quickly, trying to master her emotions again. "When can I see him? Is there any way you can arrange it? It might kill me, but I would give anything just to tousle his hair."

Owen shook his head. "That's not likely to happen anytime soon, Kathryn. Lord Catsby has been named Duke of North Cumbria."

Kathryn blanched. "You cannot be serious. That is dreadful news. What does that mean for the Queen of Atabyrion? I thought she would be the heir!"

"So did she," Owen said darkly. "But Severn won't trust one person with too much power. Even though she's Horwath's heir, she's also Iago Llewellyn's wife, and the king would rather enrich his own supporters than bolster a potential rival."

Kathryn's eyes narrowed with anger. "It is unjust."

"As you've already learned for yourself, the world has been that way for quite some time. There is little I can do about it. The decision was made before I even arrived. Catsby is already making an oaf of himself. But I came here with a particular favor to ask of you."

She gave him a startled look. "Whatever can I do? I'm a prisoner here."

"Trust me, you should prefer this cell to the one in which Eyric sits."

She flushed and shook her head. "I would rather stay in that drafty tower *with* him."

Owen believed she meant it. "It's not drafty, Kathryn. It's not like it was with Tunmore. If there were a way to bring you both together, you know I would. Some of the Espion are loyal to me, but I can't trust that they all are."

"What is this favor you spoke of?"

He swallowed. "The king fears that Iago may be a risk in the short term, following his decision. So he's bringing another hostage to join the palace. Iago and Elysabeth's eldest, their daughter, Genevieve. She's taken a fancy to your son," he added with a bittersweet smile. "They have been play-fellows. Severn will bring her to the palace. I was wondering if you would look after her. She may be frightened being so far away from Edonburick."

Kathryn's expression changed to one of sympathy and delight. "Of course I will! Dear child, of course! I will do all that I can to help her. Thank you, Owen, for thinking of me. It would help me endure the loneliness better."

Owen smiled, pleased by her reaction. "Thank you. Now for the bitter tidings." He started to pace, as he usually did while mulling through all of his problems. How best to introduce the next bit of news?

"I don't like your countenance," she told him worriedly.

"You shouldn't," he said with a grunt. "The king has ordered Etayne and me to leave the palace. In fact, we'll be leaving the kingdom shortly on a mission of . . . oh, how should we put this?" He gave Etayne a pleading look.

"Diplomacy," she supplied with a smirk.

"That's as good a word as any other. I'm going to threaten the Duchess of Brythonica. Etayne was ordered to go with me."

Kathryn's face blanched and then she started to tremble. "You're leaving me alone with *him*," she said in a subdued, terrified voice.

The look on her face made his stomach twist into knots. "Yes, I'm afraid that's true," he said softly.

Kathryn walked a few steps to a table and planted her palms on the flat surface, her shoulders quivering. "Both of you must go?" she asked pleadingly.

"The king orders it," Owen said helplessly. "I do not think we will be gone for long. You must be *strong*, Kathryn. You know the king has power in his voice. You must not let him touch you, even for a moment."

Her eyes were squeezed shut. "You don't know what it's like," she whispered thickly. "It's all I can do to keep my wits about me when he's near. Etayne is so much better at deception." She opened her eyes and turned, looking pleadingly at the poisoner. "I'm not as strong as you are."

Etayne looked at her sadly. "You must be, Kathryn. You must stand up to him on your own."

Kathryn looked as if she would collapse on the floor. "The only thing that keeps me from succumbing," she whispered, "is imagining my son with the crown on his head." Her breath started to quicken. "I can't do this. I can't endure it!"

Etayne shot Owen a worried look as he stood there helplessly and then she gave him a look that said he was being about as helpful as a brick. Etayne walked up to Kathryn and held her, gently stroking her back, the black silk fabric rustling softly.

"You can deceive him," Etayne said soothingly. "I know it's against your nature. But you must do it. You must practice. When he comes to visit you, you always stiffen up and become so distant. Be courteous. I'm not asking you to flirt with him. But smile. Stop looking at him as if he's a beast."

"He *is* a beast," Kathryn whispered desperately. "Even though the deconeus pronounced the marriage invalid, I told the king it was valid to *me*. Yet he persists in lavishing gifts. He's determined to conquer me. I can't . . . I can't endure much more of this." She gave Owen a pleading look, her cheeks wet with tears. "I'm breaking apart inside. I don't need wealth. I don't desire to be queen anymore. I miss Atabyrion with all my heart. Can you not just find a little cottage somewhere? A place where Eyric and Andrew and I can be a family together?" She broke away from Etayne's embrace and gestured to the opulent chamber. "I do not need any of this! I'd be happier as a fisherman's wife in Brugia than here. Please, Owen! Can you not make us disappear?"

Every time he met with Kathryn, it pained him more and more. "Do you think there is anywhere I could hide you that Severn wouldn't discover?" he asked her coldly. "There is always someone willing to wag their tongue when there is sufficient coin. Don't you think your father wishes to ransom you? He's tried four times! But the king doesn't want money. He wants you. Your unwillingness to yield only inflames him more." Owen rubbed his eyes. "I'm doing the best I can, Kathryn. But I understand a little about your suffering. Don't imagine I'm enjoying this."

She gave him a wary look, drying her eyes on her sleeve. She patted Etayne's shoulder and then shook her head. "Thank you for telling me. For . . . for warning me you were leaving. I'm frightened of how Severn makes me *feel*. He's twisted me with his power so that I feel compassion for him. That I even believe I *love* him at times. But I belong to another man. And it's not right for him to hunt me this way. It's not right."

Owen eyed her with pity. "No, it isn't. Seven years ago, he could have been toppled with a breeze. Now he's like flint." He sighed, disgusted with himself. "If he knew we were talking like this, he'd kill me. If he knew only a part of what I do behind his back." Owen shook his head, not daring to say more. "I must leave for Brythonica. I have a duty to perform, even though I find that duty distasteful. Bear yours the best you can. Hopefully when I come again, there will be more cheerful tidings. Farewell." He gave her a small bow.

Lady Kathryn smoothed the black fabric over her lap. She was twenty-five years old. A beauty, even in black, but much of her bloom had faded with her imprisonment. The king showed her constantly that he, not her husband, controlled her destiny. He controlled her sleeping arrangements. He controlled her wardrobe. He controlled who visited her. But he could not control her will. Owen saw the strength in her eyes, in the determined look forming on her pouting lips. She stood regally, and gave him a formal curtsy. "Thank you for all you've done, Lord Owen," she said in a firm, clear voice. "I will bear this patiently."

Owen admired her for it. He turned and went to the door, Etayne following silently save for the swish of her gown. As they exited into the hall, Owen's heart burned with unspent emotion.

"You look like you want to hit someone," Etayne said.

He glanced around before answering. There were no servants in the hall, no one nearby to hear them. "I don't know how much longer I can endure this either," he muttered under his breath.

"The solution is simple and always has been," Etayne said, keeping stride with him. "I could do it so secretly no one would ever know. Especially now that we're both leaving for Brythonica. Some powder in his gloves. A bit on his pillow. Owen, stop making this harder than it needs to be. He has become a tyrant."

Owen knew she was right, but he could not bring himself to commit murder. All of Owen's power had derived from King Severn. How could he convince the people that a young boy from North Cumbria was meant to be the next king? He had the beginnings of a plan. The original King Andrew had been raised in the household of another nobleman, unaware that he was the son of a king. A Fountain-blessed Wizr had put a sword in a fountain after professing that whoever drew the blade from the water was to be the new king. He had then used his powers to arrange for young King Andrew to draw the blade.

According to Duke Horwath, that very sword, which had gone on to transform a young Fountain-blessed girl into the legendary Maid of Donremy, was concealed in the ice caves. If he managed to retrieve the blade and secretly bring it to the fountain of Our Lady, he could say he'd had a *dream* that the new king would draw the blade. Of course, Severn was Fountain-blessed himself, so he could ruin the plan by taking the sword himself. Owen would have to approach the situation carefully.

"You're ignoring me?" Etayne said with a hint of injury to her tone.

"What you're offering you've offered before," he said under his breath. "But I can't *do* that."

"Then *I'll* do it," Etayne said darkly. "It will solve all of your problems in one stroke. Why should you be so squeamish about it?" She sniffed. "If I need to kill Marshal Roux, what is the difference?"

"The difference," Owen replied, "is that you're the *King's* Poisoner. He's ordering it done. And believe me, I don't feel right about it either. I'm going to try and find a way to threaten the duchess without killing her chief protector. Besides, Roux will not be as easily toppled as Severn assumes."

Etayne let out her breath slowly. "You are obstinate."

"This is like a game of Wizr," Owen said. "You can't always predict what will happen. How many other pieces are waiting to invade our side of the board? The lad is only seven years old. He's not ready to become a king."

"He may not get another chance," Etayne said knowingly, giving voice to Owen's own thoughts. "You are the one calling the moves. Your *dreams* tell the future, do they not? Haven't you deceived the king for years into believing that? But sometimes trickery isn't enough. Sometimes there just isn't a good move to make on the board. You have to sacrifice pieces."

Owen laughed at that. "In Wizr, one doesn't sacrifice the king. That's what ends the game."

Her lips pursed; her eyes narrowed slyly. She looked quite pretty, and it distracted him. "But then doesn't a new game start?"

♦ ♦ ♦

Owen was only too grateful to leave Kingfountain behind, though he worried what might happen in his absence. Kathryn was a strong and courageous woman. But he could see the cracks in her, the weakness of the constant stress on her soul. King Severn was nearly twice her age, but she was young enough to bear children. And the king was ever patient.

Owen and Etayne reached Tatton Hall two days later. He had sent word ahead to his herald Farnes to assemble an escort to ride with them to Averanche and from there to Brythonica. Owen had never entered the duchess's lands before. He had heard reports that some of the most fertile valleys and farmlands existed in Brythonica. The mildness of the weather was famous, and the sea air purportedly made the crops more plentiful. The duchy was renowned for growing berries of all sorts, and some had jokingly dubbed past rulers the Duke of Berries. There were ships coming and going constantly from her ports to carry the delicate fruit to the far reaches of other kingdoms.

Despite the circumstances, he looked forward to finally meeting the duchess, Lady Sinia. Although they had been neighbors for many years, she never left her domains for fear of abduction. Owen wondered secretly if the lord marshal also played a part in her reticence. Was he truly the power in Brythonica, as Severn supposed? Was she living in an opulent prison much like Kathryn? If that was the case, then perhaps disrupting it would be a strategic move.

After dismounting in front of the manor doors, Owen handed his reins to a groom. Etayne was windblown, but they had oft traveled together, and he was accustomed to seeing her this way. His servants knew her true identity and treated her with wary respect.

Farnes waited at the head of the column of servants standing to greet the duke upon his return.

"I told you I don't like the formalities," Owen said in a grumbling tone, looking at everyone standing idle and attentive.

"I know, my lord," Farnes said with a wheezing rasp in his voice. He'd had trouble with his throat in previous years, but he was determined to continue serving. His eldest son, Benjamin, was being groomed to take his father's place. Unfortunately, the son was only twelve. "But we have guests, and I thought it proper to greet you more formally this time."

"Guests?" Owen asked with concern. He had not received any messages about these guests, and as the head of the Espion, he hated surprises. He had the sudden impression that Marshal Roux was there. The man had a nasty habit of anticipating Owen's actions. "Who?"

"Lord Tidwell," Farnes said. "And his *daughter* Ida. Lord Bascom and his *daughter* Prynn. There's also a wealthy merchant from Genevar who stopped at Averanche first and then came to Tatton Hall when he heard you were returning. I think he has a daughter in tow as well. And then there is an heiress from Brugia who is staying in the village. She's forty years old and quite determined to meet you."

Owen stared at Farnes in disbelief. "You're letting them *stay* in the manor?"

Farnes looked helpless. "It would be the height of rudeness not to offer hospitality."

Owen wanted to throttle his herald. "It's the height of rudeness to show up uninvited!"

The look Farnes gave him was scandalized. "You're not going to send them away!" he hissed under his breath.

Owen shook his head. "No. They can stay as long as they like. *I'm* the one who will go." He turned back to his groomsman and whistled, startling the young man. He turned to one of his captains. "The men can rest. Etayne and I are riding on to Averanche. Join us there."

Etayne's eyes were alight with amusement. Wisely, she said nothing.

# CHAPTER SIX

## *Poisoner's Gift*

Owen was so exhausted when he reached Averanche that he fell asleep on a small couch with a goblet of wine still in his hand. His dreams of Ankarette were so vivid he could smell her scent of faded roses. In them, he was a child again, feeling safe because she was watching over him.

He imagined her stroking his hair and then realized that the sensation was not part of the dream. It was real. When he blinked his eyes open, he saw Etayne sitting at the edge of the couch, gazing down at him tenderly, her fingers slowly stroking his hair. For a moment, he forgot who she was, where he was, or how he'd come to be there, but the hard ride from Tatton Hall came back in a rush.

"I fell asleep, didn't I?" he mumbled, remembering the goblet. She had set it on the table next to the couch.

"I would have tugged off your boots, but I didn't want to wake you," Etayne said. "You looked so peaceful."

He rubbed his bleary eyes on the back of his hand and sat up, feeling the warmth from her sitting so near. She glided her fingers through his hair one last time and then nestled her hands in her lap. The look of yearning she gave him made him deeply uncomfortable.

"How late is it?" he asked, chagrined. The curtains were closed, but the room was dark. It was still the middle of the night. He scooted back until he was sitting up, but she did not give up her seat on the edge of the couch.

"I made sure the room was secured," she said, looking over at the curtained window. "The latches are all fastened and set with traps. The bed looks infinitely more comfortable than the couch. There's some cold capon and cheese over there from the earlier meals served by the castle staff. They didn't expect you to arrive unannounced, so they're staying up late to make sure things are ready in the morning." She smiled at him. "I would have left you, but the door cannot be barred from outside. I didn't want to leave you so . . . so vulnerable."

That was a good word to describe the way he was feeling. He was exhausted from the long ride from Kingfountain. He'd anticipated a quick respite at Tatton Hall, but was in no mood to humor rich heiresses.

Etayne's eyes narrowed. "You haven't told me how your trip to the North went." She reached up and smoothed hair from his brow. "Was it as painful as you suspected? You made it before Lord Horwath passed away?"

Owen let out a pent-up breath. The room was lit by an assortment of thick candles offering a small glow. He pinched the bridge of his nose, closed his eyes, and thought hard about the question.

"It was painful, to be sure," he told her honestly. "She's happy with her life. With her children. Even her husband wasn't too intolerable," he added wryly. "She's moved forward, that's clear. I feel as if I'm stranded on a foreign shore now."

Etayne nodded sagely. One of the many things he appreciated about her was that she was an excellent listener, and even though he knew she cared about him, she never tried to push her feelings on him.

"You weren't tempted to make her forget Iago?" she prodded.

"By the Fountain, no!" Owen said with a frown of disgust. "I could never do that to her. Nor could I look her in the eye afterward." He gave her a solemn look. "She wants me to be happy. To find someone else to love." He shook his head. "It's not so easy as that."

Etayne nodded sympathetically. "Your marriage will be commanded by the king, it seems. As hers was. Do you think this duchess could win your heart?"

Owen scowled. "I'm pretty confident she'll hate me for what I'm about to do. The king doesn't expect us to marry. He made it patently clear that we're going to Brythonica to start a war, not form a marriage alliance. I'm supposed to offend her, not woo her. I'm more than capable of *that*."

She gave him a knowing smile. "Oh, you are quite adept at spoiling hopes, my lord." She fussed with the front of his tunic. "There are no Espion working in Brythonica, so we are going there blindly. What have you heard about it?"

"Most of what I know is from the mayor of Averanche. The fashions in Occitania are quite different from those in Ceredigion or Atabyrion. I've heard she's a pretty lass, but it's well known that she rarely gives audiences. You'll be studying her closely, I am sure," he said with a conniving smile.

Etayne dimpled. "You know me so well."

"I'm expecting trouble from Marshal Roux. Facing him on the battlefield may actually prove a challenge."

"Not for you, surely!" she said teasingly.

Owen shook his head and chuckled. Feeling restless, he started to rise from the couch, and she stood to let him up. "How long was I asleep?"

"An hour perhaps. I thought you'd sleep longer. Aren't you tired?"

"I am," he said, stretching his arms. "I'm not going to Brythonica without an escort. A hundred men will do, I think. I don't want to appear too aggressive or distrusting."

She took a step toward the door before stopping abruptly. "In the game of Wizr, sometimes there are no easy moves left," she said. She gave him a knowing look. "Each one requires a sacrifice. Let me be blunt, Owen. You intend to topple the king." Her voice was very low and serious. "We've discussed this for years. Severn hasn't named an heir yet. You believe his heir *should* be Kathryn's son. He's the Dreadful Deadman. How can you make that happen without deposing Severn Argentine?"

Owen stared at the bed, longing to drop into the oblivion of sleep. "I'm still working on it," he said vaguely. His ideas were still not fully formed. How he wished Ankarette were here to advise him. She would have had it all figured out by now.

Etayne shook her head. "Your loyalties are conflicted. I can see it on your face. You are compelled to obey a king that you no longer respect. Out of duty. But your mind tells you that he's not the man you once served. And your support of him only strengthens his malice. The other leaders of the realm look to you to act first."

"Hardly," Owen countered. "They look to their *own* interests. Catsby is now the duke of the North and he will plunder everything Horwath built up. He'll strip Dundrennan to its bones. Evie and Iago may eventually persuade the king to give it up, but what they'll end up with will cost them more than it benefits them. I've seen the same thing happen to other lords of the realm. Even if I *were* to marry the duchess, do you think the king would allow me to keep so much power?" He snorted.

"Then what are you waiting for?" Etayne pressed with growing frustration in her voice. "The king to grow old and die? Owen, he's barely fifty. He's still as strong and hale as he was twenty years ago. Why do you wait?"

Owen stared at her. She had asked an honest question, and it deserved an honest answer. He sighed wearily. "Sit down on the couch, Etayne. This may take a while to explain."

"I'm not tired," she said, but she promptly obeyed.

He went to the table next to the couch and fetched his goblet. He took a sip of the currant wine and winced. It was a bit tart. He set it down and then perched on the edge of the couch, looking down at the poisoner.

"Have you heard the story of the Duke of Bollinger?" he asked.

Etayne frowned and shook her head. "No. Was he from our history?"

Owen nodded. "Bollinger is the name of the royal castle in East Stowe. That's where he was born, so it became his common name. Until he became king. From then on, he was known as Henricus Argentine."

Her eyes widened with understanding. "Yes, I do know that name."

Owen continued. "Elysabeth told me this story years ago. She loves history more than I do. Henricus was the Duke of East Stowe. The king at the time, much like Severn, was a brash man who pitted his nobles against each other. His marriage was childless, so he had no heir. You can imagine the infighting that occurred as the many Argentine cousins sought to be named his heir. One of these was Bollinger."

Etayne looked thoughtful. "He was banished from the realm, wasn't he? I do recall something about that."

Owen was impressed. "It was over an argument he had with another duke. The two of them were snarling like hounds for scraps, so the king banished them both. The duke of the North was banished for life. Bollinger was banished for a set time. While he was gone, the king plundered his lands to support a war against the island of Legault. The king was still embroiled in that fight when Bollinger returned, demanded his rights as duke, and proceeded to topple the king. The kingdom rallied behind him, and he was named Henricus. He spent the rest of his life trying to hold on to the power he had seized."

Owen rose from the couch and began pacing. "Do you ever get the feeling, Etayne, that history plays itself over and over? Like some sort of farce where actors assemble and assume different roles? I feel like I'm Bollinger. That events are trying to force me to play a certain part." He rubbed his jaw, feeling the untidy whiskers there. He hadn't shaved in weeks. He didn't care.

"You feel *you* should claim the throne?" she asked him softly, almost eagerly.

"No!" he shot back, dousing the flame before it struck the tinder of his ambitions. "But I can see why Bollinger was *tempted* to do it. It's the same reason Severn took the seat. He worried about losing his wife and son after Eredur died. He was the duke of the North, a powerful man, and he feared it would be stripped away from him so that the queen dowager's children could inherit. Of course he fought for it! And I feel the same destiny dragging me toward the same course. But I want to fight it, Etayne." He looked at her, his eyes blazing with energy. "I don't want to be *told* what to do. I don't want to be swept away on a current that transforms me into another Severn." His voice fell to a whisper. "I fear that most of all. Losing myself. I already *talk* like him," he said dejectedly.

Etayne rose from the couch, her look serious and contemplative. She touched the side of his face. "You are not Severn Argentine."

"*Yet*," Owen said. "But I feel it inside me. I feel the anger. The frustration. The helplessness. The role of the conniving uncle will next be played by Owen Kiskaddon!" he said passionately. "Have you ever felt that you don't have a choice? That the Fountain's current is too strong? I'm trying to swim against it, Etayne. But I'm so tired already. I'm already weary and I'm still a young man. Will there come a day when I gather children around me for fear of poison?" He gave her a pleading look.

Her demeanor was serious. His words had struck something inside her.

"That's why you won't murder him," she said, nodding. "Because that's what *he* would have done."

He shook his head. "No. Because it's *wrong*. I know all the kings use poison on their enemies, but I believe a king should be a protector, not a destroyer. When Eredur died, Ankarette was gone. She was away on some sort of assignment. I never knew what. I think she was in Occitania, but I can't remember, to be truthful. Why was she sent away? What would have happened if she hadn't been gone? I shudder to think of it. I might be a feckless young nobleman in my father's house, wishing one of those simpering girls I left back there would notice me. I'd be gibbering in fear. I would never have met Evie." He shrugged. "I wouldn't have known *you*."

She smiled at the gallant comment, her expression so pleased he regretted saying it. She shook her head. Her wig was blond. He had seen her wear so many disguises, so many faces, he wondered if she even knew who she was anymore.

"So you are swimming against the current," she said succinctly. "Trying to avoid a fate you may not be able to."

"To do otherwise would make *me* into a monster next," Owen said. "I would avoid that if I could." He turned away from her and walked over to the bed, feeling so weary. "After telling me the story of Bollinger, Elysabeth said she wondered what would have happened if he hadn't assumed the throne after all. If he had completed his exile. Who knows how long the king would have ruled. But I can imagine how furious he must have been to watch his duchy be gutted, his inheritance surrendered to others. I can imagine how Elysabeth is feeling right now. She's in a similar position."

He felt Etayne come up behind him, but he nearly flinched when her fingers began massaging his shoulders. "You have enough worries, Owen. You'll need your wits about you when you meet the Duchess of

Brythonica and her marshal. Can I stay with you? To watch over you while you sleep?"

He knew her offer was simply that, an offer to watch and protect him. He found her loyalty refreshing, for many of the Espion strove for personal glory. But she could not stay. The same soft touch that was easing the tight muscles in his shoulders was also invoking stirrings of pleasure. His body was rebelling against him. He knew everyone thought he and Etayne were more than merely friends. It would be so easy to surrender to others' expectations. She would never betray him.

But he couldn't do that. He shook his head slowly no.

Etayne's eyes crinkled a bit as the rejection came, but she was an excellent actress. She walked slowly to the door and then twisted the handle. "Don't forget to bolt it," she reminded him.

After she was gone, he slid the bolt into place. He could still sense her standing on the other side of the door. Owen felt a growl of selfishness unleash itself inside his heart. Why not find comfort and solace in a willing girl? She knew he didn't love her that way. She didn't care. He kicked the thought in his mind to silence it. When he was a young boy, old Stiev Horwath had told him a story that he had never forgotten. That inside each person lives two wolves. One was full of evil, jealousy, anger, resentment. The other wolf was kind, benevolent, generous, and dutiful.

Owen had asked how someone could survive with two such beasts inside them. Would not one of them eventually win? Duke Horwath had given him a crinkled smile.

"*Which wolf wins?*" he had asked. "*The one that you feed.*"

It was clear which one Severn was nourishing.

He walked away from the door.

# CHAPTER SEVEN

## *Lady Sinia*

Owen summoned his host, and after a much-needed day of rest, prepared to depart for Ploemeur. He carefully pored over the Espion maps of the realm, growing frustrated by the vagueness he found there. Brythonica was much smaller than Westmarch, and he could only name three cities, two rivers, and the main road. There were several densely wooded areas, game parks as the mayor of Averanche had once explained to him, several of which bordered his own lands, but as to their size and borders, the map was empty.

Giving it some thought, he decided it would be best to meet the king's expectations quickly and ruthlessly. He ordered his men not to wash their tunics, and he himself wore the most travel-stained outfit he could find amongst his possessions. He intended to arrive dust-spattered and ill-kempt. Surely the duchess was accustomed to being courted by those intending to impress her, and Owen had no intention to follow suit. His goal was to offend her as quickly as possible, laying bare Severn's machinations for her duchy, and then retreat back to Westmarch to work on his plan to make Eyric and Kathryn's son the heir of Ceredigion.

The weather could not have been more perfect, which made for a pleasant ride through the countryside. The air had the salty tang of the sea to it, for Brythonica was a jagged inlet along the coast of Occitania, full of grottos and lagoons and sweet-smelling eucalyptus trees that were towering and ancient. Etayne rode at his side, hooded and mysterious, as they crossed the border between Averanche and Brythonica. Shortly after entering the domain, they were hailed by warriors bearing the Raven tunic of Brythonica, but the border guards were totally outnumbered by Owen's men. When they learned Duke Kiskaddon was coming to meet the duchess, they blanched, let him pass, and undoubtedly sent riders dashing ahead to forewarn their ruler.

The land was full of rolling hills and valleys, lush parks, and manors with sculpted gardens that reminded Owen of Tatton Hall. The roads crisscrossed through spacious fields full of line after line of thick green berry bushes. There were strawberries, thimbleberries, honeysuckle, currants, and bilberries. The variety of colors and smells was pleasant and inviting, and Owen was impressed by the industry he saw. Everywhere he looked, foragers were working their way down the orderly rows, gently collecting the berries into small boxes strapped to their bodies. At the edges of the fields yet more peasants stacked crates of berries into wagons for shipment to the port cities. Despite all the work, there was a calm, comforting feeling in the air.

Several leagues into the countryside, they came across a road running alongside one of the game parks. The forest was thick and overgrown. It would have been difficult for horses to pass. Owen felt a strange sensation as he stared at the majestic eucalyptus and redwood trees, almost as if the forest were alive and gazing back at him. He saw squirrels rushing through the undergrowth, some climbing the trees and perching on limbs, their huge gray tails swishing as they moved. There was a ruckus from the birds lodged in the high branches.

After passing the woods, they reached another valley filled with even more farms and lush fields. These were more heavily populated than the ones Owen had seen earlier in the day. There were beautifully built villas occupying each hilltop, but no fortifications could be seen, and their walls appeared to be made of wood and plaster rather than stone. They were retreats, not structures intended for safety. Owen hadn't seen a single castle along the journey, which gave the land a vulnerable feel. It would be easy to march an army on the packed-earth roads. The only natural barriers were the occasional woods, but those wouldn't be suited for soldiers. A heartsick feeling struck him at the thought of this beautiful place being trampled and ravaged by war.

As they traveled deeper into the country, Owen felt the unmistakable sensation of the Fountain all around him, but there was no obvious source. There were none of the massive rivers and waterfalls that marked Ceredigion, and while each villa appeared to have a fountain in the courtyard, they were too distant to be heard. The lapping of the canals was so gentle it was almost unnoticeable. The gentle murmur of the Fountain seemed to be coming from the land itself, which he had never experienced before. He sensed it in the peasant farmers working joyfully in their gardens. He heard it in the air of music coming from the small villages. He saw maypoles and flowered garlands. There were many children dashing around, playing games. Their voices seemed to conjure the magic of the Fountain. In his mind's eye, he imagined what it would have been like to grow up here, playing in such a carefree way, basking in the magic of this land.

Owen turned to look at Etayne, only to catch her gazing longingly at the scene.

"Do you feel it?" he whispered to her.

Her eyes were serious, almost sad. "I feel it everywhere," she answered softly. "What is this place?"

Owen shook his head, not certain what to make of it—a sensation that only heightened as they continued to ride into the land, intent on reaching the capital of Brythonica by nightfall. The valleys and hills were so idyllic it almost felt sacrilegious to ride hastily past them. Peasants working near the roads lifted their caps and waved at the strangers, as if totally unconcerned by the foreign soldiers in their midst. Owen spied an old man resting against the trunk of a eucalyptus, surrounded by sunny-haired grandchildren, one of whom was peeling long strips of bark from the tree. The grandfather tickled a squealing girl, which made Owen smile despite his desire to appear stern.

The peasants weren't dirty and unkempt. They were cheerful, hard-working, and exuded a sense of calm and safety that didn't make sense considering the apparent lack of protection.

Ahead loomed another wood, but this time, the road went through the middle of it. It would be an ideal place for a trap, and Owen's gut began to clench with wariness. He gave orders for ten men to ride on ahead and ten to remain at the edge of the woods to alert them of an ambush. There were ravens in the trees, their black plumage stark against the silver bark and green glossy leaves. Several cawed and fluttered from branch to branch. Owen had the unmistakable feeling of being watched.

"So many ravens," Etayne muttered curiously. At her words, about a dozen lifted into the air simultaneously. Owen felt a sudden, piercing dread that the birds would attack them, but they flew away instead, their path hidden by the upper boughs.

As Owen entered the woods, he felt a shudder pass through him. The sense of the Fountain was incredibly strong in the woods. The feeling was ancient, implacable, powerful. It was like being in the grip of a shadow. The hair on the back of his neck and arms stood up with pronounced gooseflesh. His men seemed to be infected by his mood, their eyebrows scowling as they began searching the trees on each side of them.

"The feeling is thicker in here," Etayne said with worry. "But it's even stronger that way." She nodded toward the left side of the road, the woods so dense they couldn't see far.

Owen gave her a short nod. While the presence of the Fountain was overpowering, it was particularly strong to their left. He felt it drawing him, beckoning him to leave the road, to learn its secrets.

Etayne looked in that direction as well, then glanced back at him with a quirked brow. She was offering to explore it.

Owen shook his head no. But he fully intended to go there on his way out. Something was hidden in the woods. Something he didn't understand and craved to. Something that might help him in his rebellion.

One of the advance scouts came riding back around the bend, his face flushed. He reined in hard in front of Owen. "My lord, Marshal Roux is ahead with twenty riders."

*He was waiting for us*, Owen realized again, frowning at the thought. *He knew we were coming.* He wasn't surprised, but it was another sign that Roux was not an enemy he wished to make.

"How are they armed?"

"Like knights," the soldier said. "More polished than we are."

"Thank you," Owen said. He knew the confrontation was inevitable. Best to get it over with quickly. They rode ahead and found the marshal's knights blocking the road. Their tabards were clean and tidy, the white field with the black raven sigil on it. They held lances with banners as well, each knight armed for battle.

Owen grit his teeth as he approached, slowing the horse to a trot. He glanced at the woods on each side of Lord Roux, hoping to discern movement. There were only more ravens. A whole unkindness of them. He smirked at the thought. Evie had once told him about the various names used to describe groupings of birds. It had taken her nearly an hour to recite them all.

"My lord Kiskaddon, I'm surprised to see you," Marshal Roux said. As always, he looked wary, proud, and suspicious.

"Are you truly?" Owen answered with a snort of disbelief. "It seems to me as if you were expecting us."

"Word does travel quickly here."

"I imagine it does," Owen countered. He tugged on the reins, stopping his horse in front of Roux's.

"Why have you come?" Marshal Roux demanded. "We received no message from you. Nothing to state your business."

"I come with a message from my king," Owen said evenly. "And I am to deliver it to the duchess in person. Be so kind as to escort us there. As you can see," he added, gesturing to his unkempt soldiers, "we're simple soldiers on a mission for our king. There was no time for preamble."

The lord marshal's eyes narrowed. He seemed to be sizing Owen up, trying to discern the true reason for his visit.

"This is highly suspicious," Roux said.

"I can imagine why it would be seen that way," Owen replied. "We are allies, are we not? Is it not proper for us to discuss matters without a formal invitation?"

"You brought soldiers with you," Roux pointed out.

"As did you. Why should that concern either of us?"

"And who is *she*?" Roux asked, looking guardedly at Etayne, his eyes full of distrust.

Owen hesitated before responding. Then he chuckled. "You don't think I would have come this far out of Ceredigion without suitable *protection*, do you, Lord Marshal? Do you intend to talk until sunset? It is still a fair journey to the city, is it not?"

Lord Roux frowned at the comment, at Owen's evasiveness and insinuation—all of which were deliberate. Owen would not give away the purpose of his visit until they were in front of the duchess. This put Roux at a disadvantage.

"Of course you are welcome," Lord Roux said flatly, with no hint of the sentiment. "The duchess herself ordered me to bring you to her as her guests and allies. She is anxious to meet you, Lord Kiskaddon. Come with me."

He turned his horse with a sharp tug on the reins, and the pennant bearers hoisted their javelins and rode in organized columns.

◆　◆　◆

The capital of Brythonica was built into a cove off the coast and had expansive quays and docks and ships bearing many flags, especially that of Genevar. The cove was crested by hills on which sat an array of villas and gardened manors. The royal castle was built on a rocky crag at the head of the bay, and the road leading to it was so steep that switchbacks had been dug out of it, making it possible to ascend but incredibly difficult to assault. It was obvious the location of Ploemeur had been chosen carefully, for it was the most defensible structure Owen had seen in Brythonica. It reminded him of Kingfountain palace, only much smaller and more difficult to reach.

Riding up the switchbacks was an arduous affair, and the air soon filled with chalk-white dust from the constant tramp of the horses. As they ascended the rocky hill, Owen could see the beautiful estates stretched out below them, and the fading sunlight and shadows filling the bay lent a purple cast to the stones of the hill.

When they finally reached the castle, Owen was exhausted from the ride and growing concerned that he had blundered into a trap. As he gazed at the structure, he tried to examine it critically, wondering how an invading army could besiege such a place. Even with all of Severn's sizable resources, it would be no easy feat. The castle could be held for a very long time with minimal guardians. The duchess could defend from the heights while Chatriyon's army, once the Occitanian king learned about the siege, could ravage the countryside and attack at their rear. It was beginning to look like a foolish venture.

The duchess had well-dressed grooms waiting to take their horses and offer refreshment to the men.

Lord Roux dismounted and immediately made his way over to Owen, tugging off his gloves and stuffing them into his belt. "Your men need time to wash and dress. I would advise a breakfast meeting with the duchess. The view of the bay is exquisite in the morning, and I'm certain—"

"The news I bring is urgent, my lord," Owen interrupted, clapping his dusty gloves together and letting a cloud plume before him. "It cannot wait."

Roux's eyes hardened even more. "You are filthy," he said angrily.

"I'm a soldier," Owen replied with a shrug. Then he gave Roux a stern look. "I didn't come all this way to be trifled with."

Roux bristled at the choice of words. "Why are you here, Kiskaddon?" he said in a low voice.

"As I told you, my business is with the duchess. Shall we?" He gestured mockingly toward the castle.

Lord Roux tried and failed to conceal his displeasure. He started marching across the bailey at a quick pace. There were decorative urns arranged before the entryway, and Owen stopped when he saw the symbol carved on them. He had never seen it before, but it evoked the feeling of the Fountain.

How best to describe it? The symbol was like three interlocking horseshoes, the ends facing east, west, and south. In the east/west crescents, two faces in profile had been carved into the stone. One face looked pleasant, well-proportioned. The other face looked sharp, frowning, and angry. A third face pointed down with a neutral expression.

"This way," Roux scolded, noticing Owen had stopped to gawk at the urns.

As he entered the palace, Owen noticed the symbol everywhere. The floor was decorated in black and white tiles, but unlike the sanctuary of Our Lady of Kingfountain, the tiles weren't arranged like a Wizr board. Instead they formed a repeating hook design like waves, all the white ones symmetrical to the black ones. He felt the presence of the Fountain strongly in the palace, but as he'd noticed elsewhere in Brythonica, it was *everywhere*, not anchored to a specific person.

The palace servants were all dressed in fine clothes. Not opulent, but pleasant and colorful. A few servants gave him curious looks and wrinkled their noses slightly in response to his dirty tunic and boots. The interior corridor was quite long, but they eventually reached a pair of open doors guarded by six men. Lord Roux nodded to the guards as he passed, and the men responded with dutiful nods. Owen felt his chest flutter with unease as he prepared to face the ruler of Brythonica. He dreaded fulfilling the duty Severn had given him, suddenly self-conscious of how condescending and provoking the ultimatum would be.

The duchess immediately captured his attention when he entered the room. There was no wondering who she was, no misunderstanding. The mayor of Averanche had said she was beautiful, and he clearly was not blind.

Her name was Sinia Montfort, and she was the scion of one of the ancient noble houses of Occitania. She had wavy gold hair that went all the way down her back, but part was braided and coiffed behind her head. The crown she wore could hardly be called a crown. It was a circlet of gold with ornamented leaves dangling from the band, one just touching her forehead. She had on a pale blue gown studded with small pearls on the front and a surcoat of even paler fabric. Her eyes were blue, even more so than the gown, and they welled with worry. She wasn't seated on the throne, but pacing near it, her fingers fidgeting with a ring on her right hand. There was a light flush on her cheeks, as if she felt extremely unsettled.

She reminded him a little of Princess Elyse when he had first met her as a little boy. Although she was an undeniable beauty, there did not appear to be any haughtiness to her. When she noticed them enter, the fidgeting with her ring ended and she stood in a regal pose, gazing at him with an expression that was difficult to describe. Not anger, but almost as if she were nervous to see him in an excited way. As if she had been *wanting* to see him.

*Oh dear*, he thought with dread. *This is going to be awful for her.*

The lord marshal approached halfway into the audience hall and then dropped to both knees, bowing his head reverentially. All of the servants mimicked him and dropped down to both knees. That was an unusual custom.

Owen, on the other hand, did not kneel. He was a duke, his station equal to hers. He did incline his head to her.

"You are most welcome to Ploemeur, Lord Kiskaddon," the duchess said. She inclined her head to him. "Our allies are always welcome. Let me be the first to thank you for rendering aid when we were being invaded."

Owen felt the irony of her comment like a stab to the gut. At the time, he had helped her avoid a forced marriage with Chatriyon, the King of Occitania. Now the King of Ceredigion had sent him here to press his own proposal.

"No thanks are needed, my lady," he answered with a shrug of no concern. "You may want to keep your thanks for a better time. I have come on the king's errand, and he is not known to be a patient man."

Lady Sinia gestured to Lord Roux and the others to rise, which they did in a uniform manner.

"Lord Kiskaddon would not reveal the nature of his urgent summons to our lands," Roux said, giving the duchess a sharp look. "It may be best to dismiss the servants ere he—"

"That won't be necessary at all," Owen countermanded, deliberately goading the lord marshal. "I don't intend to stay very long." Owen began to saunter in the throne room, eyeing the tall columns and decorative vases. He walked up to one and picked it up as if it were his own, noticing the triple crescent symbol was there as well. He set it back down and glanced at Lord Roux, who was turning red with anger and resentment. Etayne had positioned herself among the servants, close enough that she could watch the proceedings and intervene in case things became hostile.

"Why have you come?" Lady Sinia asked politely.

Owen could only imagine how he looked in her eyes. She looked so beautiful, polished, and regal. And here he stood in his dirty boots and sweat-stained tunic. With a scraggly half beard and smudged eyes, his odor clashing with the vase of fresh flowers.

"Well, my lady, it's really a simple matter," Owen said offhandedly. "King Severn wishes to enhance the relationship between Ceredigion and Brythonica." He paused again to admire a curtain, deliberately adding to the suspense. He nodded approvingly, then turned and faced her. He hated himself. He hated what Severn was making him do. What he was trying to make him become.

*Get this over with*, he chided himself.

Owen let out a breath and then marched up to the duchess. Roux's hand went for his sword pommel, as if he feared Owen might attack her. The servants gaped at his rudeness and effrontery. Etayne reached for a dagger.

He dropped to one knee in front of Lady Sinia and took her dainty hand in his dirty one, causing a gasp of shock from some of the observers.

"I have come to Plumerie," he said, deliberately butchering the name of her capital, "to offer you my hand in marriage. My king commands me to wed you, and I must obey. Loyalty binds me, just as it will bind our duchies under the throne of Severn Argentine. What say you, my lady? I must bring my king your answer."

He stared into her eyes, gritting his teeth, loathing himself for what he was doing.

He couldn't see Lord Roux's face, but he could imagine his expression from the tone of his voice. "How *dare* you," he growled with barely suppressed outrage. "You, sir, have exceeded all propriety. How dare you speak to her thus!"

Owen tried to look abashed, to give Sinia a helpless shrug to communicate that none of this was his own choice. But he was surprised by the pleased look on her face. The delight in her eyes. This was not the reaction he had expected.

"Yes, my lord," she said, squeezing his hand. "Yes, I think I will have you."

◆ ◆ ◆

*My lord Kiskaddon,*

*The king has arrived back at Kingfountain from the North. There is much ill will between the new duke and the population of the duchy. Catsby has occupied Dundrennan for not even a fortnight and he has already shipped many of the treasures of the palace to his manors in East Stowe and Southport. I thought you'd want to know. While he tries to do this secretly, the servants are appalled and outraged at his blatant plundering. He has also dismissed many of the loyal families who have served the Horwath line for years, and brought in his own men. He may not listen to reason, but I implore you to speak to him as you are highly regarded in this corner of the realm. His actions are stirring the bitterest enmity. One final note—the king has requested companionship for the daughter of King Iago and Queen Elysabeth. There is a foundling at Dundrennan that was requested, a lad about her own age by the name of Andrew. He'll be sent to Kingfountain shortly. When do you expect to return from your visit to Brythonica?*

    *Kevan Amrein*
    *Kingfountain Palace*

◆ ◆ ◆

# CHAPTER EIGHT

*Secrets*

A pit opened up in Owen's stomach. He had the queer sensation that he had finally been outmaneuvered, though he had no idea how. Her response had so surprised him that he found himself momentarily rendered speechless, his mouth partway open. He shut it, still at a loss for words, and slowly rose, staring at Sinia incredulously.

It did not take long before Marshal Roux rushed up to his side. "It takes some gall, my lord," he said, his voice raw with anger and accusation, "to come hither with such tidings. My lady, I *implore* you to reconsider such a blatant attempt at extortion! We have not defended Brythonica these many years to surrender it to another king without a fight!"

Owen watched the duchess's reaction closely, looking for a sign that his hunch was correct, that Lord Roux was the true power behind Brythonica. Perhaps the duchess saw marriage to Owen as her only escape from the man. She still had not released her grip on Owen's fingers.

But her gaze contained no fear when she turned it to Roux. It was pragmatic, patient. "Lord Marshal, I thank you for your advice and many years of loyal service. I do not make this decision lightly; you may be sure. Long has my duchy been vulnerable to attack. We have enjoyed a long season of peace due to our alliance with Ceredigion." She returned her gaze to Owen. "I see wisdom in cementing the alliance. I know you wish to return promptly to your king, Owen, but may I beg you to remain for a few days? I would care to show you my domain and discuss terms of the betrothal that would mutually serve our interests. Would that be agreeable to you?"

Again, Owen was dumbfounded, and the throbbing vein in Marshal Roux's forehead told him he was not alone in that sensation. "My lady, I implore you to heed my warning!" Roux said. "If you allow this alliance to proceed, then everything we have fought for, everything your *father* fought for, will be ruined!"

Owen felt rankled by the objection, although he had expected it all along. He pulled his hand away and turned to meet the eyes of the lord marshal. "I don't think it's your place to reverse the word of a duchess, my lord," Owen said icily. "Is she beholden to you in some way?"

Roux's eyes blazed with white-hot fire.

Lady Sinia reached out and touched Roux's arm. "My lord, truly. I do not make this decision rashly or lightly. I hold your counsel in the highest respect and regard, as I always have."

"It would seem not," he sniffed, barely controlling his temper. Then he turned on his heel and stormed out of the chamber.

Owen watched him leave. When he glanced back at Sinia, he saw a disappointed frown tug the corner of her mouth, but it was gone in an instant. "How long can I persuade you to linger in Ploemeur?" she asked.

Owen risked a look back at the door, where all the servants were gathered, giving him hateful looks. He had come there to alienate and offend. He had succeeded with everyone except the duchess herself. Or perhaps she was just better at disguising her true emotions. He warily reached out to her with his magic, letting the ripples of the Fountain, which he had felt constantly since entering Brythonica, gently flow from him.

The reaction he truly hoped to see was from Lady Sinia herself. The magic glided from his fingertips, traveling through the duchess like a vapor. He sensed her stiffen, her eyes crinkling slightly, as if a breeze had given her a chill. Then he felt himself brushing against a huge dam of power. She was Fountain-blessed herself; he could sense her power like a vast lake. Her blue eyes met his, her mouth showing neither resentment nor intrigue. She was letting him *observe* her without doing anything to push away his intrusion. It felt insulting, so he drew his magic back.

But not without learning her weakness. If she stopped breathing, her power would be completely severed. She was as vulnerable as a sparrow. The thought of breaking her neck filled him with utter revulsion.

Her nostrils flared just a little. "Good night, my lord," she said dismissively, and turned and walked away.

◆　◆　◆

Sinia's steward, a man named Thierry, escorted Owen to one of the royal apartments in the castle. It was beautifully furnished and possessed a small fountain within it, a tiny one that chirped like a little bird as it bubbled. The floor was polished marble, the curtains expensive and thin and gauzy, and the colors light and festive. Several surfaces were decorated with beautiful vases filled with fresh flowers.

He walked like a man in a trance, only partially aware of his surroundings. He was now betrothed to the Duchess of Brythonica. Even though he had come to Ploemeur with that express purpose, he had never imagined it happening, let alone so quickly. Part of him wanted to laugh. Part of him wondered if he should break it off immediately. But while his feelings were anything but simple, he could not deny he was acutely curious about the Montfort heiress and her impressive power. He had always suspected Roux to be the strong one in her realm. He was keen to learn more about her, about this place.

Owen's men were bunked in the armory, and he had given orders to Captain Ashby to spend their stay inspecting the castle's defenses and planning siege strategies. While the castle could protect the court and the chief nobles, it was far too small to accommodate the population of Ploemeur. That left the majority of the people incredibly vulnerable. It would be easy to land an army in Brythonica and siege it, but the siege would be long and tedious.

Owen only half listened as Thierry explained the duchess's daily schedule; he was preoccupied with watching Etayne examine the doors, windows, and all other possible entrances and exits.

"My lord?" Thierry sounded aggrieved.

"Yes, what was that again?" Owen asked.

Thierry's face wrinkled with stern anger. He was an older man with steel-gray hair combed forward in the Occitanian style, and a colorful doublet, but his face was lined with crags and wrinkles. "I said, would my lord wish to join Lady Sinia at the supplicant hearing, or during the time when the artists are painting?"

Owen looked at the man in feigned confusion. "Why would I care about either of those things?"

Thierry grit his teeth. "She is very busy, my lord, and wishes to afford you the *courtesy* of her time tomorrow. It was my thinking that you would benefit from hearing about the troubles presented to her for resolution. Or you may be interested in the art of this kingdom, which is one of our great treasures." He rocked on his heels, obviously exasperated that Owen hadn't been listening. "There is also an archery tournament tomorrow," he added. "Perhaps some of your men might wish to impress us all with their talents?"

Owen sighed, wanting the conversation to be done. The ruse to be over. Thierry was assuming Owen actually intended to marry the girl, which was far from certain. He clapped Thierry on the shoulder. "I'll let you know in the morning."

The steward scowled. "The . . . the morning?"

"Of course!" Owen said cheerfully. "I'm exhausted from the ride and may sleep quite late tomorrow. I'll let you know when I'm ready to see the duchess."

It was calculated to make Thierry apoplectic and it worked. The steward had a difficult time remaining civil in the face of such an outrage. "I beg your leave then, my lord."

"No need to beg," he answered offhandedly. "You couldn't leave here quickly enough."

Thierry scowled, bowed stiffly, and then stormed out of the room. He clearly wanted to slam the door, but he remembered himself in time and shut it gently.

"You almost sounded like the king when you said that last part," Etayne offered slyly.

Owen folded his arms and stared at the door. "Sarcasm doesn't require much effort when you have ample practice." The sun was beginning to set, painting the fleecy clouds a rich orange. He crossed the room to the iron-and-glass door to the balcony and stepped outside. The platform jutted off the cliff, giving him an impressive view of the bay and the flickering lights far below. The air was salty from the sea.

Etayne joined him. "One would have to be mad or quite skilled to climb up here from below," she said. "The doors have sturdy bolts. The locking mechanisms are unsophisticated. The vases of flowers could be intended to hide the scent of poison, so we might want to dump them out."

Owen chuckled and turned, pressing his back against the rim of the balcony as he looked at her. "You think someone will try and kill me now?"

She smirked. "I think everyone here in Ploemeur is going to want to kill you after what you just did."

"She was expecting it," Owen said, shaking his head. "I didn't surprise her at all."

"Lord Roux was surprised, that much was obvious."

Owen nodded. "He was. He reacted just as I expected he would. Which surprises me, because *he's* usually one step ahead of me. But Sinia wasn't surprised. I don't think she's the helpless damsel I thought she was."

Etayne came closer so that he could hear her whispered words. "Yes, you thought Lord Roux was keeping her on a leash."

"I did," he said. "But not anymore. I wouldn't go so far as to say *he's* the one on the leash. But they are close. She respects him, not fears him."

"I noticed that as well," Etayne said. "I felt you use the magic when you were standing with her. What did you learn, if you don't mind my asking?"

He raised his eyebrows and chuffed. "She's one of us," he said knowingly. "And her access to the magic is both vast and well controlled. She could sense me probing her. She let me do it, but it offended her, I think."

She smiled playfully. "I remember when you did it to me onboard the ship all those years ago. It does make a girl feel rather vulnerable. Did you learn her weakness? Does she even have one?" The last remark sounded a little jealous.

Owen was not ready to share that information, especially not with a poisoner—friend or not. "I pulled back as soon as I realized what she was," he answered evasively. Her eyes narrowed slightly, her usual sign of disbelief.

"Have you seen the symbol on the vases?" he asked, both because he wanted to change the subject and because he wanted to know. "It's on the gate, it's—"

"Everywhere," she interrupted. "Yes. But I don't know what it means. You should ask her when you see her tomorrow. If they'll even *let* you after how vulgar you've been." She gave him another sly look. "Should we even bother disguising who I am? That you brought a poisoner with you should add to the offense you are deliberately inflicting."

Owen chuckled, folding his arms. He stared at Etayne, but he was thinking about Sinia. The duchess had always intrigued him, in part because he'd encountered Roux so often without learning anything about her. Based on the mayor of Averanche's assessment, he'd expected her to be a beauty, and she was, but his other expectations had been trumped. She was not the puppet he'd expected.

The duchess had lost her father at a young age, and her mother not too long after. As a child thrust to the helm of command, she had been guided and couched by people like Roux until she reached adulthood. That was how they did things in Occitania and its independent duchies. The people respected the authority of the family. Uncles didn't snatch thrones from children. There was a sense of honor in that. Ceredigion's rulers were known to be more ruthless, which was part of why Owen had suspected the worst of Roux.

"When we met Marshal Roux in the woods, there was something there," he said, rubbing the stubble on his lip. "I'm sure you felt it too. I want to see it. Maybe I'll ask Sinia to take me there. Or maybe I'll go there without asking."

"Or I could go on ahead," Etayne offered with a nod. "Why don't I do that tonight?"

Owen shook his head. "They're expecting something like that from us. I don't want to give them an excuse to hunt you. You're supposed to be protecting me."

"I could protect you better if I stayed *with* you," she hinted.

"No, I have other plans for you tonight. I'd like you to disguise yourself as a servant and get to know the castle. I'm uncomfortable because I don't know this place. Are there dungeons? Where is the duchess's bedchamber?" She gave him an arch look. "I'm not suggesting anything! But this is a new place, and we don't have our bearings. See what you can learn inside the castle before venturing out."

"Of course," she answered, nodding slightly.

Owen heard an unfamiliar noise, the slight creak of door hinges being clandestinely shut. His hearing had always been especially keen— it was one of his abilities from the Fountain. Then there was the soft scuff of a padded shoe on the marble floor.

Etayne heard it as well, and there was a thin knife in her hand in an instant. She always kept it strapped to her forearm beneath her gown. Owen had not changed out of his dusty traveling clothes, so he still had his sword strapped to him. He gestured for Etayne to stay put and she shook her head no.

Owen took a hesitant step to the side of the balcony door, angling his body sideways to provide less of a target if someone had come with a bow. The drapes by the balcony concealed whoever was in the room, but he could see a shadow moving slowly, as if the intruder was searching for something hidden.

Etayne stepped forward, dagger behind her back, gripping the tip between her fingers in preparation to throw it. She pushed the curtain aside, and Owen caught a glimpse of the woman who had entered his chamber.

He gripped Etayne's knife arm to prevent her from hurling the weapon.

A memory darted in Owen's mind. Recognition. He blinked rapidly, trying to make sense of what he was seeing. The woman was much older than the last time he'd seen her, probably thirty. She wore the fashionable gown of a lady-in-waiting, not a servant, and it fit her well. But it was her face that jarred him. He *knew* that face.

With the curtain flung aside, the woman saw him and Etayne on the balcony. When her eyes met his, she startled and gasped his name, her hand clutching her breast in surprise. "Owen! It's you! It's really you!"

His legs felt weak. The last time he had seen her was sixteen years ago when he watched her enter a boat bound for Occitania with his parents and other siblings. She was the oldest after Jorganon's death.

It was his sister, Jessica Kiskaddon.

# CHAPTER NINE

## *Haven*

At first Owen doubted what his heart knew. So much time had passed since he had last seen his sister. In that fraught moment, he knew one thing: he *hoped* it was her. He could sense the Fountain's whispers in the night air, but it was not coming from Jessica. And it did not reveal anything to him. His sister rushed to him and pulled him into a warm embrace. She touched him, kissed him, smearing wet tears on his cheek despite her attempts to wipe them away with her wrist, then stroked his hair affectionately, her fingers grazing the spot of white still embedded in his unruly locks.

"How are you here, Sister?" he demanded. It felt as if live coals were hissing in his chest. He had never thought to see her, to see any of them again. The wedding band on her finger winked up at him, telling him that she was a Kiskaddon no longer. His eyes feasted on her. She was family—something that had been sundered from his life for too long.

She hiccuped with emotion, shaking her head as she was unable to speak. She tried to quell her tears again and then gripped his shoulder. "It was going to be a surprise. The duchess wanted to share it with you when you arrived, but your coming was so fraught with tension." She shook her head. "Mother will be so pleased."

"Mother is here?" Owen said, eyes widening with shock.

Jessica nodded. "We are all *here*, Owen. You are the last. You who saved our family from extinction. But it was the duchess who saved us from starving."

His heart ached at the words. "Tell me what happened. I've tried to find you, to make sure you were alive and well, but I've had no word for years! You should have sent me a message!"

She shook her head. "We could not. You must understand, Owen. Our lives here have been a closely guarded secret. When you defeated Chatriyon, we had to flee for our lives. You cannot understand the depths of the Occitanians' hatred of you. Remember Azinkeep? The shame of it still haunts this land. And then you came to Chatriyon's own land and humiliated him. You weren't even a king but a duke. They sent a poisoner to kill us, but the duchess managed to smuggle us away. We've been living in Ploemeur these last few years. We were given new names, a manor house. Papan is in charge of overseeing taxes on the goods traded in our ports. It's a position of great trust. I am one of the duchess's ladies-in-waiting. She has been so good to us, Owen. She found me an honorable husband. Our brother Timond is a knight at court. Our sister Ann is here as well. We are so fortunate. But we had to keep our identities secret for fear of us being used to harm or threaten *you*."

Owen stared at her, amazed at what he was hearing. "And Lady Sinia did this?"

Jessica nodded emphatically. "She is a noble woman, Owen. A generous and thoughtful soul. She's lost both her parents, but there is no trace of bitterness. She was so young when she was named the Duchess of Brythonica. Without Marshal Roux's craftiness and courage, we would have been invaded long ago. She was going to bring you to see us at our manor house, but I couldn't bear to wait.

I needed to touch you and make sure you were real." She stroked his hair with a pained smile. "You are here. You look . . . rather ragged for a duke." She sniffed and grimaced slightly. "I was expecting you would arrive in all your state. But you look and smell like a common soldier."

"I am a soldier," Owen said with a dark chuckle. "Fighting wars for the king has been my task in life. We've had no peace since Ambion Hill."

Her eyes narrowed with some inner wisdom. "Nor will you, so I fear."

He wrinkled his brow. "What do you mean, Jessica?"

"It is not my place to say," she said, pressing her lips together tightly. "But this much I can tell you. There is a reason the duchess has chosen to stay as the ruler of Brythonica. Why she refused to become the Queen of Occitania when given the chance. Why she would refuse to become the Queen of Ceredigion if Severn were to demand it."

"And what is that reason? Jessica, you must tell me if you know."

She shook her head firmly. "I cannot, Owen. It is not my secret to share. The duchess will, if she trusts you." She squirmed uncomfortably. "Owen . . . you look so old for one so young. I can see in your eyes how much suffering you have known. You cannot understand how much it grieved us to leave you behind. You saved us. We are not ungrateful; surely you must know that." She hugged him again and planted a moist kiss on his cheek. "But our family was sundered that day. There has been the ghost of pain these many years. Maman and Papan will be so happy to see you. You must come soon, Owen. It will ease their anguish to see you again."

Just hearing her endearments caused an ache of pain inside Owen's bones. He was not a boy any longer. But the childhood hurts were still sore.

"I don't understand why you couldn't send word. Why the duchess didn't tell me." Despite how wonderful it felt to see her, to be near one who shared his blood, he was suspicious of her motives.

Jessica cupped his cheek. "I'll send word to Maman that you are here. I live in the castle, naturally. I heard about how you arrived and made your demands." She looked up to the ceiling and then shook her head. "You were very rude, Owen."

Hearing it from his sister made the shame of his actions fester. "Well, I'll admit my entrance was rather unconventional."

"Now that's calling a frog a goose!" she teased.

Owen laughed at the statement. "So I'm a frog, am I?"

"You are a handsome lad behind that dirt and dishevelment." Her eyes narrowed slightly as she gazed over Owen's shoulder. Her voice dropped very low. "Is that your mistress?"

She was talking about Etayne. He had almost forgotten she was in the room, amidst the storm of emotion. "No, of course not! She's my . . . how shall I put this? She's my protector."

Jessica's eyes lifted with surprise. "Very well, although that's quite a mysterious answer. I will send word to Maman and Papan at once. I'll see you tomorrow. I'm so glad you have finally come!" She hugged and kissed him again and then stole away from the room, blowing him a last kiss as she quietly shut the door.

Owen folded his arms, still reeling from the revelations of the evening. He heard Etayne's footsteps pad up to him.

His heart still raged with emotions. He blinked quickly, feeling close to tears, and pinched a few strands of his beard below his bottom lip and tugged at them.

"I'm glad you're here, Etayne," he said in a half whisper. "My emotions are being toyed with. I'm not even sure what to think right now."

"So that was your sister. Are you certain it was her? I can feel Fountain magic all around us."

"The endearments she used," Owen said, nodding. "That's what I used to call my mother and father." His heart was roiling like one of Liona's stews. "When you play Wizr and start losing, it's easy to make mistakes. Often fatal ones. Why have my family been here for so many years without telling me? Are they hostages? Perhaps even willing ones?"

"Why would the duchess forbid your sister from seeing you? It seemed to me that she stole in here deliberately."

Owen nodded. "Exactly. Was that happenstance? Or by design? This is an important game I'm playing. I already feel I've been outwitted. I came here to start a war, not a betrothal." He turned and looked at Etayne. "I am betrothed, aren't I? The reality is finally hitting me. I knelt down in front of witnesses and offered my hand and she said she'd take me. That wasn't supposed to happen. Weren't we supposed to negotiate terms or formulate a treaty at the very least?"

Etayne smiled with amusement. "Threat," she said knowingly.

Owen shook his head. "Somehow she predicted it. Did you notice the look on her face?"

"Whose face?" Etayne asked.

"Lady Sinia's. She almost looked relieved when I asked for her hand. She didn't look upset at all. Why is that? Because she guessed correctly? Or does she stand to gain something from this union?"

Owen started to pace, wishing he had brought his tiles with him. He rarely used them to replenish his magic now, but this unexpected invocation of his childhood made him suddenly crave them.

"From what your sister said, it's clear that you already have a reputation here. Whatever it was before has been compounded by how you acted once getting here. Let me see what I can find out tonight. What were they saying about you before you came and what are they saying about you now?"

"It can't be pleasant," Owen sniffed. "And it will not end pleasantly." He looked hard into Etayne's eyes. "I didn't come here to get married," he said flatly. "I can imagine the king's reaction if he were told." He mimicked Severn's voice. "'Good work, lad! You defeated them without a skirmish! Marry her, and let's work on toppling Chatriyon.' He won't give five figs for my feelings."

Etayne's eyes narrowed shrewdly. "What? She's not beautiful enough for you? I can imagine many men would eagerly marry her to inherit the duchy of Brythonica even if she were a homely girl."

Owen didn't like her mocking tone. "I gave my heart to another woman long ago."

He fidgeted under Etayne's stare, and his mind would not give him peace. Yes, he had given his heart to a woman. A woman who was now a queen in another realm and had two children of her own. Was he going to pine after her for the rest of his life? Would he cling to the hope that Iago might stumble during his hop on the rocks by the waterfalls and plummet to his death? Or perhaps he simply needed to admit to himself that Sinia intrigued him and he was actually considering a possibility he had never thought to contemplate.

◆ ◆ ◆

Owen slept fitfully that night. Although his rooms were spacious and exquisitely comfortable, he was not used to them. Every little noise and sound disturbed his slumber and made him worry someone was trying to enter his room to murder him. He finally fell asleep just before sunrise, and when he awoke, light streamed in through the thin veils and stabbed at his eyes. It was midmorning, and he rarely slept in that late. His mind was muddy and confused. He unfastened the bolt on his door and found Farnes outside, pacing worriedly.

"Farnes?" he asked, blinking in surprise. He had left him in Tatton Hall to handle the guests.

"You're awake," the herald said with relief. "I was debating whether I should send for Captain Ashby to burst open the door. You normally don't sleep this late."

"I have a splitting headache," Owen said. He noticed several trays of food set on tables outside the door. It had been locked, so no one had been able to enter and arrange it within his chamber.

Farnes followed him in and handed him a series of letters, many marked with Espion seals. He began breaking them open as his stomach growled noisily. While Owen started to read the first note, Farnes went to the door and snapped for a servant to bring in the food.

"How did you leave things with all those visitors at Tatton Hall?" Owen asked, tossing the letter aside. He was adept at reading quickly and remembering the key points after only a quick look. He felt the magic inside him stir with his efforts.

"You managed to offend each and every one of them," Farnes said crisply, rocking on his heels, his hands clasped behind his back.

"I'm rather good at that these days," Owen said with a chuckle, perusing the next letter.

"You didn't *used* to be," Farnes said pointedly.

Owen didn't care for the rebuke or the tone. He gave Farnes a sour look. "What did you expect me to do, Farnes? They were uninvited guests preying on my hospitality while I had business elsewhere."

"I've heard about your business," Farnes said. "The problem is how you go about it. I apologize for being so candid, my lord, but I feel it's my duty to tell you when you are creating diplomatic hazards for yourself. People are much more willing to remember a slight than a compliment. It's like salting a well you'll need to drink from later."

He was only half listening to Farnes because the second message was from Kevan, telling him that Drew was being moved to the palace to be a playmate for Evie's daughter. It did not surprise him, but he swore softly under his breath.

"Ill news, my lord?" Farnes asked worriedly.

If the king saw the boy continually, it was inevitable he would notice the boy's similarities to Lady Kathryn and Eyric. His eyes widened farther as a new thought struck him. Lady Kathryn would see her son! Would her heart tell her who he was? How would she react? The throbbing in his temples felt like the clanging of kitchen pans.

"You truly look ill, my lord," Farnes said.

"I already told you I'm not feeling well," Owen said, gazing down at the page again in consternation and rubbing his temple with his free hand. He needed to get back to Kingfountain. He had to contrive a plan to send the lad away. If Duke Catsby abrogated the commitment to rear the boy, then Owen would have to bring him to Tatton Hall where he could trust his own people to look after him. Maybe he could send the boy to Atabyrion? His mind whirled with the possibilities as implication upon implication and consequence upon consequence flooded his mind.

This was a challenge that would test him greatly. He would need to come up with a way to force Lady Sinia to break off the engagement, after all. Something that would allow him to return back to Kingfountain quickly, even if it meant losing the opportunity to see the rest of his family. At least he knew where they were. He had sensed Sinia was powerful with the Fountain's magic. She had allowed him to see that, although he did sense she resented it.

"Have some food, my lord. It will help. When did you last eat?" Farnes asked.

He shook his head. "Not since I arrived." He wandered over to the trays the servants were still carrying into the vast chamber. There was tray after tray of fruit, mostly berries in a huge assortment. Little round purple ones, long bell-shaped ones—his favorites were thimbleberries, and he'd never seen such a huge platter of them in his life. There were breads baked with them, little pots of jams and jellies. Some, like the bowl of gooseberries, were dusted in sugar. He wondered if anything on the table had been poisoned. He expected that Etayne had already examined the trays, but he had not seen her yet.

"Do you know where the duchess is?" Owen asked Farnes.

He rocked back on his heels again, hands clasped. "She left early this morning."

Owen scowled. "I thought she was going to hear disputes from her people?"

Farnes nodded. "She is. She goes down to *them*. The lord marshal also left this morning, bringing his soldiers with him. They say he has quit the palace."

Owen's mouth hardened into a frown. He reached for one of the thimbleberries and plopped it into his mouth.

It was the sweetest fruit he'd ever tasted.

# CHAPTER TEN

## Sea Glass

Even Owen could no longer stand the stench of his shirt and tunic, so he accepted the trunk Farnes had brought with him, and cleaned himself up. He deliberately did not shave, but he used the water pitcher, bowl, and towel to wipe away the grime from his travels and felt freshened by the change. While he was tugging on his boots, he was interrupted by the arrival of Captain Ashby and Etayne.

Owen squinted against the light pouring in from the silk curtains and grimaced while he pulled on the boot and fastened the straps alongside. "What news, Ashby?" he asked in a rushed manner. He wanted to leave the castle as quickly as possible and be on his way.

Captain Ashby saluted and started to pace. "We've scoured the castle grounds and taken note of the number of knights protecting it. The cliffs are especially rugged and steep. It would be difficult to lay siege to this place."

"I saw that myself on the ride up here yesterday," Owen said wryly. "What else?"

"I took some of the men down to Ploemeur last night. It can't really be called a city. There are manors on the hilltops all around, but very little down in the valleys. Mostly smaller shops that line the thoroughfares connecting the hills. They carry a variety of things to trade. What surprised me was how many of the merchants are from other kingdoms. There are many from Genevar, Legault, and Atabyrion. Truly a hodgepodge. I don't think I've seen a place like this before. Every few blocks the culture and language changes. This is a major trading hub, my lord. I even bought a few trinkets for my wife and children, little necklaces made of glass beads."

Owen set his leg down and then began tugging on his other boot. "I wasn't aware of that. How far is the harbor from here?"

Ashby shook his head. "Not far at all. The tide comes and goes regularly, bringing with it ships from every port. I heard many languages last night."

Owen continued tightening the buckles. "How were your men treated?"

Ashby shrugged. "There were so many from so many different countries, I don't think we stood out. When we got back, the palace staff looked like they wanted to spit on us, but the people down below knew nothing of our arrival. Nary a word about it."

"Thank you, Ashby," Owen said, finishing his work. He stood and buckled his scabbard around his waist. "So what you're saying is the kingdom is vulnerable. Especially by sea. It seems they'd probably try to use the woods to block us from getting this far."

"Aye," the captain responded. "If you don't mind, my lord, I'll get some sleep now myself. We were out a bit late last night, but I didn't want to keep you waiting."

Owen nodded, dismissing him. He turned to Etayne, who was dressed and coiffed in the Brythonican fashion.

"So they really hate us now?" he asked her with the quirk of a smile.

She gave him a knowing look. "I think the sentiment is more directed at *you* right now. The people here are very generous and they care about their duchess. There is an almost reverential feeling when they speak of her. By insulting her, you've offended them deeply. There is much gossiping and backbiting about you throughout the castle. They're suggesting you won't be the Duke of Brythonica. Only the duchess's consort."

Owen started to laugh. "Oh really? I'm not worthy to be a duke outside of Ceredigion? As if Westmarch isn't three times the size of Brythonica."

"I thought you didn't *want* to become the duke here?" she reminded him.

"I don't," he said, frowning. "But I also don't like being told what I can or can't have. They're insulted, though, so that makes good sense. It also gives me a good way to goad the duchess. When I talk to her, I'll ask about the history of consorts and dukes. Her father was a duke, and she holds rank in her own right. I will definitely *insist* that the marriage terms include the title. Hopefully, she'll balk and withdraw her acceptance." He fidgeted with his belt and smoothed his tunic front. "I received some news from Kevan. Drew is being sent to the palace as a playmate for Genevieve." He tried to keep from frowning but failed. "I need to get there before events unravel."

Etayne smiled knowingly and bowed. "Then you should be on your way. She metes out judgment at a place a bit lower than the palace called the House of Pillars. That's where I would look for her."

"I will. Thank you, Etayne. Are you going to get some sleep now?"

"I've rested enough," she said. "I'm going to learn more about that patch of woods we passed if I can. The one where we felt the Fountain so strongly."

He gave her a wary look. "See what you can learn, but we should go there together on our way out. Be careful."

"I always am," she answered and turned away.

◆　◆　◆

Owen did not find Lady Sinia at the House of Pillars. The building was comprised of a center main tower with a dome and spire basilica and two lower-level wings jutting from angles on either side of the tower. As Owen approached the beautiful structure, full of windows and arches, it occurred to him that the tower in the middle resembled a piece from a Wizr board. The first floor of the tower and the wings were made of brick. The second and third levels were made of plaster and wood. The roofs were slanted and steep, and there was symmetry in the windows and arches throughout, each one lining up perfectly with the ones above and below. The basilica was made of iron or bronze, a darker color than the rest of the structure. He was intrigued by the design and felt the stirrings of the Fountain emanate from the structure itself.

The duchess had already heard cases and moved to the docks, so he ventured there next, only to find that he had just missed her. Owen was feeling impatient and thwarted after spending several hours trying to catch up to her. Her servants answered him obediently, but he could see the scolding looks in their eyes. After another delay, he was led away from the docks. He had an escort of ten with him, and he could sense their eagerness to explore the trading stalls Ashby had described. He dismissed half of his guard after arranging for them to switch out with the others in an hour. His soldiers gratefully accepted the short furlough.

The uniformed servants of the duchess escorted Owen to a private cove along the bay where the surf came crashing against the rocks and sand. They had to hike down a little sandy trail to reach the basin, where he found the duchess walking side by side with her steward. Owen's boots crunched in the sand as they reached the bottom of the steps. Having noticed his arrival, Sinia gestured for the steward to leave. There were a dozen or so soldiers in Raven tunics standing back along the edge of the cove, leaving room for the duchess to wander alone.

As Owen passed the steward coming toward him, he noticed the tight frown on the man's face.

"Glad you finally caught up," the steward said with a biting tone.

"Glad you waited for me, Thierry," Owen answered mockingly.

The steward sniffed and shook his head, heading toward the soldiers by the path. As Owen approached Sinia, he saw she was walking barefoot, two sandals dangling from her fingers. His boots left large prints on the sandy shore. The wind blew some of her golden hair into her face, and she reached up and smoothed it back before turning to face him.

He was expecting resentment in her countenance—how could she feel otherwise after having a day to stew on their unsatisfactory conversation? But her look was resigned instead, as if Owen were a trial to be patiently endured. The wind carried the salty smell of the sea and the crashing of the waves.

"I found you at last," Owen said with an almost reproachful tone.

"Walk with me," she said, and then she turned toward the waves and started off. She clasped her hands behind her back, the sandals still dangling in the crook of her fingers. The sun was beginning its descent and glittered off her leaflike tiara. Today's gown matched the color of the ocean, except for the girdle and the white ruffs at her sleeves.

As Owen followed her toward the pounding surf and the hulking boulders and formations jutting up along the shore, he felt a change in the texture of the sand beneath his feet. The sand became firmer and more saturated, and his boots left crumbs in the wake of their passing. The rocks were speckled with sea life and he saw half-buried shells poking out all around them. The sun was warm, but the breeze was cool. As they approached the first crag of rock, the sand began to change again, and instead of tiny brown flecks, the shore was filled with small rocky beads of various colors. Sinia walked through it, the sticky sand clinging to her bare feet. The crunch from his boots took on a different sound.

Were they pebbles? How strange that the beach would turn from sand to pebbles as they approached the waves.

A particularly large wave crested and then hissed with foam as it approached them. Sinia walked in defiance of the wave, and it receded away from her before she reached it. She set the sandals down as she crouched and scooped up a handful of the tiny beads to show him.

They were of various shapes and hues—pink, blue, orange, red, and green. She poked at the beads with her finger, pushing them aside to show him the full variety.

"This is called sea glass," she said, and offered to drop the pile in his hand. He held out his palm and she tilted her wrist, sending the little pebbles clacking down onto his hand. The edge of her wrist grazed his and her touch sent an unanticipated jolt up his arm.

"I've never seen the like before," he said, admiring the small intricate stones, trying to shake off the feelings that were stirring within him. Amidst the ebb and rush of the ocean, he heard the steady trickle of water. As he looked for the source, he discovered water running down the craggy boulder cleft that formed one of the cove's boundaries. Little rivulets had made the stone mossy, but the water was clear. An indentation had formed at the bottom of the rock and little streams ran down the shore into the sea.

"These aren't pebbles," she said, picking up one from his hand. It was a misshapen red one. "Each one is truly made of glass. The sea has broken them into smaller and smaller pieces and then dragged them along the beaches here for centuries. This is the residue. Artisans come and fashion jewelry out of it. Just like gemstones, they take thousands of years to form. But the glass was made by men." She stared out into the bay wistfully, smoothing more strands of hair from her face.

As Owen stood there, cupping the sea glass in his palm, he followed her gaze. An enormous feeling of recognition swept into him, as if he had stood in this exact spot before. Emotions swirled inside him, hammering against him like the waves buffeting the rocks nearby. The glass fragments he held in his hand were the remains of huge windows. Thousands of windows from an enormous castle that had once risen from the heart of the bay. He blinked, almost able to see it.

Owen had felt this sensation once before, while sailing through the cove to enter Edonburick in Atabyrion. He had sensed a city buried by water beneath them.

Thousands of stained-glass windows of the most majestic designs had been smashed and pulverized to become these small bits of detritus gathered on the shore. Owen's knees buckled a bit, and a sudden dizziness washed over him, making him sway. His hand dropped and the sea glass fell back to his feet.

He felt a small hand wrap around his arm. "Are you all right?"

He blinked quickly, trying to quell the awful vision in his mind. How many people had died when the sea came rushing in? How many had drowned? An ancient ache throbbed in his heart.

"I'm . . . I'm sorry," he stammered, his throat thick with a suppressed groan.

"There are memories here," Sinia said in a peculiar way.

He turned to look at her. "What memories?"

Her eyes were wise. "Of long ago. Places now forgotten." She turned and looked back at the sea. "Like Leoneyis."

There was something she wasn't saying. He could sense the innuendo in her words.

"I've heard you collect relics from that lost realm," he said suspiciously.

She shrugged. "I'm not the only ruler who has done so," she answered simply. "The collection in Ceredigion is vast. But, of course, that would be expected. Since it was the kingdom of King Andrew and Queen Genevieve." She gave him a pointed look, a look that said so much it made his heart quake.

She was toying with him. Testing him. It was no coincidence that she had brought him to the seashore. Again he had the feeling that he was being outmaneuvered in a game of Wizr.

"I'm surprised all the sea glass isn't gone," he said stiffly. "One would think it would all have been claimed by now."

"Not so," she answered. "These beaches are guarded by certain laws and covenants. Only one chest full of sea glass can be harvested each year. It is bid upon and sold. The selling can take several months. Depending on the color, the size, and the shape, it can fetch outrageous prices."

Owen pursed his lips. "But wouldn't that drive men to come steal it at night? That handful you gave me . . . how much would it have been worth?"

"What does it matter? It's only broken glass. It's worth nothing, truly. But because it is rare, because it is withheld, it is worth so much more. No one comes to steal from this beach, Owen. No one would dare risk offending the Fountain. I've heard in your kingdom that people steal coins from the water fountains. Is that true?"

Owen shook his head. "Not often. If someone is caught stealing from one of the fountains, the thief will be thrown into the river to go over the falls."

Sinia nodded. "For that reason, the sea glass remains here unprotected. Or should I say, it is protected by the traditions that bind us." Her gaze narrowed. "When those traditions are cast aside, there are often unwanted consequences."

There seemed to be deeper significance to her words, but the meaning was veiled from him. She knew about the Deep Fathoms. She knew about Leoneyis, things that could not be learned in the history books that Polidoro Urbino studied. There were things Owen could learn from her. But he still felt he was being manipulated, and he didn't like it. It gave him a sour taste.

He decided to flip the game by going on the attack. His voice became colder and more detached. "I came a great distance to meet with you, my lady. I did as my king commanded me, no more."

"I understand," she replied graciously.

"But I'd like to make it clear what I came here to accomplish. I didn't come all this way to become your *consort*. Not just your *husband*. King Severn expects me to rule Brythonica as I've ruled Westmarch. I don't want there to be any misunderstanding between us, my lady."

He watched her eyes closely, looking for anger and resentment. Looking for defiance to tighten her nostrils.

There was none of that in her expression. Instead, she looked disappointed. As if she had expected more of him than what he was giving her.

She reached out and touched his arm again. "Of course we understand each other," she answered almost sadly. "I would expect no less." She sighed and then her eyes narrowed as she saw someone approaching. Owen turned and saw Thierry marching toward them on the beach, a messenger at his heels.

Sinia let go of Owen's arm and started forward to meet them.

As soon as she walked away, a surge of surf crashed against Owen's boots, startling him. While they had been close to the shore, none of the waves had even come near them, but this one caught him by surprise. Sinia's sandals lifted up in the swell, and he hurried to try to catch them before they were dragged out to sea. Saltwater splashed him in the face as he tried to bend over and snatch them, leaving the foul taste of brine on his tongue.

With his chin dripping, he looked back as Sinia walked away from him, her skirts pulled up to her ankles as she strode across the sand. She looked absolutely beautiful in the fading sunlight, and he simply stood there and looked at her for a moment, clutching her dripping sandals in his hand, trying to understand what he was even feeling and trying even harder to control it.

And that's when the next wave hit him from behind, knocking him down.

# CHAPTER ELEVEN

*Betrayal*

Seawater sloshed in Owen's ears as he trudged through the sand in his soaked clothes, and he shook his head to jostle it loose. Thierry greeted him with a baleful look. The messenger was from Pisan and spoke in a thick accent, but it was clearly understood. The mousy-looking fellow was wringing his hands.

Owen still clung to Sinia's sandals, which were also dripping wet, and stood by her side, asserting himself as her equal.

"The storm was brutal, my lady," the messenger said in a distraught voice. "There were four ships in harbor, and each was smashed against the wall. The cargo is ruined!"

The duchess put her hand on the messenger's shoulder. "What was the cargo? Foodstuffs?"

"Aye," he replied miserably. "All ruined by the sea. We have enough stores to last a fortnight, but without those shipments, our people will go hungry. We sought aid from the King of Occitania, but he demanded five times the worth of the cargo. Five times!"

"Who else did you ask?" she inquired.

"Most recently the court of the White Boar. He wouldn't even hear the plea in person, my lady. The lord chancellor was too busy and the lord mayor of Kingfountain said it wasn't his king's concern. He said to blame the ill luck on the Fountain."

Owen bridled at the response, feeling a frown tug on his mouth.

The duchess looked sorrowful. "It is a pity indeed. Was anyone injured by the storm?"

"Aye, a few lads drowned, and a roof collapsed on a family and crushed them. But it is the food that will be sorely needed, my lady. Is there nothing you can do for us?"

Sinia turned to Owen. "Master Torcellini, this is my betrothed lord, Duke Kiskaddon of Ceredigion. If he were at Kingfountain, I'm certain you would have met with a different response." She sidled closer to him, despite his soggy apparel, and clung to his arm. "What say you, my lord?" she asked Owen. "I was thinking we should send two ships straightaway to alleviate the people's suffering and prevent famine. Do you agree?"

He felt himself being maneuvered again, but he had been at the receiving end of her generosity before. She had sent ships to relieve the siege of Averanche seven years before.

"Let's send three," Owen answered, feeling water drip from his chin and the tips of his hair. She gave him an approving smile.

The messenger beamed with a new burst of hope. "I thank you! You both are magnanimous. I hadn't heard of this happy news. My congratulations!"

"It's quite sudden," the duchess said with a wry smile, giving Owen's arm a gentle squeeze. "The Fountain gives and it takes. We were blessed with an abundant harvest ourselves and have food to spare. Be at ease, Master Torcellini. You have not traveled in vain. Thierry, see to it, please."

"As you wish, my lady," the steward said with a bow. Then he escorted the grinning messenger away.

Sinia released Owen's arm and turned, giving him another approving smile, as if he had passed some sort of test.

"You were expecting me to be cruel, I suppose?" he asked with a snort, handing her the sandals.

She took them and shook her head slowly. "No, I didn't think that at all." She swung the sandals before her. "I'm always losing my shoes, sandals, and boots. I much prefer walking barefoot, even in the palace, shocking as that may sound. My servants are constantly picking them up from odd places. I don't even realize I'm doing it most of the time. Thank you for rescuing them from the sea." Then she turned her gaze back to the sea and the darkening sky. The sun was behind them, casting long shadows across the cove. Waves hissed and sighed along the shore.

"Do you always help those in distress?" he asked her pointedly.

She smoothed some hair back over her shoulder. "Why shouldn't I? We've been blessed by the Fountain to live in such a temperate climate. It only snows rarely, and there is a plentitude of rain. It's ideal land for growing things." She gave him a hesitant look. "We aren't a warlike people, Owen. But we fight if we must. Marshal Roux has wearied himself protecting us from those who want our fields for themselves."

Owen scratched his arm, feeling uncomfortable in the sodden clothing. "I heard he left the castle. Is he sulking?"

She narrowed her eyes a bit. "Walk with me and I'll tell you," she offered. He nodded and followed as she started across the cove. "You must understand that Brendon Roux is very *protective* by nature. He was given the trust to guard and defend Brythonica when my father died. I was only a child. In your kingdom, someone in his position might have usurped the throne. Many rulers believe that he is the true ruler of Brythonica. But the people will only have a Montfort rule them. What you saw just now," she said, gesturing to Thierry and the messenger as they climbed the rocky shelf leading out of the cove, "was not a tradition I started, but one I maintain with honor. We help kingdoms in need. We may be a small duchy compared to yours, but we feel our duty strongly."

Owen nodded, stifling a shiver as the wind knifed through him. "My king has a saying. 'Loyalty Binds Me.' It is my oath."

"I know," she said. "I've heard it before. I'm sure it chafes you at times."

He wrinkled his brow. "What do you mean?"

She cast him a furtive glance, and he could tell she was debating whether to trust him. "Our duties and obligations can feel confining," she said after a lengthy pause. Her answer showed he had not yet earned her trust.

To his surprise, she stopped walking in the middle of the beach and then sank to her knees. She pushed her fingers into the sand and began scooping up little mounds of it. He was soaked and knew the sand would stick to him if he joined her. She didn't seem to mind as she absently played with the sand, letting it glide between her fingers. They were a distance from the sea glass near the shore, but he saw occasional beads of it appear, as if they were beguiled by her.

Owen hunkered down near her, studying her face. "Do you play Wizr?" he asked.

There was a flash of a secret smile and then it was gone. "I do."

"I would like to play you sometime," he said. "I think you might be one of the few people who could actually beat me."

That earned an amused look. "I've played since I was a child. My father taught me."

"I've played since childhood as well," Owen said. But he didn't reveal Ankarette's role in teaching him. "When can we play?"

She shook her head and then gave him a piercing look. "I'll play Wizr with you if *you* provide the set." The way she said the words made his heart start pounding. Could she know about the ancient Wizr set concealed in the fountain of St. Penryn in Westmarch? St. Penryn was the vestige of the drowned kingdom of Leoneyis. This was the second subtle reference she'd made to it. They were dancing around each other, each knowing something the other did not. He hungered to know more, but he didn't think he could trust her. Not yet.

"The king gave me a set when I was little," Owen said, giving her an answer that he suspected she didn't want. "I'll bring it with me next time."

"Do," she answered, her eyes more guarded.

"Why do I feel like *talking* to you is like playing Wizr?" he said with a chuckle. He gave her a challenging look.

"Is that my fault?"

It was a soft rebuke, but a rebuke nonetheless. Owen gritted his teeth and composed himself. "No," he answered. He decided to take a risk and confide something they both knew. "I didn't come here expecting to marry you, Sinia," he said in a low voice. "I came because my *king* commanded it and I serve him. Would Marshal Roux do any less?"

She glided her fingers through the sand with one hand, her other arm propping her up. "He is as loyal to me as you are to your king. The difference, I think, is that he is loyal because he *respects* what he serves. He doesn't fear me." She met his gaze, and Owen swallowed.

"Severn Argentine is not the monster everyone says he is," he said defensively, falling back on an old argument that had once been true. Ankarette had once told him that Severn was influenced by what people thought of him, which he knew to be true.

Sinia looked down again, tracing a circle with her finger. "I think he became the monster everyone said he was." Her eyelashes fluttered, and when she looked up at him, it felt as if her eyes were seeing *into* him. Her expression said, *Is the same thing happening to you?*

Owen squirmed with discomfort. He didn't like the way the conversation was going.

She must have sensed his reaction, for she changed tack. "We tend to resemble those we interact with the most. The Argentine temper is legendary, especially in these lands. The first Argentine king married his third son to the Duchess of Brythonica. Did you know that?"

"I did," Owen said, grateful once again for Evie's deep knowledge of history and their endless discussions about it.

"It was a tragic marriage," she said, using the flat of her hand to smooth away the circle she'd drawn. "The king was unfaithful to her. She rebelled against him and tried to put her son on his throne. Owen, do you ever have a feeling that the past keeps coming back? See how the tide is creeping up toward us. In a few hours, this entire cove will be underwater. Then it will recede again. In and out, wet and dry. I feel like that sometimes. That the past is inescapable." There was a haunted sense of longing in her voice. She didn't look at him, as if she were suddenly shy.

"You're asking if I will betray you?" he said, his insides roiling from her observation about the recurring nature of things—one he had often considered himself.

She pursed her lips. "You admitted that you came here to offer your troth because your king *forced* your hand. He will not be king forever. No one ever is." Her hands stopped moving through the sand, her fingers suddenly taut and talon-like, digging into the sand. She was struggling with some unspoken emotion. "It doesn't bode well for our marriage," she added softly.

Owen suspected she knew all about his past with Elysabeth. Pain stabbed his heart, and once again he cursed Severn for the poison the king had forced him to drink. It was a bitter cup still. Did the duchess question his motives for bringing a beautiful woman with him in his entourage? Did she even know Etayne was a poisoner?

He felt muddled and miserable. The tendril of a wave came up to them, close enough that he watched the foamy bubbles pop and the sand drink in the moisture.

"We'd better go," Sinia said, sitting upright and brushing her hands together. Owen was still squatting, his knees aching, and he rose to his feet. Then, in a gallant gesture, he extended his hand to her to help her stand.

She looked surprised by the offer, but a pleased smile spread across her face. Her hand was so warm, and he could feel the specks of sand still clinging to her skin. He pulled her up and she straightened, shaking the sand loose from her skirts.

"Thank you," she said and started away from the oncoming tide. The sea was flat and gray on the horizon.

She had left her sandals behind again. He smirked as he bent down to retrieve them, keeping a wary eye on the waves. Though he caught up to Sinia, he didn't give her sandals back until they reached the smooth rocks and she turned to look for them.

An embarrassed but relieved smile touched her mouth when she realized Owen was holding them.

"Your parents and siblings will be joining us for dinner at the House of Pillars," she said, tugging on one damp sandal while balancing herself against the stone. "I thought you might want to see them. I know Jessica told you they were here. She's dear to me."

"I would indeed," Owen said, feeling a flush of gratitude, even though he knew she'd done it deliberately. "Thank you." He'd come looking for her so he could make his excuses and return to Kingfountain to deal with the news about Drew. But their conversation had altered his urgency. Perhaps he could make time to see his parents after all.

"You're welcome," she said, smiling at him again. She was about to turn away when he caught her wrist.

"Did you know why I had come to Brythonica?" he asked her pointedly.

She seemed taken aback by the question. For an instant, she looked worried, frightened. The emotion was quickly suppressed, but he noticed it. She hesitated before responding, her mood becoming less playful. "Isn't the point of Wizr," she answered enigmatically, "to anticipate your opponent's next move?"

◆ ◆ ◆

*My lord Kiskaddon,*

*The king commands you return at once to Kingfountain. There is no mincing words on this news. Eyric and Dunsdworth have escaped the tower. Their guards were undoubtedly bribed or murdered, for there was no watch on them this morn. We have hounds and men tracking them, for it seems they have gone upriver. You can only imagine the state of agitation at present. Would there was a way we could contact you more directly. Hopefully they will have been recaptured by the time you receive this news. I've never seen the king so wroth. Return at once, my lord.*

> *Kevan Amrein*
> *Kingfountain Palace*

◆ ◆ ◆

# CHAPTER TWELVE

*Traitor*

Before meeting his parents, Owen arranged for a change of clothing since his were damp from the dunking he'd taken at the beach. He was very nervous about the encounter, not just because it was so unexpected but also because he didn't know how his parents and other siblings would react to him after so many years apart.

He needn't have worried.

The dome of his father's head was completely bald, but he still had a fringe of graying hair around the sides and back, shorn close to his scalp. His skin was marked in places with liver splotches and craggy wrinkles, but he was fit and strong. Mother had crow's-feet around her eyes, but she also had aged well, and the instant Owen entered the room, she engulfed him in a fierce, motherly hug. She kissed him repeatedly on the cheek, by his ear, and on the patch of white in his hair. Then, gripping the front of his fashionable tunic, she pulled him so close their noses almost touched.

"I have *never* stopped thinking about you," she whispered to him, looking into his eyes with such intensity. Her voice was thick with emotion. "Not one day. I rejoice at every scrap of news I hear about you. But a mother's love holds true. Even though you're taller than me now, you are still my little miracle."

Jessica was beaming, wiping tears from the corners of her eyes as she waited for her turn to greet him once more. Then the entire family crowded around him, pulling him into the center of a vast embrace. And while they felt a little like strangers, he could *feel* memories of his childhood at Tatton Hall begin to emerge from the haze of the past.

"Welcome to Ploemeur," Papan said. "I cannot wait to hear about your adventures."

"You *must* tell us all of them," Jessica implored, tugging his tunic sleeve.

Owen was uncomfortable with so much attention, but it was from *them*, and that made a difference. Through the crowd, he spied the Duchess of Brythonica, watching the reunion and keeping to herself. She had staged the moment deliberately.

He was still unsure of her motives, but he was grateful nonetheless and tipped a nod to her from across the room.

"Are you *really* Fountain-blessed as they say?" said his other sister Ann. She had long blond hair that went down to her waist. He had vague memories of her constantly brushing it at the window seat while staring outside.

"Tell them about the battle of Averanche!" Jessica suggested.

"I don't care about battles and war," Maman said in a scolding tone. "Did you truly come here to marry the duchess? I would blame your mother for your manners if I dared."

"Where to start?" Owen said at last.

◆　◆　◆

The moon was gleaming silver in the sky as Owen and Sinia left the House of Pillars, walking side by side. They were followed by her entourage, all of whom were a little bleary-eyed due to the lateness of the hour. The air was brisk and calm, the weather very mild. Owen admired the glittering stars in the sky.

"Is it always this bright out at night?" he asked.

"The fog will come in soon," Sinia said. "It usually does."

"I'm not looking forward to the ride back up to the castle," he confessed. "Do you take a carriage, or ride?"

"Neither, usually," she answered with a playful smile. The hint of mischief in her eyes made him return her smile.

"This way," she said, capturing his arm with a little flash of possessiveness and pulling him to the rear of the House of Pillars. At the rear, there were workers hoisting huge crates off wagons. As Sinia approached, they doffed their hats respectfully. Sinia flashed them a smile and led him over to a small crowd of people, horses, and wagons.

"Do you see it?" Sinia asked, pointing ahead. Workers were securing thick ropes to the crates. The ropes were connected to some sort of crane, like the kind used in the ship docks, only Owen couldn't see the top of it. He craned his neck and realized that they were at the foot of the cliffs, the palace high above them.

"You're not serious?" Owen said, looking back at the crates.

"It's the opposite of falling," she said, pulling him with her. The crew seemed to be expecting her. A few members of the entourage shook their heads and said they'd take a horse up instead, and she dismissed them good-naturedly.

"Up you go," said one of the workers, hoisting Sinia onto one of the crates by her waist. There were four ropes coming up at the corners, meeting at a metal hook and ring. Owen studied the contraption for a moment and, not to be outdone by his host, swung up onto the crate.

"You have to sit over there," she said, pointing to the other end, then clasping the ropes with both hands. "Or it will not be balanced."

Owen felt a stab of fear in his middle, a sensation that became more acute when one of the foremen gave a signal. There was a grinding, clicking noise, followed by a sudden lurch from the ropes. Owen's insides fluttered with panic the moment his boots left the ground. Sinia laughed sweetly. He turned and saw the breeze ruffle her long, lovely hair.

"Don't be frightened," she said, her tone suddenly serious. "Nothing will happen. Do you see the docks? Over there!"

She pointed again, and this time his stomach lurched with fear for her. He wanted to warn her to hang on, though she seemed at ease here as she had been at the edge of the beach. They were rising at a rapid pace, the roofs shrinking beneath their feet. There were the docks with boats secured for the night, having brought their cargo during the day. The ropes groaned under the crate's weight and the contents swayed a little, making Owen tighten his grip. It was an interesting feeling—like a bird soaring.

"Thank you for arranging the dinner tonight," Owen told her, watching in wonder as a bank of fog rolled in off the coast. He could see the lights of the sanctuary on the distant island.

"You're welcome, Owen. I thought you'd wish it."

She was thoughtful. But there was still so much he didn't know about her. It was as if he were looking at her through the haze of that fog.

"Do you see Averanche?" she asked. "It's that speck of light just on the horizon."

"I think so," Owen said. "Do you do this often then?"

"I did it more when I was little girl," she answered, giving him a sidelong look. Almost a knowing look. "I liked to explore."

"We have that in common then," Owen replied.

"Perhaps you'd care to join me on a journey across the duchy?" The noise of the machinery above grew louder as they approached the landing where the crates would arrive.

He wasn't sure he wanted to refuse. But he needed to get back to Kingfountain. Etayne was probably chafing, and it was his duty to protect Drew.

"I'll think about it," he answered. She seemed a little disappointed by his answer.

◆　◆　◆

It was late in the evening when Owen returned to his chamber in the castle overlooking Ploemeur. He felt like collapsing on the bed with his boots on, but there was a pile of correspondence awaiting him on the desk.

"You saw your family this evening," Etayne said, slipping out from the curtained balcony. "I thought you were planning to leave earlier?"

Owen rubbed his eyes, his heart still raw from the emotional reunion. "I felt obligated to spend the day," he said flatly, planting his knuckles on the desk by the mound of letters. "When did these all arrive? Or did the ones from yesterday breed? Look at this stack. It will take half the night to read and answer them all, and that will delay us even more." He grimaced at how petulant he sounded.

"I can stay and help you read through them," Etayne offered. "The ones from Kevan I put over there. Farnes brought new ones earlier this evening. He said that one came in a hurry."

Owen scrubbed his fingers through his hair, frowning. "If it's more bad news, I'm going to have him flogged," he muttered. Etayne seemed eager to speak with him, but she seemed to sense his poor mood. "I will accept your offer," he said, shoving part of the pile toward her. "I don't have time to woo a duchess *and* run a duchy *and* the Espion." He shook his head. "The weight of all of this is crushing me tonight."

She gave him a sympathetic look and then sat down beside him. She looked at the vast pile of correspondence and picked out one, breaking the seal. "Your parents are well?"

Owen snatched a letter and opened it. "More than well, it seems. They aren't hostages, that much is clear. Everything my sister told us is true. They go by Occitanian surnames to help hide their true identities.

They have a comfortable manor on a hill to the west, and my father oversees the taxation of trade. My mother wasn't sure what to make of me," he added with a chuckle. "It's been sixteen years after all, and she remembered a little lad who used to clutch at her skirts." He sniffed, scanning the letter quickly and then tossing it aside. "I don't know why the duchess has rewarded them with so many favors. It's certainly not something Severn would have done."

Etayne murmured in agreement as she read another letter. "And how goes the wooing?"

Owen smiled wearily at the veiled attempt to draw him out. "I suppose that depends," he said, careful of his answer, careful of her feelings. "The king deeply believed that this suggested alliance would provoke Brythonica. In that regard, his plan is utterly failing. It seems Sinia anticipated his move and resigned herself to marrying me before I even arrived. Poor girl." He wanted to laugh at the absurdity. "Marshal Roux has thrown a fit and skulked off to his own manor to brood."

"No he hasn't," Etayne said softly.

That caught Owen's interest. "What do you mean?"

"His men were guarding the forest we passed on our way to the castle. I came in disguise to see the place, but for all my tricks, I could not get past the sentries. They were vigilant. What are they keeping from us? I wonder."

Owen looked at her, his brow furrowing. "You're sure it was the marshal?"

Etayne nodded. "I didn't see him, but one of the sentries let it slip that he was there in person."

"He knew you were coming," Owen said angrily. "He always seems to know!" He slammed his fist onto the table, his frustration spilling over. "The offense he feigned was a ruse, a trick. I should have seen this. He must have left for the woods the very night we arrived." Another memory struck Owen like an arrow shaft. "Hold on a moment."

"What?" she pressed, her eyes full of eagerness, the pile of correspondence momentarily forgotten.

"This was years ago, after the mayor of Averanche surrendered the city to me. Some visitors came to find me in the North. One of Roux's knights—he was a giant of a man. And also a lawyer from Averanche." Owen started pacing, his mind working furiously to recall the moment. He snapped his fingers quickly. "There was something about disputes. Border disputes about the hunting forests. The knight sought reassurance that I didn't intend to encroach on Brythonica's boundaries. Especially the forests. I thought nothing of it at the time. I'm not all that fond of hunting and hawking, nor do I have the time!" He turned and looked at her. "Roux doesn't want us to see whatever's in those woods. I'm not sure Sinia knows what it is." He shook his head. "Or maybe that's an errant presumption. She is far more clever than her demeanor suggests."

"How so?" Etayne asked, walking toward him.

"So many times during our conversation today she hinted at things. Like she was trying to prompt me to ask certain questions. The Wizr set, for example," he said, naming one of the instances. "I challenged her to a game of Wizr, and she gave me this strange look and said that *I* needed to provide the set."

Etayne's face darkened. "You think she meant the one you hid in the fountain of St. Penryn?"

Owen held up his hands. "That is exactly what I suspected. But her words were so innocuous she could have meant anything. I feel as if a game is being played around me. This feeling has been nagging at me for years, and I'm frustrated that I haven't learned the rules yet."

"You could ask the duchess directly," Etayne suggested, giving him an arch look.

"How does one have *that* conversation?" Owen said with a laugh. "I sense you're hiding something from me, my lady. Would you please confess while I keep my own secrets?" He tapped his mouth. "No, I'm going to ferret this out. I have to find out what makes that forest so powerful with the Fountain. What we need is a way to get past the guards. What we need are . . ." He stopped, his eyes widening. "Disguises."

He gave Etayne a serious look. "Your power might be exactly what we need. Being a local didn't help you get through. But if you *looked* and *sounded* like Sinia, they wouldn't stop you. I've spent time with her today. You can use my memories like you've done in the past."

Etayne's eyes flashed with mischievous intent. "And what if I were to disguise you as well?"

He stared at her. "Do you think you can do that?"

"Let me try," she said. "Hold still a moment. I've been wondering if I could change others and not just myself, and this would be a perfect opportunity to test it. Roux would be able to sense the power, but if he's stationed by the forest, where there is already so much Fountain magic, he may not be able to figure it out. Here, I think I need to touch you for this to work." She reached out and took his arm at the elbow, then opened herself to the Fountain. He sensed it immediately and, not for the first time, marveled at how much her strength in it had grown over the years.

He felt the magic wash over him in warm, gentle waves. Once again, he felt part of him resist it, a certain feeling of rebelliousness that balked from letting another change him. But he allowed the magic to suffuse him, taking care to keep the core of himself intact.

"Look at yourself," Etayne breathed excitedly, her eyes delighted. Still gripping his arm, she steered him over to a large mirror so that he could see his own reflection.

He was almost startled to see Lord Roux staring back at him. The image seemed to flicker under his scrutiny, but he allowed Etayne's spell to cling to him. His powers from the Fountain made him impermeable to the powers of others who were Fountain-blessed. As far as he knew, his abilities were unique. No one else would have cause to doubt his disguise. Owen raised his hand to touch his chin and watched the doppelganger mimic his motion.

"You *can* do it," Owen breathed. "Can you still change yourself? Or must you hold your focus on me?"

Suddenly the duchess was standing at his side, her hand resting on his arm as if they were attending guests at a ball. "For me," she told him, "the magic is like carrying a weight on my shoulders. It's a weight that grows heavier the longer I use it. Over the years, I've been pushing and training myself. But it helps when other things contribute to the disguise. See how I've made your tunic into the standard of the raven? That requires concentration. If I stole you a tunic, it would lessen my burden. I'm strong in the magic now, Owen. I can hold this illusion for some time, and we'll only need it to get past the sentries. Of course, it won't work if Roux is still among them."

She let the magic fall away, and Owen watched in fascination as the illusion shed from them instantly. She gave him a determined look in the mirror. "I could do this with more than just the two of us. Naturally, the more people I try to disguise, the heavier the toll and the less time I would be able to maintain it."

"You are amazing," Owen said and watched a little flush creep across her cheeks at the praise.

"You taught me," she demurred.

"I think those woods hide another clue that may help me figure out what game is being played against us. I don't like losing," he said with a growl of ambition in his voice.

"No man ever does," she said, squeezing his arm. "Back to the letters then, so we can go." From the smug-looking smile on her face, he could tell she was pleased with her accomplishment. It made him chuckle to himself, but then his eyes fell to the pile of letters. Groaning, he grabbed the stack and went over to the couch, languidly draping his leg over the armrest in a casual manner. He broke another seal and read the message quickly before tossing it aside.

Then he remembered the one Etayne said Farnes had brought in a rush. "Where's the one from Farnes again?"

"It was that one. There's a stain on it."

He spied it and then cracked open the seal. His stomach spun and then lurched as he read the message. He pulled his leg off the rest and hurried to his feet, his pulse quickening.

"No," he muttered darkly, feeling the calamity growing larger and larger. Eyric and Dunsdworth had escaped their confinement. They were missing. Owen had entrusted Kevan with watching over them. What could have happened to upset things?

"What is it? Tell me—your expression is frightening me!"

His heart hammered in his chest. "I can't believe it. How? How could it happen?"

"Tell me!" she demanded.

"Eyric and Dunsdworth escaped," he said in frustration. "They were under heavy guard. The Espion should have been able to prevent this from happening." He cursed the constant flood of troubles that had plagued Severn's indecorous reign. "I'm to return at once," Owen said, glancing at the words again. "I tell you, Etayne, I am heartily *sick* of this! To constantly defend a man who I . . ." He caught himself, frowning and swallowing the bitterness, to keep treasonous words from spilling out of his mouth. "By the Fountain, why must we go through this again and again? This is because of Brugia. This is Maxwell's hand. I can see the smears. He wants to be lord and master of all. Severn is the strongest ruler, so he gains the most enmity. This constant fighting and scheming. This unending intrigue. It makes me want to retch." He sighed, shaking his head. "The duchess tried to persuade me to spend the next few days visiting other towns in Brythonica. I wish I had the freedom to do just that, but we must get back at once." The words tumbled out before he had a chance to consider them. The look of hurt that formed on Etayne's face made him wince. He rubbed his eyes. "What is it?"

"Only that you seem to be breaking your vow," she answered. "You swore you'd bar your heart, Owen. You told me to remind you in case you lost your senses."

He did not appreciate her reminder. "Go wake Farnes," he told her, trying to curb the tone of resentfulness that threatened to make things worse. "Get him in here. We'll need to beg our pardon and leave tonight." He snapped his fingers. "Actually, you and I will ride on ahead like we normally do so we can make our stop in the forest first. He can stay behind and soothe any hurt feelings, make our excuses." *Plan my wedding.* He caught himself in time before saying it aloud.

"I'll get him," she said, her eyes narrowing as she left.

When the door shut, he read Kevan's note again. *I've never seen the king so wroth.* Owen couldn't be sure how to interpret that statement. But queasy feelings sucked on his insides like leeches.

What would Severn do if the missing princes were finally caught?

What had Eredur done to those who posed a threat to *his* throne?

Owen turned and stared at the closed door, imagining he could hear the poisoner's footsteps fading down the hall.

He grabbed the next letter on the pile. It bore the king's seal. He blinked with surprise and cracked it open.

The words were scrawled in splotchy letters, but he recognized the king's handwriting, the hastily crafted message addressed to Owen, Lord Kiskaddon, Duke of Westmarch.

*I know you've betrayed me.*

# CHAPTER THIRTEEN

## *Threat*

That brief hand-scratched note in the king's own style had opened up a pit inside Owen's stomach and filled it with terror. He was a child again, a helpless creature trapped inside a prison of fear. His throat seized up, and sweat began to trickle down his cheeks. Slumping onto a nearby couch, it was all he could do to keep his supper inside his body. It was a battle he soon lost, and a few warning pangs later, he rushed to the privy and vomited noisily into the garderobe hole. He crouched there, humiliated, and then sank to the floor. It felt as if his bones had turned into paper.

He sat there a long while, pondering the king's message. He wasn't a child anymore. He wasn't a helpless boy. He was a man now and needed to act like one. Even though his heart felt weighed down with despair, he rallied his wits to try to think of what was happening.

What could the king be referring to? Had he finally learned about Ankarette's role in saving Owen when he came to Kingfountain as a young child? That was a secret Mancini had carried to his watery grave. He and Etayne and Elysabeth were the only ones who knew the truth.

He wrinkled his brow. No, it was unlikely that the king knew. Did that mean he had discovered the truth about Andrew, the boy Owen had rescued and hidden? The king had asked him to investigate how the boy had come to the North. Owen had gone through the motions, ensuring all the while that the search would be in vain. But maybe something had happened at court—perhaps Kathryn had indeed recognized through her mother's intuition that the child was hers. His stomach twisted more violently still. That was entirely likely. Kathryn had been so distraught before they left; perhaps she had discovered the truth and revealed herself in some way. Then the king could have used his magic to persuade her to reveal the whole truth.

Yes, that was the most likely possibility. He stiffened when another implication struck him. Eyric's escape from the tower. Was that related as well? Had Kathryn helped her husband escape? Was the tiny family trying to flee together? He knuckled his forehead and began counting off curses under his breath.

*I know you've betrayed me.*

What to do about it? How to respond? In one letter, he'd been summoned back to Kingfountain to help deal with the missing captives. In another, he'd been accused of treason. Had both letters arrived simultaneously? There was no date affixed to the king's note. Squeezing his hand into a fist, he slammed it onto the floor, full of frustration.

What were his options? Well, he could refuse to obey the king's summons, but that was tantamount to confessing his guilt. He doubted he'd find any welcome in Chatriyon's court. He knew the Occitanian king both hated and feared him, which Jessica had confirmed. The thought of fleeing made him sick with shame. That was a coward's answer. He thought of the tawny-haired lad whom the Fountain had entrusted him to protect. He could not step down from that duty.

One option would be to throw himself at the mercy of the king. To admit to the lies and deceptions. To attempt to persuade Severn that he needed to step down and give the child his crown. No king of

Ceredigion had done that before. In all the tales that he had heard Evie tell about the history of their country, kings had always been forced to yield their thrones. And it was usually a rebellious duke who made it happen. Another role, played over and over again—a waterwheel spinning in a river.

He sat there for a long time, plucking at the strands of hair from his unkempt beard, staring into the void of his festering conscience. The question that had tormented him for years reared its head again. Could Owen rise in rebellion against the king? None of the other dukes had the power. Catsby was new and untested, and besides, he had been plundering Lord Horwath's dominions. He'd find no one willing to die for him. Jack Paulen of East Stowe? Laughable. Lovel had been loyal to Severn since their early friendship, and while he was well-meaning, he was totally incapable of rallying men.

Owen knew Severn well enough to guess the king would not have sent such a note without making precautions against a possible rebellion. In fact, Owen imagined there would be soldiers waiting for him at Tatton Hall. Was the king trying to force him into rebellion? So many possibilities. He continued to stack up the various possibilities and weigh them against one another. It was his primary gift from the Fountain.

"Owen?"

He had not heard the door open, but he recognized Etayne's voice. He had lost track of time in the privy and was only faintly aware of his surroundings. He tried to stand on trembling legs. He must have made some noise because Etayne came rushing in after him, and when she saw the look on his face, her eyes widened with fear.

"Are you sick?" she demanded, rushing to his side. She touched his face and examined his eyes, his mouth. Obviously she feared he'd been poisoned.

"I'm not sick," he said, warding off her efforts. "Well, not in *that* way."

"I noticed you hadn't bolted the door, so I waited outside," she said with agitation. "Then when I came in, I didn't see you. I thought you'd gone." Her voice was sounding more desperate by the moment. "What's wrong?"

He did make it to his feet finally, and she looked so concerned it made him wonder about his own appearance. Not wanting to say the words aloud, he thrust Severn's note into her hands.

She blanched when she read it.

After walking past her out of the privy, he noticed the small fire had burned low. The only light came from a single candle Etayne had brought. It was probably after midnight. He stretched his arms, weary from the exhausting day, but his mind was too thick with the dilemma to rest.

A foot scuff came up behind him. "I won't let him hurt you," she whispered in a low, threatening voice.

He turned and saw the fierce eyes, the serious expression that told him she'd murder the king if he tried. It gave him some small measure of comfort that someone cared that much about him.

"I won't ask you to—"

"You don't *need* to ask me!" she said passionately. "We both know that he is not *worthy* of the loyalty you've shown him. It's been in your power all along to rid the kingdom of that tyrant. I will ride ahead. They won't even know it was me. Why am I even asking you? I should just leave now and do the deed."

"No," he said, shaking his head. "If Severn is going to die, it will be on a battlefield, not in a bedchamber. There is a deep tradition, Etayne. I even think the people would rally to me if I did rise up."

"They would." She nodded fervently. "Do it, Owen. For the Fountain's sake, do it! Claim the throne for yourself and then give it to the boy. You can become the protector. The people would accept you. They *love* you!" She stopped short, but he could sense the words she hadn't said. The air sizzled with them.

"I have to go back and face him," Owen said.

She looked at him, aghast. "No! That would be foolish. When you next ride into Kingfountain, it should be to siege the castle."

He shook his head. "No. I'm going to return and face him."

She came up and gripped his arms, her fingers digging into him. "He knows how to kill someone who is Fountain-blessed! I won't let you do this."

"Let me do this?" he said, grabbing her arms and pushing her back slightly. "Etayne, I'm counting on you to get me out of it! I'm going to face him. He's not going to throw me into the river. There will be a trial, there will be the Assizes. Maybe the truth finally needs to be let out into the open. The truth about Eyric and the boy. The truth about Kathryn—that she's still another man's wife! If the king won't see reason, if I must compel him through force, then I will need you to rescue me. I don't think . . ." he paused, shaking his head. "I know he's cruel, but I don't think he'll just kill me. Especially if I come and submit to him. He's expecting a rebellion. He's undoubtedly preparing for it. He will not expect this." He breathed out a sigh. "I have to trust my instincts. I have to trust my gift from the Fountain. This is the right course."

Her look was beginning to soften. She pressed her fingers against her lips and started to pace. "I'll go ahead of you. In disguise, of course. I'll find out what's happening. What the Espion knows." She looked at him with a burning gaze. "If he's already preparing your death, then I won't let you surrender to him."

He chuckled. "Fair enough. Did you tell Farnes we were leaving?"

She nodded briskly. "I have horses and disguises waiting for us. We'll change after we ride out."

"I have neither the intention nor the ability to sleep right now," he said with a laugh. "You must keep me alive, Etayne. I need you."

She looked mollified, some of the danger ebbing from her eyes. "You still want to examine the woods on the way out?"

"I do," Owen said darkly. "They are hiding a secret. And I grow weary of secrets."

◆　◆　◆

The vales of Brythonica were quiet in the night. A haze of fog had rolled in from the sea, giving the air a mysterious aspect while also concealing them from the gaze of others. There were no stars to be seen and the roads looked different in the fog, but Owen had help. He could sense the Fountain drawing him to the woods. It was like the tower bells of a sanctuary pealing, pointing his mind in the right direction. The dew from the mist clung to his eyelashes and he could feel the wetness when he blinked.

The earth was loamy and rich, the smells drifting on the cool breeze. He wore his chain hauberk, but it was topped with a tunic bearing the black raven of Brythonica rather than the standard of his own duchy. Etayne kept pace with him, and he could sense her brooding. She was probably plotting a dozen different ways of saving Owen from his sense of duty. He was grateful that Stiev Horwath was dead. He could not have borne the look of disappointment in the old man's eyes. He had no doubt, however, that Iago would gladly join in a rebellion against Severn if it meant reinstating Evie's rights to her grandfather's land.

They rode in stillness, the mists getting thinner as they left the coast and moved deeper inland. They rode until the first flushes of dawn began to smudge the sky. He didn't know how many leagues they had crossed, but he felt they should be reaching the woods soon. He felt them drawing closer.

"There," Etayne said, pointing.

The horizon showed the hills and woods, which were blacker than the brightening sky. As they came closer, he spied movement on the road and discerned the white tunics of knights blocking the way.

Owen lifted the chain cowl to cover his hair. His sword was strapped and ready, but he hoped he wouldn't have to fight his way through. As they came closer, he felt the magic start to flow from Etayne as she concocted their disguises. He didn't look at her, but he used his thoughts to feed her magic with the small details from his memories that would make the illusion more believable.

They reined in before some startled troops who were holding lanterns and hailing them as they approached.

"M-my lady!" the knight gasped in recognition, seeing the Duchess of Brythonica ride up in the dark. "What are you . . . what are you doing here in the midst of the night?" He looked absolutely startled.

Etayne looked down at him imperiously. "I do the Fountain's will," she said, her voice perfectly matching Sinia's.

"Blessed be the Fountain," the knight said, bowing reverently. They pulled aside, asking no more questions. Owen concealed a smirk as they rode past. He wanted to compliment her, but didn't know who might be listening. None of the soldiers guarding the road followed them, though he could hear them talking in low voices amongst themselves, gossiping as soldiers always did.

They took the road, and the sky began to brighten more rapidly. Owen's heart began pounding as they drew closer to their destination. He could feel the presence of the Fountain magic coming from the woods on the right. The cluster of trees was especially dense there, which would make riding difficult.

*Leave the horses here.*

The whisper was unmistakable and startling. Owen jerked on the reins, stopping. It had been some time since the Fountain had spoken to him directly.

"What is it?" Etayne asked, her voice full of dread.

He dismounted and she followed him. Owen led his horse to the edge of the road and secured the reins on a tree branch. She did the same.

"We go the rest of the way on foot," he said. "It's not far. The Fountain told me to leave the horses."

"It spoke to you?" she queried.

"It did."

They started into the woods together, the ground suddenly uneven and full of treacherous footing. Instinctively, he sought her hand to prevent them from getting separated in the shadows. A few birds trilled to welcome the imminent dawn. Etayne let herself be guided, and he felt how cold her hand was from the long night ride. She gave him surreptitious looks that he pretended not to notice.

Ahead, Owen could hear the lapping noises of a fountain or small waterfall. His sense of curiosity grew with each step, as did the worry and fear welling in his gut. Branches clawed at his face, and he used one arm to ward them back and clear a gap for the two of them to pass. He was trying to be quiet, but it sounded like they were marching with an army for all the noise they made.

The woods encircled a small clearing centered around a huge mound of massive boulders that towered as big as houses. The trees were ancient and huge, and some younger ones grew from cracks and seams in the rocks. Moss and lichen riddled the stones, barely discernible from the fading gloom. Water was coming from the rocks, little rippling waterfalls that pattered in endless drips. Looking more closely, Owen saw a shaggy oak tree growing amidst the stones, pregnant with leaves and acorns and mistletoe. The trickling water seemed to be coming from the tangled roots of the tree. The ground had gotten relatively steeper as they crossed the woods, and a small trickling stream tumbled from the boulders and oak tree and disappeared back into the woods.

"Look," Etayne said, squeezing his hand and pointing with her finger.

At the base of the rocky terrain there was a marble plinth—a flat altar-like sheet of rock that was definitely human-carved. It was set away from the mass of boulders and strewn with detritus from the trees. On the flat marble sheet was a silver bowl. An iron chain fastened the bowl to a ring driven into the side of the marble. The chain was loosely coiled.

It was the source of the magic. Owen sensed power coming from the bowl—it thrummed inside his skull and filled his reservoirs of magic to the brim. Despite his lack of sleep and anxiety, he felt alive, quickened, and alert.

"What is this place?" Etayne whispered in awe, staring at the boulders, the trees, the naked sky. A single star seemed to burn in the sky above them, a pinprick of torchlight.

*Fill the bowl with water from the fountain.*

Owen blinked in astonishment, his mouth suddenly dry. Releasing Etayne's hand, he approached the marble slab. She followed at his heels, casting her gaze around for a sign of danger. The caw of birds clawed the air, and Owen saw several ravens come and land on the branches. They were different from the birds he'd heard earlier, their tones darker and more ominous. That they were ravens—the standard of the Montforts—made him deeply suspicious and gave him the sense he was being watched.

"I don't know," Owen said, but he knew what he needed to do. He marched up to the silver bowl while his courage lasted. It was not heavy when he hefted it. The chain rattled slightly.

"What are you doing?" Etayne whispered.

Owen looked at the waters tumbling from the roots and down over the rocks. It was a curious sight, and he found himself breathing hard. Then, carefully, he crossed several larger broken stones with the bowl until he reached the small waterfall and held the bowl under the stream. It filled quickly, and he pulled it back carefully, worried the weight of it would cause a spill. The sky had turned a faint blue overhead. He could see Etayne's worried eyes on him, but he couldn't explain what he didn't understand.

*Pour it onto the plinth.*

Cautiously, Owen carried the bowl to the plinth, letting the chain drag beneath it. He caught himself from tripping, breathing in deep gasps as the magic tingled against his skin. The waters in the bowl rippled, reflecting his image back at him. He looked terrible. When he reached the marble slab, he stood by it, cradling the bowl. He'd trusted the whispers of the Fountain so far. There was no turning back. He upturned the bowl and splashed the water onto the plinth.

As soon as he'd done so, a crack of thunder boomed from the cloud-less sky overhead, so loud and deafening that Owen dropped the bowl to shield his ears. Though he had been in thunderstorms before, he'd never heard a boom so loud that it felt like the sky itself was shattering. The sound frightened him out of his wits and he looked at Etayne, who was holding her ears as well, staring up at the sky.

It started to rain. Heavy fat droplets began to gush from overhead. Wind kicked up and sent the desiccated leaves whirling into his face, little pricks of pain that made him shield his eyes.

The rain turned into hail.

Icy chunks began to crash into the plinth and the detritus all around, growing bigger and bigger by the moment. Etayne shrieked in pain as they started to strike her. Owen's heart beat wildly in his chest, and he felt he'd made a terrible, life-threatening mistake. The hail ham-mered down on them relentlessly, but strangely, Owen did not feel the wetness strike him. In fact, none of the ice struck him.

"We need shelter!" Owen bellowed amidst the deluge. The woods were farther back, and they'd find some protection there. The boulders behind him were all curved and rounded. He didn't see any pockets or small caves that would offer them shelter.

A walnut-sized chunk of ice struck Etayne on the head and she crumpled to the ground. The hail beat down on her mercilessly.

Owen bellowed in surprise and rushed over to her, watching the pelting stones hammer down on her body. He knelt by her side and scooped up her legs, intent on running into the woods for protection, but the ground was full of pebble-sized hailstones and he heard a rushing noise coming from the sky that made him shudder and quake. It was as if a waterfall of hail had opened above the plinth and they were caught in the rapids. Owen pulled her tightly against him and covered her body with his own, waiting to die. Death was the only outcome. He had tampered with magic beyond his ken; he had opened up a flood that would destroy all of Brythonica.

The hailstorm came down on him, but somehow, he was protected against it. He was freezing and trembling, with water dripping into his face, but the chunks of ice did not strike him. Was Etayne even alive? Her face was crushed against his chest as he clutched her tightly to him, shielding her from the devastating storm he'd unwittingly summoned.

He would protect her for as long as he was able, but he felt certain he would drown. They were both going to die.

And then the storm ended as suddenly as it had started. He shook with cold, unable to believe that somehow he'd been reprieved from death. The magic swirled around him, and he noticed his scabbard was glowing. The raven etched into it was made of livid fire, a fire that slowly faded and could only be seen by the user. That whisper of insight had come from the Fountain to his mind.

His scabbard, which the Maid of Donremy herself had used in all her famous battles, had protected him. He had found it in the cistern at the palace of Kingfountain, one of the lost treasures of a bygone age.

"Etayne! Etayne!" he pleaded, pulling her away. Her face was pale. There was blood coming down her ear.

Then the trilling songs of birds filled the air. Owen jerked his head up and saw that the oak tree near the waterfall was completely barren of leaves. It had been stripped clear by the violent storm. Some of the branches had crashed down as well. But birds were alighting on the bare limbs, singing the most beautiful song he'd ever heard. These weren't ravens—they were songbirds—and as he hugged Etayne to his chest, his heart wanted to weep from the purity of their music.

The song melted the ice in moments. Owen blinked, watching the heaps of sharp-edged ice vanish. Amidst the song, he heard the clomp of hooves coming from the woods.

Owen bent his ear to Etayne's lips, listening closely for the sound of her breath. She was breathing; thank the Fountain, she was breathing. "Etayne, someone's coming. Etayne!" He tried to jostle her shoulders, but she remained limp.

Turning his head, Owen saw a horse as black as night coming from the woods. The rider was garbed in black armor and a matching helmet that concealed his face. Fixed to a spear on the horse's bridle was a pennant, also black, with a white raven on it. The spurs on the knight's boots poked the horse's flanks, making it snort and start up the terrain directly toward Owen. The knight drew his sword with his right hand, steadying the spear and pennant with his left.

Owen wanted to get Etayne to safety, but he could sense the knight's ill intent as he charged up the hill.

Gently, Owen settled Etayne onto the muddy ground, cradling her head on her arm. He rose, grimacing, and stepped away from her as the knight closed the distance between them. Owen unsheathed his sword.

"I have no quarrel with you," Owen said, summoning the magic of the Fountain to him. His reservoir was full of power. He sensed, however, that his words were utterly futile.

A mist of steam snorted from the horse's nostrils.

And then the rider charged at him, his spear lowering toward Owen's heart.

# CHAPTER FOURTEEN

## *The Knight at Dawn*

The ground shuddered from the charging mount, its nostrils flaming with white mist as it raced toward him. Owen blinked rapidly, drawing upon the Fountain's magic. His eyes narrowed on the mystery knight's spear, and he tightened his grip on his sword, angling it slightly forward. If he parried wrong or misjudged, he would be skewered. It was no longer time for thinking. It was time for instinct. For survival.

He moved away from Etayne's limp body, forcing the knight to change position. The spear wavered slightly. His magic revealed much about the man's weakness. This knight was battle-hardened with expert reflexes, but his left ankle was a source of pain. Owen could sense it throbbing now, even from this distance. The horse had weaknesses too—it was experienced, but it was nervous about Owen and his magic. The steed's natural trepidation would be an asset so long as the beast didn't collide with him.

Owen brought his sword up to an overhanging guard, both hands twisting the pommel fiercely—one over the other—the blade poised above his head. He walked crossways, moving slightly downhill. It was much easier to strike a stationary target, and Owen had no intention of being easy prey.

The knight suddenly lunged with the spear, trying to catch Owen off guard. Dipping the sword, Owen deflected the charge effortlessly, spun around, and sliced the warhorse's flanks as it rushed past him. The animal screamed in pain.

The black-garbed knight reined in hard and then flung himself off the horse, landing well but with an obvious favoring of his left leg. Owen had not dealt the horse a killing wound, and the animal stamped and seethed, thrashing its mane wildly. The knight stood solidly. He'd exchanged the spear for a sword. Owen could only see the man's eyes through the visor, but his own face was revealed to his opponent. At least the helmet would limit the knight's ability to see.

The two began squaring off, circling each other warily, swords at the ready. Owen's senses felt sharp and alert. The magic of the Fountain pulsed inside of him. Strangely, he did not sense it coming from his opponent.

Then the black knight came at Owen with a whirlwind of blows, his dark sword coming at his head and then his chest. This was not the training yard of Owen's youth. Even with the weak leg, the knight was formidable and very experienced, and Owen was forced to retreat and defend himself. A sting cut against his arm, shearing through the hauberk links. Then his thigh. The pain shot through him, but his heart was beating too wildly for him to feel it. He sensed blood, torn skin. And then he felt something peculiar. The scabbard at his side began to glow, the raven sigil igniting once more with magic. The wounds in his arm and thigh were soothed.

Owen deflected another thrust at his throat and then kicked the knight in his weakened leg to break off the attack. The man grunted with pain and limped slightly, but he shook off the discomfort and came at Owen again, hobbling just a little. Their boots crushed through the twigs and shards of leaves, threatened by the unstable footing and broken stones. The black knight butted his shoulder into Owen's chest, his superior weight nearly sending Owen onto his back, but the young duke caught his footing and swung his sword down against the other man's breastplate, sending up a shower of sparks.

The men began circling each other again, panting heavily. Owen went on the attack next, driving fast and hard, hammering away on the knight's left side, forcing him to defend, to use his legs to move and react. Owen kept at it, drawing around him in a narrower circle, thrusting and blocking, looking for vulnerable spots where he could nick his opponent. The man was wearing gauntlets, so he wasn't likely to drop his blade. The young duke forced him to spin around in circles, hoping the extra movement and the weight of his armor would dizzy him.

It seemed to be working. The labored breathing of the black knight was growing more pronounced. Most battles rarely lasted this long. Owen was younger, had more stamina, and was driven by the need to survive.

"Yield," Owen said, bashing away a feeble attempt at a strike. The man was starting to wobble.

"No," answered a gruff voice, echoing strangely in the helm.

With that, the black knight charged him, swinging high and then low. Owen did not catch the feint in time to avoid a shallow cut, but the hauberk absorbed the blow. Then the knight's elbow struck Owen's jaw, spinning him back and making his eyes dance with pricks of light. Owen went down hard, unable to see, so he cleared the way with his sword, swinging it indiscriminately like a scythe.

He felt a shadow loom over him, saw the tip of the knight's blade rushing down toward his nose. Owen twisted his shoulders and heaved himself to one side, thrusting his blade out. The knight collapsed on top of him, and Owen felt his blade shearing through metal and then skin as the black knight impaled himself in his fall. The weight of the knight came down on Owen like anvils, knocking him flat onto his back. He squirmed and wriggled to get free and saw with horror the tip of his blade appearing from his enemy's back.

It was a death wound. His magic revealed the truth instantly as blood began to well through the slit in the man's breastplate. Shoving the gasping knight onto his side, Owen saw the man's legs twitch with spasms. His life was fading quickly, his heart as wild as a bird's. Owen scrambled backward in shock, weaponless. The black knight's sword was on the ground next to him.

Owen hadn't intended to kill him. He had defended himself as best he could, and his wounds still hurt, although the pain was lessening by the moment. The knight groaned in agony and began tugging off his helmet as if he couldn't breathe.

Owen knelt by his side, dismally aware of the pool of blood leaching into the ground. His heart was struck with remorse. Then the helmet came free, and Owen found himself staring at the face of Brendon Roux, the lord marshal of Brythonica. Blood dribbled from his nose and lips.

"My lord!" Owen gasped in sudden despair. "Why did you attack me? I didn't mean for this to happen!"

The marshal gritted his teeth, in obvious and excruciating pain. He looked at Owen not with accusation but with mercy. "My turn . . . is done," he gasped, his lips in a rictus. He panted, trying to speak again. Owen knelt closer, his heart ripping in pain. "Your turn now," he groaned. "You must protect her . . . now . . . the duchess . . . you are her . . . protector."

Owen felt as if he'd been struck. The duchess? She would hate him for killing Marshal Roux. But the man's words implied this terrible combat had been inevitable. That he had known all along he would die. It felt as if they were part of a giant Wizr set—two pieces had clashed, and Owen emerged as the victor.

"Let me heal you," Owen said desperately, grabbing Roux's shoulder. He tried summoning the magic, but it fled from him. He'd felt spent after healing Justine, Elysabeth's maid, but that wasn't the way he felt now. The magic was abandoning him, its purpose complete. He tried to draw it in, but it was like trying to clutch water with his arms. Frustration and fury battled inside him.

Why had Roux attacked him?

Owen stared into the man's waxy face, which grew paler and paler as his blood ebbed away. "I am done," the older man said slowly, his eyes growing vacant. "I've done all . . . I could." Then his eyes sharpened and hardened. He stared at Owen with a look of desperation. "You are the only one who can . . . save her. Or kill her. Only . . . you. Your gift by the Fountain . . . so rare. So is . . . so is hers. Protect her. Or they will all . . . drown."

"Who will drown?" Owen pleaded in fury, tears stinging his eyes as he knelt next to the crumpled knight.

The faint puffs of air from Roux's mouth became shallower. "On my hand . . . is a ring. It is yours. You are master now. Master of the Woods."

Owen watched his chest fall, and this time it did not rise. Marshal Roux stared vacantly, lips slightly parted. A trickle of blood welled from his eye like a tear.

The young duke knelt in the mushy ground, casting his gaze around in wonderment and confusion. There were the stone altar and the silver dish. The strange tree that had shed all its leaves. He saw Etayne lying still. And the fallen knight and his wounded horse. A horrible sense of guilt settled across him like a blanket. He had summoned the conflict by pouring water on the stone. Somehow that had prompted Roux to fight him. He hadn't known it would happen.

But he was beginning to wonder if Sinia had known all along.

♦ ♦ ♦

A small fire crackled in the woods, and an owl hooted somewhere in the night. The two horses were tethered nearby, both eating from sacks of provender slung around their necks. It was an ancient grove of yew trees, similar to the ones Owen had seen as a boy riding toward Beestone.

Etayne finally stirred while Owen was feeding another stick into the fire.

"Where are we?" she asked groggily.

"The woods bordering Brythonica and my lands," he replied. "You've been unconscious all day."

He had laid her out on a blanket and covered her with his own. She tried sitting up, and winced in obvious pain. "The last thing I remember was a noise. A terrible noise, louder than thunder. And then something struck me. Hailstones?"

Owen nodded, feeding another small stick into the fire. He was fidgeting inside, swollen with secrets and mysteries and unfathomable conflicts. His thoughts were so desperate, he wondered if he were falling into madness. He needed someone to talk to. Someone to help him piece together the clues. He had discovered that the scabbard he wore held special healing properties—all the wounds from his battle with Marshal Roux had been miraculously cured, and Etayne's head wound had healed before his eyes after he strapped the scabbard around her waist.

"I'm wearing your sword," Etayne said, as if reading his thoughts.

"The scabbard healed you," Owen said, looking into her eyes. "I've often wondered why my wounds at the battle of Averanche vanished so quickly. I gave your training credit all these years." He let out an anguished sigh. "Roux is dead."

Etayne blinked in surprise. "How? Where?"

Owen picked up another stick and snapped it in half with his hands. "After the hailstorm, the tree limbs were bare. Then a flock of birds came and sang away the frost. It was the strangest thing I've ever seen. Before they were done singing, a knight garbed in black galloped into the grove and fought me. I didn't know who it was until after I dealt him a mortal wound." He tossed away the broken fragments of wood and stared into Etayne's eyes, letting his anxiety pour out of him.

"Something is going on. I need to tell you something. I must say it out loud for fear I've gone mad. Help me see reason, Etayne. Help me see if I'm understanding the situation." He wiped his mouth, grateful for the solitude of the night. All day he had battled with himself whether he should return to Ploemeur and tell the duchess what had happened in that grove. Owen had slain her marshal while defending himself. But there was something more to it than that. It felt as if the Fountain was summoning him back to Kingfountain. In the grand Wizr game, a piece had fallen. It was only one move, and more were to follow.

"I haven't seen you this distraught in a long time," Etayne said worriedly. "Tell me what's troubling you, Owen."

"This may come out all jumbled," he said with a half chuckle. "Forgive me. I've been wrestling with my thoughts all day. As you know, we can't go back to Averanche or Tatton Hall. So I thought we'd camp here tonight. This is my forest now." He gazed up at the trees towering above them. "They're all mine."

Etayne waited patiently, saying nothing.

"When we sailed to Atabyrion, do you remember entering the cove of Edonburick?" She nodded. "When we were crossing the bay, the Fountain told me that the city had drowned. I could sense beneath the waves that the castles and houses and manors of Atabyrion had long been destroyed. I was horrified by the scale of the devastation. It's happened before, you know. St. Penryn is all that's left of the kingdom of Leoneyis. It too was drowned. After I fought Marshal Roux, as he lay dying, he said I was the duchess's protector now. And he warned me that if I did not protect her well, another kingdom would drown." He stared into the flames, lost in thought again.

"But he didn't say who would be destroyed?" Etayne asked.

Owen shook his head. "I'm assuming Brythonica. Have you noticed that all the residences are on the hilltops in Ploemeur? The duchess's castle is on the highest ground of all. I think she knows of the risk. I think she's prepared her people to survive if the flood happens again. But it wouldn't be the sort of flood caused by nature, Etayne." He clenched his fist and quelled his desire to hammer something. "It's part of the legend of the Deep Fathoms. When I poured the water on that stone, there was not a cloud in the sky! Not a single one. And yet it deluged on us, a violent hailstorm unlike any I've ever experienced. It nearly killed you."

She looked at him with amazement. "I remember you shielding me. I thought we were going to die, but I felt safe when you were there."

The warm look in her eyes made Owen squirm. "For some reason, the magic doesn't affect me. I have this strange—what's the right word—immunity? The duchess is Fountain-blessed. I learned that the first night we met her. She has a vast power that surpasses even Severn's. Even my own! I've wondered how that power manifests itself, but now I think I know. I cannot be sure, but I think she has the gift that I've been pretending to have all along." He looked at Etayne with a wild feeling of helplessness. "I think she knows the future. Like the Wizr Myrddin did. Think on it, Etayne. I've never been able to surprise her. When the king sent me and Lord Horwath to defend Brythonica, we attacked Chatriyon's army in the middle of the night. And Marshal Roux was there. When we went to Atabyrion to confront Eyric, who came? Marshal Roux. When Chatriyon began sieging Averanche, who helped us? Marshal Roux. I've thought all along that *he* was Fountain-blessed. Yet when we fought this morning, I sensed nothing from him. Not even a little trickle of the magic." He hung his head. "Tell me I've mistaken all of this. Tell me I'm a muddled fool. I've tried all day to sort this out, to make sense of it."

He took another stick and flung it into the trees.

When he looked at Etayne, he saw her eyes staring into his. She didn't look baffled. She looked impressed. "You're not mad, Owen," she said. "You're bloody brilliant. The duchess wasn't surprised when you came demanding she marry you. Everyone else was, even Roux. But she knew."

And that's what troubled Owen the most. Why had she not prevented it?

# CHAPTER FIFTEEN

## *St. Penryn*

Owen and Etayne separated at dawn. Her injuries had sufficiently healed for her to ride. She returned the magical scabbard to him and started off for Kingfountain palace to try to determine the danger he would be facing upon his return. They agreed to meet at a popular tavern called the Coxcomb, on the bridge to the sanctuary of Our Lady of Kingfountain, in three days' time. He would rent a room under the name Owen Satchel, which would alert her of his arrival.

There was a stop Owen wanted to make on the return trip. He intended to go to St. Penryn and draw the chest with the ancient Wizr board out of the waters. He had studied it many times before submerging it in the fountain, but he could not discern how the pieces moved or who was supposed to move them. He had a suspicion that the duchess was one of the few who could tell him.

Upon entering his domain, he removed his tunic and livery and rode toward the sanctuary alone. Etayne would have at least a day's head start, but with her abilities, she would be able to slip in and out of the castle unnoticed. He felt an invisible current drawing him back to Kingfountain. Part of him wanted to go to Brythonica and face Sinia again. Was she part of the massive game of Wizr unfolding in the world? If so, was she an ally, or an opponent? His mood turned dark with the memory of how offensive he had been to her and her people. It had been deliberate on his part, but she had endured his provoking words with admirable patience. Was that patience an act? A way to lure him into lowering his defenses? Or was she truly a benevolent soul, a ruler whose people were utterly devoted to her? Her personality and temperament suited him well—too well. Though he had ridden into Brythonica with no intention of marrying the duchess, in their short encounters together, he had found himself impressed by her and unexpectedly drawn to her. He had Elysabeth's permission to fall in love. But the wound in his heart was still a grievous one.

◆  ◆  ◆

As he rode through Westmarch, the sights and sounds becoming ever more familiar and comfortable, he thought with fondness of Tatton Hall. He had expanded his domains beyond what his father had accomplished. Yet, though his father's dominion had shrunken considerably, he seemed at ease in his new role in Brythonica. If Owen and Sinia did marry, Owen's domain would stretch across a vast seashore, bridging the lands that had long been separated by war. It would make him even more powerful in the kingdom, drawing resentment and bitterness from his rival dukes.

He followed the coast, steering the horse wide of Averanche. The jagged coastline was hauntingly beautiful, but as he stared at the sea, he was struck with the knowledge that this very ocean had buried the kingdom of Leoneyis and drowned its inhabitants. The sea was a vast power, a relentless force that hammered away at the coastline, pulverizing rock into sand. It went by many names, but the most hallowed was the Deep Fathoms. A place where lost treasures lay hidden and buried.

A place where the dead went to rest after they finished their worldly labors. A place that had existed before the world came to be.

In the afternoon, Owen spied the sanctuary of St. Penryn in the distance. He had kept a punishing pace, and his horse was weary. He would need to change horses, but knew the deconeus would willingly let him borrow from his stables. The salty smell filled his nose and lungs, and the road became gritty with sand the closer he approached.

He reached the sanctuary by late afternoon and found the grounds quiet except for the screeches of gulls. The clop of hooves on stone announced him, and the sexton came out to interview the new arrival. Owen slid out of the saddle. His disheveled appearance did not mark him as a duke, so the man didn't recognize him until Owen gave him a knowing look.

"My lord!" the man gasped with surprise. "We did not expect your arrival! There has been much commotion in the kingdom since you left. Have you heard the news? It reached us only earlier today."

"What news?" Owen asked, tugging off his gloves and stuffing them under his belt.

"The two who escaped from the tower. Lord Eyric and Lord Dunsdworth. They've been captured."

Owen blinked with surprise. "I'd heard about their escape. That's why I returned. They were recaptured?"

The sexton nodded vigorously. "They did not make it far before the Espion surrounded them. There's a trial underway. We've heard the king intends to put them both into the river."

It felt as if someone had punched Owen in the stomach. He was suddenly quite ill. "This is grim news. Is the deconeus here?"

"He awaits within. I will have your horse tended. Will you stay long?"

"I cannot. I came to borrow another horse. Can you arrange it?"

"Of course, my lord! Right away."

As Owen strode into the sanctuary, memories assailed him. What would have happened if he had helped Eyric seize the throne all those years ago? He'd confronted him in this place. But if events had unfolded differently, he wouldn't have been present for the Dreadful Deadman's birth. Drew's birth. He had cradled the bloody infant in his hands and breathed life back into him. All of it had felt like the Fountain's will. Why had events unfolded this way? Why hadn't the Fountain commanded him to bring down Severn then?

He reached the rim of the fountain in the center of the sanctuary, planted his hands along the edge, and stared down into the calm water. He could hear the sigh and roll of the ocean beyond the stone walls as the waves crashed violently against the rocky shore below. His troubles felt as inexorable as those waves. Perhaps there would never be a moment's peace in his life.

Closing his eyes, he breathed in deeply, trying to calm himself. So many events had unfolded in his absence, and he was too far away to influence them. Oh, he could imagine Severn wanting Eyric dead. Killing him in public would free Kathryn at last. Would Severn finally rid himself of the ghost of his nephew by destroying the man he believed was only pretending to be him? Of course, Owen knew the truth. Piers Urbick *was* Eyric Argentine. He always had been.

Opening his eyes, he saw the chest submerged in the water. It had appeared suddenly, drawn to him through its mysterious powers. Owen hiked up his sleeve, reached into the cold water, and grasped the handle. He pulled it out and set it down on the edge of the fountain. After sitting down next to the chest, he withdrew the key he wore around his neck and slid it into the lock, twisting it carefully until he felt the click. The chest wasn't even damp. Though he did not understand why, the waters protected enchanted treasures from the Deep Fathoms.

He lifted the lid and stared at the Wizr board inside.

The ancient set had faces carved into the individual pieces. What struck him immediately was that some of the pieces had moved since the last time he'd looked at it, years before. The white Wizr was back on its own side. He distinctly remembered seeing it in play during the battle of Averanche. One of the knights that had been on the board before was missing. He swallowed guiltily. It was the white knight. The image of Lord Roux's face came to his mind, with blood streaming from his eyes like tears. How strange that he'd been wearing black armor.

He stared at the board, feeling hopelessly lost. He examined the pieces more closely. Two kings were still present; the dark one was Severn, but who played the white? Chatriyon? A dark knight was missing. One that had been there previously. Only one knight remained on the board.

Then the white Wizr began to move unbidden and untouched, sending a shiver of fear down Owen's back. He watched it slide across the tiles, moving in an unobstructed path toward the dark knight's position. His heart began pounding, and he felt an ominous sense of dread. The waters of the fountain began to churn, and the presence of magic hung heavy in the air.

He quickly rose from the rim and backed away, his hand going to his sword. The waters churned, and a spray of mist came leaping from the once-placid waters.

A form emerged from the mist, a person whom Owen immediately recognized.

It was Lady Sinia.

His bones felt weak and he experienced a sensation of utter vulnerability. The swell of the Fountain magic that flowed with her was vast. He had sensed it before, when her power was dormant, but now it was active, living, and he felt like cowering before its majesty. Then the sensation subsided, like the violence of a wave that retreats calmly back from the shore to build up its strength.

Some of the pieces began to fit together in his mind. She was there, standing before him, holding a pair of sandals in her hand. She extended her other hand to him and moved toward the edge of the fountain.

Owen wasn't as afraid as he'd been moments before. He'd thought, for an instant, she'd come to destroy him.

When he took her hand, she smiled and stepped over the edge of the fountain. He was expecting her gown to be soaked, but it was perfectly dry. Not even a drop of water came from her bare feet as she touched the stone tile on his side.

"Thank you," she said with a pleasant smile. She set her sandals down on the edge of the fountain. "I'm sure you have many questions. We didn't have a chance to talk before you left."

Owen stared at the Wizr set and saw that the white Wizr and the dark knight were occupying adjacent squares. She noticed his attention to the board.

"Have you discerned the board's truth yet, Owen?" she asked.

He looked at her warily, but with budding hope. "Are we enemies?"

There was a delighted look in her eyes, and a slight flush came to her cheeks. "I'm not *your* enemy," she said simply. "I want to be your ally. If you will let me help you."

Owen walked closer to her. Could he trust her? So much of his fate would depend on that. One wrong turn could destroy him. But he also felt it could destroy her. He wanted to test some of his knowledge. To make her *prove* she was trustworthy.

"Can you see the future?" he asked her pointedly.

"Yes," she answered. "My gifts from the Fountain are mantic in nature."

"Romantic?" he asked in confusion.

She smiled at the mistake. "No, Owen. They are *mantic*. I can see the future. And the past. My parents hid my gifts when I was little. I've learned to hide them also. To be very guarded of who knows of them. I'm trusting you, as you can see."

He nodded slowly. "And you are a Wizr. A true one. That brings me answers to some of the questions that have puzzled me. You knew

I'd be looking for you that morning in Ploemeur, and you deliberately avoided me."

"I'll admit, I was teasing you a bit. Do you understand now that our lifting contraption isn't the only reason I don't need to take a horse or a carriage up to the palace? I can travel along the anchor lines quickly and efficiently."

"Anchor lines?" Owen asked, perplexed.

She nodded again with calm deliberation. "Another secret. It's not often shared because Wizrs are killed in this world, Owen. We are too powerful and misunderstood. You see my true form on the set. Just as I see yours." She looked over at the pieces. "You understand now that the rows are geographical? This side represents Ceredigion. This one, Occitania. There are anchor lines of magic that connect the boundaries between earth and sea and intersect with one another. There is a map I can show you that reveals where they are."

"We've been on opposing sides," Owen pointed out.

"I know. It's my hope that will change when you learn the truth." She gave him an imploring look.

Owen bit his lip. "Are you asking me to betray my king?" he asked hoarsely. He wanted so much to tell her that he was willing to do it. That perhaps the Fountain was using them *both* to change events in the world.

She shook her head. "I think it's the Fountain's will that you save your people."

He wrinkled his brow in confusion. "What do you mean?"

She looked down at the arrangement of the remaining pieces in the Wizr set. It appeared as if the game were winding to a close. "This particular game has been drawn out for centuries," she said, her finger lightly touching one of the pieces. "This side represents the Argentine family. This side, the Vertus family. The game plays out over several generations. Severn is the king now," she said, touching the dark king next. "The problem, Owen, is that he was never meant to be king, and now he is defying the rules of the game. He violated the rights of sanctuary. He has threatened to harm innocent children again and again. The rules were set in ancient times by great Wizrs who had mantic gifts like my own. When they are disobeyed, the Deep Fathoms will reclaim the land." She looked up from the board and into his eyes. "If you do not stop Severn, his choices will destroy your people. Left unchecked, he will continue to violate every custom, every boundary set up by the Wizrs. He wears the hollow crown, which has its own magic. With its power, he can destroy his entire kingdom in winter. You know the legends of the sanctuary of Our Lady. How long will the privileges of sanctuary exist?"

Owen stared at her, his heart yearning to know more. "Until the river stops flowing."

"Until the river becomes *ice*," she corrected.

# CHAPTER SIXTEEN

*Alliance*

Because of the Wizr set, the king's deeds and misdeeds wielded control over the weather. He did this unwittingly, but the more evil his actions had become, the more the snow had fallen on Ceredigion. Owen nearly gasped aloud from shock.

"I think you're beginning to understand," Sinia said, giving him a prodding nod. "You must say it, Owen. I can't tell you everything, but I can tell you if you've figured it out. Knowledge about the game isn't forbidden. But I can't share the mantic truths with you directly. You must learn them for yourself."

Owen stared down at the set, at the king representing Severn. There were so few dark pieces left on the board. "Are you saying that the words were changed over time? That the protection would last so long as the river flows, meaning until it's frozen over?"

"Precisely," she said earnestly. "The one who wears the hollow crown can *make* the river stop flowing through his violation of the principles upon which the sanctuaries were founded. When a ruler stops being just. When they are unfaithful. These are examples."

Owen nodded in understanding. "That is why Tunmore was so desperate for the set to be moved!" he said, beginning his habit of pacing. "This was years ago. He thought Severn was going to freeze the kingdom! He needed someone who was Fountain-blessed to move the chest to St. Penryn because he couldn't. Why here?"

Sinia smiled with excitement. "Yes . . . why here? What does your intuition tell you?"

Owen snapped his fingers. "Because St. Penryn isn't part of Ceredigion at all. It is by tradition, but it was once part of Leoneyis. Once the set left the borders, the curse stopped."

She gave him a lovely smile and an encouraging nod. "You're close, Owen. It did not stop the curse; it merely slowed it. If you return the Wizr set to Ceredigion, the curse will set in once more—and quickly. The game plays on. It *must* play on. Have you not noticed the winters in Ceredigion growing ever colder and bleaker these last seven years? We each have a role to play. I don't want Ceredigion to be destroyed. I don't want its people to be trapped in a blizzard and frozen to death, just as much as I don't want my own people to drown."

Owen stared at her, feeling the awful weight of pending doom. The memories of the drowned cove of Edonburick and the ruined buildings of Brythonica still made him tremble. "You've been helping me all along, haven't you?" He looked her in the eye. "When your people aided mine during the battle of Averanche, I saw the white Wizr piece on the board. That was . . . you were *there*, Sinia?" He stopped his pacing and stared at her in shock.

She reached out and grasped his hands in excitement. "I was! I couldn't *tell* you. Do you remember the storm?"

"You caused it? Through the water bowl! The grove! By the Fountain, that was you!"

Her smile was even brighter. "I was there. I have been helping you. The Fountain needed you to protect the true king of Ceredigion. You know the prophecy of the Dreadful Deadman. You know who it is, don't you?"

Owen nodded. "I do. And he's at Kingfountain palace right now if I'm not mistaken."

"You're not," she added knowingly.

Owen sighed and looked up at the support struts of the chamber. "And there's a good chance I'll be a dead man if I return." Her hands were still holding his. He pulled away and wiped his mouth, his mind whirling with the flurry of revelations. He looked over and saw the deconeus standing beneath an arch, his eyes full of reverence and awe.

"Don't be so sure of that," Sinia said meaningfully. "Your man Farnes left a message that you'd been summoned back to the king."

Should he trust her? If the duchess could see the future, then aligning himself with her might be his only chance for survival. Assuming, of course, that she wasn't deliberately misleading him. It came back to the ability to read someone's intentions. Ankarette had decided to trust Evie after meeting her in the kitchen of Kingfountain. Owen had to make the same fateful decision.

He glanced back at the deconeus.

"He cannot hear us," Sinia said. "All he can hear is the lapping of the fountain waters. He sees me as a manifestation of the Fountain. He thinks you are having a vision."

Owen chuckled. "So do I."

"Do you trust me, Owen?" she asked hopefully. "I've tried to show you that you can. Neither of us wants our people to perish. But they will, Owen, if you don't stop the king."

"I believe you. Trust is difficult for me."

Her look changed dramatically, into one that was full of pain. "I know it is," she said emphatically. "You've made many decisions without knowing the consequences. The Fountain has guided you during those critical moments. Even knowing the future, I cannot tell you what will happen. If I tell you something out of order, it may influence your decisions. In the end, it's our choices that affect what happens in the world. You must be the one to choose, Owen. I will guide you as best I can."

"How can you trust me?" Owen said. "My lady, I killed Brendon Roux. I didn't know who he was, but I left him for dead. I think you already know this."

She let out a mournful sigh and nodded. "Let me put this simply. In order for *you* to change sides on the board, another piece needed to be removed. You are meant to be my protector now. If you choose to accept your fate, if you put on the ring he gave you, if you make a promise of fealty to me, then your piece on the board will change color. You will become a knight on the white side. I cannot make you do this."

Owen wanted to laugh at the absurdity of it all. "Chatriyon's side?" he chuffed.

She shook her head seriously. "No. King *Andrew's* side."

Her words cut him to the quick, melting his smirk away. "This is real, is it not?"

"All too real," she answered. "This game of Wizr is perilous." She stepped up to the board, admiring the remaining pieces. "The Wizrs of old made the rules. The game wasn't called Wizr back then. It was called the Siege Perilous. The Wizrs *survived* when kingdoms fell. Then they would offer the game to another man ambitious enough to rule." She looked at him pointedly, but could not say what she was thinking. He saw the secrets hidden in her blue eyes, the longing to tell him that which she could not share. "Do you have a plan, Owen? A way to defeat the king?"

"I've been working on one," Owen said, shaking his head at the vastness of the task. "It was rather simple. I'm afraid you'll laugh."

She reached out and touched his arm. "Never fear that."

He firmed his courage, deciding to make the leap. "Everyone knows the legend of King Andrew. How he pulled a sword from the waters of the fountain of Our Lady. No one else was able to touch it. He had that ability because he was Fountain-blessed. Something similar happened to the Maid of Donremy."

Sinia's smile encouraged him to continue.

"She too pulled a sword from a fountain before helping to crown the Prince of Occitania."

"The story repeats itself over and over," Sinia said. "Go on."

"I think I know where her sword is," Owen said. "If the legends bear true, it was also King Andrew's sword." Lord Horwath had made him swear he wouldn't tell the Occitanians. But did that promise include the Duchess of Brythonica, who had been Ceredigion's ally for so long? If he was going to accept her help, he needed to trust her. And he did believe what she had told him. The feelings from the Fountain had been compelling, and he had learned to trust them. "There are ice caves in North Cumbria. Duke Horwath told me of them before he died. I think the sword is there. I thought . . . well, I thought to fetch it and bring it to Our Lady of Kingfountain. I have the power to put ancient relics into the water and remove them. So I hoped to trick Severn. To trick everyone, actually. I was going to say I had a dream that the true king of Ceredigion would be able to draw a sword from the fountain of Our Lady. That it's a sign the Dreadful Deadman has returned. And then I was going to arrange for it to happen. Basically, I was going to cheat!"

Sinia stared at him with a smile of pleasure. "And why would that be cheating, Owen? Did not the Wizr Myrddin do the same thing?"

Owen looked at her, startled. "He did?"

She nodded. "Andrew *wasn't* Fountain-blessed, Owen, he simply surrounded himself with those who were. It was Myrddin who allowed him to draw the blade, and Andrew's greatest knight was a man named Owain."

His heart shuddered at the words. "I've never heard that," he gasped. "I've never heard that name in all the legends I've read."

"Of course not," she answered simply. "Because the record was lost when Leoneyis drowned. That version of the story stopped being told. The version that talked about Owain. And how he married the Lady of the Fountain."

A small pink flush rose on her cheeks, and she looked down, suddenly abashed.

"But you know the story," he whispered, his heart hammering painfully in his chest. She looked so beautiful in that moment, so vulnerable. Like the butterfly she was named after.

She nodded, still unable to meet his eyes.

Then another question struck him, fast as an arrow bolt. "If you know their story, then you know how it ends. Don't you, Sinia?"

She was uncomfortable now. He could see her anguish in the curl of her mouth, her clenched fists, and her trembling arms.

"Tell me," he insisted.

There were tears in her eyes as she looked up at him. "I can't say it," she whispered.

But he already knew. Her look told all. "Owain betrayed her," he said, feeling disgusted with himself even though he hadn't done anything. The same story had been told over and over. Different men and women playing different roles. "Am I right?" he pressed.

She looked at him steadfastly. Then she nodded once.

Owen breathed in through his nose. "Are these stories preordained? Must they always happen the way they did in the past?"

She shook her head no. "There is always a choice. Always."

He realized that so much in life depended on choices. He had chosen to forsake love after losing his chance with Evie. His choice had deprived him of opportunities. It had also prepared him for this one. Could he open his heart again? Could he risk the pain? But he already knew the answer—he had to. This was the decision that would help him serve the Dreadful Deadman. And he could not deny that the choice appealed to him for other reasons. That *she* appealed to him.

Stepping up to her, he grabbed her hand. "Then I'm making mine," he said, almost roughly. "You've risked everything to try and help me. I don't know why, truly. I've been nothing but rude and disingenuous to you. But I will not betray you, Sinia. What must I do? How can I join your side? You said I must swear fealty? I won't let my people be destroyed, not if putting the lad on the throne will prevent it. The road ahead will be difficult, but I will not stray from it. I promise you."

She dabbed tears on her sleeve and gave him an encouraging smile. "So will I. You must, formally, plight me your troth. And I to you. Then the knight piece will change color when you put on the ring."

"I think we need witnesses, no?" Owen asked her.

"Yes, that is the proper way."

Owen took her hand with one of his and waved impatiently for the deconeus to join them. He felt light-headed, filled with a strange sensation of both utter terror and happiness. Having someone like Sinia on his side, having a partner and ally to help him counter Severn made the impossible seem possible. He'd felt nothing but hopelessness while carrying the burden on his shoulders. Now she was willing to share it with him. To plot and maneuver with him.

The deconeus reached them, his eyes wide with wonderment. He hastily knelt before Lady Sinia. "My lady," he breathed solemnly. "You do honor us. How may I serve you?" His words were fraught with reverence.

Sinia stared down at him, smiling sweetly. Then she turned to Owen and nodded for him to continue. While the proposal he'd made in Ploemeur was likely binding because of the witnesses, he wished to make their betrothal more official by actually pronouncing the oath.

"I, Owen Kiskaddon, do hereby plight my troth to you, Sinia Montfort, to be my lawful wife and to become your lawful husband. I swear to be true and faithful to this pledge, on my life and on my honor."

The deconeus's face trembled with joy. He clasped his hands together.

Sinia squeezed Owen's hand. She looked radiant, but there was a smudge of wariness in her gaze. As if she wanted to believe his words but couldn't quite trust them. "I, Sinia Montfort, do hereby plight my troth to you, Owen Kiskaddon, to be my lawful husband and to become your lawful wife. I swear to be true and faithful to this pledge, on my life and on my honor."

The deconeus rose shakily from his knees. "May the Fountain bless it so and bind you to your oaths."

The knowing, encouraging look the old man gave him was confusing until Owen realized, abashedly, that he was supposed to kiss her.

When he turned to face the duchess, she was blushing violently, looking rather embarrassed. Owen had not imagined his first real kiss would be in a sanctuary next to a gouty old man, a babbling fountain, and an ancient Wizr set.

He clung to Sinia's hand and pulled her to him. He was so nervous his heart was racing and his knees were trembling, returning him to the bashful little boy he had once been, and he thought, in a moment of utter terror, that he might actually faint from fear. Trying to rally himself, he bent his head lower and caught her fearful look—which no doubt matched his—and then he shut his eyes and tried to kiss her.

He missed her mouth.

In their fumbling way, they managed to kiss the corner of each other's mouths and then both of them pulled away. It was tantamount to a kiss on the cheek.

Owen felt humiliated. Sinia looked disappointed.

"Well," the deconeus said, clasping his hands in front of him. "That was . . . sweet. You are now officially betrothed. You have sworn your troth in the presence of the Fountain and man. I wish you joy!"

Sinia looked away, rubbing her hands up and down her arms in a nervous gesture.

"Thank you," Owen said, nodding for the deconeus to waddle away. This was not how he had hoped it would unfold. He gritted his teeth in frustration, wishing someone were there to flog him for his ineptitude.

"I must away," Owen said. "I need to go back to Kingfountain to see what damage is done."

"The ring?" she said, looking at him hopefully. He was so scatter-brained he'd forgotten. He opened the pouch at his belt and withdrew Lord Roux's ring.

She gestured to take it from him and he gave it to her. She played with it, turning the gold band end over end. The ring was a mix of white and yellow gold. There were carved overlapping circles that went all around the ring and caught the light. Then she took his hand and slid the ring onto his finger, uttering a word in an archaic language as she did so. The ring fit perfectly.

She held on to his hand, gently stroking it. Her eyes had lost most of the embarrassment of the failed kiss. "You needn't fear a return to Kingfountain," she told him. "Why do you think the king sent you that note?"

He didn't need to ask how she knew about it. Not that she could have answered him anyway. "The problem is I *have* betrayed him. In many ways. But now that I think on it, this could be another one of his tests of loyalty. To see if I *will* return."

She smiled and patted his bearded cheek. "You have more power over him than you realize," she said. "As with any game of Wizr, how you approach the end makes a difference. We've made this choice, you and I. Severn will make his own. We'll defeat him together. It will continue to be my hope that we can do this *without* killing him. Please know that. The king doesn't need to die to lose. He just needs to be defeated." She then escorted him to the edge of the fountain. "What will you do with the chest?"

Owen glanced at it and noticed that the two adjacent pieces representing them were now the same color. "I think I should bring it with me. I could leave it in the waters of Our Lady. When I tell the king about the dream I had, I can say that it will start snowing as a sign. The chest will make sure it happens."

She smiled at him. "You are a clever one, Owen Kiskaddon. I like that about you. How will you get the sword from the cave? You have an opportunity already brewing."

"Indeed," he said. "Catsby is making a fool of himself. I just need to spark a little rebellion in the North. We'll need other allies as well. I have a feeling Iago will join us. Sending him a message will be difficult, though . . ."

"I can send him a message," Sinia promised. "Just write the note and leave it in the chest in the waters of the fountain. We'll be able to communicate with each other that way. Now, here is another trick about this Wizr set. Only certain people can move the pieces. The boy is the Dreadful Deadman. He can. So can Severn, but if *he* does, he can use the game to win. When you bring it to Kingfountain, have the boy move the pieces for you. What he chooses to do will influence how events play out in this world. Teach him the rules of Wizr. Teach him to play. With this set, we'll be able to defeat Severn and put the rightful Argentine on the throne." She closed the lid and then handed the set to Owen.

"Now is the time for you to return. Come into the water with me. I will send you there."

"I can be back in Kingfountain today?" he asked in surprise.

She gave him a meaningful look and reached out to take his arm.

◆ ◆ ◆

*Lord Kiskaddon,*

*I'm cautious writing this to you as I do not want to add to your overwhelming burdens. It is a difficult thing watching all that my grandfather built be ruined. Not a day has passed since leaving Dundrennan that we haven't heard of some insult, depredation, or foulness coming from Lord Catsby. It was a time that deserved solemnity and mourning. Feelings are flaming brightly, and we continually receive petitions to take up arms and reclaim my birthright. Please, Owen, there must be something you can do to stop Catsby from plundering it all. Every story I hear grows more wicked. Kiss my daughter for me.*

*Elysabeth Victoria Mortimer Llewellyn*
*Queen of Atabyrion*

◆ ◆ ◆

# CHAPTER SEVENTEEN

## *Misprision*

Owen had always wondered what it would be like to plummet off a waterfall. This . . . it would be like this. Sinia had gripped his arm and they had stepped into the fountain of St. Penryn together, Owen with the Wizr set clutched to his chest. It felt as if the floor had vanished and they'd dropped into an abyss. It was nothing like jumping with Evie into the cistern at Kingfountain. If he could have screamed, he would have, but it felt as if they were caught inside a waterfall on its way down, all white turbulent foam and surging power and freefalling, falling, falling . . .

There was no bone-jarring crunch. Just stillness, a sense of floating, and then he had firm footing once more. The gentle ripple of water lapped against their ankles, although the wetness could not penetrate them. Owen's knees shook violently from the surge of power, his stomach more than queasy. He would have stumbled, but Sinia was still clutching his arm. A strange mist rose up from the waters, like an impenetrable fog.

"I must leave you here," she said. "Severn may be able to sense my presence, though he will not understand why there has been a surge in the Fountain. I must away back to Brythonica. But I will leave you messages in the chest, and you can do the same for me. I will look forward to it."

He turned and gazed at her, taking in her lovely smile and the look of tenderness and excitement in her eyes. His sensations struggled to reconcile the fact that they had crossed from one end of Ceredigion to the other in a mere moment.

"This is one of your powers?" he said, shaking his head in wonderment. "I never knew."

"I trust you can keep it a secret," she replied. "While the mist is up, no one can see or hear us. This particular fountain is not in the main hall of the sanctuary. Set the chest down inside the waters and then entrust it to the Fountain. It will disappear from view from all who aren't Fountain-blessed. And not even everyone who is Fountain-blessed has the power to do so."

"You mean the king could see it?" Owen pressed.

She nodded. "If he came here."

"But you've seen the future and know that he will not?"

She gave him a warm look of approval and a single nod. "He will not come here." She glided her hand along his arm, a possessive gesture. "Write to me soon, Owen. I want to help you."

"And I'll need your help," he said with a chuckle. "Thank you, Sinia." Before setting the chest into the waters, he opened it to examine the Wizr board. Sure enough, the white Wizr had moved across the board and was now adjacent to the dark king. There was a white knight next to it.

Sinia nodded to him, but said nothing. He shut the lid and then settled the chest back into the waters. Just as his hands were about to enter it, the waters were repelled back, clearing a dry space on the floor of the fountain. It amazed and astounded him still.

"May the Fountain guide you, my beloved," she said, her voice full of longing.

Her words caught him off guard. He had pledged himself to marry her. They had thrown the dice together to unseat a king. But the thought of being loved by someone, of being cherished, filled him with conflicting emotions.

"And you," he replied. She gave him an awkward look, then pressed up on her tiptoes and kissed his cheek, grazing his thick stubble. And she vanished in an instant. Before he could kiss her back.

He stared at where she had been standing and realized with a chuckle that she'd left her sandals back on the rail of the fountain of St. Penryn. He stepped away from the fountain, and the mist fell away, sloughing off like powder. His heart burned with purpose as he walked away from the fountain. There were few visitors in the sanctuary that day, so no one seemed to notice him. When Owen left the building, he saw a black smudge of cloud starting to fester in the northern sky.

◆  ◆  ◆

Owen entered the palace grounds through the Espion gate he had once used as a child. He did not want word of his return spreading too quickly. By his estimation, Etayne would not arrive for another day or two. He had already left a note for her at the inn where they'd arranged to meet, explaining that he had returned ahead of her and to look for further messages from him inside her tower.

The sunlight was fading, filling the sky with the ink of darkness. Taking care to avoid people, he made his way to the Espion tunnels without being seen. Then he grabbed a lamp and maneuvered his way to the king's council chamber. The sound of voices emanating from beyond the wall made him slow his approach. He found the latch to open the spy hole and extinguished the lamp before releasing it.

He pressed his eyes to the slits for a view inside the room. Severn was there, pacing back and forth, and so were several of the lords of the realm, including Catsby and Paulen. Kevan, Owen's second in command of the Espion, was leaning against the far wall, shaking his head and frowning in frustration. The air was charged with enmity. The voice of the king's chamberlain rang out, announcing dinner, and the mood changed as the meal was brought in. Owen sensed the subtle flow of the Fountain coming from the room, which made him wary.

Owen concentrated on the draw of the magic, trying to get a sense of the source. At first, he suspected the king, but it was coming from deeper in the room. He dared not use his own magic for fear of revealing himself to the king and whoever else was there. Listening in eagerly to the conversation when it resumed, he discovered quickly that the fate of two men's lives were being discussed over seasoned beef.

"The Assizes have found them both guilty of treason, just as you wished," Catsby said to the king after the servants had cleared out. "Eyric and Dunsdworth are doomed. They both know it. I don't understand why we can't sentence them now, my lord, and throw them both into the river this very evening?"

Owen's stomach lurched with dread.

"My lord!" Kevan said imploringly.

"Shut it, man!" Catsby snarled. "You had your chance to bring evidence. It's the king's decision. Why do you hesitate, my lord?"

There was a miserable look on the king's face. He was frowning, his face full of agitation. "Don't press me, Catsby. I warn you."

"Shall we not pend the sentence until Lord Owen returns?" Kevan demanded. "Let him see the evidence. Would it not be more just to add his voice to the council?"

Catsby had daggers in his eyes. "I told you to be quiet."

"You are not the master of the Espion," Kevan growled. "The evidence is murky at best. There were others involved who helped Eyric and Dunsdworth escape. It seemed as if . . ." He hesitated.

"Go on," Severn said, much to Catsby's chagrin.

"The circumstances of their escape and capture are *highly* suspicious," Kevan said.

"Say more," Severn pressed.

"I dare not," Kevan replied, looking worriedly at the others in the room.

"You have an accusation to make, then make it!" Catsby growled. "You think I was behind their escape? Pfah! Why would I care a green fig about them! I came all the way from the North to help since Kiskaddon is *conveniently* absent. When did you summon him back, my lord? How many days ago? He could have taken a ship. Why would he delay so long?"

"You have no idea how far he must ride," Severn said impatiently. "Even if he left right after receiving Kevan's news of their escape, it would still take him another day to reach us. Give him time. He will come. I assure you, he will."

"My lord," Catsby said, a battle between impatience and forced courtesy playing out in his voice. "You have a guilty verdict. Do you think having Kiskaddon's opinion will make your decision any easier? You *must* execute these two rivals. They are the last threat to your throne. Dunsdworth could not fulfill the role of king without sending all of us to the river. He's much too damaged and dangerous."

"And it's my fault that he is, I suppose?" Severn asked huskily.

Owen tried to sense if the magic was coming from Catsby, but though it was the right direction, he couldn't be sure.

Catsby put away his napkin and rose. "You've been far more lenient than other kings would have been. Your brother used a poisoner to put Dunsdworth's father to death. Is that why you hesitate? And what of Eyric . . . or should I say Piers? He's the son of a fishmonger's wife. You should have killed him years ago."

Severn's gaze burned hot, and Owen was about to enter the room to startle them all, but some impulse held him back.

"What say you, Jack?" Severn said, his burning eyes fixed on Catsby.

Jack Paulen was busy devouring his meal, but he paused to wipe the grease from his mouth with a napkin, then said, "I sat on the Assizes, my lord. The evidence may be murky, but that doesn't shroud the result. The two are a threat to your throne and your power. They must be put to death in the river."

"Go," Severn said curtly. "All of you. Leave me."

Catsby gave the king a disdainful look and stomped out of the chamber. They all left, one by one, leaving Severn standing by himself in front of the hearth, his eyes lost in thought. It was the perfect opportunity to approach the king alone, but Owen still hesitated. Intuition plucked at him, warning him to wait, to see what the king would do all alone.

"Are you still here?" the king said in a low, angry tone.

Owen blinked with surprise. Had the king somehow detected his presence? Then he sensed the ebbing of the subtle power of the Fountain, which had filled the room throughout the meeting, and a man appeared in the farthest corner. He was a square-faced man with dark sideburn whiskers and thick unruly hair, dressed in a jacket and breeches. He pulled a long-stemmed wooden pipe from his belt and began chewing on the end. Owen recognized him instantly, although his look and manner had changed dramatically. He'd last seen this man crouching nervously in a cell. It was Etayne's father.

And Owen realized immediately that he was the Fountain-blessed one he had sensed.

"Of course, my lord," the man said gruffly, chewing on the stem.

"You've done your work well, Dragan," Severn said wryly. "Of course, it wouldn't have worked at all if Lord Kiskaddon had been here. He would have sensed you, just as I can."

Owen's heart seethed in uneasy anger. What was going on?

The man shrugged with unconcern. "Best to get it over with quickly, my lord. Break it off quick and sudden. That's what I say. He'll never know. You seemed contrite enough. I think you fooled them others."

"It may surprise you, Dragan," Severn said with a cunning look. "But I do care about the lad's conscience. He won't accept the throne willingly. But I need an heir, and he deserves it. He deserves it without all the complications I've had to endure."

"It's so kind of you, my lord," the man said with a low chuckle.

"You'll get a bonus, of course," Severn said. "I said I'd pay you double what Maxwell was offering to rescue the lad."

Dragan clenched the stem within his teeth. "Money is money, my lord. I'm not picky as to who's paying it."

"Of course not. I need a man like you around, Dragan. Do you have the Espion ring I gave you? Maybe I'll let you keep it a while longer."

Dragan smiled charmingly. "If you say so, my lord. If you say so. Might I have some of these fixings? It would be a shame not to eat it up."

"I'm not hungry. I must go prepare to console a soon-to-be widow."

Dragan smacked his lips and helped himself to the food trays while the king exited the council room and shut the door behind him. The thief took a bite from a piece of succulent beef and smacked his lips.

"Poor lass," he said with a wicked grin. "He'll get her in the end. She's been wearing black for so long she *looks* like his queen now."

# CHAPTER EIGHTEEN

*Loyalty*

As Owen stalked the dark Espion tunnel, his emotions churned. The implications of what he had witnessed made him burn with conflict. It appeared to Owen that Severn was going to position him as his named heir. The idea made his ambition squirm to life inside him. Owen Kiskaddon—King of Ceredigion. But Severn had told that to the thief. Was it even true? And if so, should Owen willingly accept the role and use it as an opportunity to abdicate in favor of Drew? That question brought forth another—one that poked at the very essence of Owen Kiskaddon. Would he have the strength to let go of power once he had a taste of it?

He feared he might not, a thought that troubled him deeply. As he walked through the Espion tunnels that snaked through the walls of the palace, he brooded on how the years had altered him, making him more and more like Severn. His tongue had developed the same sarcastic sharpness. His moods grew ever darker, and everything smelled of treachery and deceit. No, Owen could not allow himself to play the role of the usurper. Perhaps everyone expected it of him. But he would defy that fate. He would not betray Sinia. He needed to get her a note about what had happened upon his return. Their plan to topple Severn had to start immediately.

The end of the journey found him deep in the secret wings of the palace at the Star Chamber, where he hoped to find Kevan Amrein alone. He listened at the portal for a moment, then rapped on the door and opened it.

The older Espion was sitting in a chair opposite a desk stacked with a tottering tower of missives. He looked beleaguered and fretful as he glanced up at the intrusion, looked back down at the letter, and then started and rose from his chair.

"You're back!" Kevan said with unfeigned surprise. "I've not had word from you since you left. I'd begun to fear you'd come to harm in Brythonica!"

Owen smiled at the remark and quietly shut and bolted the door behind him.

"Does the king know you've returned?" Kevan pressed.

Owen shook his head. "Not yet. I wanted to see you first. I eavesdropped on the meeting you just had with him."

A relieved exhalation came out of Kevan's mouth. "I'm glad you did. I've been trying to stave off disaster, but I'm afraid I've been failing. Thank the Fountain you made it back. What can I tell you? What do you need to know most? Did you get my message about Eyric and Dunsdworth?"

"It's why I returned so quickly," Owen said. "Tell me what happened—how they escaped."

Kevan walked around the desk so they could face each other. "That's the problem. I don't understand how it happened. Your orders were to hold Dragan for a few days, then release him and follow him. He escaped from his cell the day you left."

Owen's brow crinkled. "How so?"

"I wish I knew!" Kevan said with surprise. "The jailor came to feed him and found the chains in a heap on the floor. The door was still locked, but the man was gone. You saw his cell. It's not very big. The jailor's key went missing, so I had him arrested for being part of the conspiracy."

Owen shook his head. "The jailor's innocent. I know how he escaped."

"But how? I told the king about it, and he blamed the Espion for bungling things. He was furious, as you can imagine. Then shortly afterward, Eyric and Dunsdworth escaped. Set free by Dragan, no doubt. I had every man available on the hunt."

Owen tapped his lip and started pacing. "Let me guess. You didn't have trouble finding them."

Kevan looked at him in surprise. "You're frightening me with your clairvoyance, my lord. Did you have a portentous dream? You *have* been in Brythonica, have you not?"

"I have indeed," Owen said with a smirk. "After your meeting with the king, everyone left. Except for the king. And Dragan."

The Espion's eyes bulged. "Dragan was there?"

"He was in the room with you all the while. I sensed him, but couldn't see him. The thief is Fountain-blessed." Etayne's gift made so much sense now. "He can turn himself invisible. A handy skill for a thief, wouldn't you say? So when you found chains on the floor in the cell . . ."

Kevan's eyes widened. "He was still there. He'd managed to slip out of the cuffs, but he was waiting there all along. And he managed to steal the jailor's key in the hubbub."

Owen nodded. "Dragan is working for the king now."

Kevan blew out softly. "I'm . . . I'm bewildered, my lord. All of our information showed that Dragan was working for Maxwell of Brugia."

Owen shrugged. "Severn paid him off. I think he's using Dragan to create an opportunity to destroy his two rivals. Then he will be able to do as he's long wished and wed Lady Kathryn. I must stop him."

"My lord," Kevan said, looking disturbed. "There's something else."

"Why not ruin my evening completely? Say on, man. I can't be in a worse mood."

"I think the king plans to replace you as head of the Espion. Whenever I report the news to him, he asks me many pointed questions about the Star Chamber and which men are the most loyal to you personally. I get the sense that he plans to cast you aside, like he's done to others. That he isn't comfortable with how much power you've accrued. I think he means to put someone else in the role."

"Do you know who?" Owen asked.

Kevan shrugged. "It's not me. He knows I'm loyal to you. Now that I know he was behind Eyric's escape himself . . ." He paused, looking disgruntled. "I fear what he may do with you."

Owen scratched his neck. "He sent me to Brythonica to get me out of the way. I see he appointed Catsby to lead the Assizes while I was gone."

"And you know how quick *he* is to do what Severn wants. What he's doing in the North is nothing short of rapine and plunder. Catsby hates you. He's envied you for years and sees himself as your replacement if you should fall."

"He can have anything he wishes," Owen said snidely. "He may be plundering Dundrennan, but he'll get his fair share." He chuckled to himself. "I think the king will be very surprised to learn the duchess and I are now betrothed."

"You can't be serious!" Kevan said with a cough of surprise. "How did you manage that! Everyone believed it was a fool's errand. A pretext to start a war with Occitania because you *know* Chatriyon would rather let you spit in his eye than allow Ceredigion to occupy one of the larger duchies."

"I truly believe the king intended for me *not* to be successful," Owen replied with a grunt. "But what can I say? The duchess was wooed by my many charms." He stopped pacing and turned to face the Espion. "I may not be head of the Espion for much longer, but I am head of it now. I need you to send word of my return to the king, and tell him that a messenger came just ahead of me with news of my engagement with Lady Sinia Montfort. Inform him that I'm coming to his great hall to share the news of a dream. Make sure the other dukes know about it. I want everyone there."

Kevan's eyes gleamed with excitement. "What news, my lord?"

Owen shook his head. "You'll see in time. I'm going to slip back into the city so I can make a proper entrance. I want all of Kingfountain to know that the Duke of Westmarch has returned."

The Espion nodded vigorously. "Are you going to try to save Eyric and Dunsdworth from being thrown into the river?"

Owen clapped him on the back. "I'm trying to save everyone. Now go."

Kevan smiled with relief as he unbolted the door of the Star Chamber and quickly slipped away. Owen bolted the door behind him, his heart throbbing with the desire to hurry. He had to think fast and act faster if he wished to prevent the kingdom from meeting its icy fate.

He took a sheet of paper, snatched an ink-stained quill from his desk, and scrawled a hasty note to Sinia.

*My dear, things are unraveling quickly here as I'm certain you already know. Severn wants Eyric and Dunsdworth executed for treason, though he himself arranged their escape. He intends to seduce Kathryn as soon as Eyric is gone. I'm enclosing another note for you to deliver to Elysabeth and Iago as soon as you possibly can. I will predict an invasion of the North in order to give myself an excuse to go there. I don't think Catsby will be up to the task, and Iago will find loyal and willing subjects ready to revolt. When the king orders me to put down the rebellion, I can then explain my plan in greater detail to Iago. According to the prophecy of the Dreadful Deadman, each kingdom will invade Ceredigion simultaneously. Help me manifest the prophecy. I hope you are safe and well. Would it be possible for you to take Genevieve with you and safeguard her in Brythonica? I will sneak her away from the castle to the sanctuary; you need only tell me when to meet you there. I've never written a love note before. Sorry that this one includes so much intrigue. I'm grateful we met at long last. I've thought of you often. Tell me something about yourself. Tell me we can win.*

Owen stared at the paper, wincing over his choice of words, but there was no time to second-guess himself. He scrawled his first name, leaving off his titles and so forth, folded the note, and stuffed it in his tunic pocket. Then he withdrew another sheet and wrote a quick note to Evie.

*I promised that I would keep your daughter safe. I've learned some news that forces me to act. I will safeguard her as I promised. You can trust me in that. But I need you and your husband to reclaim your rights and territories in the North. It is a matter of utmost urgency. The king must be stopped or else the entire kingdom is doomed. Learn what you can about Edonburick and how its people drowned. I seek to prevent a similar disaster here. I need your help. I will bring my army to join Iago's in the North, and then he and I can discuss this together in person. If there were another way, I would take it. But the king has forsaken my trust and his duty. I cannot stand aside and risk so many lives. I will look for your husband at the inn where we once met in Blackpool in twelve days' time. Have faith in me, my dear friend. Trust I'm doing this because I must.*

Owen signed and dated the paper, then folded and stuffed it in his vest with his note to Sinia. He stood at the desk for a moment, staring down at the mound of papers. He wouldn't miss being the head of the Espion, he realized. The thought of letting another man carry the burden wasn't terrible to him. Something so much . . . *more* was happening. Tension hung in the air, and he had a sense that the pieces on the board were already moving. It was as if the earth were groaning beneath his feet.

He slipped out of the Star Chamber and was grateful for the cover of the coming night, which would help him flee the palace grounds without being noticed. If he did not hurry, he would be locked out of the sanctuary when they shut the gates after sunset. But no one paid him any mind as he slipped out of the palace and into the city, which meant he could push his way through the crowded streets as quickly as he pleased.

Owen entered the gates as the mass of visitors started to leave, which earned him some strange looks.

"My daughter is ill, and I must make a wish!" Owen babbled feverishly to the gate warden who barred his way.

"Make it quick, man. Make it quick! The sanctuary closes after sunset. You know that."

"Thank you, sir!" Owen said with a convincing look of humility, and quickly strode up the steps to the sanctuary. The main chamber was empty and his boots clapped loudly on the stone floor. The waters of the fountain were at rest, and hundreds of rusting coins filled the basin.

Owen glanced around and slipped into the side alcove he'd emerged from earlier. He brought the chest to mind, picturing it in as much detail as he could recall, and there it was, waiting for him in the waters. After tugging on the handle, he drew it out and set it on the side railing. He heard the sound of footfalls coming across the hall after him, so he hastily opened the Wizr set. The white Wizr piece was back across the board on the Occitanian side, indicating that Sinia had returned to Brythonica. He smiled at the piece.

And then he noticed a tightly folded piece of paper waiting for him in the crook of the set. He hadn't expected a note from her so soon. He quickly took the two letters he had written and exchanged them for the one he took. Gently, he closed the lid of the set and then broke the wax seal, embellished with a butterfly, on the note left for him. The handwriting was exquisitely done, each word and letter painstakingly and delicately flourished.

*My dearest Owen,*

*By the time you read this note, it will be too late. Eyric is dead. It's not your fault. It was his choice. I know this news grieves you, and I'm sorry to be the one to tell you. I will come for Genevieve in two days. Bring her to this fountain at noon. When you see the mist, have her step inside. I will keep her safe. Be you safe, my lord. Until we next meet.*

*Sinia*

# CHAPTER NINETEEN

### Poisoner's Grief

With a heavy heart, Owen went to the inn on the bridge where he had reserved a room for Etayne. He didn't expect her to be there yet—she would arrive the next day at the earliest—but it was somewhere he could sit and think. Once in the room, he changed into a fresh set of clothes and washed his face in the water dish. And then he sat in a chair and stared once more at the note Sinia had left for him, his mood as dark as the night sky outside the window.

Eyric was already dead.

He had not heard that news from Kevan, so he assumed the Espion did not know. Had Severn ordered the executions upon learning of Owen's return? He frowned. It was technically murder if the king had arranged for them to escape so that they could be tried for and found guilty of treason. He stared at the burning wick of the table candle, focusing on it so keenly he could see the different colors in the flame.

The door shut softly behind him, so quietly he nearly didn't hear it.

Owen spun out of his chair and drew his sword halfway out of the raven-marked scabbard before he realized it was Etayne, a dagger in her own hand.

"How did you get here ahead of me?" Etayne whispered in shock. "When I saw the light under the door, I assumed someone was waiting to kill me."

His heart was still thudding like a galloping stallion. "I wasn't expecting you until the morrow."

"I've not slept since I left you," she said, and he could see the shadow smudges under her eyes that confirmed it. Her body was still rigid with wariness. "How did you get here so quickly?"

Owen licked his lips. "I see I caught you off guard. Let me explain. Would you put down the knife?"

She lowered her arm, but did not release her grip on the weapon. "How do I know it is truly you?"

"Sinia brought me here." He ran a hand through his hair. "Let me try and explain this quickly. She's powerful with the Fountain, Etayne. She's a Wizr." Her eyes widened with shock at the news. "She brought me here through the fountain of St. Penryn, and I emerged yonder at Our Lady." He nodded in that direction. "I stole into the palace and used the Espion tunnels. Your father is working for the king. He's Fountain-blessed himself. Did you know?"

"No," Etayne said, shaking her head. "I had no idea." He could see the truth of that statement in her eyes, and he heaved a sigh of relief.

"It's true. He was there in the privy council meeting—I could sense his presence—but his power rendered him invisible. I only saw him after everyone else left and he emerged to speak privately with Severn. He arranged Eyric and Dunsdworth's escape *and* recapture."

The poisoner's face betrayed a sudden rush of emotion. She blinked quickly, her lip trembling.

"What is it?" Owen pressed, walking toward her in concern.

She was struggling to maintain her composure. "What else?" she said, her voice choked.

"I hardly know how to say it," Owen said weakly. "I learned about the Wizr board from Sinia. Apparently, the Wizrs of old set up the game on this particular board, bestowing it with an enchantment to control the destinies of kingdoms. The two sides are Occitania and Ceredigion, and their rivalry has lasted for centuries. The problem is that if one side loses or breaks the rules the Wizrs set up, their kingdom will be destroyed. Remember when Severn allowed Mancini to violate the sanctuary of Our Lady by dragging Tunmore out? That triggered some unnatural consequences. Specifically, the weather."

"There is a storm heading this way," Etayne said. "Before nightfall, I could see huge storm clouds coming from the North. They'll be here by tomorrow. Are you saying this Wizr board summoned them?"

Owen nodded vigorously. "Remember the unnatural snow that happened all those years ago? It was induced by the Wizr set Tunmore was hiding in the fountain of Our Lady of Kingfountain. This Wizr game allows certain individuals to manipulate the pieces, but only if they have that right by blood. I'm to teach Drew how to play the game so he can move the pieces to defeat Severn. If we don't defeat him, Ceredigion will be destroyed under a curse of ice. The duchess is trying to stop this as well. We've made an alliance. She will help overthrow Severn."

A distrusting look crossed Etayne's face. "She told you all this?"

"She did," Owen said. "It makes sense, Etayne! I've seen evidence of it throughout my life. And the Fountain told me that Drew is the Dreadful Deadman. He's the fulfillment of the prophecy, the only heir of the Argentine family that will allow the game to continue on. Every kingdom is going to attack us. That's what the prophecy says. Severn is the kind of man who would sooner let everyone be destroyed than yield the hollow crown voluntarily. Do you doubt it, Etayne?"

She put away the dagger. "I don't doubt that, Owen. But the duchess may have other motives for helping us. Is she really as benevolent as she's made you believe?"

Her words stabbed a sliver of doubt into Owen's heart. "I think she's trustworthy, yes," he said, infusing the words with as much conviction as he could muster.

"So what is your plan, Owen?" Etayne said after a moment's pause. "What happens next?"

Owen wasn't certain she was convinced. "Do you believe me, Etayne? Judging from your expression, you're more wary than usual."

She shook her head and sighed. "You caught me off guard, and I'm not used to that. I truly didn't expect to find you here ahead of me. I came here to make sure it was safe for you to return to Kingfountain, and then there you were. The first thing you told me was that my *father* is in league with Severn. Owen, you must understand that he is the most untrustworthy man in all of Ceredigion. He is a liar and a thief, and he's not been faithful to *anyone* in his entire life." Tears danced on her lashes as she spoke. "I think he saw me when we went into his cell. If he suspects I'm still alive, he'll try and find me so he can manipulate me as he's always done." She was trembling, which surprised him. She knew a thousand ways to kill a man, yet memories of her father, the thief, still haunted her. She clenched her fist and pressed it hard against her lips as she struggled to maintain her composure. He couldn't see the awful memories playing through her mind, but he sensed them. A tear trickled down her cheek.

Owen hurt for her. How many times had she comforted him in his moments of grief and despair? Her failure to regain control of her runaway feelings sliced at him, particularly since he knew how keenly it would cost her. She was his friend, his confidante. The one person he had been able to fully trust over these last brutal years.

He couldn't bear to see her suffer, so he stepped near and wrapped his arms around her shoulders. She stiffened at his touch, but then let herself lean against him, stifling a sob. He held her close, feeling the tremors shake her body. She leaned her forehead against his chest. The moment between them was bittersweet; he felt both drawn to her and afraid of her. Sinia had warned him he'd be tempted to betray their troth. Now he and Etayne were alone in an inn, night had fallen, and his dear friend was the most vulnerable he'd ever seen her.

Then she lifted her head and looked into his eyes with a fierceness that startled him. She pushed away and lifted the cowl to hide her face. "I'll be back before dawn," she whispered. "Bolt the door."

"I told Kevan that I needed to see the king and his councilors at once," Owen said worriedly.

She shook her head. "You're not going into that castle again until I've made sure it's safe. Stay here."

◆   ◆   ◆

Owen barely slept that night. Every knock, every footfall startled him awake. Hours later, Etayne's soft knock roused him from a fitful slumber, and he rushed to the door and unbolted it.

She swept in, all business, her look grim.

It was still dark, but the dim light in the sky marked the coming dawn.

"What did you learn?" he asked cautiously.

"The king is having the bodies dumped into the river this morning. At dawn."

Owen's stomach lurched. "So Eyric is dead," he whispered. "Dunsdworth too?"

She shook her head. "Dunsdworth was allowed to drink himself into oblivion. He's passed out. I saw the bodies as they were being strapped into canoes. They'll be launched from the quay on the palace side. I told Kathryn you'd meet her there."

"You saw her?" Owen asked.

She nodded. "She's grieving. You can only imagine. I told her you'd bring her son so he could watch Eyric go into the river. She knows about the boy. I made arrangements with Liona to fetch him and dress him, and they're expecting us in the kitchen. The king knows you're coming. They'll be expecting you at breakfast in the great hall. He plans to name you the heir of Ceredigion today, in front of the hall. But it's a ploy, Owen. He fully intends to marry Kathryn, and any son will supersede you. The announcement will allow him to strip you of the Espion and half of Westmarch."

Owen gritted his teeth. "How did you find all this out? Who knows you are back?"

She shook her head. "No one. I dosed Catsby with nightshade. When he awakens, he won't remember telling me anything. He's going to run the Espion now, and he knows all about Dragan. He's your chief adversary. If I were to advise you, I'd ask Iago to invade the North. The people hate Catsby so much, they'll welcome him with open arms. Thus begins your rebellion. The king will command you to subdue them."

Owen smiled. "That's my plan exactly, and the first steps have already been taken. But first I must tell the court about the dream I've had. It's time to rock Severn's throne. This will be my most impressive dream yet. Thank you," he said, smiling eagerly at her. "You've done well. I couldn't manage any of this without you."

"Glad you realize that," she said with a smirk. "I'll disguise you so you're not recognized when we fetch the boy from the kitchen. I brought you a tunic to wear," she said, opening her cloak and revealing a small satchel. Inside was a black tunic with the white boar insignia. She helped Owen rebuckle his scabbard after he donned the disguise. She cinched the buckle and stuffed the added leather through the band. "Wish we had time to shave you before going," she said, shaking her head. "Severn's knights aren't bearded. I'll have to use magic to disguise you."

Owen nodded, and they left the inn together, walking rapidly across the bridge. Somewhere a rooster called, the sound barely noticeable amidst the rush of the waterfall. Owen tugged on his gloves as the chill of morning crept into his hands. He looked at Etayne and saw puffs of mist coming from her mouth.

"It's not normally this cold," he said, looking up at a sky thick with gray clouds that hid the stars. "It's already happening."

She shuddered and nodded, holding her arms to her chest for warmth as they walked briskly. Etayne showed her Espion ring at the gatehouse, and then they slipped into the woods to approach the palace from the secret entrance. It was dark, and the woods looked menacing in the dimness, putting Owen in mind of the woods in Brythonica where he'd found the silver bowl and the marble slab. Memories of his battle with the black knight made his insides crawl. When they reached the kitchen, Liona and her husband were feeding the boy a buttery roll in the corner. The kitchen was empty but for them. The boy looked tousled and tired, and his brow furrowed when he saw Owen enter. He said nothing, keeping his thoughts to himself.

"Hello, Drew," Owen said.

"Would you like something to eat?" Liona asked him. Her husband patted the young man's shoulder and Owen noticed how silver his hair had become of late.

"I'll have breakfast with the king," Owen said, although his stomach did complain at his refusal. "Come with me, lad. There is a place I would like to take you."

Drew looked at him for a long moment before nodding. Owen tried to hide his disappointment that the lad wasn't as demonstrative with him as he'd been with Lord Horwath. But then, Owen's own unhappiness had made him a poor uncle figure. He promised himself that would change.

After stuffing the rest of the roll into his mouth, Drew stood and followed Owen and Etayne out of the kitchen. They walked around the edge of the castle wall toward the yard leading down the hill to the quays. Owen and Evie had wandered the grounds together as children, and he found he still knew the way.

"I'm cold," Drew said, chafing his arms.

"Here, walk between us," Etayne said, drawing him up next to them. "That should help."

Drew gave her a suspicious look, then turned his gaze back to Owen as he walked. "Where are we going?"

"There's something I wanted to show you," Owen said. "You won't understand it now, but you will later."

"I'm tired," Drew complained.

"So am I," Owen said, trying to curb his impatience. "But a knight must learn to fight even if he's cold and tired."

"That's true," the boy said thoughtfully.

They had to cut across a lawn as they approached the gatehouse leading to the docks. He made a subtle gesture to Etayne, and she summoned her magic to disguise him as a common soldier. Her magic seeped from her like a delicate breeze.

Two guards wearing the badge of the white boar stood watch at the doors. Owen could hear voices rising from the dock beyond. One of the guards held up his hand, warning them to slow their approach.

"Shhh," the guard said, shaking his head. When they reached him, Owen caught sight of the scene beyond the latticework bars of the gate. His heart skipped fast. Two canoes had been set down on the path, and the soldiers who had hefted them were milling around.

Kathryn was kneeling beside the boat that contained the body of her husband. She wept over it with grief and misery. A white mist came from her mouth as she gasped and swallowed and sobbed. Owen's heart panged him to see her in such a state. Severn. Severn had done this. Etayne's eyes narrowed with simmering fury.

Drew wrapped his little hands on the bars and watched the woman who, unbeknownst to him, was his mother.

"Poor lady," the boy whispered. "She's my friend."

"Give her time to mourn, lad," the soldier said softly to the boy. The soldier looked at Owen, though he didn't recognize him through the disguise. "He jumped down the tower stairs last night," he whispered with a grimace. "Broke himself on the floor. Like Tunmore. Poor fool knew he was going in the river today. Poor, poor fool."

Owen joined Drew at the gate, his heart wrenching with pain. He clasped the boy's shoulder with his hand. The lad had a dark countenance, a look of sadness.

"Why did you want me to come?" Drew asked, looking up at Owen, and then started when he saw a stranger's face looking back.

It was time to finally tell him the truth. *That* was why he'd brought him here. "It's all right, lad. It's still me," he whispered.

Before he could continue, he heard the unmistakable shuffle-step coming from the path behind them. The halting limp he had known since he was Drew's age.

Severn was coming.

# CHAPTER TWENTY

## *The Widow's Spite*

Owen's heart jolted at the sound of the king's shuffling footsteps, and Etayne's eyes widened with fear. They could not see Severn amidst the shadows, and it was not likely he could see them yet, but he would be at the gate in moments.

There was little time to react, and Owen needed ideas. He was still under Etayne's disguise, but with any luck the king would be too distracted by his task and the noise of the river to notice someone using the magic nearby. What could he do to conceal Etayne and the boy? His mind raced as he heard the king's footfalls approach. The guards posted hadn't noticed it yet, and Owen seized on the first idea that bloomed in his mind.

"The king sent us on ahead," he said to the guards. "Open the gate for him. He wanted to see the bodies put into the river this morning." He gestured quickly for them to open the doors.

The soldier looked startled and then listened as the sound approached.

"He *is* coming," one of them grunted with surprise. "Come on, be quick about it!" The two men wrenched on the heavy barred door, and Owen nodded for Etayne to drag the boy into the gap between the door and the wall, letting the heavy bars conceal them both. Owen kept his back to the approaching king and directed with a gesture for the soldier to stand at attention after finishing the maneuver.

"Long live the king!" Owen said in a crisp salute. The soldiers milling around on the other side suddenly scrambled. Several bent down and hoisted up the canoe with Dunsdworth's comatose body. The man did not so much as grunt.

"My lady," one of the guards near Kathryn whispered in a pleading voice. "The king comes!"

Owen heard the boots coming up behind him and felt the skin on his neck prickle. He adopted the persona of a rough soldier, hoping it matched his disguise. "Be quick about it! Be quick about it! The king comes!"

"Shut up, you fool," Severn snarled to Owen as he passed, not giving him a second look. Etayne and Drew could be seen beyond the gate, but the shadows were thick enough to conceal them. Owen's heart raced with fear, but so far his strategy was working.

"Beg your pardon, my lord," Owen mumbled apologetically and stood aside.

Several soldiers bent down to hoist the staves supporting Eyric's boat, but Kathryn still knelt beside it, cradling her dead husband's face with her hands.

"My lady!" one of them pleaded, glancing worriedly at the king as he crossed the threshold of the gate.

"A moment longer, I beg you!" Kathryn wailed, consumed by grief. Owen watched as the king slowed his approach, one hand gripping his dagger hilt.

"You heard her, leave it alone!" the king barked with anger. The soldiers hastily retreated from the bound corpse. The dawn was quickly driving away the shadows. Owen gestured for Etayne subtly, preparing to send her and Drew away. This was *not* how he planned to tell the boy about his true parentage.

Kathryn looked up at the king, her eyes wet with tears, her mouth twisted with grief, and the look she gave him was like spears. Any fear she'd had of the king lay broken. Her eyes were so full of hate they made Owen want to retreat.

"Of course you would come," she said in a broken voice, "to witness your handiwork. You've long wanted my husband dead, my lord king. Now it is done. He is broken. He is no more."

"He leaped from the tower, my dear," Severn said coldly. "Because he was not man enough to face the river. He knew the Fountain wouldn't save him."

Kathryn straightened, her fingers stiffening like claws as she dug them into her black skirts. "How *dare* you speak of courage. He had more courage than you've ever known. At least he'll rest from his torments now. The Deep Fathoms will bring him peace."

"Then you should *thank* me," the king said with a coughing chuckle. "He'll soon be in a better place. At least you are rid of him now."

Her face contorted with fury. "I never wanted to be rid of him! He was my husband! Can you not understand this? I was his wife."

Severn took a dragging step forward. "But you were fit to be a *queen*. Not a pauper's bride. You are worth more than he ever gave you."

Owen felt the magic of the Fountain begin to churn all around them, tendrils of it wrapping around the king's voice. Severn scooted closer to Kathryn, and Owen saw his hand tentatively start to nudge toward her. For a moment, all he could do was look on in mute horror.

He gave Etayne a sharp look and nodded for her to escape with Drew. Her eyes riveted to his, she nodded back. It would mean the loss of his disguise, but with any luck, the king wouldn't pay any attention to the guard he'd so casually dismissed. The poisoner's hands tightened on Drew's shoulder and she started to draw him away, but Drew clung to the bars, straining against them, eager to witness what was happening. He would not leave without drawing attention to himself, which they could not allow.

"Do you think I would *ever* have you after what you've done?" Kathryn said with astonishment and outrage. "Send me back to Atabyrion. Send me back to my father. Why must I remain your prisoner a moment longer? You have tormented me long enough! If you were a man, you would leap into the river yourself. Your people fear you. You are a coward and a knave and deserve to drown more than either of these poor mistreated wretches!"

Owen had never seen Kathryn so passionate before. She stood like a lioness, facing the king with the very power and indignation that had earned his respect.

The king's voice was full of mocking. "You think the destroyer of these two should go into the river? Then take my hand, Kathryn, and we can go into the flood together. *You* were the cause of their fates. Why did I hate your husband? Because of you. Why was I pleased to hear he'd escaped? Because it would prove to you what a coward and traitor he truly was. Any torments he underwent in the tower, I put him through because I knew they could not compare to the torment I daily endured by having you at court without being able to have you. Love killed your husband. And you are the cause of it."

The king continued to approach her, like one would approach a dangerous animal, one hand on his dagger, the other tentatively reaching toward her. He was very close and Owen wanted to warn her to get away from him. He'd warned her many times that the king's magic was amplified by his touch. In her distress, she was not realizing the danger. What could he do without giving himself away?

"You blame *me*?" Kathryn said with open contempt. "You are always quick to blame everyone else for the failings of your character. I cannot love you, Severn."

"The angel speaks my name at last!" the king crooned.

"Would my words were poison to kill you," she replied in kind.

"But they are, they are!" he said pleadingly, his voice filling with emotion. "I've offered you a crown. I've offered you my love. I would give all that I possess to claim your heart. But you will not have me. You, who shine as bright as the sun even in widow's weeds, could never care for such a misbegotten lump of deformity as myself. Even the sun refuses to shine on me these days. Dogs bark at me when I pass. I, who am hated above all, who would give everything for one . . . sweet . . . kiss from those lips."

His fingers encircled her arm, and Owen felt the king release his magic in a flood against her.

"You have never been hated, Kathryn. Everyone who sees you must love you. How could I prevent myself? How could I stop my heart from feeling? Yes, your husband died because of me. But it was you who drove me to it."

She spat in his face.

Owen stared at her in surprise and wonder.

But the magic of the Fountain did not ebb. It grew stronger. The soldiers shrank back, unable to stop gawking at the scene in front of them.

The king did not release her arm, and Owen watched as Kathryn began to tremble. When the king spoke next, his voice was low and full of emotion, a sound like triumph. "Even *you* spit at me?"

"Out of my sight," Kathryn stammered, her resolve beginning to crumble. "You infect this place with your presence. This was hallowed ground moments ago."

"Your presence hallowed it," Severn whispered powerfully, his voice becoming stronger as his will crushed against hers.

"I pray the Fountain will curse you," Kathryn said, but with less violence and passion.

"It already has, for your sake," the king said. He slowly knelt in front of her, still clinging to her arm, and grunted in pain at the maneuver. "Do not weep, fair lady. Your eyes were made to love. Love *me*."

His words caused a shudder of magic.

"I hate you. I cannot . . . I could never—"

"Your lips were not meant to scorn," he said soothingly. "Teach them to rescue instead. Only you can rescue me, my lady. Only you can tame the boar. If you cannot forgive me, then destroy me." He jerked free the knife from his belt and pulled her closer to him, so close her skirts rustled against his crouching knee. He planted the blade in her hand and closed her fingers around the hilt. "Take this blade and have your revenge." With his free hand, he tugged loose his tunic strings and exposed his chest. "Sheath it here," he said, tapping his heart. "End my suffering and your confinement. Rid the world of this savage beast. Nay! Do not hesitate! Look at me! You hold power over my life or death. It was loving you that drove me to my worst. Tame me or finish me. I would just as soon go over the falls this morning than spend another moment seeing such hate in your eyes."

The king was using up all his magic. Owen sensed the vast dam giving way, the force of the flood insinuating Severn's thoughts into Kathryn's mind. Owen gritted his teeth. If he had been closer, his magic would have prevented the king's from working against her.

Her will melted before such power, and the king's dagger dropped from her hand and clattered onto the cobbles.

Severn's voice was thick with triumph. "Take up my dagger. Or take me."

Her shoulders slumped with despair. "I will not kill you. Though you deserve it."

He shook his head. "Then do it with your words. Tell me to leap into the river, and I will."

Owen wished she would look over at him. If he could have caught her gaze for a moment, he would have nodded violently. *Yes!* He did not believe the king would willingly destroy himself. This was a ruse, a deception, a way of conquering her heart. This was unlike any battle-field Severn had faced before.

"Did I not tell you earlier to jump into the river?" she asked tremulously.

"You were insulting me. Bid me the command now, and I will do it."

The fiery look on the widow's face was passing with the rising sun. Birds were chirping playfully from trees nearby. It was such a strange scene to witness.

She wiped tears on the back of her hand. Owen noticed that the king's hand had slowly traced down her arm and was now nestled in hers. The magic was ebbing, but the spell was done.

"I wish I knew your heart," she whispered, her fingers tightening around his.

"I've already confessed it with my tongue. Will you forgive me, Kathryn? Will you be my queen?"

"That you will know later. Cannot a widow be permitted to grieve?"

"You've been a widow these many years," he said ardently. "Put aside your grief. Accept what is yours by right. All that I have, I give to thee. This heart. My crown. Take this ring from me. Say you are mine."

He quickly withdrew a ring from a pouch at his belt. It was all planned. Owen stared at the king, so shrewd and cunning. His heart ached for Kathryn, who had never truly been given a chance or a choice. He saw the tenderness in her eyes. The castle had been breached. She would relent at last.

Unless Owen could stop it before the wedding.

"I will take it," she said, accepting the ring. Owen noticed the other guards gawking at the scene, some in disbelief and some with impressed amazement.

The king strained and started to rise, wincing with pain. Kathryn's expression softened with sympathy and she took his arm to help him up. She did not loosen her grip on his arm once he had come to standing.

Severn bent his head, looking at the ring in her hand. "Put it on."

Owen glanced back at the gate and saw that Etayne and the boy had vanished. When he looked back, Kathryn was admiring the ring on her finger, the gold band winking in the light.

She looked up timidly at the king's face, and he saw her heart in her eyes. All the hate and anguish was gone. She rested her cheek against Severn's chest, and he wrapped his arm around her shoulders.

"Let us pay our respects to the Fountain's offering," Severn said. He nodded to the soldiers to hoist up the boats, and started marching toward the end of the dock. Kathryn glanced back at her dead husband once more before the guards lifted the boat cradling his body. Her expression was no longer wounded. It was as if the grief had left her.

Owen watched Severn's slow walk alongside Kathryn as they followed unhurriedly behind the guards. His heart simmered with fury at what the king had done and how he had wooed her. His lips twisted in resentment and defiance.

Severn may have won the lady. But he would not keep her long.

# CHAPTER
# TWENTY-ONE

### *The White King*

The palace corridor resounded with the thunder of Owen's boots as he walked firmly and purposefully to the throne room. Servants steered away from him, and his path was marked by the muted whispers that followed him. The Duke of Westmarch had returned to Kingfountain, summoned by the king because of all the treasons in the realm. There were rumors in the palace that the young man from Tatton Hall had had another dream. When Owen reached the main doors leading into the throne room, he saw it was packed to nearly overflowing.

Perfect.

The familiar bubbling of worry and doubt rose up inside Owen's chest, threatening to suffocate him. As he passed the guards, he felt the subtle presence of Fountain magic and then spied Etayne in disguise near the doors. Per their arrangement, she had positioned herself there in advance, and though she looked like any of the elegant noble beauties in the room, he saw through her disguise. The subtle nod she gave him indicated he should proceed with the plan.

The crowd parted before him, clearing a path directly to the throne itself. Owen saw the numerous tables lined with food, and for a moment, he could almost see a younger version of himself there, nervous eyes gazing at the crouch-backed king, nervous legs trying to escape him. This time, Owen would be confronting him directly.

The king was already sitting on his throne, hand on his dagger hilt, his posture calculated to diminish his deformity. Lady Kathryn stood near the dais, and even at this distance, he could see the new ring glittering on her finger. As he approached, he caught sight of the three other dukes of the realm—Catsby, Paulen, and Lovel—clustered together in a corner, whispering urgently to one another. Catsby's eyes were full of loathing as he watched Owen's approach. Paulen whispered something behind his hand to Catsby. Lovel sipped from a wine goblet, not paying attention to the conversation but watching the king and his conquest. To one side of them stood Kevan, his keen eyes taking in the scene with interest.

It was tradition to kneel before the throne of kings before speaking. Severn had dismissed Owen from that obligation years ago because of his service to the crown. But Owen deliberately dropped to one knee and bowed his head before the king.

"I told you he'd come," the king said snidely to the other dukes. "Did I not? But lad, you could have changed into some new clothes. You haven't shaved in weeks by the look of you. Have a bath first next time."

A few tittering chuckles came from the huge assembly. Owen ignored the jab and began to summon the Fountain's power into himself. He knew Severn had used up most of his reserves in his confrontation with Kathryn, but Owen wanted to impress this memory on the king and all others who were present.

Before he spoke, he caught sight of Evie's daughter standing alongside one of the trestle tables with Drew. The two were positioned quite close to each other, and Genevieve was whispering something in Drew's ear as she watched the long-absent duke kneel in front of the king. Seeing the two of them together sparked something unexpected in his heart. It was no accident those two had been thrown together. The water-wheel was circling up again, ready to dip and plunge back into the river.

"My lord," Owen said respectfully. "You summoned me home, but I come with urgent news."

"Stand," Severn said, gesturing for him to do so. "So the Espion tells me. But before you share this news, I wish to announce publicly my faith and confidence in—"

"My lord!" Owen interrupted, rising quickly to his feet. A sudden chill of silence swept the hall at Owen's declaration. Rarely did people defy the king or gainsay him. Owen saw the king's gray eyes narrow in consternation.

The young duke took several strides forward, drawing on the power of the Fountain to bolster his words.

"There is a prophecy," Owen said, his voice rising. "It is native to Ceredigion and has been passed down in various forms for centuries. It is the prophecy of the Dreadful Deadman."

As he said the words, it felt as if an invisible thunderclap had stricken everyone present. He felt the Fountain magic seething inside him, rushing from his mouth, from his fingertips. The air was suddenly charged with emotion. The king straightened in his throne, his expression turning grave.

Something whispered in the room, a voice that came not from any person but from the silence itself.

"That prophecy," the king said sharply, "is nothing but an empty legend used to trick and fool the gullible. Even my brother Eredur claimed to be the Dreadful Deadman." Severn tried to laugh, but it was a broken sound.

"The prophecy was written down by Geoffrey of Dundas," Owen said, letting his voice ring out in the hall as he approached the king. "Master Polidoro has shown me copies of the original. We all know the saying, my lord. *When E is come and gone, then take heed to yourselves, for war shall never cease. After E is come and gone, then cometh Ceredigion to destruction by seven kings. The Fountain shall cease to flood the land and after that will come a Dreadful Deadman with a royal wife of the best blood in the world. And he shall have the hollow crown and shall set Ceredigion on the right way and put out all heretics."*

Owen paused, letting the words of the prophecy fade into silence. The prophecy was common knowledge to most of the realm, and it was common practice among the lesser born to name their children after the letter E.

Severn's face had turned a shade paler, his lips twisting into an angry frown. Some whispering broke out, loud enough to reach Owen's ears, about how the pretender had taken the name Eyric, beginning with the letter E.

"That doggerel," the king said tightly, "has been common gossip for centuries. What mean you to come in here and—"

"My lord, forgive me," Owen said, interrupting him again. "But while I was in Brythonica, I had a vision. The magic of the Fountain is strong in that land. Stronger than in any place I have ever been. My lord, the prophecy of the Dreadful Deadman says that a man shall rise from the dead. Not a grown man. A child. I saw in my dream a stillborn baby. A child wrapped in bloody rags." He looked at Kathryn, piercing her with his gaze. She stared at Owen, trembling, and then her eyes went to young Drew, who wasn't watching her at all.

"The child came alive. The child lives in the realm at this moment. He must be eight years old by now. I saw him walk into the sanctuary of Our Lady. All the people had gathered to watch. The boy then reached into the waters of the fountain and drew out a sword."

There was an audible gasp at Owen's words, and Severn's face began to quiver with fury.

"A sword, my king," Owen continued gravely. "It was the sword of the Maid. It was King Andrew's sword. It was the sign from the Fountain that he was the Dreadful Deadman, the rightful ruler of Ceredigion. The White King."

Owen turned and faced those assembled in the hall. He spied Etayne watching him, trying to conceal her smile of approval. "You all know my history. You all know that I was stillborn. But I am *not* the Dreadful Deadman. I could not see his face in my vision, but I know he is still a child. Like I was when I started having visions. He will save us from destruction." Owen turned and looked at the king. "My lord, the Fountain whispered to me that it will not stop snowing until the boy is crowned king." He dropped again to one knee. "That is my vision, Your Majesty. If it is true, then we will soon be invaded by seven kingdoms. What would you have me do to defend our lands?"

"Out," the king said in a low, snarling voice. Then he rushed to his feet and waved his hand. "Get out! All of you! Only my privy council will stay. Out, I say! Get out!" He was nearly screaming in fury.

There was a rush of bodies toward the door and then suddenly a voice rang out from the hall. "It's snowing! By the Fountain, it started to snow as he spoke!"

Owen felt a throb of giddiness at the news. The timing was perfect.

Pure chaos filled the hall as people began shoving against each other to be the first to leave. Someone knocked over a table, and food spilled onto the floor in heaps. Owen kept his eyes locked on Severn's, not wanting to risk exposing himself by staring at anyone else. He'd rarely seen the king so agitated, so apoplectic. He did his best not to smile.

It took some time to clear away the crowds, but the guards drove them out and bolted the door, leaving the king and some of the dukes in the chamber. Lady Kathryn stared worriedly at Severn, her hands reaching for his arm before pulling back.

The door burst open, and Catsby entered. Owen hadn't seen him leave. He waited on his knee, determined not to rise before he received the king's command. His legs were throbbing.

"It *is* snowing, my lord," Catsby said in a worried voice. "I saw it with my own eyes. The castle bailey is already dusted with white."

Jack Paulen snorted with amazement. "By my troth," he grunted.

The king pressed a knuckle against his smooth mouth, his eyes turning balefully on Owen. "You did this in front of the great hall," he said angrily. "In front of a room full of witnesses! What on earth compelled you to make such a scene?"

Owen remained on bended knee. "I followed the Fountain's bidding," he replied meekly.

The king rose from his throne and began to pace. He glanced at Kathryn, his expression turning from pain to triumph. Kathryn looked away. "Wait for me in the anteroom," he told her, his voice tender. She nodded and silently left through the side door from which the king usually entered.

Severn grimaced once she was gone. "I was going to make an announcement this morning," he said angrily. He gave Owen a hard look. "Before you spoke, I was going to name you my heir and—"

"Your heir?" Owen said, interrupting him again. "I am not an Argentine, my lord. I *cannot* be your heir. I *will not* be your heir. You accused me of treason in the note you sent me."

Some of the dukes looked at Owen in startled surprise.

Severn waved it off. "A test, lad. It was only a test. I knew you'd come. I knew you were faithful, despite some who would argue otherwise." He looked over at Catsby before glancing down at Owen with exasperation. "Get up, man. I told you not to kneel before me."

"What are we going to do, my lord?" Catsby said with worry. "If the prophecy is true, we cannot defeat all the kingdoms if they attacked us at once. Only King Andrew could hope to defend a kingdom against so many enemies."

"Once word gets out," Jack Paulen added. "They'll all seize the opportunity regardless of the prophecy."

"Not *all* of them," Severn said defiantly. "Iago wouldn't dare. This is absurd. I can't believe you all trust in such superstitious nonsense. We are men of the world, not given to fancy. Winter has come early, that is all. It happened years ago and nothing came of it, remember?" He turned and shot Owen another angry glance. "You should have seen me privately, lad. You should have resisted the impulse to make such a show of the news." He swore under his breath. "You were summoned home after Urbick and Dunsdworth escaped. Well, that problem has been solved. They were both found guilty of treason by the Assizes and ushered into the river this very morning. Urbick, mind you. Not Eyric." He glanced at the door Kathryn had used to make her exit. "His name never started with an E. It was all a trick. A . . . coincidence. There is no sword in the fountain of Our Lady. There is nothing but the rusty coins that the sexton shovels and collects for the royal treasury. You all *know* this! Lad, I appreciate you coming to me with your vision. It may indeed presage that war is coming. But it does not mean the Dreadful Deadman has returned."

"But the snow," Lovel said earnestly.

"Who didn't see the clouds coming yesterday?" Severn snapped. "Now heed my orders and serve me well, Dukes of Ceredigion. I command you to return to your duchies and make preparations."

Catsby looked greensick. "What about the Espion?" he whined.

"Can you not see past your own greed for a quarter hour!" Severn roared at him. "I'm not changing aught until this storm blows past. And it will, mark my words." He snapped his fingers. "I know what I'll do. We'll send out a royal decree to summon all the children of the kingdom to the palace. *All* of them." He turned to Owen. "I want you to post Espion to guard the fountain night and day. Stop this sniveling and fidgeting. I am the master of this realm. No little brat is going to steal my crown." He chuffed and began pacing.

Then he turned to Catsby. "Prepare the summons and then get your body to the North. Of all the duchies, it's the most vulnerable. Because of your greediness. But thankfully, I thought ahead and prepared a way to keep Iago in line. He loves that little girl, you see." His face turned menacing. "She's his weakness, and he'd never allow anything to happen to her."

# CHAPTER
# TWENTY-TWO

*Mantic Gifts*

The king dismissed all of the dukes except for Owen. Lovel, Paulen, and Catsby left—Catsby pausing to cast a suspicious glance over his shoulder at Owen before he walked out—and the door thudded shut with an ominous sound, leaving Owen and Severn alone together.

Torches hissed and fluttered in the throne room sconces. Owen stood still, but he felt the nervous impulse to reach for his sword hilt. The king was pacing again on his crooked leg, his brow knitting with consternation. He stopped and then fixed Owen with a wary stare.

"Why did you announce your dream in a hall full of witnesses?" he asked in a low, seething voice.

Owen held his ground and met the king's gaze without flinching. "Why did you execute Dunsdworth and Eyric before I returned?"

Severn's face darkened. "I did it to spare your sensibilities, lad."

"How considerate of you," Owen said. "I'm glad you've always kept my *feelings* in the forefront of your thoughts."

The king gave him a measuring look, as if Owen's words had caught him off guard. "Have you finally found your tongue after all of these years?" he said with a snort. "The boy who used to quaver in this very hall at breakfast each morning?" He swept his hand in a wide circle, indicating the food-laden tables that had been ransacked earlier.

Owen took a deliberate step closer. "I'm not a child anymore."

The king's anger was growing, but he looked uncomfortable as well, as if his conscience was suddenly bothering him. "You should have told me privately about your dream. Now the entire realm will hear of it within the hour. You owe allegiance to *me*, lad. I gave you everything you have. And I can take it from you just as easily."

Owen couldn't have cared less, and he hoped it showed on his face. "I returned, did I not? Even after your threat. Even after your test. Can you not stop such antics, my lord? Have I not proven my loyalty again and again over these many years?"

The king shook his head. "I do trust you, lad, but Catsby has been whispering that it's a mistake. That you've had too much power for one so young. He said that some of the Espion are more loyal to *you* than to me." He gave Owen a meaningful look. Did he mean Etayne? Kevan?

Owen held up his hands. "Then strip it from me, my lord, like you did to Ratcliffe. If Catsby wants the burden, he's welcome to it. If he's done ruining everything Stiev Horwath built in Dundrennan, why not turn him loose on your Espion next, as he wishes?"

The king looked at him again in surprise. "Do you hear yourself?"

"I do. I sound like you, don't I?"

The king nodded. "You are young and you've carried a heavy burden. Perhaps it is time that I eased some of it off you. What news from Ploemeur? I've heard the duchess wasn't opposed to the match after all?"

Owen wondered how he could keep his face disinterested, but he tried. "She's no fool, nor was she Roux's puppet."

"Was? What do you mean?"

Owen bit his tongue, cursing himself for the slip. "I only meant that she's not his puppet after all. She sees the value in the deeper alliance with Ceredigion. We are betrothed."

The king looked surprised and a little envious. "So quickly?" he murmured. "You think this is a ruse? Or does she mean to go through with it? I hadn't intended you to actually marry her, you know."

"Then you shouldn't have sent me to offer an engagement," Owen rebuffed. "I was rude, cantankerous, and unkempt."

"You still are," the king said snidely.

"Is it any wonder?" Owen answered. "The assignment is complete. If you have no further plans for me, I'd like to return to Westmarch and prepare my army."

The king shook his head. "No, Owen. I need you here. Send word to the duchess to be alert for signs that Chatriyon is stirring and seeking to reclaim his lost cities. I might send you to Pree to lay siege there."

Owen wrinkled his brow, feeling the tangles forming in his plan. "You want me to attack him?"

Severn shook his head. "I believe you had a dream, Owen. Too many of your visions have come to pass for me to doubt them. But I don't intend to forsake my crown, and I'd just as soon attack seven kingdoms at once than risk being defeated on my own ground. Make you ready. I want you near me as my advisor."

Owen bowed. "I'll send word to Ashby to begin the preparations."

The king nodded. "Very well. See to it."

Owen was about to turn, but the king signaled him to stay a moment longer. "You are not the only one who is recently betrothed," he said, his expression softening. "Lady Kathryn has agreed to be my wife. She will be the queen my people have long desired." He frowned, his brow turning more serious. "That's another reason your news upset me. I'm fully intending to sire a son. An heir. I was going to name you protector should that happen." His gaze narrowed. "Can I trust you, Owen? Can I trust you with that?"

Owen felt the squirming conflict inside of him. The duplicitous role the king had forced him to play sickened him, but he could not reveal himself now. He gave the king a stern look. "Loyalty binds me," he said softly.

"Good lad," Severn answered. "I want you to see Polidoro for me. I have no patience for his long-winded answers, but I want you to ask him about the Dreadful Deadman prophecy. From what I understand, he hasn't been able to validate the myth of King Andrew at all. There are no records dating back to his court at Tintagel. Polidoro tells me the story is a myth. That the common story about the origins of this city, this very palace—Kingfountain—is simply a legend. There is no evidence that any sword was ever drawn from the water. I want you to talk with him, Owen. Then you can see for yourself why I have doubts about your prophecy."

Owen bowed deeply. "I will, my lord. And congratulations on your betrothal. I know you have long desired it." He did his best to keep the bitterness from his voice.

The king dismissed him with a nod.

◆　◆　◆

Etayne walked alongside Owen as they headed to the record room where Polidoro Urbino had been working for so many years. The history he had written on the people of Ceredigion was lengthy and consisted of seven volumes. The man certainly was loquacious. He had traveled the land collecting documents, assembling the largest body of sources from castle records to sanctuary journals kept by the deconeuses.

"How did the king handle your news?" Etayne murmured to Owen.

"He was upset, of course. But then I threw it in his face that he'd had two men executed while I was gone. That kicked him off the holy pedestal he was attempting to mount."

Etayne smirked at the joke. "I remember Mancini saying how much he hated debating with you."

Owen chuckled. "He always lost. No, I've been around the king too long. If I opened my mouth, you'd find thorns on my tongue." He sighed. "I'm going to have to learn to control my temper."

"I like your temper," Etayne said with a smile. "There is nothing about you I would change. Not even those whiskers."

Her inviting tone made him a little uncomfortable, and he was grateful when they reached the heavy oak door leading to the record room. When they entered, they found Polidoro giving instructions to several young scribes whom the king was paying to work for him. They brought him books at his request, scanning passages for the references he sought.

"No, no, not volume six, I asked for volume seven!" Polidoro complained, shaking his head and shooing the young man at his elbow away. "Tanner, bring me another jar of ink, would you? Good lad. Lord Kiskaddon!" he said, brightening instantly as he noticed the new arrivals. "Come in, come in! It has been too long since you've visited this humble court historian." He bowed with a flourish and rose, coming forward to give Owen's hand a vigorous shake.

"It has been too long, Master Urbino," Owen said. "I don't come nearly as often as I should."

"It's understandable," the historian said in a grave tone, looking serious and concerned. "You used to come quite often with a certain young water sprite long ago." He clucked his tongue, his eyes growing misty. "I rather miss her, you know. She used to talk to me often before leaving for Edonburick. Those were fond memories. I see you mourn her as well. Well, best to wave aside the clouds, and face our fate with courage. What can I do for you, my young lord? Is there another battle you would like to reference? I do have several I've been saving for you." He grinned knowingly at Owen and butted him with an elbow.

"Actually," Owen said, hoping the man would stop speaking long enough for him to issue his message. "The king sent me here on an errand. He says you can dispel my notion about King Andrew being a historical figure."

The lanky historian swiped his hand across his gray-haired scalp and pursed his leathery lips. "Did he now? Well, what I told him was that there is no *evidence* of it. I'm a historian, after all. I've been looking at records that go back hundreds of years, to the first Argentine family. But the story of King Andrew is older still. Did you know there is a tapestry in the royal palace of Pree that shows Ceredigion's invasion by Jessup the Conqueror?" His eyes grew animated whenever he shared obscure historical facts, and he started to gesticulate with his hands. "History told in art! You can see the stories painted instead of printed. So it should not surprise you to learn that there are also pictures of a young boy drawing a sword from a fountain. But it's impossible to tell *when* it happened. In some of the pictures, there is a woman in the water who hands Andrew the sword. The sanctuaries have been built to commemorate the event and, as you know, people still toss coins into the fountains and make wishes. It's a deeply ingrained tradition, Lord Owen. But just because I can't prove *when* Andrew lived, doesn't mean I don't believe he did. After living here for so many years, after studying the references over and over again, I've come to appreciate them like the sound of beautiful music."

Owen started pacing and rubbing the growth on his chin, then caught himself when he noticed Etayne watching him with an amused smile. "The king asked specifically about the prophecy of the Dreadful Deadman."

Polidoro nodded. "You know almost as much about it as I do, of course. You've often asked me about the mantic prophecies."

That word, Sinia's word, caught Owen's attention. "The *mantic* prophecies?"

"Yes, that's the word we used to describe them. They are prophecies of the past or the future. There have always been certain Fountain-blessed individuals who possess mantic gifts. The Wizr Myrddin, for example, had that gift. As do you, naturally. The Sirens shared that gift, but they weren't mortal."

Owen held up his hand. "The Sirens?"

Polidoro looked at him in surprise. "They are mythological creatures, Owen. Very nasty. I thought you knew of them. They are a type of water sprite—one of the more malevolent ones."

Owen glanced at Etayne and then back at the historian. "I've not heard of them specifically. Tell me more?"

"It's an ancient legend," Polidoro said, sitting on the edge of his desk and rubbing his hands briskly together. "The legend comes from Genevar, I believe. There are many islands in that area, and they've always been a trading nation. According to their history, any sailors who traveled too close to the rocky islands of the Sirens risked destruction. Sirens were beautiful female creatures . . . not mortals, but from the Deep Fathoms. Their song would entice the sailors—so much so that they would crash their ships into the rocks. The songs were mantic, personal to each sailor. Only one man survived the Sirens. He was Fountain-blessed, so their song could not drive him mad. The Sirens are a myth, of course. Shipwrecks are caused by storms, not water sprites, but just because something isn't real doesn't mean people won't believe in it."

Owen's heart hammered in his chest as Polidoro spoke. Water sprites. He remembered hearing about the water creatures who lived in the Deep Fathoms when he was a child. Mancini had even accused Evie once of being one. According to legend, some water sprites were left to parents who couldn't bear children to raise them in the mortal world. Pieces began to tumble together in Owen's mind. When he and Sinia had stood on the beach with the smooth glass, none of the waves had touched her. He had seen her step into the Fountain and the water had appeared to disperse from her. Was it because she was a Wizr? Or was it because she had other powers he could not understand? If she was a water sprite, was she the benevolent or malevolent kind?

"You look astonished," Polidoro said, quirking his brow. "Have I troubled you?"

He swallowed. "These water sprites—the Sirens—from mythology. Did they have names?"

The historian nodded. "Oh yes, they had names listed in the myths. Let me think." He tapped his chin and scrunched up his brow. "Aglayopee, Lukosia, Ligeia, Molpine, let me think . . . hmm . . . Thelxia, Kelpie, and . . . what was the last one? I can't quite remember . . . oh, I've got it!" He snapped his fingers loudly. "Peisinia!"

◆  ◆  ◆

*My dearest Owen,*

*I enjoyed the note you wrote and have read it through often. It shows me part of your heart, and while ink is but a poor substitute for words, it is better than silence. Difficulties face us. The king will not accept defeat willingly.*

*About myself, as you requested. My father made me practice my penmanship repeatedly as a child. I apologize if my words are written too fancifully, but it pleased my father, and I wished to please him. I am also fascinated by drawing, so I have always treasured illuminated manuscripts and imagined the little pictures on the pages coming to life. I thought that if I could make a picture seem real enough, it would become real. When I learned about my gifts, I discovered a word from the ancient language of the Wizrs. The word means "breath," but it also means "life." Do you know what I speak of? Here is a little picture I have drawn for you, of the breed of butterfly I am named after. A little gift for you, along with some berries from the gardens of Ploemeur.*

*Sinia*

◆  ◆  ◆

# CHAPTER
# TWENTY-THREE

## *Myrddin*

The name—Peisinia—was so hauntingly close to the duchess's, it made Owen's stomach lurch with dread. His gaze sought out Etayne, who stared at him with open worry and surprise on her face, emotions she quickly subdued.

"You have a remarkable memory," Owen said to the historian, struggling to control his tone. Sinia did not *seem* like a negative influence in the world. Her people admired and respected her, and he had witnessed evidence of her compassion more than once. He did not relish the idea of being duped by anyone, though, and the mere possibility that she was not what she seemed twisted his stomach into knots.

Polidoro waved it off. "I do have a prodigious memory for minute details. It serves my occupation. The king wished to know about the Dreadful Deadman prophecy," he said, tapping his long fingers against his chin. "Is there anything in particular he wanted to know?"

With difficulty, he managed to choke out, "You named the source as Geoffrey of Dundas. Can you tell us anything else? Anything from deeper in the past?"

"Certainly," Polidoro said, wagging his finger at Owen. "Geoffrey was merely transcribing one of the prophecies of Myrddin. The ancient Wizr had the mantic gifts, as you know. With him as an advisor, King Andrew was able to make his empire grow ever stronger. There were always plots to do away with the Wizr and prevent his counsel from reaching the king. The old man could use the Fountain magic to disguise himself, and he was known to wander the kingdom, visiting people and telling fortunes. Sometimes as a little child. Sometimes as a doddering ancient. Several kings of the day would send poisoners to try and kill him, but he foresaw their attacks and eluded them."

Owen's interest was piqued yet again. "If I recall correctly from my reading, Myrddin eventually stopped protecting the king, and that's when King Andrew was mortally wounded and passed on to the Deep Fathoms."

"Precisely," Polidoro said, nodding in agreement. "Once the king's Wizr was removed, the king's realm began to fall into chaos. He was betrayed constantly, and his dominions crumbled. In those days, the king taught the people the code of Virtus."

Owen wrinkled his brow. "Isn't that the family name of the kings of Occitania?"

"Indeed. They've carried it for generations. But it is also an ancient ideal. The kingdoms of Ceredigion and Occitania were founded on it. The more common use of the word is 'virtue' today, but in ancient times, it encompassed many meanings, including *prudentia, iustitia, temperantia,* and *fortitudo.* 'Prudence,' 'justice,' 'self-control,' 'courage.' This is what King Andrew taught his people. To become a knight in his realm meant a person had to embody all of these traits, to demonstrate them in all aspects of their lives *before* they were bestowed the rank of knighthood. These attributes are famous in the literature, though they are no longer requisite. The early Argentines espoused them publicly, but in their private lives, the burden often felt too heavy."

"You've given me a lot to think about, sir," Owen said, trying to make sense of it all. "I thank you." Another thought came to him. "How did they destroy Myrddin in the end? I seem to recall that he disappeared from court and never returned. King Andrew said he was taken away by the Fountain."

Polidoro gave him a wise look. "Well, *that* is a story in itself. The Wizr eventually fell in love."

"Truly?" Owen said with a chuckle.

"Of course. Love overthrows the strongest of men. And women. It was love that united the first Argentine king with the Queen of Occitania. She tricked her husband into divorcing her and then married King Ursus and founded the dynasty that has gone on for centuries now. Love is a powerful force, my lord. More powerful than the Fountain itself, I fear." He sighed deeply, his thoughts turning more introspective. "Myrddin fell in love with a nobleman's daughter. The history does not state which kingdom she was from. She persuaded him to teach her his magic so that she might become a Wizr as well. He knew from his visions that she would betray him. But even though he knew it, he could not stay away and he could not prevent it. The water in a river cannot escape the boulders strewn in the path ahead. They can only crash against them. She betrayed Myrddin and captured him beneath a mound of giant stones. They say Myrddin was immortal and could not die. That he is trapped there still. No one knows where he was lost, for he traveled with the girl willingly as she led him to his doom. A sad end for a great man. His last prophecy was about the Dreadful Deadman and the return of the White King. You tell this to King Severn, my boy. As I've told you both before, there is no proof that these legends of King Andrew are more than stories. But then again," he added wryly, lifting his eyebrows, "perhaps the records were drowned in Leoneyis, eh?" He gave Owen a conspiratorial wink.

◆  ◆  ◆

When Owen returned to the Star Chamber with Etayne, she hastily bolted the door behind them.

"I hardly know what to think," she said. Before continuing, she rushed to the various spy holes to make sure no one was eavesdropping. Her whole manner communicated agitation and bewilderment.

"What do you mean?" Owen asked, looking for some paper to craft another note to Sinia.

Having finished her inspection, Etayne turned back to him and folded her arms. "You've only just met the Duchess of Brythonica. You two are betrothed. It never occurred to me that she might be otherworldly! What if she's a Siren, Owen? What if her magic is clouding your mind?"

Owen shook his head. He had managed to regain most of his control. "Fountain magic doesn't work on me unless I permit it. You could try your best to deceive me with one of your disguises, Etayne, but I'd still know it was you. I don't think I'm under a spell."

Etayne started to pace. "I don't trust her."

"Who? Sinia?"

"Who else?" she said angrily. "She's been manipulating you from the start. If she truly has mantic gifts like Myrddin, who's to say she's not using them to prevent Severn from using Brythonica as a base to attack Chatriyon? She could be defending herself through intrigue."

Owen took a moment to sort through this possibility, for her words made sense and he was not going to discount them. But his *heart* told him that Sinia wasn't deceiving him. She had been truthful when confronted with his suspicions. And she had known about Eyric's death before it happened. He had the note from her to prove it.

"I don't know everything," Owen said after a lengthy pause. "But I've decided to trust her. Based on what Polidoro said, not all water sprites are harmful. She's trying to prevent the destruction of our kingdom. When we brought back the Wizr set, it started to snow. The evidence backs up her claims."

Etayne looked unconvinced. "I have a bad feeling about her," she said.

Owen gave her a wary look, wondering if that bad feeling was jealousy. "I've already cast the die, Etayne," he said. "What I intend to do," he continued, gesturing to the paper and quill, "is ask her directly about the name Peisinia. Is she an otherworldly creature?" He shrugged. "Perhaps. At this point, it wouldn't surprise me. Did you hear what Polidoro told us? About how Myrddin trained a woman to become a Wizr? How he shared his power and was then trapped under stones?"

Etayne blinked. "The woods in Brythonica. The silver bowl!"

Owen nodded approvingly. "I knew you'd catch on. It all fits. Perhaps Myrddin is still there. Do I dare ask her about it? Is she expecting me to figure it out so she can confirm it? There are riddles inside riddles, and I feel as if I've been chipping away the layers to reveal the gem glistening beneath."

Etayne's eyes were fearful. "What if she destroys you?" she asked.

Owen sighed. "To be honest, I don't think she can. Her powers are vast. I sensed them. But I don't think she can use them against me any more than any other Fountain-blessed could. I'm immune, like that sailor was to the Siren's song. Back and again, back and again," he muttered.

A fist pounded on the door, startling them both.

Heart racing in his chest, Owen hurried over to the door and unbolted it. Catsby waited on the other side with two of his knights. The duke of the North looked furious, and when he spoke, his tone was thick with accusation.

"I hear that you're betrothed to the Duchess of Brythonica."

Owen felt a blistering retort come to his tongue, but stopped himself from releasing it. He took a steadying breath. "That is true, Catsby. Thank you," he added, as if the man had congratulated him.

Catsby's fury heightened to outrage. "Westmarch, the Espion, *and* Brythonica? It was a ploy all along."

Owen looked at him in confusion.

Catsby tossed up his hands. "The king's!" he snorted. "He assured me that the duchess would sooner wed a scorpion than you, that it was a pretext to go to war and nothing would come of it. Now I see that he only wanted to enrich you more."

"Have a care," Owen warned him. "You're not lacking for treasures yourself, man."

"But he always rewards *you* the most." Catsby frowned bitterly. "Well, I'm off to Dundrennan to do the impossible. The people can't abide me and now I must force them to muster soldiers. It's not fair that you get all the rewards. I've served the king loyally for years."

Fearing that he'd unleash one of the insults dancing on his tongue if he were to open his mouth, Owen simply nodded.

Catsby gave him a look of disapproval and then snapped his fingers for the knights to follow him.

Owen shut the door and turned back to Etayne, letting out his breath as he slumped against the wood. "It was harder than I thought it would be."

"What? Being civil?" Etayne said.

He glowered at her, but couldn't hold back a grin. She knew him well.

"What are you going to do next?" she asked him.

Owen rubbed his hands together. "I'm going back to the sanctuary. I was going to write the note here and bring it with me, but seeing Catsby and his soldiers reminded me that it would be foolish to carry treasonous notes in my pocket. That's how Ratcliffe met his end."

Etayne nodded. "Do you need a disguise before you go?"

"No, I'm going to bring a coin and make a wish at the fountain. What further pretext do I need?"

After collecting a little bottle of ink, a quill, and some paper, he took his coin pouch and walked hurriedly to the sanctuary of Our Lady.

There were still piles of correspondence to read, orders to write up for Captain Ashby, who would summon Owen's retainers for war, but his thoughts still turned to Sinia as he walked. Snow drifted lazily down onto his expensive cloak, adding splotches of white. The air was crisp and cold. Winter had come early. And Owen had brought it with him in a Wizr set.

The grounds of the sanctuary contained fewer people this day, the chill having kept many indoors. Owen brushed off his sleeves as he entered and stood by the main fountain, deliberately choosing to stand on a white tile. He withdrew a coin and studied it a moment. He had intended to feign a prayerful stance and fling the coin in like a pious young man would.

But to his surprise, he felt the desire to commune with the Fountain stir inside him. He had not done so in a long while.

*Bless me with courage and not fear. Bless me with the wisdom to know whom to trust and to be worthy of trust. Bless me with the strength to serve and not the desire to be served. Bless me with the humility to be ruled and not the will to rule. Give me the faith to do the Fountain's bidding. Bless me to rise to it.*

After waiting silently, listening for an answer that didn't come, he tossed the coin into the water, watching the surface ripple after the coin plunged to the bottom. He stared at the ripples, the expanding circles that chased after each other, never touching. One action caused so many consequences. He watched until the ripples vanished and the water became smooth again.

He glanced around the hall and saw a few families and individuals milling around, mostly admiring the structure or, like him, paying their devotions. When he was certain no one was watching, he surreptitiously made his way into the alcove by which he had returned to Kingfountain. He walked around the smaller fountain, the waters lapping and bubbling soothingly. From that vantage, he would see if anyone was approaching.

He sat down at the edge of the fountain, feeling a few droplets land on his arm. When he was certain no one was watching, he summoned the Wizr chest, reached into the waters, and dragged it out by the handle. Using the key around his neck, he unlocked it and lifted the lid.

Inside the box awaited a note addressed to him in Sinia's elegant script. There was also a small towel full of berries nestled into an empty portion of the board. He smiled as he plopped one of the fruits into his mouth; it was absolutely soft, sweet, and delicious. Reaching down, he lifted another one, imagining she had plucked it from the field with her own fingers.

He read the note quickly, learning about her father's desire for her to have perfect penmanship, and her love of drawing. Reading her words brought a little smile to his face, and her openness made him feel that she was deserving of his trust. The little butterfly she had drawn was impressive—as realistic and beautiful as he'd seen in any book. The insect was a shade of blue-gray with black spots on its wings and little intricate designs along the edges. Two long antennae protruded above its black eyes. It was meticulously done, though small enough that it would not have taken long to draw. Owen lacked that ability himself. He finished the letter, reading the words about "breath" and "life."

His heart began to race again. It was no accident she had phrased the last sentence just so. He *knew* the word she meant, for he had used it twice before. Owen stared at the little drawing, feeling his heart well up with curious emotions. He had become so accustomed to equating love with pain that he'd forgotten how gentle and delicate it could feel. A drop of water landed on the paper and he lifted it higher to keep it away.

Owen stared at the image of the butterfly, drawn by the hand of his betrothed, and he felt the Fountain magic stir inside him. For a strange moment, it felt as if Sinia were sitting beside him, her fingers close to his on the edge of the fountain wall. If he closed his eyes, he wondered if he would hear her breathing.

"*Nesh-ama*," Owen whispered to the image.

He felt the magic tug loose inside him and watched in awe as the lines of color wriggled to life. A sinia butterfly flapped its tiny wings and escaped the paper to flutter in front of him, so helpless and weak. He found himself laughing in childlike delight, amazed when it came up and landed on his shoulder. In his mind's eye, he thought he saw Sinia sitting at the edge of a fountain elsewhere, smiling shyly at him.

◆  ◆  ◆

Sinia,

I am not one for endearments, and your name is suitably short that an abbreviation isn't necessary. While I was tempted to begin this note by calling you my sweet butterfly, I resisted it because it sounded silly even to me. One cannot improve on perfection. My attempt at gallantry has probably failed.

   Not only is your penmanship exemplary, but your art is equally impressive. Sadly, my gifts tend to be in the battlefield or across a Wizr board. You did promise me a match, you may recall, if I brought the set.

   Since our departure, I have spoken to the court historian at Kingfountain. I suspect you may already know that, so I struggle how to write this without coming across as overly apprehensive. He related to me certain legends. One regards the imprisonment of a famous Wizr. Another story he told me was about a race of water sprites and one of their daughters. Her name was rather similar to yours—Peisinia. There are certain things I have noticed about you that give me questions I cannot answer. I will speak more freely when we next meet. Until then, I am ever your rough soldier and erstwhile intemperate friend.

   Owen

◆  ◆  ◆

# CHAPTER
# TWENTY-FOUR

*Genevieve Llewellyn*

Owen returned to the Star Chamber, but he could not focus on the heap of correspondence that awaited him despite the fact that such work strengthened his magic. He found himself gazing off into the stone hearth, plucking at strands of hair below his lip, experiencing the roiling guilt of a man in the process of betraying his king. Were it not for the snow falling silent and deadly on the grounds of Kingfountain at that very moment, he may well have reconsidered his brash act of defiance. But the soft flakes of white were a testament to Sinia's words. The boundaries set by the ancient Wizrs had been violated years ago when Severn broke the laws of sanctuary to capture Tunmore, and retribution would fall on Ceredigion until the hollow crown was passed to the rightful heir—a quiet young boy who had been groomed at Dundrennan to be a knight. Before dawn, Drew had watched his father's corpse being carried away and had seen his mother ensorcelled by a crouch-backed king whose passion for her had finally won the moment. Of course, Drew did not yet understand his true connection to any of them.

Owen sat back in his stuffed chair, feeling the quiet of the room enfold his shoulders. He was alone, mercifully alone, and his mind assembled the pieces of his strategy together like tiles to be knocked down. Orders had been sent to Captain Ashby to muster the army of Westmarch. If his other message had been received and heeded, Atabyrion would soon invade the North. Catsby would be forced to beg for help. Owen needed that to happen so he would have the excuse to go to Dundrennan and seek out the sword of the Maid of Donremy from the ice caves. Would it be difficult to find? Or would the magic of the blade call to him as the silver dish had done in Brythonica? He suspected he knew where to find the caves. The same river that gushed and tumbled outside Our Lady had its origin in the ancient glaciers in the North, beyond Dundrennan. The caves would be there, he surmised. If he got close enough, he thought he'd be able to sense the blade.

But before Iago Llewellyn would attack, he would need assurance that his daughter Genevieve was safely away. Owen rubbed his mouth and then steepled his fingers beneath his nose, thinking swiftly. Etayne could easily disguise the child and sneak her out of the palace. But there would be too many eyes watching. Owen shook his head. No, he needed to get her out at night or early in the morning, before too many people were watching. A memory sparked in his mind. The cistern beneath the palace led to the river. It was far enough upstream that the current would take them directly to Our Lady. Overshooting it would be fatal, of course. But that's how Tunmore had originally escaped to the sanctuary. As master of the Espion, Owen had ensured there was always a boat in that location. It was a secret way to flee the castle—one of Owen's many escape plans.

Genevieve was the tile that knocked over the rest. He saw that clearly in his mind. Once she was gone, his plan would take on momentum, and there would be no turning back. As the head of the Espion, Owen would be in charge of the investigation regarding her disappearance. He could confuse the situation by sending Espion to investigate possible treachery from Brugia, keeping all eyes away from the sanctuary and the little girl from Atabyrion.

A child could be unpredictable, as he well knew, but he would need to tell Genevieve at least part of his plan. Could he trust her? He was discomfited by the idea of putting his life in the hands of a little girl. One false word on her part could jeopardize everything. The thought instantly reminded him of when he, as a child himself, had pled with Ankarette to trust Evie with their secrets. What a risk the poisoner had taken. He would have to take the same risk, all the while knowing what the punishment would be if he were caught.

If Severn captured him, he wouldn't be sent over the falls. No, the Fountain-blessed could not be killed by the very waters that gave them their magic. Like the Maid of Donremy, Owen would be taken to a frigid mountain, chained there, and left to freeze to death. He closed his eyes as his heart thrummed with terror. For a moment, the panic was so paralyzing that he could only sit there in the stuffed chair, staring at the tongues of fire that taunted him from the hearth. He breathed out slowly, trying to regain composure. Was this all a horrible mistake? After all, his entire life had been devoted to Severn, to the belief that loyalty should be binding. And Duke Horwath, who had become a second father to him, had expected him to take on that oath.

The answer came to him quick. His promise of loyalty had been delivered to a different man, a different king. Severn was no longer the misunderstood regent he had once been. He had allowed himself to become corrupted, and now he was on the verge of destroying his own kingdom. Owen felt the press of duty like iron bands around his heart. He had a duty to the kingdom that superseded his duty to the king.

He had heard the Fountain's voice and message: Kathryn's son was the rightful Argentine to inherit the throne. It was his duty to see to it that it happened.

Owen leaned forward in the chair and swept his arm across the desk, spilling the mound of correspondence to the ground. He rose, walked purposefully to the door, and unlocked it. He marched down the hall, not stopping until he encountered Kevan Amrein bent in conversation with another Espion. As soon as he saw Owen, Kevan dismissed the other man.

"Grave news?" he asked.

Owen shook his head. "Trouble with Brugia, I think. I'm worried about our defenses at Callait. Can you send some men across the channel immediately? I've had some news that worries me. Can the castellan there be trusted?"

Kevan's face twisted with surprise. "Lord Ramey? He's a fine fellow, one of the staunchest allies in the realm. I wouldn't have a concern at all. Why? Do you suspect him?"

Owen shook his head. "No, he is a good fellow. But I have a suspicion, and it would ease my mind if you send some Espion there to poke around the defenses."

"Immediately, my lord," Kevan said. "Anything else?"

"I have a note for Genevieve from her mother that came through Clark." Clark had been assigned to Edonburick after Lord Bothwell's treason so he could be with his wife, Evie's maid, Justine. He missed his old friend. "Do you know where she is?"

Kevan thought a moment. "This time of day, she's normally in the king's library with Lady Kathryn. It's too frostbitten to play outside, or she'd be running around the grounds like a terror." The words were said with a small smile that revealed a fondness for the child.

Owen nodded and quickly slipped into the Espion tunnels to avoid being seen. When he reached the corridor adjacent to the library, he

slipped open the wooden slat so he could survey the room before entering. He found Genevieve as expected, kneeling on the floor over a Wizr
board. Drew was lying on the ground on the other side, and she was
teaching him different moves. Her hair was a lighter brown than her
mother's, but she shared many of the same expressions and features,
and it heartbreakingly reminded Owen of his first love. They too had
played Wizr together.

But as he watched the children, the pang of agony quickly dulled.
The wound wasn't as tender as it had once been. Owen blinked in
surprise. The sadness, which had long ago become a part of him, was
finally starting to dissipate. The memory of a little butterfly came to
him in that moment, bringing with it a curious warmth. It was a form
of magic, a powerful kind, and even he was not immune to it.

Looking past the children, he saw Kathryn standing by the window.
The whiteness from the sky beyond made her glow like some mystical
being. Her gaze was far away as she twisted the ring on her finger—the
one Severn had given her—and there was an interplay of conflicted
emotions on her face. Her mouth was twisted with sadness, but there
was hope in her expression as well. Her back was to the children, perhaps in an attempt to hide her struggle.

Owen softly released the latch and opened the hidden door so he
could slip into the room unobserved. The air had that musty quality
that prevailed wherever old books were kept, and he found himself
reminiscing about all the time he'd spent in this library himself, poring
over stories of other Fountain-blessed individuals.

Now that he was inside the room, he could hear the chattering
voices more clearly.

Genevieve was doing most of the talking. That wasn't a surprise.

"It's like this, Drew," she said patiently, adjusting the pieces again.
"Here, then here—threat and mate! You defeat them in four moves."
Strands of her nut-brown hair were braided around the back of her
neck, where they joined into a single braid going down her back. She

had hazel eyes, but they did not shift colors with her mood like her mother's did. Owen smiled to himself.

"And to block it," Drew said, his brow knit, "you bring this pawn over here at the beginning. Or move the knight over there." He tapped both pieces.

"Exactly!" she purred. "That's how you keep from being defeated in the first moments of the game. I have my own Wizr set at home. It's gray and white. My papa gave it to me when I was five. Do you have a set?" Even her voice sounded like Evie's!

Drew frowned a little. "No. I don't have very much."

She looked concerned at that. "Not even a set made of wood?"

He shook his head. "No one has ever let me play. But I like to watch."

"That's not right," she said a little indignantly. "I'm going to get you a set, Drew. It's not fair not to have one if you want one. I wish you could come back to Atabyrion with me. There is a place there called Wizr Falls!" She began to launch into a vivid description of a place Owen had once visited, and he watched with interest as Drew listened to her, his eyes widening with fascination as she spoke.

*The White King's queen.*

The whisper from the Fountain echoed his own thoughts. *The same story is told, over and over*, he reminded himself. These two children had been thrown together in a miasma of politics and intrigue. Genevieve was the king's hostage, just as Owen had once been. And while the names Andrew and Genevieve were commonplace now, it was perhaps more than coincidence that the parents had named their children thusly. The original Andrew's queen had come from a foreign alliance as well.

Owen looked up and noticed that Lady Kathryn had left the window and was staring down at the children, giving little Drew a heart-rending look of longing and pain. She slowly approached them and knelt down to watch them play and talk. Her fingers delicately grazed the boy's golden hair, and he looked up at her with a shy smile.

The realization that the boy didn't understand the tender gesture nearly broke Owen. Drew turned back to the game, listening keenly to Genevieve as she explained another series of maneuvers between the pieces.

"Now the Wizr piece is the most powerful one. It can move the farthest and challenge any other piece. One of the strategies people use is to try and kill that piece near the beginning of the game."

Drew frowned. "Why would they do that?"

"Because it's so powerful. Some people will sacrifice two or even three pieces to destroy it, even though it upsets the rest of their defenses."

Drew nodded with concern. "That's not fair. Do you think there are real Wizrs today?"

Owen chuckled to himself and both children turned to look at him.

"Oh, I didn't see you there," Genevieve said brightly. "You're Lord Owen."

"I am," he replied, dropping down on his haunches to be on their level. "Your mother taught you Wizr?" he asked her. From the corner of his eye, he noticed Lady Kathryn had tears swimming in hers as she stared at Drew. She quickly covered her mouth and retreated from the room, shutting the door quietly behind her.

Genevieve nodded briskly. "She did, but she learned it from you!"

Owen felt a little jolt of pain at the words, but behind that pain he felt a flush of gratification—Evie had told her children about him. She had attributed her knowledge of the game to him.

"It's true. I did teach her." He shifted his gaze to Drew. "And I can teach you as well, if you'd like."

Drew's face beamed. "I would!" he stammered. He looked surprised by the offer since they had rarely spent time together. Owen had treated him with no special regard until recently.

He took a deep breath and then lowered his voice. "Do you miss your parents, Genevieve? Do you wish you were back in Edonburick?"

Her eyes widened with surprise. "Of course! I like *visiting* Kingfountain. It's beautiful here. But the king is rude and mean and I don't like him very much. I think what Lord Catsby is doing to the North is abhorrent!"

Owen was startled by her use of the word. "Abhorrent is a *big* word for such a little girl."

"I know *many* big words, my lord," she said proudly. "I'm teaching some of them to Drew."

The boy seemed in awe of her.

"Can I ask you a question?" Genevieve asked him, her voice falling lower.

"You can ask me anything," he answered, his face becoming graver because he suddenly knew what she was going to say.

Genevieve sidled up closer to him, her face full of honesty and childlike courage. Just like her mother's had been at her age.

"Do you still love my mother?" she asked him.

She was so serious in her look, so trusting, that he knew he could not lie to her. Children could handle complex truths better than simplified falsehoods. He let out his breath, trying and discarding several answers before choosing one.

Finally, he gave her a wry smile. "How could anyone who knows your mother *ever* stop loving her?" Her smile became radiant. "Now that was a very delicate question, Genevieve Llewellyn. Let me add to my answer that while I still care for your mother, I would never do anything that would compromise or insult her in any way. We are friends. At one time, we hoped to be more, but life does not always pay us in the coin we expect."

Genevieve sat back a little and smiled knowingly. "I knew it. I've heard many stories about your mischiefs together. Like when you pulled her into the fountain in the outer lawns!"

"She pulled *me* in," Owen said.

Genevieve began to giggle infectiously. "I love hearing those stories. Thank you for telling me the truth, Lord Owen."

"There is one more truth I need to tell you," Owen said, trying not to be completely charmed by the little girl. Drew sat there mutely, listening to every word.

"I promised your mother at Dundrennan," Owen continued, "that I would help you escape."

Genevieve's eyes grew to the size of saucers. "You did?"

He nodded once.

"When?" she whispered eagerly.

"Tomorrow," he answered. Drew's face transformed from excitement to dread as he realized his playmate was about to be liberated and he, once again, would be left behind. Owen had to swallow a bulge in his throat.

He looked at the young man in a kindly way. "Don't worry, lad. I have plans for *you* as well."

# CHAPTER TWENTY-FIVE

## *A Game of Tiles*

There were so many threats, stratagems, worries, and heart-flutters colliding inside of Owen that he locked himself inside his state room at the palace with a box of tiles he'd stashed in an ancient wardrobe. He set it down in the middle of the floor and carefully removed the lid, staring down at the oblong pieces with a wistful smile. As he had grown older, his ability to replenish his Fountain magic had changed subtly. It wasn't the tiles themselves that did it, but the quiet solitude that helped him think and reason through difficult situations. A ride on horseback from one part of the realm to another could provide the same benefit. But with all his troubles of late, he relished the idea of immersing himself in the old craft he'd taught himself as a child.

Piece by piece, he began arranging the tiles into an elaborate structure. This was to be a tower he would knock over, a tower made of precarious tiles that would collapse in a rush when struck at its most vulnerable point.

As Owen worked, his mind turned to Sinia. He was anxious to check the box in the fountain for a note from her. He craved to see her delicate handwriting again. What would she write to him? How would he interpret it? There was a sort of deliciousness about the feeling that was new and exciting.

A memory struck him so keenly he felt as if he could physically see her. It was from that night on the beach with the glass beads. The wind had tousled her hair, and her hand had reached up to smooth it back. Her sandals had dangled off the crook of her finger. He blinked in surprise at the sudden rush of emotion that swelled his heart. After staring down at the tile in his hand for a moment, he continued to build his structure with a new objective. He would solve the riddle that was Sinia Montfort.

His mind combed through all their interactions as he stacked tile after tile, and a little flush of embarrassment came to his skin at the remembrance of how he'd treated her upon their first introduction. He'd been shamefully rude, but it hadn't angered her. There had been another look on her face instead—one of disappointment. How curious. How could someone be disappointed in a stranger?

It may have been the first time they had met, he realized, but it was not their first interaction. She had caused the storm at the battle of Averanche. She had told him as much. So why hadn't she revealed herself to him then?

He felt the Fountain magic flow inside him, sharpening his instincts and insights, as he continued to stack the tiles. Pieces started to slide together in his mind, disparate joints forming a unique whole. He started to look at the events of the past from her point of view, and suddenly it all began to make sense.

There was a child in Ceredigion reported to be Fountain-blessed. A hostage of King Severn who could see the future, like Myrddin of old. How would such news have been received by a young girl, his own age at the time, who actually *did* possess that power? Wouldn't it have excited her? Did she know the truth about Owen, or did the stories ignite her imagination?

But if she had visited him through the Fountain, she would have realized how close he was to another little girl, the granddaughter of the Duke of North Cumbria. Had their obvious affection for each other disappointed Sinia? Is that why she had remained aloof?

Owen placed the pieces on the tower faster now as it grew in size, each new row shorter than the one below it.

A memory stirred to life in his mind—the first day he had seen the treasure of the Fountain in the waters of the cistern. Evie had not been able to see it, and it had angered him that she didn't believe him. And then Ratcliffe had tried to kill them by opening the cistern to drain it into the river. Owen had struggled to save his own life and Evie's. In that panicky moment, he had felt the Fountain magic bidding him to . . . to *breathe*.

*Nesh-ama.*

A prickle of gooseflesh shot down his arms. Had the voice truly been the Fountain? Or had it been Sinia's?

His hand wobbled, and he almost ruined the tower he was building. He dropped his hand into his lap, his eyes widening with wonder. Had Sinia been communicating with him all this while? Was *she* the voice of the Fountain? Had she, a little girl herself, seen visions of the Kiskaddon boy through her mantic gifts? Had she used her magic to save him from drowning?

What if she had continued to watch him from afar? Perhaps she had known for years they were fated to meet for the first time in Brythonica, when he came to propose marriage to her. Is that why she hadn't extended herself to him before?

He sat still, his mind whirling. Then another memory came. She *had* reached out. Not to him directly, but through Severn. The King of Occitania had been determined to force Sinia to marry him. To escape his advances, she had reached out to Ceredigion for help. Had she known Owen would be sent to help? Of course she had! Just as she'd known he would surprise Chatriyon's army in the middle of the night. That was why Marshal Roux had been waiting for them that night. Owen and Sinia had worked side by side to keep the Occitanian king at bay. Because she hadn't *wanted* to marry Chatriyon.

She had wanted to marry Owen.

The insight crystalized inside his mind, shaped into certainty by a surge of Fountain magic. Sinia had known he was in love with Evie, and she had known what was going to happen to his heart when his first love was denied to him. He realized with astonishment that she had suffered the same pangs herself because she, as a little girl, had fallen in love with a boy she'd never met. One she had seen only in her visions.

Sinia had been in love with him all along, suffering silently while watching him consume himself in grief and despair. She'd probably hoped to comfort him, since it was her nature to want to alleviate the suffering of others. He had never considered it a possibility. Her quick acceptance of his proposal wasn't an indication that she had outsmarted him. It was her greatest hope. And *he* had handled the whole thing in the most shameful and offensive way possible. He'd alienated her entire court, ridiculing their governor and ruler, whom they respected and admired. *That* was why she had acted disappointed.

He got on his feet and began pacing. "You fool, you fool, you fool," he muttered to himself. He wanted to pore over her notes again, but he had taken to storing the notes in the Wizr box.

"I am the world's biggest idiot," he said again, shaking his head. He looked down at the mostly completed tower, a monument representing years of folly.

He and Sinia were suited for each other. She was calm and peaceful. They shared gifts from the Fountain, gifts that would be a huge help to any monarch they served, but especially to a young boy who would be on the verge of manhood in a few years.

*Elysabeth*, a voice whispered in his mind.

Genevieve had asked him directly if he still loved her. Of course he did. They had shared so many memories. She'd been his truest friend and faithful companion. There was nothing in their relationship that he regretted now, no liberties taken that could sully their connection. In his heart, Owen knew that the marriage had made Iago Llewellyn a better man and king, and in his estimation, Atabyrion's queen had improved her new country's standing in the world through her wisdom, guidance, and strengths. Elysabeth loved her husband and her children. Owen had secretly hoped it would be otherwise, that she would pine for him as he had pined for her.

That had to stop. Immediately. He was betrothed to a person who loved him, one he knew he could love. The raging inferno inside his chest was evidence that he could feel again. The time had come.

He hungered for a way to demonstrate to her that his heart was changing. When would he be able to see her again? She had written in her note that he should send Genevieve into the mist when it appeared. Would he have the opportunity to see her? He wanted to apologize for his early behavior, to learn more about her true nature and whether she was in truth a water sprite. But more than that, he wanted to prove to her that she hadn't waited for him in vain. Wasn't it her greatest concern that he, like the Owain of legend, would be unfaithful to her?

Why had she fallen in love with him in the first place, knowing how things would start between them?

The idea struck him like a thunderbolt.

Perhaps she had foreseen who he would *become.*

"I am right, I know I am," he whispered to himself. The magic inside him confirmed the truth.

He heard a noise, and as he turned, he saw the secret door swing open, and Etayne rushed inside, shutting it forcefully behind her. The look of fear and dread in her eyes made Owen's stomach sink.

"What is it?" Owen asked, fear snaking through his legs.

"My father found me," she whispered in terror.

# CHAPTER
# TWENTY-SIX

## *Poisoner's Revenge*

"Tell me what happened," Owen said in a steady voice. It required all of his self-discipline not to panic. He would try to turn whatever news she brought to an advantage.

"Somehow he discovered my tower," Etayne said, pacing back and forth in the short space between them. "His power concealed him from me, but I sensed the Fountain magic in the room with me."

It was the king who had turned the skilled thief loose in the palace. He'd even given him an Espion ring. Owen was flooded with a new rush of anger; yes, Severn had fallen far.

"I drew my dagger, and that's when he appeared," Etayne said, shuddering. "He'd been rifling through my things. My poisons were in disarray. I still don't know if he took any. He'd gone through my clothes, stolen jewelry." Her lips were tight with fury. "That has been *my* sanctuary, my refuge! He's spoiled it! I can't stay there anymore, not now that he knows where I live. I should have killed him when I had the chance." She shook her head furiously. "I should have!"

"What did he want?"

Her scowl turned into a grimace. "He wanted me to help him get access to *you*."

Owen started. "What?"

She nodded. "It was all I could do not to slit his gullet. I hate him, Owen. You can't know how much I hate him! I'm sorry I'm so emotional right now. Give me a moment to calm down."

"You have every right to be upset!"

"I'm better than that. He caught me by surprise, that's all. I didn't think he'd find his way into my tower, but I should have realized he would eventually. I was right. He recognized me that day the two of us went to see him in the dungeon. He's been asking around about the King's Poisoner." She shook her head in frustration. "He's happy to betray anyone for the right price. First the Duke of Brugia to set Eyric loose. Then Severn to capture him. He admitted to it all, Owen. He's only after the money. The only thing that binds him is greed!"

Owen felt his resentment grow hotter. "I can't have him running about like this."

Etayne threw up her hands. "He can turn invisible! He told me he *let* himself get caught by the Espion. Owen, Chatriyon is furious about your betrothal to the duchess. Word has spread like a spilled chalice of wine, and everyone is talking about it in foreign courts. At least that's what my father said. Chatriyon has ordered his poisoner to remove you. We've met him before."

"Bothwell?" Owen said, aghast.

Etayne nodded. "Foulcart. That's his poisoner name. Remember how he duped us on our visit to Atabyrion? He wants revenge for personal reasons too, I assure you. No poisoner likes to be bested, and he hasn't forgotten how we unmasked him in Iago's court. My father said he's in the city already, and has offered him a sizable sum to get him access to you." Her eyes were livid. "That's why I didn't kill him. If he knows how to find Bothwell, then perhaps we can turn the tables on him."

Owen let out his breath. "What did you tell Dragan?"

She was tormented by her feelings and it showed. "I . . . I hesitated. Probably too much. He's very suspicious. I said I take my orders from the king. That he pays me more to keep you alive than Bothwell was offering." She twisted her hands together. "My father said that blood is worth more than gold. That I should help him out of duty." She put one hand on the table to steady herself. "You don't understand how much I hate him. He doesn't know . . . he thinks I'm only a poisoner because of the coin. He said that Chatriyon would pay me far more than Severn if I betrayed you to him." She gave him a look full of anguish. "But he doesn't know that I could *never* hurt you. What do we do? You're the clever one. I can't think clearly right now."

Anger crashed inside Owen like waves at the sight of his old friend so vulnerable. So King Chatriyon of Occitania wanted retribution for past humiliations? Bothwell's disadvantages were considerable. Owen and Etayne both knew what he looked like. He also wasn't Fountain-blessed, which gave them additional advantages over him. They needed to strip Dragan of his power. An idea struck him and he straightened, snapping his fingers.

Etayne gave him a hopeful look.

"Thank you for coming straightaway," he told her, and he meant it. He hadn't taken her loyalty for granted before, and he certainly wasn't going to do so now. "I can't imagine how difficult that encounter must have been for you. We can't allow someone like Dragan to poke around the palace any longer. There is too much at risk. We need to get Genevieve out of here tonight, under the cover of darkness. I don't want to wait until morning. You'll come with us. I want you to use your magic to disguise me as your father."

She looked horrified by the idea of Owen impersonating her father.

He smiled at her expression. "Just long enough for people to see us, Etayne. When she goes missing, I want witnesses to implicate *him* in her disappearance. If Severn thinks he's betrayed him, your father's life will become infinitely more difficult, and he'll be too busy trying to save his own neck to help Bothwell. When he next comes to you, arrange for a meeting. Tell him you want fifty thousand crowns. A hundred thousand. The higher the better. Then arrange a place to meet, and I'll have Kevan swarm it with Espion. See? We'll use this news to our advantage. I don't fear your father as you do."

Etayne looked somewhat mollified, but he could tell she was still reeling from the encounter. "You should, Owen. I've never known a man so relentless and cruel. He will get what he feels he's due. And he probably knows he'd survive a boat over the falls."

Owen looked at her seriously. "Oh, but we wouldn't send *him* over the falls. He'd be taken to the North and dragged atop an icy mountain." He took a step toward her. "I won't let him hurt you, Etayne."

The room filled with tension, and he could tell part of her misery was due to her feelings for him. She shook her head. "No . . . I won't let him hurt *you*."

He sighed. "I want you to take your things and move them here. This will be your room for now." Her tower was compromised. She couldn't return now that Dragan knew how to find her.

A look of surprise and hope brightened her eyes.

"I will find lodgings elsewhere," he said quickly. "In fact, it might be best for me to bed down somewhere different every night. Having a routine will make it too easy to find me. If I were Bothwell, I'd be at an inn on the bridge with a view of the palace gates. He's probably planning to wait for me to ride back to Tatton Hall so he can ambush me on the road."

"I don't want you to give up your rooms," she said, her tone thick with disappointment. "There are places I could go as well."

He shook his head no. "But if anyone comes here to kill me, you'll be able to capture and question them."

She smiled slyly at him. "Very well, my lord. What next?"

He rubbed his hands together. "Have you ever steered a boat in a river headed toward the falls before?"

◆ ◆ ◆

The palace of Kingfountain never truly slept. There were guards who roamed the corridors at night, carrying torches to brighten the way. But the Espion tunnels behind the walls made for a faster mode of travel. Etayne had arranged disguises for all of them. She'd used her powders and pencils to line her face and the corners of her eyes, transforming herself into a matronly looking woman. Owen had seen her impersonate her mother before and realized what she was doing. She had used a blade and lathering soap to give Owen a shave, keeping the whiskers on the side and a mustache, but removing the rest. In the morning, she said she'd shave him smooth the rest of the way to make it less conspicuous.

After darkness fell, they stole into Genevieve's room through the secret passages and found her wide awake, unable to sleep due to her excitement for the coming dawn.

"We're leaving tonight instead?" she repeated eagerly after Owen explained the situation. "And we're taking the secret tunnels in the palace? This is just like the stories Mama used to tell me!"

"Exactly so," Owen said. "You will have stories of your own to tell her when you get back to Edonburick."

Her eyes gleamed. "What about Drew?"

Owen shook his head no and saw the disappointment fall over her face. "He'll be worried if I don't at least say good-bye. I don't want him to worry."

Owen felt his patience begin to slip, but then he remembered how Ankarette had always treated him. He dropped down on one knee and put his hand on the little girl's shoulder. "I will tell him good-bye for you, Genevieve." He glanced at Etayne before looking back at the girl. "We learned tonight that a poisoner is coming to the castle."

Genevieve's expression was a mixture of fear and wonder. "Truly?"

Owen nodded. "I promised your mama I'd keep you safe. We're getting into a boat and going into the river. Drew must stay behind, but do not worry. I will look after him for you." He felt a tug in his heart. "I feel certain you'll see him again."

She beamed at that and then nodded eagerly.

Owen rose and led the way back into the tunnels. He used his magic to reach out around them, feeling for hidden dangers or threats. Stacking the tiles earlier had filled him to the brim with Fountain magic, and he thought it wise to anticipate trouble instead of reacting to it. He also kept his senses alert for signs of other magic, in case Dragan was lurking in the dark tunnels.

When they reached the cistern, the moon was hanging high overhead, casting their shadows on the ground. The moon was ringed with frost-light and their boots crunched in the snow as they crossed the courtyard. The walls of the castle were outlined in white, and drifts had already begun to gather in heaps. The cold air stung his nose. Owen paused at the dark opening that allowed the water to drain into the cistern. Genevieve had linked hands with him as they walked in the tunnels, as children were wont to do. It was strangely comforting feeling her hand in his own, and it made him think about what it would be like to be a father himself someday. She tightened her grip and bent over the hole, gazing down.

"You two jumped down here?" she asked him, staring into the gloomy cistern hole. Owen knew from experience that it was a long drop to the waters of the vast cistern that ran the length of the palace.

"We did," he answered with a wry smile. "But the water will be too cold right now. There's another way down. Over there." He pointed.

They walked over, and before Owen tripped the latch, he used his magic to once again feel for any threats awaiting them. Etayne, who was bundled up in a cloak, walked behind them, and she continually looked for any sign of pursuit. Only stillness met them, and Owen felt satisfied no one was lying in wait for them.

He tripped the latch of the door and led Genevieve down the dark steps without a torch. Etayne shut the door behind them.

"Careful," Owen said, his voice suddenly echoing. "It drops off into the water on that side. There's no railing." Now that they were belowground, he drew a torch from his bag and handed it to Etayne so he could smash two flint stones to light it. The rippling flames from the torch radiated warmth and light, revealing how pink Genevieve's nose had become in the cold. She looked fearful in the vast underground chasm, but if all went well, she would soon be safe. The boat was right where Owen had left it. Still, he examined both the craft and the oars carefully before hauling it into the water.

Etayne held the light, but she turned around and cocked her head, listening to some distant sound. Owen froze.

After a moment, she shook her head.

Owen got into the boat first and felt it bob with his weight. Using an oar to hook the edge of the platform, he reached for Genevieve's hand and helped her inside. She sat on a small wooden ledge and gazed up at the cavernous ceiling as the waters lapped fitfully against the hull. Etayne entered next and the boat swayed more, but it steadied as soon as she sat down.

Using the oar, Owen shoved off and began rowing them down the vast corridor. As they traversed the waterway beneath the palace, the torchlight exposed the thick stone columns that held up the colossal structure. The light reflected off the surface of the water, and Owen could see the secret treasure of the Deep Fathoms glistening at the bottom. He looked up and almost did a double take when he saw Etayne gazing over the side of the boat with wide eyes.

"You can see it?" he asked her.

"See what?" Genevieve interrupted.

"Do you see anything in the water?" Etayne asked the girl, putting her hand on her shoulder.

Genevieve looked over the edge for a moment and then shook her head. "No."

Etayne met Owen's gaze and then subtly nodded.

They glided to the end of the cistern, where the gate controlled the flood of the water. This was where Owen and Evie had nearly drowned or been swept away. Owen could see the control winches and levers in the dim torchlight. He also saw the breath wafting from his mouth and felt the numbness in his fingers. Winter was coming on fast—yet another sign they needed to move quickly.

He brought the boat up to the edge, maneuvering it until it was sideways along the grille. "The cistern drains into the river from here," he told them, including Genevieve to help reassure her. "It's nearly full. When you pull the lever, the winch begins to open, and when you let go, it takes a few seconds to close again. You can lock it open if you want to drain the entire cistern, but we won't be doing that." He looked at both of them with an adventurous smile. "Ready?"

Genevieve was almost aglow with excitement. Etayne waved the torch in the direction of the water, asking him silently if she should douse it. Owen gripped the lever handle and then nodded. The torch hissed as it hit the frigid water, leaving them in pitch blackness.

The darkness was so acute that sounds took on new significance. Owen could actually hear Genevieve's teeth chattering. He pulled the lever, and the current dragged them out of the cistern in moments, sending them onto a pitched slope that would jettison them into the river. Releasing the handle, he grabbed the other oar.

Genevieve let out a little squeak of fright as the boat rushed down the short ramp and then splashed violently into the river. The roar of the falls instantly surrounded them, and Owen felt a pang of fear as he began to steer toward the island ahead of them. Sanctuary. His heart was pounding in his chest, but he couldn't help but grin a little at the audacity of what he was doing. The little girl gripped each side of the boat, facing forward, and smiled brightly, as if she didn't comprehend the danger of the powerful falls.

Owen had made the journey twice before, so he knew what to expect, but it still sent a little thrill through him. The moon shone brightly overhead, revealing both his path and his companions. While Genevieve looked as excited as her mother might have, Etayne was clutching the side of the boat. The river was such a vibrant force of nature—a creator of both destiny and death. The island of the sanctuary of Our Lady loomed up before them, and Owen carefully steered toward the inlet on the opposite side. There were little docks nestled there and a few small boats. It took several very strong men to row against such a powerful current. This journey would be one-way.

Owen maneuvered the boat to the dock, using the flat of the oar to slow them down so they wouldn't collide with it. The boat began to pitch and tug back toward the river current, but he paddled hard to correct it. When they reached the edge of the dock, he grabbed the mooring post.

"You first," he told Etayne, trying to keep the boat from rocking. The water from the river churned beneath them, colliding with the rocks before veering toward the roaring sound farther ahead. The falls. Etayne bent low and then scuttled up to the dock. It was dark and cold, and Owen was full of nervous energy. Anxious to get ashore as quickly as possible, he grabbed the chain and began anchoring it to the mooring post.

"I can get out myself," Genevieve said, standing up. Her sudden movement made the boat wobble alarmingly.

"Take my hand," Etayne said, reaching down from the dock to grab the girl.

"I can do it!" Genevieve said, looking up at her with the type of confidence reserved for the young and inexperienced. Owen felt a surge of unease, and then watched in horror as she missed her footing. At exactly the wrong moment, the boat lurched and the edge dipped below the river. Water rushed into the tiny boat and jerked it hard against the chain. Everything went into chaos in the blink of an eye.

There was a splash as the little girl went into the river.

◆  ◆  ◆

*Dear Owen,*

*Thank you so much for your letter and your warning. What is happening in Ceredigion feels unnatural. Iago and I have felt helpless to do anything. But thanks to you and your offer to rescue our daughter, Atabyrion will faithfully join your cause. We must tread carefully, my dear friend. History is full of examples of both successful usurpations and the consequences of failure. But I am equally certain that you are more canny and cunning than your king. If you feel this is the only way, then I will trust it. I'm sending this note by my husband's hand. Thank the duchess for her willing help and assistance. I will be so relieved when I'm holding Genevieve in my arms once again. Every day without her has been a torment.*

> *Yours with loyalty,*
> *Elysabeth Victoria Mortimer Llewellyn*
> *Queen of Atabyrion*

◆  ◆  ◆

# CHAPTER TWENTY-SEVEN

### *The Fountain's Ring*

There were no words to describe Owen's feelings when he heard the sound of Genevieve plunging into the river. There wasn't even time for him to think about what he should do; he leaped into the water after her without pausing to rationalize or debate. There was no way he was going to face the child's mother without her. He'd rather die himself.

As the shock of the frigid river water smashed into him, the cold so fast and sudden he feared even his memories would freeze, he groped to catch some piece of her cloak, her hair, anything. He had a vague sense that he might survive the waterfall because he was Fountain-blessed, and he could only hope that having her with him might make a difference.

And then light and pain exploded from his hand.

The river still had him in its grip, but suddenly his hand was burning with pain. His knees bit into harsh stone and he found himself in some sort of roaring pit. The light was everywhere, and it took a long moment for his eyes to adjust to it. The roar of the river and the falls thundered in his ears, and to his shock, he felt himself gasping and breathing air and not water. He heard someone screaming for help, the tiny voice nearly lost amidst the cacophony.

Owen's clothes were no longer soggy and weighing on him, and even his hair had dried. He lifted his head and hand, trying to ward off the rays of light, only then realizing that the light was emanating from the ring on his finger, the ring he'd pulled from Marshal Roux's dead hand. The betrothal ring that Sinia had placed on him herself.

There was Genevieve.

She was huddled on some dry stones just ahead of him, reaching out to him and crying. Just past her, the water of the river had converged again, a violent mass of waves that threatened to suck her back into the river.

Owen clambered forward, grabbed her outstretched arm with his right hand, and pulled her to him. She grabbed his tunic and buried her face against his shirt, sobbing with combined terror and relief. Lifting his head, Owen saw that the river had been shunted away from the rocky wall of the island through the power of the ring. The dock posts were exposed, as were the slick, smooth stones that normally lay beneath the waves. The relentless power of the river had broken away the boat he had attempted to tether there, and it was now hurtling downstream to meet its fate at the falls. He saw Etayne kneeling at the dock, reaching out to them, her face full of panic and awe as she beheld the river parting away from Owen and the child.

The ring burned on his finger so fiercely, he feared he'd lose his entire hand as a result of its magic. His mind could not grasp a power that was strong enough to turn a river out of its course, especially a river as mighty as the one serving Kingfountain. Trying not to look at the blinding light of the ring, he carried Genevieve clumsily up the rocky cliff.

He stumbled a bit and then hoisted the child up into Etayne's arms. As he moved closer to the dock, the river began to fill in behind him, showing that the protection he had experienced was limited and temporary. How long would the magic last? He had no desire to test it. The dock posts were black and slick, and he stumbled against the uneven boulders strewn at their base. Genevieve was safe again, thank the Fountain, so he reached up and caught Etayne's hand himself, letting her help him up next.

As soon as his boots cleared, the light in the ring vanished and he felt the river hammer once again at the dock, the power of the water rocking and shaking it. He knelt there, breathing down his terror in fearful gasps, and saw Genevieve staring at him with huge eyes.

"Mother was right. You . . . you truly *are* Fountain-blessed!" she said reverently. Then, with all the effusion of a child, she flung her arms around his neck and started to weep again, this time with gratitude. She thanked him over and over, mumbling her apology for being so clumsy.

Owen rocked back on his boots a bit, feeling so grateful for the ring he wore on his hand. He patted her back with one arm and then examined his hand, afraid of what he'd find. The finger that held the ring was dark and bruised beyond recognition. It hurt terribly, but he felt a surge of warmth envelop his body, sending healing waves. He noticed the scabbard was glowing again, although the incandescence was only visible to his eyes.

Etayne was kneeling beside him, looking at him with so much relief, her hands folded prayer-like in front of her. Even though she'd disguised herself as her mother, he could see the true woman beneath the concealment.

Genevieve pulled away and looked down at Owen's hand. Just like him, Genevieve was dry, as were her clothes and hair. He smoothed down her dark tresses, astonished at this demonstration of the Fountain's power. Had Sinia known he would need the ring's protection? He suspected so, and felt a throb of warmth for her.

Etayne took his hand, and he watched her press her lips to the ring like a benediction. His breath was finally starting to calm.

"Let's get away from the river," he managed to say.

Etayne looked like she wanted to start weeping. She smiled through her tears and nodded vigorously at the suggestion.

◆　◆　◆

At dawn, the sexton of the sanctuary of Our Lady unlocked the gates and pulled them open with a groan. There were many who had gathered outside in anticipation, waiting with their coins in hand to make an offering to one of the many fountains. One young couple whispered of their hope to be blessed with a babe. A grieving father had spoken of his boy slipping on an icy street and cracking his skull the night before. When the gate finally opened, Owen led Genevieve through the aperture, Etayne's magic rippling gently around them.

The sexton gave Owen a wary look of recognition as he passed, something he had been counting on. The man's lip curled into a warning sneer, but he said nothing. Owen tipped his head at the man and gave him a mocking smile, knowing full well that his face was the twin of Dragan's.

"Come along, lass," he said gruffly to Genevieve. "Shan't keep your papa waiting."

Once inside the grounds, the supplicants gathered into the interior of the sanctuary where the cold of the early winter was dispelled by braziers lit with fresh coals. The trio stood by one of them, chafing their hands and trying to get warm again.

A man sauntered up to Owen, someone who, judging from his expression, clearly knew Dragan.

"What's this about, eh?" the man said with a bit of defiance in his tone. "Who's the chit?" he demanded, nodding to the little girl.

"Never you mind," Owen said, mimicking Dragan's tone of voice. He felt Etayne's magic washing over the man, convincing him utterly. "What news?"

"That Espion bloke Amrein has been snooping around for ya. I'd knife him if I wuz you. Watch out for him. Any luck inside the palace?" He looked cautiously around. "Bothwell's in a temper. He needs to get this done, and fast. It's a lot of *money*, Dragan." He was almost whining in anticipation.

"I've got it all figured, you see. You tell Bothwell I can get him in. Now go, the sexton's looking this way. Go!"

The man nodded and then hurried off.

Owen traded glances with Etayne. "I think our visit served its purpose. If we wait here until noon, who knows who might show up to talk."

"I think this is wonderful," Genevieve said in a low voice. "I've never seen such magic. Even though I know who you *really* are, I still can't tell for sure. I'm a little afraid. Where are we going?"

"We're meeting the Duchess of Brythonica at one of the fountains in the back," Owen said. "We agreed on noon, which is hours away. But maybe she'll be able to sense us if we go near. Walk with me. We won't stay there long if she doesn't come right away."

Etayne nodded and fell in step with Owen. He felt the magic moving along with him, giving his walk a little limp and swagger. The power came from the poisoner's intricate memory of the man, and while he could resist the magic, he let it work on him to complete the illusion. There was power in wearing masks. He actually felt decades older, even though he knew it was just a mirage.

When they reached the little alcove, he stared into the fountain's placid, coin-speckled waters and summoned the chest. There was no one else in the immediate area, but there were many passersby near them. Owen tugged on Genevieve's hand and directed her to the other side of the fountain, where they were less likely to be seen. As they'd planned, Etayne lingered by the entryway, glancing at the crowd and keeping an eye out for her father.

"Look!" Genevieve said with excitement, pointing at the waters as they started to froth and bubble. A thick, roiling mist rose up from the churning surface, veiling the room. Owen could no longer see Etayne. Genevieve looked at the mist eagerly, without any apparent fear. "Is she coming?"

"She is," Owen said, feeling his own heart begin to mimic the waters.

Then Sinia appeared in the mist, walking from the center of the pool toward them. She wore a different gown than the last one he'd seen her in—it was lavender in color with a lacy bodice and cuffs. Owen didn't want to greet her as Dragan, so with a thought, he repelled Etayne's magic and let the facade slough off.

"Genevieve Llewellyn, meet Sinia Montfort, the Duchess of Brythonica," Owen said. He gave her a look of warmth and pleasure, trying to tell her without words that he knew all. That he was grateful for her and all she had done for him.

Sinia started when she saw the look on his face, but she regained her composure quickly, her anxiety turning to smiles and tenderness as she looked at Evie's daughter. "Hello, Genevieve," she said. "Your papa arrived with the tide this morning."

"He did?" Genevieve asked, startled now. "Where is he?"

"At the sanctuary of Our Lady of Toussan," Sinia replied. "Where I just came from. It's the chief sanctuary in my realm, like Kingfountain is in Ceredigion. He's as eager to see his little girl as you are to see him! Come with me. I told him I'd be back straightaway."

Genevieve reached out to take the proffered hand, but then she looked up at Owen once more and threw her arms around him. "Thank you for saving me," she mumbled. "I can never thank you enough. Here, I must kiss you. Kneel down."

Owen felt chagrined, but he dropped down to one knee as requested. Sinia was staring at him with something like amazement, one hand covering her mouth. He'd never seen her look at him that way, but she looked—it wasn't distraught—overwhelmed.

Owen felt the warm lips press against his cheek where Etayne had shaved him earlier. Relief flooded him. For just a moment, he had experienced the utter devastation that had haunted Severn for so long. Losing his brother's children was a blow from which the king had never recovered. Owen did not understand how someone *could* recover. The insight made him feel an unbidden pang of sympathy for the man he'd served—the man he was now betraying.

"You're welcome," Owen said, patting the little girl's cheek in return. "I promised your mother I'd keep you safe."

Genevieve gave him another radiant smile and then took Sinia's hand and stepped over the wall of the fountain. Owen stood and met his betrothed's eyes, surprised when he saw they were wet with tears.

"You didn't know what would happen?" he asked.

She blinked quickly, trying to regain her composure. "Years ago," she whispered, "I had a vision of you saving a little girl's life. In the vision you had whiskers and such, so I thought it was more deeply in the future." She swallowed again, her emotions filled to the brim. "I saw the ring save you. So I knew, back then, that you needed to have that ring for such a moment." She shook her head. "But I had no idea it would happen this soon. You had shaved it into a different shape, after all," she said shyly, reaching out and grazing the edge of her finger against his chin. The touch made him shiver.

She glanced down at his hand. "It's healing quickly," she said, nodding with satisfaction. "The ring is powerful. If you hold on to the magic too long, it *will* kill you. But with the scabbard, you will not be scarred."

Owen liked seeing her so discomfited on his behalf. He smiled at her and watched her cheeks flush with pink. "Well, I had to shave to look the part," he said offhandedly. "But I don't intend to keep the whiskers long. Unless you like them?"

She looked agitated and flustered, which made him long to reach out and touch her. She shook her head no, but wouldn't meet his eyes.

"That's good, because I plan to shave the rest off this morning," he said. He gave in to temptation and reached out and took her hand. "Thank you, Sinia. Thank you for making sure I was wearing that ring." He kept his voice low. "I wouldn't have survived otherwise."

She looked up, seeing his face again. A timid smile crept onto her mouth. "I know," she answered. Then she blinked. "I almost forgot. Iago wanted me to give this to you. It's from her *mother*." Owen was impressed that she'd mentioned Elysabeth without flinching. She withdrew the sealed note from her girdle and placed it in Owen's hand. He stuffed it quickly into his pocket to read later, but did not let go of her hand.

"It has begun," he told Sinia.

"It has," she agreed.

It was the breath before the plunge.

# CHAPTER
# TWENTY-EIGHT

### *The King's Wrath*

The hearth in the throne room had been stoked with enormous logs and was blazing, but the cavernous space had an unshakable chill. It was the second morning since Genevieve's disappearance, and the king's wrath was terrible to behold. He'd cast out the guests in a fury so he could receive an update from Kevan.

"I said, begone!" Severn shouted at a serving girl who was hastily trying to clean up a spilled platter. The girl went white and fled the room.

Owen had positioned himself near the doors, and was watching as Kevan brooked the king's temper with as much courage as he could muster. The Espion were in disgrace again. Owen struggled to conceal a smirk—his ruse was working exactly as he'd planned, although he hated to see Kevan endure the brunt of the king's anger. He saw Drew approach the door, trying to slip away with the rest. The lad had a worried look on his face, but Owen caught his eye and winked at him as he neared the door.

Drew's face brightened in an instant. Owen nodded to him and then whispered the word *library* as he passed.

Lady Kathryn was still standing by the dais, and she too bore a worried look. Genevieve's disappearance had caused her deep anxiety, but Owen hadn't dared tell her the truth. He would try to later if he could manage it discreetly.

Owen nodded to the guardsmen to shut the door and then approached the king, who continued to rail on Kevan.

"What is it, I ask you, about the Espion being unable to keep track of little children!" Severn said contemptuously. "I want answers, Kevan, and they best be good ones!"

"My lord," the Espion said, discouraged. "I've had everyone I can spare—"

"You can spare!" the king thundered, interrupting him. "I told you to put every spy in the city on alert!"

"Let him speak, my lord," Owen said, closing the distance. "Curb your temper a moment, if you can."

The king shot Owen an angry look, his lips trembling with rage.

Kevan gave Owen a grateful nod and shrugged helplessly. "We don't know how she got out of the castle. She simply disappeared. When her chambermaid arrived in the morning to light the fire, her bed was empty. It would appear she's been kidnapped."

"But how? How could she have been removed from the city without anyone knowing?" the king asked in exasperation.

"We've secured the roads, the port, searched every ship in the harbor, Atabyrion or not," Kevan explained. "The only lead we had has led to nothing."

"What lead?" Severn demanded. "I should toss out the lot of you. Why do I pay for a spy service that botches everything!"

"Tell him, Kevan," Owen said.

"Tell me what?"

Kevan swallowed, as if to banish his rising impatience. "I heard a rumor that the sexton of the sanctuary may have seen her yesterday morning. I went and spoke to him myself. He described a man and a woman who were at the gates when the sanctuary opened. They had a little girl with them who matched Genevieve's description. The sexton swore by it. The man he described to me may have been Dragan. Do you remember him, my lord? The thief we captured who tried to release Eyric?"

Owen watched as the expression on the king's face shifted from anger to recognition, then to betrayal. Kevan may not have noticed the subtle changes, but Owen had been studying him closely.

"Yes . . . yes, I do," the king stammered.

Kevan scratched his ear. "The sexton swears he saw them enter but not leave. I asked the deconeus if the girl had claimed sanctuary, but he looked as surprised as I've ever seen a man. No one had claimed sanctuary that day, and it was the first he'd even heard about the girl. I had men search the entire premises yesterday, from basement to loft. Every crate, every bushel, every closet. I thought I'd have good news for you today, my lord, but there was no sign of her there or at the port."

Owen stepped forward. "My lord, after hearing Kevan's report, it's my belief that this Dragan fellow was involved in Genevieve's disappearance. I also believe, my lord, that he has some sort of special access to the palace. I don't have any proof, but I believe he may be Fountain-blessed. If so, that makes him a dangerous threat. Imagine what will happen if Iago finds out. You would be blamed for it."

The king's eyes narrowed at the deliberate reference to his nephews who'd disappeared.

"I had no hand in this," the king said, but his voice had lost confidence and bluster.

"Of course not, my lord," Owen said sympathetically. "But that won't stop Iago and Elysabeth from assuming the worst. I fear my vision will come to pass and we will be invaded by all the other kingdoms. I know you sent Catsby to the North, but I have a suspicion that they will turn on him like wolves if Stiev's granddaughter shows up with war banners. If we lose our grip on the North, we lose a significant number of once-loyal soldiers, the core of your supporters!"

The king rubbed his mouth and started pacing with a pronounced limp.

Owen glanced at Lady Kathryn, who seemed keenly interested in the conversation. Was she piecing the clues together on her own in a way that Severn couldn't?

"What do you suggest then?" the king asked Owen.

"I've ordered the Espion to hunt down this Dragan fellow. I think there are some questions he must answer."

The king looked firm and resolved. "I want you to bring him to me when you catch him."

Owen bowed respectfully. "Kevan will see to it right away."

Severn looked confused. "If he's Fountain-blessed, shouldn't you oversee it?"

Owen shook his head. "My lord, I think it would be wise if you sent me to the North. Catsby has managed to offend every lesser noble and the entire staff of Dundrennan. I know those people, having spent much of my childhood there. Let me see if I can rally them. I've already ordered Captain Ashby to muster my army and start marching to Beestone castle. Then, depending on where we're invaded, I can split the army if needed. I've sent word to the Duchess of Brythonica to watch her borders for movement by Chatriyon. Do you agree?"

The king stared absently at the flames. Owen suspected he was cursing himself for trusting Dragan. He had hoped the king would admit to his double-dealing, but he wasn't surprised that he had not, especially in front of his lady.

Severn brooded awhile over the flames. Then he turned and shook his head. "I won't send you North, not yet." His eyes shone with burning anger. "I want you to lead the search for Dragan yourself. I think you may be right about his gift, and if so, you'll have a better chance of finding him than anyone Kevan sends. Bring him to me. I know how to kill someone like him. You may get your chance to go North after you've caught him. There is a snow-covered peak there where the Maid of Donremy froze to death. Bring me this thief lord. I'll show him no mercy if he's harmed the girl."

Owen had manipulated the king by asking to go North right away. The pieces were falling just as he'd hoped and planned.

"Very well, my lord," he said stiffly. He bowed curtly and then turned to leave.

◆　◆　◆

"Lord Owen?"

It was Kathryn's voice. She'd followed him into the corridor leading off the throne room. It was empty, but the palace was riddled with spy holes and he couldn't know if it was safe to speak frankly with her.

"Yes, my lady?" he asked.

She wrung her hands as she approached. Her eyes were worried and puffy, and he could tell she hadn't slept much.

"I know you are doing everything possible to find her," Kathryn said softly. When she reached him, she cast a look back at the double doors leading to the throne room. The guards stood at attention, but they were too far away to hear their conversation.

"I am, my lady," he answered simply, keeping his expression neutral.

Her voice dropped lower. "No need to disguise yourself with me, Owen," she whispered. "I'm not fretting because of Genevieve. I'm worried about the king. I'm worried about what he may be planning."

Owen wrinkled his brow and said nothing.

Her voice was very quiet and confidential. "I asked him about whether he believed in your prophecy," she said. "He won't let himself accept it as truth. At least not yet. The snow is an early winter, he says. He's convinced himself the Fountain's portents are childish superstitions." She bent her head closer to his, giving him a pleading look. "I . . . I asked him what he would do if it *were* true. What if a boy does draw a sword out of the fountain?" She blinked rapidly, and he saw her eyes fill with tears.

"What did he say?" Owen asked.

"He said it would never come to that," she whispered. "If we get invaded, he plans to round up all the young men in the kingdom and summon them to Kingfountain. He said he'd prove the Fountain's power wasn't real."

Owen stared at her. "How?"

She shook her head. "He wouldn't say. But the look in his eye made me afraid. My lord, you promised me my son would be safe. That you'd protect him. I almost feel that if I *told* the king the truth, he'd see reason and relinquish the throne voluntarily. Maybe we can avert all these troubles? But do I dare risk it? When he is *such* a man?"

Owen looked at her with growing concern. He shook his head slowly. "Don't tell him."

Kathryn squeezed her eyes shut, and a single tear raced down her cheek. "I won't."

"I need to go speak to your son," Owen whispered. "Come with me. He's in the library. I think it is time he knew the truth."

# CHAPTER
# TWENTY-NINE

*Thief's Ransom*

Drew was nestled on a cushion by the window, poring over a book, when they entered the library. The light shining on his hair gave him an otherworldly cast. His eyes were so earnest and absorbed that he reminded Owen of himself, how he had always found sanctuary in this place. He wondered how many times the boy and Genevieve had found their way into the library together. Kathryn paused at the threshold, staring at the boy with such tenderness and longing that it pained Owen to see it.

He gave her an encouraging nod and gestured for her to approach the lad first, which she did. She nestled at the edge of the cushioned window seat, her eyes caressing his face.

"What are you reading?" she asked softly, reaching out to brush away a piece of his hair.

Drew didn't look away from the book. "A book about the Lady of the Fountain," he said, chewing on his little finger. "She was an Ondine."

"A what?" Kathryn asked.

"An Ondine," Drew replied. "A water sprite."

As the words came out of the child's mouth, Owen felt a ripple inside his heart that made him shudder. He walked closer, stepping so softly his boots didn't scuff on the carpets.

"I've not heard of them," Kathryn said with a curious tone. "The Lady of the Fountain was one, you say?"

"Mmm-hmmm," the boy said, gazing down at the words with an almost dreamlike expression. "Ondines are gifts from the Deep Fathoms. They look like us, but they aren't truly mortal. People find them on the shore after storms. The Lady of the Fountain who helped King Andrew was an Ondine. They are very powerful and good."

Owen swallowed, his heart wrenching with emotion. He could feel the magic of the Fountain pulsing around and inside him. He needed to ask Polidoro for more information about Ondines. Perhaps that was Sinia's origin instead? A feeling of certainty rang through him like a bell.

"I've always liked this library," Owen said, announcing himself as he approached the corner of the window seat.

Drew lifted his head at Owen's words. "I didn't hear you." He closed the book and set it down, his body suddenly tense. His eyes were penetrating for one so young. "Is she safe?"

He knew instantly whom the boy meant. "Yes."

Drew looked relieved. "I wish I could have told her good-bye," he said with a hint of melancholy.

Owen suppressed a smile. "She felt the same way. She's with her father again, on her way back to Atabyrion." He kept his voice pitched low deliberately, but they were alone in the room. The spy holes were all along one wall, and the window seat was far away from them. Kathryn glanced up at Owen and then looked down at the boy, her lip trembling.

It had to be done. The secret was wriggling furiously now, trying to escape. Owen felt it tearing him apart inside. He didn't know what was going to happen. But he felt he could not contain it a moment longer.

"When I told you to meet me here, I wanted to let you know that she was safe," Owen said. "But there is also another reason."

Drew dangled his legs over the edge of the cushion. He patted the book and a sad look crossed his face. "I'm leaving again. Aren't I?"

An exquisite pain wrung Owen's heart. He wanted to tell him all of it, but he couldn't. It was too much to unload on such a young boy. One secret at a time.

"Do you want to go?" Owen asked.

Drew shook his head miserably. "Duke Horwath is dead. Catsby hates me, and he doesn't want me to become one of his knights. Can I go back to Tatton Hall with you?" he implored. "I think my mother is from Westmarch. I'd like to go to Westmarch. I've never been there before."

Looking at the child's despair was heartbreaking. Was this how Ankarette had felt? Kathryn was struggling to keep her composure. The boy looked so forlorn and unwanted that Owen experienced physical pain in his chest.

"You were born in Westmarch," Owen said thickly, reaching down and tousling the boy's fair hair.

Drew nodded, but didn't meet his gaze. "You don't want me to go with you?"

Owen stifled a snort, amazed at the power of the feelings twisting him apart. "It's not that, lad. I just don't think it would be right. To separate you from your mother again."

He watched as his words wriggled inside Drew's body. The boy was staring at the floor, but then a look stole over his face—confusion, recognition, realization. He raised his head and looked at Owen with a sort of hesitant hope. Then he turned and looked at Kathryn.

The young boy's face continued to contort as the knowledge swept through him like a flood. "You? You are my . . . my maman?"

Tears rained down Kathryn's cheeks as she nodded vigorously and then clutched the boy to her bosom, pressing hot kisses against his hair.

His small arms clung to her, and Owen heard the shuddering sobs start in his chest.

Taking a step back, Owen stared at the two, his own eyes stinging with tears, which he roughly brushed away. He had to be strong. He had to do all that he could to bring this boy to the throne.

Owen knelt down by the side of the window seat and put his hand on Drew's knee. "I had to tell you now, lad. There is more I cannot tell you quite yet."

Drew wiped his nose and looked at Owen in astonishment. "Are you my father?" he demanded.

Owen chuckled softly. "No, lad. I'm your protector. The Fountain put you in my charge when you were born. All the times I came to Dundrennan? It wasn't just to consult with the duke. I came to check on you."

Drew was beaming with newfound joy. "I'm not a foundling," he whispered to himself.

Owen nodded. "You are not. I will tell you more later, but know this. You cannot tell the king what you know. You must stay away from him, do not let him even touch you. He has power in his words. He can make you *want* to tell."

Drew stared a moment and then he pumped his head up and down. "He's done it to me before," he said. "In Dundrennan!"

"You're going to stay at the palace for now. I'll be leaving for the North soon, if all goes well. When I return, I will tell you more of the secrets surrounding your birth. It has not been easy for your mother to have you raised away from her. She loves you, boy. She loves you deeply. As if I needed to tell you that!" Kathryn's arms were still wrapped around the boy.

The boy was positively beaming. "I want to take a coin to the fountain," he said seriously. "I have a crown I've been saving. I'd like to put it in the fountain now. I've been meaning to use it to ask the Fountain who my parents were." He smiled. "I feel I should give it the coin now just to show how grateful I am."

Owen rose and mussed the boy's hair again. "I'll take you there myself. Now, I have some business to attend to. I think the two of you should spend some time alone together."

Drew nodded eagerly and turned to Lady Kathryn. "I always imagined you were beautiful," he whispered shyly. Kathryn took his hands in hers and then kissed them. "Parting with you was my greatest sorrow."

Owen left mother and son alone.

◆   ◆   ◆

Back in the Star Chamber, Owen picked through the heap of missives that were back on his desk after he'd scattered them days ago. After he'd sorted them in the order he wanted, he slumped into the chair and tried to summon the motivation to start reading them. He was hopelessly behind in his duties as master of the Espion, but his attention was more focused on dethroning his king than on preserving him. He tapped one of the scrolls against his lip and then opened it and started reading. The words blurred before him as he thought about young Drew's reaction to meeting his mother. The memory warmed him and only added to his distraction.

A knock sounded at the door, and Owen gave the order to enter.

Kevan appeared with a small tray of berries. "These just arrived from Brythonica, I was told," he said. "A gift from your betrothed?" On the tray was a note written in Sinia's elegant flourishes.

Owen saw the tray and smiled, nodding and gesturing to the desk. Kevan popped one of the berries into his mouth and blinked in surprise. "Quite tasty. I've heard good reports about the berries of that land. Perhaps you can arrange a change in my assignment once you become the Duke of Brythonica?"

Owen smiled and scooped up a few berries himself. They were delicious and sweet, so very sweet they made him blink in surprise. "Are you so anxious to leave Kingfountain, Kevan?"

The Espion chuckled, his hands clasped behind his back. "I don't know how much longer I can endure it, to be honest," he said. "The king's temper is getting worse, if that's possible."

Owen smiled and picked up another berry. Kevan looked longingly at the tray, and Owen gestured for him to help himself; he did.

"You're a capable man," Owen told him. "And I appreciate you. I have been known to assist others to assignments better suited to their interests." He smiled, thinking of Clark and Justine.

"I'm not asking for an assignment in Atabyrion, if that's what you mean. I was Clark's mentor long ago, but I have no desire to follow him there. If I may speak freely, my lord?"

"Of course."

"I have a feeling that the king will still replace you as head of the Espion when this is over. I've enjoyed serving you, Lord Owen, and I would gratefully follow you to Tatton Hall or Ploemeur or wherever else you go. I speak this truthfully."

Owen felt a flush of pleasure at the man's words. "I value loyalty," he said, wondering if he should take the Espion into his confidence. He'd tested Kevan with his magic before and found him to be genuine and forthright. And he was quite capable with his diplomacy skills; he could be an asset.

"I know you do," Kevan said, nodding. "I hope I've demonstrated mine."

The secret door in the room opened and Etayne rushed through it, startled to see Kevan there. He bowed to her and turned to leave.

"No, stay," Etayne said, forestalling him.

Kevan turned with curiosity on his face.

"I've arranged a meeting with Bothwell. My . . . *contact*," she said, giving Owen a knowing look, "said he agreed to meet me at the Candlewood Inn."

"I know where that is," Kevan said. "It's near the sanctuary. Bothwell is Chatriyon's poisoner, correct?"

"Yes, the one who poisoned our people in Edonburick," Owen said. "He's in the city. I've meant to tell you, but I've been too distracted of late. I told Etayne to arrange a meeting—"

"So you could swarm it with Espion," Etayne finished for him.

Kevan looked flummoxed. "Most of my men are busy seeking Iago's daughter. Let me gather as many of them as I can. If he's at the Candlewood, it's an opportunity worth seizing. How recently did your contact give you this news?"

Etayne flushed, but her expression was full of steel. "Just now. Bothwell's there. I'll go with you. I've defeated him before."

The Espion looked relieved. "We'll be grateful to have you with us. The longer we delay, the more we risk losing him."

"I agree," Owen said. "If you can capture him, then do so, but I wouldn't shed tears if you impaled him with a crossbow instead. Well done, Etayne."

She flushed and gave him a smile before turning and leaving the Star Chamber with Kevan.

Owen sat back in his chair, nibbling on berries from the tray. After getting rid of Bothwell, the next man to fall was Dragan. But how can you catch a man who can't been seen? What a cunning gift from the Fountain. He rolled one of the scrolls from the table across his palm, imagining how he could set a trap to catch the thief. Etayne's father had managed to infiltrate the dungeons, and somehow the king. Did he know about the Espion tunnels? It was likely he did. A sour feeling crept into Owen's stomach.

Dragan was no fool, and the fact that he'd use his own daughter to further his interests was evidence enough of his lack of morals . . .

Owen's stomach turned over, and he squirmed in the chair with discomfort. He was thinking about how to set a trap for a man like Dragan, but perhaps the thief may have already set a trap himself.

The onset of cramps in Owen's stomach was so violent that it was an unmistakable confirmation of his suspicion. He moaned and felt his legs turn to jelly as all strength left them. The tray of berries on the table was eye level with him.

Owen reached out with his magic, trying to summon it, and felt the sluggish response as his bowels flexed and twisted like the ropes on a ship in a storm. The magic crept out of Owen nonetheless, and he detected the trace of poison coming from the tray of fruit. In the Star Chamber, he was isolated from the rest of the palace.

The raven sigil on his scabbard started to glow, responding to the pain roiling inside of Owen. He tried to pull himself up on the desk with his arms, despite his weak legs. If he could get a servant to run after Etayne . . .

The secret passageway opened, and Bothwell entered with a dagger already in hand.

# CHAPTER THIRTY

## *Poisoner's Kiss*

Owen's access to his magic drained rapidly as the poison worked through his system. The scabbard he wore had invoked its magic to try to sustain him, but he didn't know how long it would last.

"I think you'll forgive me for not making any little speeches," Bothwell said in a snide tone, shutting the passage door behind him. "I've been looking forward to this *reunion* for many years now. Killing someone who's Fountain-blessed isn't easy."

Owen leaned against the table, using his arms to hold himself there. His legs were trembling and certainly not ready for a fight. He had no time to draw a sword, but he grabbed at the nearest thing he could reach—a metal tray containing scrolls and letters.

As Bothwell brought his arm back to throw the knife at Owen, the duke brought up the tray. The knife slammed into it, disrupting the attack.

"You think *that* is going to stop me?" Bothwell said with a derisive snort. He charged into the room and kicked Owen in the ribs, knocking him to the ground. The pain in his stomach was already debilitating, and the blow knocked the wind from him. Owen did not let it stop him. He summoned his magic to defend himself, searching the room for anything he could use to save himself. Grabbing the hem of Bothwell's tunic, he twisted his body, trying to drag the poisoner down on the ground next to him. There was a flash of metal, and then Owen felt a blade sink into his side. He groaned with pain and watched as the poisoner drew the weapon out and stabbed him again. Owen bucked and heaved, and the dagger caught his arm, slicing down to the bone.

"Hold still, you piddling sop!" Bothwell snarled, trying to get the blade to Owen's neck. The tangle of Owen's arms was the only thing that stopped him.

There was no longer any time to think or reason. The instinct for survival took over, sending a spurt of energy through Owen more powerful than the poison that flowed in his blood. He brought up his legs to protect himself and then kicked out, catching Bothwell and knocking him backward. Owen scrabbled across the floor and grabbed the poisoner's fallen dagger off the floor.

"Nuh-uh-uh," Bothwell sang, kicking the dagger out of his reach. "How are you still moving?"

The wounds on Owen's arm and leg burned, and he expected them to leave a trail of blood behind as he crawled, but they did not. Somehow the wounds weren't bleeding very much. The scabbard was working for him still. Even so, his stomach felt as if his enemy's dagger were jabbing him relentlessly. This had to be the same poison that had nearly made Clark plummet off a cliff into a raging river. Owen's head spun with nausea, and he felt himself growing weaker. His magic continued to dwindle.

The poisoner knelt over Owen and grabbed the scabbard belt. The thought of losing its protection filled him with a paroxysm of terror, and he jabbed his fingers at the poisoner's eyes, trying to reach his nose, his ears, anything that would cause pain. Bothwell slammed Owen's head against the ground—a blow that stunned him into a groggy stupor. He felt a loosening at his waist as the poisoner slit the leather strap and the scabbard fell away. Once its magic was no longer protecting him, the wounds in his side and arm swelled with blood. Owen barely saw the crimson bloom because he immediately went light-headed with pain.

"No more tricks, shall we?" Bothwell growled. "Be a good lad and *stay* dead this time. This will help."

He stabbed Owen in the stomach again with the dagger, plunging the knife all the way to the hilt. The pain rocked down to his toes. Then the poisoner withdrew a cord and vial from around his own neck and unstoppered it quickly. "This is a little cocktail I invented. Three types of poison at once."

Owen twitched and writhed on the floor, seeing spots dance before his eyes. He felt his grip on the tether of life slipping, and he experienced the sensation that he was about to fall. Was it all to end here?

"Drink up," the poisoner laughed, pressing his fingers roughly into Owen's cheeks to force his lips open. Then he upended the vial into the gap, spilling the black ichor into Owen's mouth. The taste was fire and ash, and it instantly created a burning sensation.

The door of the Star Chamber burst open, and Owen heard Etayne gasp in horror. Bothwell looked up in surprise, and it was the opportunity Owen needed to shove the vial from his mouth. He lolled his head to the side and tried to expel the poison, but Bothwell pressed his thumb against Owen's throat and forced his swallow reflex. He felt the poison burn a path of fire down his throat.

"No!" Etayne howled in dismay. A dagger sailed from her hand. Bothwell turned in time to avoid being struck in the heart, but it embedded itself in his shoulder. The poisoner rushed to his feet as Etayne launched herself across the room.

Owen's lids were growing heavy as he tried to scoot himself away. The scrolls of the desk exploded in a plume of parchment as Etayne and Bothwell fought each other without words, without taunts. He watched as Bothwell's head collided with the brazier, but moments later he managed to entangle Etayne's heels and force her off her feet. Owen distantly watched as she dodged Bothwell's attempt to crush her skull with an inkwell.

Owen's limbs slackened as the poison traveled through his system. He began to tremble uncontrollably and lost feeling in his legs, his hips. The dagger still protruded from his stomach, and he stared at it, amazed he was even alive. The scabbard lay near him, the raven sigil dull and lifeless. He tried to reach for it, but his arm was quivering too much. The path of fire down his throat blazed to life. The well of his magic was trickling now, almost completely spent. It would not be long.

There was a cry of pain from Etayne and then a grunt from Bothwell. He heard the crack of bone and then a man's howl cut short by a hiss and a bubbling sound.

Etayne rose from across the desk, blood trickling from her temple, and rushed to where Owen lay convulsing.

"No! No!" she moaned, her look full of agony, not for herself, but for Owen. He stared at her, grateful he wasn't alone in this moment. Grateful he would have a friend to see him to the other side. He could hear the distant murmur of the Deep Fathoms coming closer. He was going over the falls. There was nothing to stop him.

"Please, no!" Etayne gasped, her chest racked with sobs. She bent over Owen in bewildered torment, and her hand reached out toward the vial on the ground by his neck, surrounded by a small puddle of the black dreck. Owen stopped breathing, feeling the last bit of air pressed from his chest as his throat closed. He looked at her in wild panic. He couldn't breathe.

His fingers clawed numbly for the scabbard, unable to function. Sensing his intention, she lifted the scabbard and put it on his chest, closing his hand atop his sword's pommel as if she were dressing a corpse for the canoe. She slid the dagger out of his body and let it tumble to the floor. He felt nothing.

"I love you," she whispered feverishly, her face so near his. He was slipping away, and he felt certain her words would be the last that he heard. At least they were good tidings to hear at the end. He stared into her eyes, trying to focus as his vision dimmed.

There was a jarring sensation, the feeling of a glove being pulled off a hand. Suddenly he was looking at her from a different angle, from above rather than below. There was a pool of blood on the floor beneath him—his own lifeblood drained away. His body had stopped twitching and rested still. Owen felt the strange realization that he had died, and he felt a *pulling*, like a river current was trying to take him away.

Etayne was sobbing, pressing her face against his chest. How could he hear her still? He felt all of her love, all of her regret, all of her thwarted passion roiling inside her. Then she lifted her head as if startled by a sound.

The thief's daughter cupped Owen's cheeks tenderly, and he felt her magic swell as wide as the moon's glow. She bowed her head, her mouth hovering just above his.

"*Nesh-ama*," she whispered. *Breathe.*

And then she kissed him.

Etayne had been present when he used the magic to save Justine's life. Her kiss was not as tender.

The tug on Owen's soul reversed, and suddenly he was falling, a sheet of light blinding him as he tumbled back into his body and his chest filled with air and life. His back arched with pain, for his wounds were brought back to life as well. He felt her mouth on his, and he could taste the poison there.

*No!*

The realization struck him like an iron hammer on an anvil. His eyes blinked open and he could see the tears of happiness streaking down her face. He sensed her magic was completely spent. She had used it *all* to save him. Her lids began to droop. She clutched his hand and then fell next to him.

The raven sigil on the scabbard started to glow, and he felt the magic work on him once again. He was so weak he couldn't move at all, he could only breathe and stare into her eyes. He saw the wet poison on her lips.

She looked peaceful.

He tried to sit up, but the pain racking his body prevented any such movement. "No, Etayne! No!" he croaked.

Her face looked like a child about to fall asleep. "I knew I would die of love," she whispered faintly. "You could never be mine." Her hand lifted weakly, and she stroked the white tuft of hair amidst his thick locks.

Memories of Ankarette's death slammed into Owen, and he thought his heart would burst if he lost this other friend, this other protector. He reached out and touched the side of Etayne's face, grazing the skin with his fingers. Her eyes closed and a pleased smile spread across her face. "At last," she whispered.

"Etayne," Owen said in a broken voice as he watched the first convulsions start to twitch in her body. Her face went pale, but she didn't fight the poison. Owen thought the pain in his heart would kill him. He had no magic left himself. His well was absolutely void. If he could have traded places with her, he would have done so in an instant.

The poisoner's lips parted. There was no reproach in her eyes. No regret. "She's better for you," she whispered. "I see it even if I have not admitted it to you. I envy Sinia."

The eyes opened with panic as a tremor of pain rocked through her. "Good-bye, my love," Etayne breathed, and said no more.

Owen watched helplessly as his best friend died in front of him.

◆  ◆  ◆

Dear Owen,

*I have sent this note by way of the Duchess of Brythonica, who has assured me it will reach you swiftly and beyond the notice of the Espion. I am grateful to have Genevieve back, and she tells me that you literally saved her life. Children are prone to exaggeration, but if her tale is true, I owe you more than I can ever repay. You have my trust and allegiance. By the time you receive this, our invasion of the North will be underway. We plan to rally the people by striking at the heart of my rightful lands. Thanks to your cleverness, we can depose Severn with little bloodshed. That is my hope. I cannot take this step without great pain of heart and conflict in my soul. Were you not the one instigating it, I would never have dared. Iago bids me tell you that we will both be landing in the North. We've entrusted our children to faithful allies here, including Earl of Huntley, who longs to see his daughter again. The injustices we have all suffered under the hands of King Severn may hopefully come to an end.*

*Yours with loyalty,*
*Elysabeth Victoria Mortimer Llewellyn*
*Queen of Atabyrion*

◆  ◆  ◆

# CHAPTER
# THIRTY-ONE

*Raven's Feast*

Owen walked with a pronounced limp down the torch-lit corridor, but the sight of his shadow on the wall made him stop and stare. His bandaged arm was clenched to his side, and his posture looked strikingly similar to that of a young Severn Argentine. Dread knifed through him as he stood silently in the walkway, still staring at the shadow.

Thanks to the scabbard, his injuries were healing quickly and the court doctors were amazed that he was already out of his bed after losing so much blood. Owen chafed with impatience, hating the coddling and disgusting drafts the doctors had made him drink. He had been abed for nearly a full day before insisting he be released.

The drama had shocked the entire court. A poisoner from Occitania had somehow managed to infiltrate the castle and attempt to murder the head of the Espion and his chief lieutenant. Both had survived, but the king's own poisoner had been murdered. Only Owen knew the full truth, and he was keeping the facts to himself. He had warned the king that Dragan was behind the plot. The manhunt for the thief had become pressing in its intensity, but no one had seen him. Nor could they.

Owen started walking again, gritting his teeth against the pain roiling throughout his body. Etayne's body was going to be set loose in the river that morning, and Owen was determined to be there to pay his last respects to the woman who had given her life for his. It was painful to think about her, and he knew it was a wound that would never fully heal. She had spent most of their years together nursing an unrequited love for him, and it saddened him that she had only found happiness in her final act of self-sacrifice. Tears threatened him, and he could not help but wonder if he was cursed to spend his life alone. Perhaps Sinia too would be ripped away from him.

He reached the door leading to the outer yard and found two soldiers waiting there in black tunics with the white boar insignia. They stiffened and exchanged a knowing look as he limped toward them. Owen said nothing to them as they hauled open the door to let him out.

Pathways had been cleared through the yard, the drifts shoveled up against the walls, but elsewhere the land was thick with snow. The miserable cold reminded Owen of the Wizr board hidden in the secluded fountain of Our Lady. The board's magic was causing the weather. And it would continue to get worse until Severn was defeated or until the entire kingdom lay under a cataclysm of ice. He walked with a burden of pain and duty inside his heart, listening to the crunch of the ice crystals beneath his boots.

After crossing the frozen grounds littered with leafless trees, he arrived at the gate where he'd watched the king seduce Lady Kathryn. Etayne's identity was a state secret, so there would be no crowd to send her on her way back to the Deep Fathoms.

The king was already there, swathed in a heavy black cape lined with silver fur. Next to him was Kevan Amrein, leaning on a crutch.

The Espion's face was gaunt and feverish, and Owen was surprised to see him out of bed.

The sound of his boots announced him, and the men turned. Owen wondered if Dragan was also present, hidden by his magic. Owen's connection with the Fountain magic had been temporarily severed because he had no reserves left. The necessity for him to plot and plan had begun to bring it back, but he didn't want to waste what limited power he had. The well needed to be filled, drip by drip. He had not been so drained for years.

"You look hale for a man who was nearly dead," the king said to him with a wary smile. "I don't think I've ever seen you so poorly."

"I can't remember when I ever *felt* this poorly," Owen countered. He glanced at Kevan, who gave him a somber-faced nod.

The king sniffed in the cold air, but he didn't seem bothered by it. "It's a sad day, to be sure. It's like the game of Wizr when two pieces of the same value get exchanged. It would have been much worse if Chatriyon had claimed your life as well." His lips curled into a snarl. "I am ready to crush that upstart's skull. He's provoked me for the last time. When you are fit for the saddle again, you will launch a war into Occitania that will water their gardens in blood. I want to spit on the corpse at Queen Elyse's feet." His voice throbbed with hatred, and Owen felt a blackness settle in his heart.

"This was not a game of Wizr," Owen growled. "Etayne was a person, not a pawn." Fresh pain bloomed in his chest as his eyes shot to the boat where her body lay. It had been covered in a shroud, which, in turn, was decorated with freshly fallen snow.

Severn snorted. "She was a pawn, if a powerful one. Do you know how much she cost me? How much Mancini spent on her training?" He shook his head at the loss of capital, while Owen ached at the loss of his dear friend.

He didn't trust himself to speak, so he said nothing. He caught a sympathetic look from Kevan, who wisely joined him in his silence.

"Well," the king said after a long moment. "At least she's going into the river in winter. The ravens have all flown south."

Owen turned and looked at the king with morbid curiosity. "What?"

The king didn't look at him, but Owen saw a flash of disgust on his face. "Haven't you ever wondered, lad, what happens to the bodies we release into the river? And why there are so many carrion birds in this kingdom? The bodies don't disappear. They are fought over." His face tightened. "When I was a lad, no older than you were when you first came to the palace, I walked with my brother down to the base of the falls. I saw something black, something I couldn't identify." His voice took on a haunted sound. "Eredur threw a stone at it, and suddenly the heap of black moved and lifted. They were ravens, feasting on a corpse." The king shuddered at the memory. "I can't abide them. I hate this duty most of all, for it reminds me of that time. I was just a child, but it terrified me."

Owen had never given it a thought. The pageantry and splendor of the rite had always appealed to him. Even as a child he'd wondered what it would be like to be sent into the river as he'd seen happen to others.

"What happens during the winter months then?" Owen asked.

The king stared off into the distance. "Wolves," he said simply. Then he shook his head as if to ward off the evil portent. "Let's be done with this!" he barked to the soldiers.

The sound of approaching boots filled the air, and the three men turned in unison to see Lord Catsby rushing toward them from the palace. His boot slipped on a patch of ice, and the man went down with a yip of pain that sent him onto his backside.

Owen chuckled at the sight, unable to help himself, and the three of them started toward the injured lord.

"What are you doing here, Catsby?" the king demanded. "I sent you to the North."

"I never . . . even . . . made it there," Catsby grunted. His effort to stand ended in another slip that sent muddy snow spattering across his rich mantle and tunic. He made it to his feet on his second try and dusted off the slush from his knees, scowling darkly.

"What prevented you?" Severn asked with concern.

"The Mortimer girl!" Catsby snarled. "Iago's chit. She's occupying the fortress of Dundrennan while her husband is off sacking all of my men!"

Owen was angry at his choice of words, but he bit his tongue. Severn's eyes widened. "So soon? When did they land? Why haven't we gotten word of this ere now? Surely you could have sent a horse on ahead?"

Catsby shook his head. "I came myself, my lord. I need men, an army! You gave me those lands, my lord! It was my right to do with them as I chose! Now I need force to set this right."

Severn looked exasperated and furious. "Yes, I did bestow them to you, and in your *greed*, you pillaged the coffers and insulted everyone living there. Didn't I warn you to go easy? Now look what you've done! If we lose the North without even a skirmish, it will cost treasure *and* blood to win it back. How could you be so shortsighted!"

Owen suppressed a smile as he looked for Catsby's reaction. The petulant chancellor defended himself with indignation. "I have done naught but serve you, my liege! You must help me get it back. You cannot let Iago hold lands within Ceredigion. He'll be after your crown next!"

"No thanks to you!" the king shot back. He blistered the air with some choice curses. "You are useless, Catsby! Useless!" He turned to Owen. "How close is your army, lad?"

Owen was careful not to look too eager. "A few days' march from here, my lord. Would you like me to bring them North and repulse the invasion? I think if you offered some . . . concessions to Elysabeth and Iago, they might relent."

"It's mine!" Catsby blustered.

Severn scowled and shook his head. "I can't show weakness, not now. When word of this gets out, every duke and prince within the seven kingdoms will arrive with a fork and carving knife." He gave Owen a stern look. "I want you to *crush* her, Owen. She has not lived up to her grandfather's memory. She has betrayed me."

Owen held out his hands. "You drove her to it, my lord," he said, shaking his head. "You rewarded *her* loyalty by making *him* rich. This is the consequence of your own decision."

The king's face twisted with wrath. "How dare you speak to me thus!"

"I must dare it," Owen said, shaking his head. He took a pleading step forward.

"My lord," Catsby said, obviously worried about his spoils. "Don't listen to him. He's long tried to poison you against me. I've feared my life would be forfeit if I spoke more plainly to you, my lord. You cannot trust him, particularly not with the Espion. It's as I've told you time and again; they are more loyal to him than to you!"

Owen felt his own anger surge. "I've told the king more than once, Catsby, that he can take what he likes from me. I've proven my loyalty to him over the years. What have you done?"

Catsby's face twisted with fury. "If you weren't so obviously wounded, my lord—"

"Stop!" the king barked, his eyes glowering, his cheek muscles twitching. "We have enemies enough without snapping at each other! I am your king, and you will obey my orders. Owen, I want you to go North and bring her to heel. I've heard you, but I cannot tolerate disobedience. Iago must have been behind the disappearance of his brat for his attack to be timed thusly. You go North and persuade her to relinquish Dundrennan back to Catsby. Don't argue! Just do it. Catsby, you come with me. You're still my chancellor, and I want my own army summoned. If Chatriyon invades Westmarch, I will chase him all the way to Pree and break down the stones one by one. Let them all come and snap at me. They will feel the might of the boar!"

The king turned back to Kevan. "See the girl's body into the river. I've had enough of this macabre scene. We are at war, and I will prove to all of them that this snowstorm has nothing to do with the Fountain!"

He took Catsby by the arm as if he were a child, and the two of them marched back to the castle, leaving Owen and Kevan behind with the shivering soldiers waiting to fulfill their duty.

"Is that a smile, my lord?" Kevan asked him curiously, and only then did Owen realize his composure had slipped.

"Sometimes if you don't laugh at the world, your only other option is weeping," Owen said with a tone of bitterness. He clapped the Espion on the shoulder and turned around. "We haven't spoken since our last meeting in the Star Chamber. What happened to you? I'm grateful you're still alive."

Kevan flushed and leaned his weight on the cane. "I owe her my life," he said, shaking his head. "As do you, by the look of it, though you got the worst of it."

Owen shook his head. "No, she did."

"'Tis true," Kevan agreed. "We were walking together to gather men for the meeting with Bothwell. She was stymied by something that kept her quiet along the way. I felt my insides start, and we hadn't even made it to the outer wall when I collapsed in pain. She asked me what I'd eaten, and I mentioned the berries from Brythonica. She deduced the rest. If I hadn't eaten a few of those berries, the poisoner's plan would have worked."

Owen chuffed in surprise. "I didn't even consider them a risk. I was only being generous."

Kevan smiled. "I know that. She recognized the poison because he'd used it before, back in Atabyrion. She had been carrying the remedy with her in preparation to face him. She knelt by me and gave me a swallow of it—bitter stuff—and then raced back to the Star Chamber, expecting to find you sick as well. Looks like she arrived just in time to stop Bothwell from murdering you, only she died instead. How did it happen?" he asked.

Owen's heart wrenched. "Poison," he said simply, and sighed. He stared at the shroud and then hobbled up to it. Wincing, he knelt down and lifted the cloth from her face. It was like looking at a mask, not the woman he'd grown to care for and admire. A knife of grief stabbed him sharply in the heart. The feeling of loneliness came down on him like the falling snow.

"She was a . . . a capable lass," Kevan said, standing just over Owen's shoulder. "I wouldn't have wished to face her in a fight."

Owen stared down at the waxy face, the clay that no longer had the spark of life. She had given that spark to him. He gently set the cloth down and tried to stand, though his legs protested. Kevan nodded to the soldiers and gripped Owen's arm, helping him up.

"She was my friend," Owen said in a low voice after the soldiers bent down and lifted the poles to carry the canoe to the river. The sound of it filled his ears, mimicking the magic that had forsaken him.

The two men followed the soldiers as they walked to the platform constructed at the river's edge. Standing vigil, they watched as the four soldiers upended the poles and the canoe pitched forward and landed with a splash in the frigid waters. Owen felt his eyes growing moist, and a lump lodged in his throat as he watched the canoe speed away toward Our Lady and the waterfall beyond. Memories of the night he'd fallen into the river surfaced. The water was so very cold. He couldn't stand the thought of Etayne being cold. He couldn't bear the thought of her body washing up on shore to be devoured by wolves.

"If you would, my friend," Owen said thickly. "Send some men down to retrieve the corpse at the base of the falls. Bury it under a mound of stones."

Kevan put his hand on Owen's shoulder and gave a small nod. "Consider it done."

They started back toward the palace in silence, but the king's royal butler met them on the path.

"What is it?" Owen asked the grim-faced man.

The butler bit his lip. "They caught a man called Dragan in the castle," he said. "The king bids you come at once."

Owen gave Kevan a worried look, and they both followed the butler to the throne room. The castle was much warmer than the exterior, and Owen's ears began to tingle back to life. How had the Espion managed to capture a man who could disappear at will?

"Do you know aught of this?" Owen asked Kevan.

"Nothing at all," the man said with concern.

Owen wiped his nose. "Someone wants to earn the king's favor, no doubt."

When they reached the throne room, Owen noticed that it was full of soldiers wearing the badge of the white boar. There were easily twenty or thirty men, and they stared at Owen with open hostility. His pulse began to race as he limped into the room. The servants were all gone. Catsby stood by the king, arms folded, and his smug, self-satisfied look confirmed that something was very wrong.

Then Owen saw it. The Wizr chest was sitting at the base of the throne. *The* Wizr chest.

Severn was seated on the throne itself, holding an unfolded piece of paper with a broken wax seal on the edge. The other letters Sinia had written were spread across the king's lap. The look he gave Owen was full of daggers and condemnation.

Owen saw Dragan off to the side, sipping from a cup of wine. He nodded it in a mock salute, a cunning smile wrinkling his face.

"I believe this letter," the king said coldly, "is for you."

# CHAPTER THIRTY-TWO

## *The King's Traitor*

The sensation of panic and guilt struck Owen in the pit of his stomach like a physical blow. His mouth went dry, his entire body began to tremble, and the blood drained from his cheeks. The Wizr board was open, and he could see the black king's scowl. It would hardly have surprised him if the stone eyes had turned him into a statue as in the legends of old.

"At a loss for words, my lord duke? For excuses?" the king said in a low voice, but the rage behind it was growing as Owen's feeling of helplessness intensified. Severn rose from his throne, gripping the dagger hilt so tightly his knuckles turned white. The look on his face was full of condemnation.

Owen hadn't expected to get caught, not in a hall full of witnesses, but it was almost a relief not to carry the burden of secrecy any longer.

"My guilt?" Owen said in a short, clipped tone. "I have not read that letter, my lord king. How can I respond to your accusation without knowing what it says?"

"By all means," replied the king. He stood atop the dais and extended his arm, his eyes glittering with wrath. "Read it to your doom. I have seen Lady Llewellyn's script often enough to recognize her hand. This is no forgery. And she implicates you in the deepest of treasons."

It felt as if he were falling off a cliff and the world were rushing past him. As he crossed the distance to where the king extended the letter, the sound of his boots echoed in the hall as loud as thunder crackling in the sky. He reached the dais and took the letter from the king. Should he try drawing on what little magic had trickled back into his banks? The king and Dragan would sense it, though, and it would give them a sense of his current weakness. He decided against it and quickly scanned the letter Evie had written to him, which—by any possible interpretation—condemned him of treason. As he read her words, he wondered why Sinia had sent the letter along to him if she'd known what would happen. But as he'd come to learn, the timing of her visions was not always exact. Or perhaps she did know what would happen, and there was some reason it needed to unfold this way.

The king stroked his bottom lip. "You were always more loyal to *her* than to me," he said accusingly. "Thick as thieves, the two of you. Is this your revenge, Owen? You would dare take the throne yourself!" The last words had built into a roar.

It was over. The ruse was completely destroyed. Owen had rolled the dice, and he had lost.

"I would never seek to usurp your throne for myself," Owen said tightly.

"Oh, how magnanimous of you! How saintly! But do you think anything you say to me right now could justify your treason? After all you have seen, after all you've witnessed, you too have chosen the kiss of betrayal. There is no man nor woman left in Ceredigion who knows true loyalty. So be it."

Owen stepped forward. "I speak truly, my lord, whether or not you believe me. It is treason to oppose the king. But you are *not* the rightful king of Ceredigion. And you've always known it. You stole the throne from your brother's children. You were their uncle, and should have protected them."

"I will not be spoken to in such a way by a traitor!" the king screamed. He gestured. "Take him to the dungeon and prepare him for execution. Catsby, charge him!"

A greedy smile stretched across Lord Catsby's face as he made his approach. Guards appeared at Owen's side in an instant, seizing his arms so violently he winced and nearly lost all his strength from the surge of pain it brought to his wounds. The look on Catsby's face made Owen want to spit at him.

"I charge thee of high treason, Owen Kiskaddon, Duke of Westmarch," he said with wicked delight. He hooked fingers around the chain of office around Owen's neck and then snapped it off and tossed it to the ground at their feet. "Prepare to face your death, boy. It will not be long in coming."

Owen looked past the triumphant lord to meet the king's eyes. "If you do not abdicate your throne, you will destroy us all!" he said accusingly. "You've brought a curse on the land that will only stop when the Dreadful Deadman wears the crown."

"Silence!" the king shouted, flecks of spit spraying with his words. He quivered with rage.

Owen tried to shake loose the grip on his arms, but he was too weak. "The winter will destroy us all, my lord. Every man, woman, and child! Even you. I beg of you, my lord. Relinquish what you have unrightfully claimed!"

"Take him away!" Severn snarled.

The guards started to drag Owen to the doors, but he persisted in pleading with the king. "Look at the board, my lord. I'm sure you've realized it has special significance. The pieces are all arrayed against you. If you fall, we all perish with you. The Dreadful Deadman is here! Do what you will with me. Throw me into the river, I don't care! But this storm will not end so long as you are king. It will bury us all in frost."

"You think you're going into the river?" Severn snarled. "I know how to deal with the likes of you. I'll leave nothing to chance. We're riding North to reclaim Dundrennan from your wicked little friend and her faithless husband. And you'll be bound in iron atop a mountain to freeze to death! You will be the *first* to perish by the cold you foreshadow!"

◆　◆　◆

Owen was confined to Holistern Tower directly. There was frost on the window and chinks in the stone that made it drafty and miserable. Two Espion handlers had been assigned to him with orders to sleep in his bed at night, watch him when he used the privy, and keep an eye on him night and day until the king decided it was time to leave. Memories of Eyric and Dunsdworth haunted Owen—this had been their fate, one which he had always pitied them—but at least he would not spend years this way. No, his remaining life span would be limited to days.

The heavy chains secured around his wrists tired him. They'd stripped away his sword and scabbard, removing the source of the magic healing that had helped him recover so swiftly in the past. There was nothing in the room to substitute for his tiles—no ready way to fill his supply of magic. He only had his mind, and so he spent his days pacing and trying to figure an escape from his dilemma. Atabyrion's invasion of the North had been prompted by his assurances that Westmarch would rise in rebellion against the king. Now Severn could join Owen's army with his own and bring the North to heel himself. What would happen to Evie when she found out? Dundrennan was an impressive castle. It had never been breached in the past. But how long could it hold out against the determination of a man like Severn, whose own position in the North had been unquestioned?

He shook his head as he continued to pace back and forth, shivering against the cold. A brazier had been lit, and the two Espion huddled near it, chafing their hands.

The feeling of misery and hopelessness spread across Owen's shoulders like a mantle. So he was to meet his fate as the Maid of Donremy had met hers. He had hoped to provoke Severn into throwing him into the river. The ring on his hand would have protected him from the falls and helped him escape. If he could somehow escape and make it to the river, he felt he'd stand a chance. If only Etayne were still alive. Grief at her death struck him so hard he clenched his fist and pressed his knuckles against his mouth to subdue the hot rush of feelings. Etayne would have helped him escape. What about Sinia? Did she even know what had happened to him? Even if she did, was there anything she could do to help? The thought of not seeing her again made his heart wrench with anguish and dread.

Almost as if in answer to that thought, he sensed Fountain magic emanating from the stairwell. It had an oily feeling to it, though, and instead of offering hope, it made him uneasy. He stopped and stared at the door.

"What is it?" one of his protectors asked. He didn't know either of the underlings who'd been chosen for the assignment.

The other man snorted, shrugged, and spat, continuing to chafe his hands before the flames. Then he stiffened. "I 'ear boots coming up the steps." He straightened and put a hand on his dagger.

The sensation of the Fountain grew more pronounced, and Owen found himself breathing hard, the cold seeping into his bones.

There was a jangle at the lock and then the door opened. Much to Owen's surprise, the king was the first to enter. Kevan stood next to him, his face troubled but studiedly neutral. In his arms, he carried the chest with the Wizr board. Several guards wearing the king's colors filed in behind them, and Owen felt the presence of an unseen man enter at last. Dragan was there, but he was using his power of invisibility.

"I wasn't expecting a personal visit, my lord," Owen said, feeling confused and anxious. He tried to pinpoint Dragan's location, but only got a subtle impression that the thief was against the far wall by the window.

"Well, we are heading out on the morrow to crush an invasion," the king said with a strange calmness. "I want some answers from you before you die, Owen. To satisfy my curiosity, I suppose. I didn't want to discuss this in the hall in front of so many."

Owen swallowed and shrugged.

"Where did you get the Wizr board?" Severn asked. "It's been missing since Eredur died. I used to watch him play it. It holds many memories for me."

Owen was surprised. "You knew of it?"

Severn nodded. "Of course I did. It's been handed down in my family for generations. It's been stolen so many times, it's almost laughable. My brother believed he couldn't lose a battle so long as he held it. He was superstitious, of course. I'm certain he would have won his battles without it. But I know Chatriyon's father and grandfather feared the Wizr board. He tried to have it stolen several times." He smiled shrewdly. "But as I said, it disappeared while my brother was king. Where did you find it? Did the duchess give it to you? Was it in Brythonica all this time?"

Owen shook his head. "No, it was in the cistern beneath the palace. I first saw it there when I was your *hostage*."

The king pursed his lips. "Remarkable. I never thought to search there. My brother had many treasures that weren't found in the royal vaults after he died. I assumed his *wife* had taken it with the rest and brought them to sanctuary." The king started pacing. "It's all a bunch of rubbish anyway. I don't have a magic Wizr set helping *me*, and I've never been defeated either." He snorted derisively.

Owen narrowed his eyes. "It's not superstition," he said in a low voice. "The Wizr set is *causing* this storm."

"When my wife died, there was an eclipse," Severn scoffed. "Fools are always quick to attribute ill omens to the stars or the weather."

"Fools convince themselves their enemies are their true friends," Owen countered. "There are rules in the game of Wizr. Even though you're a king, you cannot change the rules of the game. The storm has come because you broke the rules of sanctuary years ago."

"Then why did the storm *stop*, I ask you?"

Owen clenched his fists. "Because it was taken outside your domains! It was inside the sanctuary of St. Penryn until I brought it back."

The king pointed his finger at Owen. "*You* brought it back."

Owen swallowed, trying to rein in his emotions. "I believe in the omens, Severn. I've seen evidence of the Fountain's judgments all my life. You are Fountain-blessed yourself, how can you deny what gives you your own power?"

Severn looked at him with disdain. "I believe in the magic. I used to believe in the source," he answered in a quiet way. "I used to *trust*. But no more. If I lived in the days of King Andrew, I would have been one of his knights. I would have *believed* in the principles of Virtus. But that's not the world we live in, Owen! This is a world of princes, poison, and power. Andrew was a myth. A legend. There is no Dreadful Deadman. You invoked a legend to usurp my crown for yourself, do not deny it. Oh, you would have used some *child* to make your claim legitimate. Especially one who bears resemblance to my dead nephews. I've uncovered your trickery, Owen. How convenient the Espion couldn't locate the boy's birth parents. I know how your mind works. And that prophecy you made! It's all the people are talking about now. Some *boy* is going to draw a sword from the waters of Our Lady. Well, I'll tell you what *I'm* going to do once I've drowned Iago and Elysabeth for treason. I'm going to summon every lad of eight summers to Kingfountain." He stepped closer. "And then I'm going to push them all into the river to see who survives! Even your little puppet." He snorted maliciously and lifted his hands. "Every prince and every king who has lifted a heel or raised a finger against me will ensure that the children in their kingdom meet the same fate."

Owen stared at him in growing horror. "Your heart is already ice."

The king met his eyes without flinching. "One grows numb to cold after a time. As you are to experience yourself." He looked at Kevan. "We leave before dawn. Make sure the roads are shoveled ere we leave the city. I've already sent my army North with Catsby." He turned to leave.

"Are you taking Dragan with you?" Owen said in challenge.

The king stopped, a look of annoyance on his face. Without speaking, he motioned for the guard to open the door. Kevan gave Owen a forlorn and helpless look over the chest he still clutched. Severn nodded to the two Espion protectors to leave as well. The door shut behind them, leaving Owen alone in the room, in chains, with Dragan.

The thief appeared before him. He drew a long-stemmed pipe and sauntered over to the brazier. With a pair of tongs, he lit the bowl, and the mash inside began to sizzle and spread noxious fumes in the room.

Dragan stuck the pipe between his teeth and breathed in deep, hooking his thumbs in his belt.

"I asked the king for a special promise ere you left on the morrow," he said smugly.

"I'm sure you did," Owen said, feeling nothing but hatred and disgust for the man.

"A small favor. He wasn't against the notion, I tell you. I thoughts to myself, I did, I thoughts, 'Dragan, that lad turned your own flesh and blood against you.' Aye, he did. A most unnatural thing he did. A child's first loyalty should be to his parents. You've always been an unnatural child, I sez. Betrayin' your own kin and serving Lord Severn. Unnatural. Well, you had my daughter kilt protectin' you." His eyes smoldered with anger. "Bothwell promised he'd spare her because I asked it. But she died because of you."

"Because of me? You let him into the castle!" Owen said, affronted and furious.

Dragan shook his head. "I'm a simple man. I seez what you did to her. How you turned her away from her own father. Well, I wants compensation for that. I took her jewels and such from her room. Hardly worth ten crowns, if you ask me. Some fancy vials, little knick-knacks." He began cracking his knuckles. "But it don't pardon ye in my eyes. And besides, Chatriyon said he'd pay fifty thousand for your left hand. The left hand, mind ye. I don't know what such a lord needs for your claw. But it's fifty thousand all the same. And I'll be checking out that cistern too. Might be more baubles down there, eh?" He drew a knife from his belt. "Now be a good lad and hold still while I cut it off. The king promised me my due. And you won't be needing it no longer anyway, I reckon, when you've frozen."

# CHAPTER
# THIRTY-THREE

*Helvellyn*

As Owen listened to Dragan's little speech, he gently, surreptitiously summoned his own magic to prepare his defense. He had small reserves and knew he would not be able to sustain the onslaught long, but he wanted to test the thief's defenses, to learn of his vulnerabilities. As his magic seeped away from him, Owen learned some immediate facts about Etayne's father. First, he was a coward at heart and would flee in an instant should a situation turn against him. Second, the somewhat stocky man had an unhealthy heart. He enjoyed his feasts and mugs of ale, and had spent most of his life without doing an honest day's work.

The insights gave Owen courage he otherwise might have lacked, considering his own circumstances. He didn't need his magic to reveal to him that he was unfit for mortal combat at the moment. His wounds were still healing, and sudden motions could easily rip the sinews binding his skin closed.

But just like in the game of Wizr, sometimes it was better to go on the offensive when facing a threat.

"Well, if you're determined to have it," Owen said, "best to get it over with quickly." He planted his iron-encircled wrist on the small wooden table in the corner, pulling the cuff higher to expose his wrist. He stared into Dragan's eyes and locked wills with him.

"That's mighty generous of you, lad," he said distrustfully. The thief seemed to sense something in the room had changed, and his whiskers twitched as he sniffed at the air.

"Be quick about your work," Owen chided, nodding to his exposed wrist.

"It's usually better to be quick in moments like this," Dragan offered with a shrug. Then suddenly the dagger plunged down, the tip heading straight for the tendons in Owen's arm. Not to slice off the hand, but to impale his arm to the desk.

Thankfully, Owen had suspected the move, and jerked his hand away just in time to watch the dagger sink into the wood rather than into his flesh. He leaned forward, putting his weight on his arms atop the table, and swung his leg forward to kick Dragan hard in the groin. The thief's eyes bulged with pain, and he crumpled over double, eyes widening with panic.

Owen yanked the dagger out of the table as the thief lord scurried backward and used his magic to vanish. But Owen had been expecting that as well, so he took a large step forward and kicked again, catching the man on the shoulder or the side of his head, hearing the body flop to the ground and roll. He could hear Dragan's breathing, his tortured gasps and stifled groans, and used the sounds to locate him. Owen knelt down and hammered the dagger's pommel into the blank space before a boot kicked him in the stomach, knocking him back.

The blow was a solid one, and Owen found himself crashing into the table. There were scrabbling sounds as Dragan struggled to reach the door.

Owen's blood was up, and he sought vengeance against the father who had done so much to hurt and frighten Etayne. He grabbed the edge of the wooden table and flung it hard toward the door. As he twisted, he felt some of the stitches rip in his side, making him double over in pain. The table smashed into the door with an echoing crash, sending fragments of wood everywhere.

Owen tried to control his rage, his thundering heart, as he reached out with his magic.

"The debt owed to you is a life," Owen said in a voice shaking with emotion. "And I intend to pay it in full. Your daughter lost hers saving mine. And I will end yours to pay her back. You betrayed her. You betrayed us all. Come here, thief, so I can *kill* you!" Owen felt dizziness wash over him, but his magic spread out across the room, doing his bidding.

There he was—skulking against the wall, cowering in fear.

Owen raised the dagger to throw it, but at that exact moment, the door of the tower cell burst open and Kevan entered with two Espion guards.

Dragan used the commotion to slip unseen out of the room. Owen nearly threw the dagger anyway, but he realized he might hit his lieutenant in the process.

"What's going on here!" Kevan said in surprise. "How did he get a dagger?"

Owen flipped the blade and then caught it by the tip and handed it over to one of the men coming to subdue him.

"You should search people more carefully next time," he grunted, gasping in pain. Looking down, he saw the bloodstain blooming on his shirt.

◆　◆　◆

Before dawn, Owen had been hoisted up onto a horse and had ridden from the bailey surrounded by the king's men. Leading the way was the king himself, his black cloak spotted with chunky flakes of the snow that continued to fall on the city. The hooves crunched through ice and clinked loudly against the stone cobbles of the road. There were already chunks of ice in the river. Owen's side throbbed with pain, and the cold stung his nose as he breathed.

Winter had come to Ceredigion.

They left while the city of Kingfountain was still abed, but as they passed the empty streets, Owen saw men and women peering from behind curtains to watch the king's procession.

Owen saw that the chest with the Wizr set was strapped to the back of the king's saddle. Alongside him rode Lady Kathryn, also swathed in black, a silken veil covering her hair. Her mantle was lined with silver fur. Her face was pallid, and puffs of steam came from her mouth as she breathed. As Owen examined the others accompanying them, he spotted Kevan. A much smaller pony rode next to the Espion, and he recognized it was the boy Drew, bundled in jackets and hats to protect him. Owen's heart pained him as he realized they had all come to watch him die. But he grieved even more for the boy Severn was preparing to murder. Of course the king had brought Drew along. He assumed it would add to Owen's misery. To him, the boy was yet another pretender to his throne—he didn't seem to realize the lad's significance beyond his resemblance to the Argentines.

Normally, the king slept out of doors while traveling, even in the winter, but because he was accompanied by his lady and a child, he had chosen to stop at certain hamlets and villages on the road heading north. News reached them at various points of the day. Owen wasn't included in the messages, but he heard his captors discussing it amongst themselves and gleaned what he could from it.

The Duke of Brugia had sacked the port city of Callait and hoisted his banners from the tower. Word of his imminent invasion was spreading throughout the kingdom. It was said that boats were assembling off the coastal towns to prepare for the invasion. Rumor also had it that

Chatriyon had stirred and was marching an army against Brythonica to prevent anyone from Ceredigion from marrying the duchess. It was said that the duchess's banners were flying and her army had assembled to resist Occitania, but without Ceredigion to protect her domain, the duchess was likely to fall.

The different reports coming in at various times along the journey made Owen grow sicker with worry. He was never given even a moment alone. His fare was simple and foul-tasting, and he was deprived of all the luxuries his rank had once afforded him. He was a dead man, he realized. His plan had failed, and all who had supported him would be punished.

As they rode the snow-packed roads leading to Dundrennan, Owen began to lose hope of finding an opportunity to escape. His magic still returned to him in small trickles, but his usually vast reservoirs were shallow. He thought about Evie and what would happen to her. She would be wise to abandon the North and seek refuge in Atabyrion before the king arrived. They would stand a better chance holding against Severn Argentine in their own lands rather than trying to cling to North Cumbria in open rebellion. Perhaps even a peace treaty could be arranged? But Owen's thoughts had turned as black as the sky was white. Severn would never forgive Evie or Iago, not now. He would punish them in ways that would stab their hearts. They had a little boy, an heir to the throne. Owen agonized at the thought of the child being sacrificed to sate the king's hunger for revenge.

He worried also about Sinia, though with any luck her powers would help protect her. Brythonica was so small compared to Occitania. Her duchy had always staved off invasion through alliances and treaties, but Severn wouldn't defend her now. Chatriyon was already married, so he couldn't press his claim. Still, he could force her to marry one of his loyal dukes and punish her peaceful realm for the years of disobedience. Owen's shoulders drooped as he thought about how much suffering would blast the people as a result of his own failure.

After days in the saddle, the clouds finally parted, revealing a vast blue expanse over the North. The mountains were fleeced with snow. The pines were laden with it, weighed down and drooping under the heavy load.

"There it is," the king announced, reining in and pointing. "See her yonder. The peak Helvellyn. That is where the Maid perished." He turned and gave Owen a look colder than the frost. "That's where you perish, lad."

A rider wearing the king's colors rode hard toward them from farther up the road. Severn kept his beast subdued until the man arrived.

"What news?" Severn asked.

The man's cheeks were flushed and he had snow in his beard. He shook his head. "The Queen of Atabyrion still holds Dundrennan, my lord. They know we're coming and they didn't flee. Your army is camped less than a league ahead. We've overtaken the lower city. Most of the populace fled into the castle to weather the winter *and* the siege."

Severn scowled. "A winter siege. She's going to make me earn it. Any word from her?"

The soldier nodded and snow sloughed from his beard. "She states her claim to the land as the rightful heir of Stiev Horwath. She demands that Lord Catsby return the treasures plundered. Once that is done, she promises to swear fealty for her lands to the King of Ceredigion."

Severn's face darkened with anger and Owen smiled at Evie's pluck.

"She owes her allegiance to me *now*," Severn snarled. "Well, if she wants to play at war, then she will have it. How many men do we have gathered here?"

The soldier wiped his beard. "Twenty thousand strong and loyal, my lord. The army from Westmarch under Captain Ashby will arrive in a few days. That will bring us to nearly thirty thousand. Even with men from Atabyrion, she can't have more than fifteen, and if they're all crammed inside that castle, they'll be dying of their own fumes ere long."

The king smirked. "Well done. Take my lady and retinue to the city. The journey is cold. I'm going to bring the rest of the men to Helvellyn to see to the king's traitor." He turned to Lady Kathryn and reached out, taking her hand. He kissed the glove. "I'll join you tonight, my love."

Lady Kathryn gave Owen a look of sad farewell. Then she turned back to the king and nodded deferentially.

Owen's stomach soured as if he'd swallowed spoiled wine.

"You're coming with us?" Kevan asked the king in surprise.

Severn nodded. "I don't trust any man to see this done for me. Especially no Espion. In fact, *you* are the one who is not coming with us. I want you to ride into the city and see what news the Espion has of Iago's troops and movements. Is there a secret way into the fortress? Prove your loyalty to me in this, Kevan, and you may lead the Espion yourself when this is all over."

◆　◆　◆

The Maid of Donremy had been taken by mule to the peak of Helvellyn, the second or third largest peak in all of Ceredigion. Owen had read the records of her trial, including her confession about hearing the whispers from the Fountain and the documentation of her many gifts as one who was Fountain-blessed. But all the records were clear about one thing: She had frozen to death in the snow-capped mountains, wearing only a shift. She had been chained to a rock while several soldiers huddled by a few coal-burning braziers and waited out her death. After the deed had been done, they'd dragged her body down for the king's men to verify that the Maid was no more.

The horses carried Owen, Severn, and the dozens of trusted soldiers up the slope of the mountain. Owen's ears and fingers were numb. His toes felt like pebbles. They'd already stripped away his cloak, and his shivers were uncontrollable. The cliffs of Helvellyn were especially steep facing the valley of Dundrennan. But along the far side, the slope was much more gradual, making it easier for the animals to bear their burdens.

Partway up the mountain, a stone effigy of the Maid had been carved into one of the boulders protruding from the snow. The image was worn and glazed in ice, and Owen felt heartsick looking at it. The air was more difficult to breathe, and Owen felt chunks of ice sticking to his whiskers and lashes. The blue sky from earlier had become veiled in white, as if the storm that was descending on Kingfountain had moved along with them.

At last, they reached the craggy peak. It was midafternoon, though the sun was hidden by thick clouds. The soldiers set up a little shelter on the leeward side of a boulder and added fuel to their sconces. Flames licked the chilled air, and the men huddled close to them, chafing their hands. Owen was kept away from the warmth, and it tortured him to see the tongues of fire without being able to savor them.

Severn remained on his pony, seemingly impervious to the cold. He wore the crown on his head, a reminder of his position to himself and all others who saw him. He watched the whole scene unfold dispassionately.

Two soldiers helped Owen dismount, and he nearly stumbled because of his leaden feet. How long had the Maid survived before perishing? Owen didn't think he would last the night. He stared at the king without flinching.

"You may do with me as you please, my lord," Owen said, his teeth chattering with cold. "But this fate that awaits me also awaits the people of your realm. This *unnatural* winter was brought on us because of you. I will not be the last who perishes from cold. You bring this doom upon all of your subjects unless you relinquish that crown."

The king looked disdainful. "So you've warned and so I've heard. Even in death you persist in your lies. Maybe you've even convinced yourself. But know this. I won this crown by right and by might. I will not give it up willingly. Even if the doom you prophesy comes to pass."

Owen frowned. "I can do no more then."

"Indeed. You've done quite enough," the king said with iron in his voice. He nodded to the soldiers. "Bring me his corpse in the morn. Be faithful, lads. You will see for yourselves that his bluster is no more than empty noise. I don't want any of you to miss the action as we humble Elysabeth *Victoria* Mortimer Llewellyn. Queen of Ashes."

The king departed with a dozen men, leaving six behind to watch Owen die.

He was taken to the very boulder where they'd chained the Maid of Donremy, and his cuffs were attached to the iron rings fastened there. His legs trembled as he stared at the torture of the flames. The wind keened through his thin shirt.

"Good luck, Evie," he whispered through clenched teeth.

He decided to stare at the flames awhile, to imagine what it would be like to cup his hands over them. In his mind, he thought back to his time in Dundrennan as a child, sitting before the raging hearth, his knees touching Evie's as they talked and played together. From this vantage point, he could see the valley so far below, see the smoke billowing from many chimneys to feed the clouds in the sky. Perhaps it would be the last thing he ever saw.

Then, from behind the gathered soldiers, part of the snowbank seemed to . . . lift. The soldiers hidden there beneath snow-covered canopies stole from their hiding places and fell on Severn's guards with brutal efficiency, killing all six before a single one could cry out in warning or pain.

Two men wrapped in thick furs trudged through the snow toward Owen. As they unwound the scarves covering their faces, Owen's heart began to hammer again. Sparks of renewed hope began to fly.

The first man he recognized was the Espion Clark, whose life he had saved at Wizr Falls in Atabyrion. Clark was normally very stoic, but he betrayed himself with a crooked little smile.

The second man under the hood and wrappings was Evie's husband, the King of Atabyrion.

"You look a little chilly, my lord," Iago said triumphantly in his native brogue. "I think we can spare you a jacket and boots, eh?"

# CHAPTER THIRTY-FOUR

## *Carrick*

Snow sloughed off Owen's cloak as he dismounted in the castle bailey of Dundrennan. The boots covering his frozen feet had helped ease his discomfort, but he still felt leaden and stiff. Even so, his heart was full of fire and emotion for his rescuers. A few dogs barked in greeting as the doors of the keep opened and Elysabeth rushed out into the slushy ice, a wool blanket draped around her shoulders. She embraced her husband, giving him a passionate kiss on the mouth, and then rushed over to fling her arms around Owen's neck.

"You're safe," she breathed in his ear before pulling back and staring at him with a jubilant grin. Her eyes were very green at that moment, and he found himself beaming back at her.

"Thanks to you," he replied sincerely, still bedazzled by his unexpected reprieve.

Evie shook her head, and only then did Owen notice the other man approaching them. It was a sheepish-looking Kevan Amrein.

He held out the scabbard with the raven insignia on it, offering it to Owen.

Owen felt another flush of warmth in his heart, and his throat suddenly felt thick as he stared at his old friend. "It was your doing?" he said.

Kevan looked abashed. "I've known you were plotting something for quite some time, my lord," he said. "I thought it strange you kept bringing Eyric books. I had them snatched while he slept and learned to read the love notes he shared with Lady Kathryn. I've tried in many delicate ways to show you I was on your side. When the king finds out I too have rebelled against him, I will need another job. If you'll have me."

Owen started to laugh. The sound just came bubbling out of him. He took the scabbard with one hand and then pulled Kevan into a hug and clapped him hard on the back. "Have you?" he chuckled. "I have a feeling that stopping my execution is only part of your plan."

Owen noticed Clark and Iago had drawn close to them. He glanced from face to face, each full of courage and determination. A feeling of profound relief flooded him. He was not alone in trying to bring down Severn. He never had been.

"Must we have this council in the middle of the freezing bailey?" Iago drawled. "Best to move it to the solar?"

Elysabeth nodded with encouragement. "The cold normally doesn't bother me, but tonight it's excessively cold."

Together they tromped their way back into the castle, where the flames from the hearth and torches forced back the chilly winter air. The castle was crowded with soldiers wearing the badge of the Pierced Lion and there were servants everywhere, bringing food and drink to satisfy those who had hunkered down inside the walls. The commotion abated when they reached the solar, but Owen didn't mind the stares. His hope had been restored to him. He belted the scabbard around his waist and instantly felt the magic begin to work through him, warming his frozen extremities and mending the festering wounds from his ordeal with Bothwell.

Owen stood by the hearth, staring down at the huge cedar logs nested amidst the coals, and savoring the warmth. The others entered, and he watched as Iago slouched into the duke's old chair, quite comfortably, and accepted a flagon of wine from his wife. When Evie stroked Iago's shoulder tenderly, and he smiled up at her, the evidence of their mutual affection made Owen's heart clench, but this time the feeling was a little different, a little less covetous. He found himself wishing Sinia were here to enjoy the reprieve with him.

Turning his back to the fire, he faced his allies. Kevan and Clark were speaking in low tones with each other, but they both fell silent when they saw Owen looking at them.

"First, I must thank you all," Owen said, shaking his head. "I was not looking forward to spending the night chained to Helvellyn. I'm not talented at these kinds of speeches, but my heart compels me to speak the gratitude I feel. Thank you all, again." He folded his arms and began to pace, dropping into the familiar habit. Ripples of Fountain magic added to his warmth as he began to sort through their situation as he would the first blocks of one of his tile structures. "Kevan—how did you arrange this?"

A wry smile twisted the face of the Espion lieutenant. "It did not require much imagination to figure out where the king was planning to execute you. I had someone stationed at the river in case he planned on throwing you in, but I thought he'd keep with tradition. It's part of the historical record that the Maid of Donremy was taken to Helvellyn for her execution. I sent word to Clark, knowing that he was already at Dundrennan."

Owen smiled at the man and nodded. "And it was your idea to hide under blankets in the snow?"

Clark was not the type to appreciate such attention. He nodded curtly.

Iago laughed. "He's too modest. It was bloody brilliant. He's an excellent hunter and spy. I tell you, I was tempted to try and kill Severn myself when he came up the mountain so unprotected. If we could have hidden fifty men, it would have been the perfect trap. But I didn't truly believe he'd leave his army, and we couldn't risk that he would kill you before we got to him. All went well enough, though, so I shouldn't complain."

Evie squeezed his shoulder and he quieted down.

"Let my lady speak," Iago said with a flamboyant gesture. "This was her strategy after all."

Owen cocked his head to get a better look at her.

"When we found out you were compromised," Evie said, "we needed to adjust our plans quickly, knowing we'd face the brunt of the king's army. I think it's better this way. He'll be surrounded and cut off from his supplies. He's coming to lay siege to the North, but he'll be trapped here."

"How so?" Owen asked. "Why can't he retreat back to Kingfountain?"

She smiled mischievously. "Because *your* army is blocking the retreat."

"Captain Ashby?" Owen asked with growing delight.

"Is on your side," Kevan answered with a nod. "As are your men. And the Duchess of Brythonica's forces will be arriving in two days. We'll more than outnumber the king's."

Owen smiled. "She's coming?"

Evie gave him a knowing look, a small smile on her face. "She's kept us informed of her actions. There is more. Kevan? Tell him about the enemies of Ceredigion."

Kevan nodded and clasped his hands behind his back. "The Duke of Brugia has breached the defenses of Callait. I see by your look you already knew this. He's preparing ships to attack Kingfountain.

Chatriyon is also marching with his army. They've swept into Westmarch behind the duchess's forces. They've been joined by the Legaultans, who seek revenge on Severn for sacking their cities years ago. Westmarch is being fought for like scattered table scraps by hounds."

Owen stared at him, his stomach clenching with worry. "That makes seven," he whispered.

"What?" Evie asked him.

Owen stopped pacing. "The prophecy of the Dreadful Deadman says that seven kings will unite against Ceredigion, but I don't think it literally means kings. Back in the days of King Andrew, each duchy was led by a king. It was a title, a rank, similar to that of a duke today." He snapped his fingers. "Occitania, Brythonica, Leoneyis— that's Westmarch—Atabyrion, Legault. In the past, North Cumbria was its own kingdom. And Brugia. That makes seven. Seven kings, or seven *rulers*, each invading Ceredigion. Severn brought his forces to the North because that is where his most loyal supporters have traditionally come from. This is the fulfillment of the prophecy. Only a new king can unify us again. A young man, hardly a boy, who is the rightful ruler of Ceredigion and who will restore the ancient rights of the sanctuaries."

"And where is this rightful king?" Evie asked. "Is he still back at the palace? Should we send someone to fetch him?"

They were all looking at him. Only Lady Kathryn, Sinia, and the Deconeus of St. Penryn knew the secret now that Eyric and Etayne had gone on to the Deep Fathoms. "He's down in the king's camp with a Wizr board that can destroy all of us."

Owen rubbed his forehead. It was time to tell them all the truth. He looked at the doors to make sure they were closed. "I must tell you about what I've been planning. It's time you all knew. But before I do, I have a question to ask of you." He turned to Evie. "Do you know of a boy in the castle named Carrick?"

Evie nodded. "He's the son of my grandfather's huntsman, Fergus. They've been out hunting meat to feed the soldiers. The boy is the best hunter in these parts. He has a gift."

Owen smiled. "He's Fountain-blessed."

◆   ◆   ◆

Owen's legs ached from the long climb into the mountains behind the fortress of Dundrennan. He was wrapped in bearskin leggings, thick gloves, and several shirts and tunics, yet it was barely enough to suppress the chill of the descending night. Clark hiked alongside him, longbow at the ready, as did Evie, dressed in her sturdy leather boots. They followed Carrick, a sinewy lad with gray eyes and shorn hair, and his father. Fergus had a salt-and-pepper beard and an animated manner, but Carrick was quiet and sober-minded. He seemed older than his seventeen summers. They had warned the others that they were hunting in bear country and the beasts were especially hungry due to the early winter. They should be hibernating, but there was still the risk that some would be out looking for meat to sustain them.

Iago had remained behind with Kevan to oversee the castle's defenses. He'd given Owen a wary look before they left, conveying the message that he had better protect Evie . . . or else. It was clear that while he trusted his wife on the jaunt, he was not happy about the risk they were taking by leaving the safety of Dundrennan.

They followed the river at the head of the waterfall high into the mountains, where water melted from a natural glacier older than any of the kingdoms. It was this glacier that was the source of the river of Kingfountain.

"There's the cave," Carrick said, pointing. There was nothing but ice and shattered rock this high in the mountains. The river was narrow enough to span with their legs at this point, but the ice cave extended deep into the throat of the glacier.

Fergus whistled with respect. "My boy found it," he said boastfully, turning to Evie. "I've been by this way a dozen times without ever thinking it more than a crag of ice and rock, but he felt something calling to him from inside it. He can hear things we can't."

Now that he was close, Owen could sense something too. The Fountain's magic welled in this place, as much as it did in Brythonica. He could sense power emanating from the mountains. The closer they'd come to the source of the river, the more he'd felt his magic reserves fill up.

They paused before the ice caves, and Carrick and Fergus brought out torches and lit them with flint and iron. The ripples of the flames would help them see as night shrouded the sky. Stars had begun to appear in the liquid expanse overhead, higher than the clouds that hung oppressively over Dundrennan.

Carrying the torches, the hunters led the way into the caves. The river was frozen just inside the cave, a sheet of continuous ice that led the way in, but the travelers' boots were equipped with leather straps covered in nail spikes. The torchlight glimmered off the strange walls that were clear and warped like glass. The light from the torches made dazzling colors that illuminated the way ahead.

"I told you I couldn't miss this," Evie whispered to Owen as they walked, her breath coming out in great puffs of white. "We always wanted to visit the caves."

With a gloved hand, Owen touched the rippled ice of the walls as Carrick led them deeper into the cave. The only sounds were the scratching noise of their boot spikes and the puffs of frosty air they exhaled.

Around the first bend, there was a cleft of solid stone that had been split down the middle. Owen stared at it in surprise. The rock looked like it had been cleaved down the middle by an enormous axe, though the boulder was too big for any mortal weapon. Fragments of rock lay askew around it. As Owen passed the area, he rubbed his hand along the sheer surface of the rock, his mind alive with the Fountain.

*It is the power of the sword,* it whispered to him. *The power of ice. It is the White King's blade.*

Owen shuddered as the knowledge passed through him.

"It is this way," Carrick said solemnly, pointing.

Around the next bend, the cave ended reaching the face of the glacier. Suspended in the ice, about a foot deep, was the outline of a sword trapped inside. A feeling of magic and reverence hung thick in the air.

They all crowded around the blade, the torches casting their shadows on the ground.

"I thought to bring a pickaxe," Carrick said softly, "but I dared not."

Owen's heart beat wildly as he stared at the ancient weapon. The sword of the Maid. The sword of King Andrew.

When he pulled the glove off his hand, he felt the cold bite into his skin. The ring on his finger began to glow. He readied himself, preparing for the pain he was expecting. As he reached out to grasp the sword, the ice began to billow out like fog. He plunged his hand into it, experiencing cold so intense that it burned. Wincing with pain, he pushed harder. When he gripped the sword, the ice around it became as insubstantial as a cloud, and he drew it out of its prison. The pain immediately began to recede, the scabbard at his hip sustaining him, and he stared in awe at the weapon he had drawn out.

The Maid's sword had been dubbed Firebos, so named because it had been drawn from the fountain of St. Kathryn in the village of Firebos in Occitania. With the sword, the Maid had driven the Ceredigion army back to their prewar borders, putting the duchy of Westmarch as the borderland between the warring kingdoms that had once, centuries before, been united.

The weapon that Owen drew from the glacier matched the description he'd once read about. The sword had five stars on the blade, and the metal was striated like wood grain, except in various shades of gray and silver.

When Owen held it in his hands and gazed on it, he felt a surge of magic shoot up his arms, and he knew without a doubt it was the Maid's blade—the weapon of King Andrew himself. Images from countless battles flashed through his mind in quick succession. A sound like a ringing bell filled his ears.

"This was worth the climb," Evie said after a pent-up breath. She gazed at Owen with eyes full of wonderment, and he allowed himself to relish her admiration for a moment.

"Praise be the Fountain," Fergus uttered reverently as he stared down at the hole in the solid ice.

◆　◆　◆

*To the king's traitor:*

*I, your sovereign lord, have played Wizr against you enough times to know when the game is lost. You have outmaneuvered me, and I submit to your claims. While you prepared a young boy to miraculously claim this unruly realm, I know you have secretly coveted the power for yourself. May your stint as lord protector prove more favorable to your fortunes than mine did. I relinquish my authority willingly and will submit to the ignominy of the dungeon or the river as many of my fore-bears have patiently endured. I send you Chancellor Catsby to negotiate my surrender. The hollow crown is yours.*

*Severn Argentine, Lord of Ceredigion*

◆　◆　◆

# CHAPTER
# THIRTY-FIVE

### *The King's Word*

Owen sat astride his horse, ready for battle, with a thick chain hauberk beneath his heavy fur cloak, bracers on his arms, and a shield strapped to his saddle harness. The hilt of Firebos protruded from its scabbard, and he felt the magic of the blade thrumming against his hip. The blade sensed the looming battle, and was eager for it. A flock of young squires stood nearby with spears, in case they were needed.

The road was covered in freshly fallen snow, but trample marks showed the paths of the horses that had been ridden to and from the village throughout the night. Hastily built pavilions had been erected in the woods on either side of the road, but no one had slept that night, especially not Owen, for fear the king would try to slip away in the dark. The Espion who were loyal to Kevan had revealed that the king was still sequestered in a wealthy lord's house. His army had marched the streets all night, expecting a night attack from Owen that hadn't come. The two armies had faced each other silently, waiting for dawn to break the deadlock.

Kevan Amrein sat astride as well, but he was only there to relay intelligence about the king's movements. He was not a warrior, and would not ride into battle should one break out.

Severn was in a terrible position. He had the mountains of Dundrennan at his back. Evie and Iago held the high ground and the keep. If the king attacked Owen's army, they would attack him from the rear. If he tried to assault the castle, Owen would flank him from behind. The two armies were evenly matched, but Brythonica's forces were already hastening to join them.

"How far is the duchess by your reckoning?" Owen asked Kevan, leaning on the saddle.

The Espion had a day's growth on his chin from not shaving. "Two days, maybe less," he said. "The roads are getting worse by the day. Will this infernal storm ever end?"

"No, it won't," Owen said, gazing down at the road toward the village. "Not until it's over." The biggest question in his mind was whether Severn would fight. Owen could have arranged for the king's abduction. It would not have been easy, but there were many who would be willing to do such a thing to prevent bloodshed. But Owen did not want to topple Severn through trickery. A king deserved the chance to die in battle if he so chose. But it was not a battle Owen was anxious to start.

Captain Ashby's horse rode up from the camp and aligned next to his.

"What news, Ashby?" Owen asked. "How are the men?"

Ashby had a serious cast to his face, but he looked confident too. They had led many battles together, and the older man had learned to trust Owen's instincts and strategies.

"They are nervous, as you can well imagine," the captain said gruffly. "You've not lost a battle. That bodes well. But neither has the king. Money is going to change hands when this is through. I put my money on you, my lord."

Owen smiled and chuckled softly. "Thank you." He stared at the lonely road, feeling warm beneath his cloak, gloves, and armor. In fact, he was a bit too warm. The scabbard was snug around his waist, and he felt the soothing, healing influence of it chase away his aches and pains.

"It's no small matter rebelling against a king," Owen said. "I'm sure the men have mixed emotions, as do I. But I swear to you, this winter will not end if Severn keeps his throne. His actions have doomed us all. The duchess and I could not let that calamity fall without acting against it."

Ashby sniffed and then straightened. "Riders."

The sound of hooves in the snow followed his warning, and men appeared on the road ahead. Owen saw the herald hoisting the banner of the king, the White Boar. A chill rattled Owen's bones when he saw it, and his breath quickened. Three men approached the line.

"We have visitors," Owen said, glancing at the cloud-veiled sky. The hour was indistinguishable in the wintery haze, but he guessed it was still before noon. He glanced at Kevan. "Get Farnes over here. Quickly."

As the riders drew closer, Owen recognized Catsby. The third person was the king's personal squire.

"Interesting," Ashby said under his breath.

Owen wondered if the king would surrender or summon them to battle. The king had the Wizr set, which meant he would be difficult to beat. He also had Drew, the boy he believed Owen was positioning to be king. But did Severn truly understand the importance of his advantages? Did he know that the board possessed powers of its own? That the boy in his tent was the only other person in Ceredigion who could use it? Owen hoped not. He'd considered sending a man to steal the set and rescue the lad, but if the man were captured, it would reveal too much. Owen knew his next moves needed to be very careful. He couldn't risk the boy's life. Nervous energy raced through him as the trio arrived.

"My lord Catsby," Owen said, nodding in wary respect.

"My lord," Catsby said. "I bear this message from the king. He told me to entrust it to no man but you."

Owen smirked. "He knows I'm alive?"

Catsby looked as if he'd tasted something sour. "He knows you aren't *dead*. He realizes he's surrounded, on unfavorable ground, by a rebel force that is likely larger than his own. You've cut off our supplies and all hope of succor. The longer this *farce* continues, the more damage the true enemies of our realm will do. I saw him write the note myself. I can assure you, it is his will."

Catsby swatted his horse's flanks and came closer to present the note bearing the royal seal. Owen accepted it, using his replenished Fountain magic to detect weakness or trickery. There was no poison on the note, nothing but ink and wax. He used his power on Catsby and found that all the man's weapons were clearly visible. Catsby was not that capable a soldier, and Owen sensed the man's secret fear of his own reputation with a sword.

He broke the seal and quickly read the message declaring the king's surrender.

"What does it say, my lord?" Ashby said in an undertone.

Owen felt a surge of relief flood his heart. He hadn't realized he'd been holding his breath until this very moment. The words were definitely Severn's. There was plenty of spite in them. His accusation that Owen intended to rule the realm was particularly vengeful. But the king still had the boy, and Owen needed to separate them.

"The king has surrendered," Owen said with relief as Kevan and Farnes drew near.

"Truly?" Farnes asked with surprise.

"Read it for yourself," he said, handing the note to him. He nodded for Kevan to do the same.

"There is no cause for bloodshed," Catsby said. "I am authorized on the king's behalf to negotiate his surrender. Is it your desire to execute him? He especially wishes to know your intentions on that front."

Rather than relief, Owen felt a strange sensation of dread. A feeling of heaviness had settled on him. Years earlier, Ankarette had told him a story that had never left him. A story about how a prince had persuaded a rebel army to lay down its arms. In the moment of relief that followed, the prince had broken his word and attacked his unprepared enemies. The leaders were all taken to the river and drowned because they were wearing heavy armor.

Owen remembered being stricken with shock—his young mind had struggled to understand such deep lies.

He still remembered the look of sadness on her face. *That is the way of princes and power, Owen. That is the nature of the kingdom of Ceredigion. In truth, it is the nature and disposition of most men. So think on this. If you were one of the rebel leaders and the prince promised you forgiveness and reward, it would matter, very much, if you had discernment. He needed to make a decision based on what type of man he believed the prince to be. Was he a man of honor? Or was he willing to say anything, do anything to help his father keep his crown? That is why discernment is the most important thing you can learn, Owen. It takes time and experience. Sadly, one wrong judgment can lead to . . . well, you heard the end of the story.*

Yes, he knew the feint well.

"The king sent you with this note?" Owen demanded hotly. "He intends to surrender?"

Catsby looked confused. "He told me so himself, Lord Owen, in no uncertain terms. He will surrender to you. He sent me to negotiate the terms. I swear it!"

The man's face was convincing. His words were convincing. And Owen felt magic in his words—magic pressing against his own in an effort to persuade him the king's words were true. But Owen's magic prevented others from controlling him this way.

"Well, this is the best news that we could possibly have received!" Farnes said with triumph. "I'm quite relieved, to be honest."

"It's not true," Owen said, shaking his head. "This isn't a surrender. It's a trap."

"Are you certain, my lord?" Ashby asked him with a worried tone. "The king knows *he's* been trapped."

A cheer arose in the distance. It sounded as if it came from the walls of Dundrennan itself. Horns began to blow. Not war horns, but the blasts of victory.

Owen discerned what was happening. The king had also sent word to Evie and Iago. He had used his magic to convince his messengers that he was serious. That the surrender was true. Catsby's manner was not that of a duplicitous man. He appeared convinced that a surrender truly was underway.

"Trumpets?" Kevan asked with concern.

Catsby nodded. "The king sent word to the castle. Our soldiers are half-frozen. He's asking if they can fall in with the garrison after we've concluded the negotiation. I tell you, Lord Owen, the king is sincere! He put his hand on my shoulder and told me most emphatically that he was surrendering. He wanted to be sure I *convinced* you he was in earnest. All that is required is—"

"Captain!" Owen interrupted. "Marshal the sergeants. We're about to be attacked. Do it now! I want archers and pikemen lining the road. Prepare for battle!"

Catsby looked outraged. "How dare you!" he shouted. "This is bloody murder! The king has surrendered, I say!"

"Then why is his army marching up behind you!" Owen snarled as the ranks of archers jogged up the road in the distance. He unstrapped the shield from his saddle horn and snugged it up his arm. Then he drew the blade, Firebos. As it cleared the scabbard, the sky rumbled with thunder.

◆　◆　◆

Blood seeped into the muddy snow. Owen's arms were weary from combat, but he gripped the hilt of Firebos tightly to counter the thrust of a spearman. The magic of the blade thrummed when he brought it down on the haft of the inferior weapon, and a blast of power sent the spearman flying backward as if he'd been struck by a battering ram. Owen's ears rang with the feeling of power that came from his blows. Several archers had aimed for him specifically, but their arrows had pierced him without bringing him down. The scabbard's magic was burning white-hot against his hip, keeping his wounds from bleeding.

The two armies slogged through the mire of slush and carnage to strike at each other. *This* was how it was supposed to end. Owen was almost relieved that the king hadn't truly surrendered. His respect for the man would have diminished. No, Severn would fight. But where was he?

"My lord!" Ashby warned. "We've drifted ahead of our men. Fall back!"

An archer bearing the standard of the white boar impaled a knight with an arrow before he could be hacked down. Then he turned his bow on Owen, aiming for his mount this time. The arrow struck the horse's withers, causing him to scream in pain and begin to fall. Owen managed to scrabble off the thrashing beast before it pinned him beneath it. Owen had lost his shield in the tumult, and he gazed around the battlefield, amazed at the number that had fallen. Tunics with the stags on blue were intermingled with the White Boar, the dead bodies frozen as the snow continued to come down in never-ending waves.

"Grab my hand!" Ashby said, riding up alongside Owen.

But as he reached for it, a spearman rode up and stabbed Ashby in the back. A rictus of pain transformed the spattered face, and Ashby yelled in agony as he arched and then tumbled from the saddle.

A dozen knights emerged from the woods to flank Owen, among them the king, his crown affixed to his helmet. Seeing him made the world suddenly totter, as if a giant had slammed his boot on the ground and caused an earthquake. The king was pointing at him with his sword, but Owen could not hear any words over the sudden ringing of the magic within the Maid's blade. He felt a grinding sensation, and images of the ancient Wizr board filled his head. He saw the black king move to occupy the space of the white knight, and his stomach filled with dread.

He felt a blade slice into his arm and realized he was surrounded by enemies. The sting could not be felt over the rush of panic. Owen twirled and swept his blade around. When it struck the knight who had attacked him, he felt the invocation of the sword's magic. The knight flew backward, leaving his arm in the muck at Owen's feet. Another knight dressed in a boar tunic charged Owen, but Owen deflected the attack and then used his magic to find the man's weakness. The sword's magic was building up again, preparing for another thunderous blast that would repel his attackers.

They came at him in droves, but Owen beat them back, the sword blasting them away like a catapult. His breath came thick and heavy. He was wounded in a dozen places, but the magic of the scabbard kept him alive and on his feet. Bodies of dead kingsmen were scattered around him in a wide arc. Where were his own men? He was in the thickest part of the fight.

The sight of the king filled him with despair, for he sensed the piece on the Wizr board moving.

Owen clenched the blade tightly, summoning its power. But his strength was failing, and Firebos felt heavy in his hand. His cracked lips pulled back into a snarl as Severn approached, a sword in one hand, a dagger in the other. The two men circled each other, but each step

Owen took made his head spin, his knees tremble. It felt as if a huge mountain were suspended over him. Was this what Roux had felt the night of his death?

"You thought to beat me!" Severn said with fury. "You thought to wear this crown! Take it from me, boy! If you can!"

Owen knew this was his chance . . . and he also knew that he was doomed to fail. Somehow the king had discovered the power of the Wizr set. Owen could sense the whorl of magic around him, making him heavier and heavier. The pieces had already been moved, and not in his favor.

He let out a grunt of rage and rushed at the king, hefting Firebos high over his head and bringing it down toward the king's shoulder. But it was like swinging against a huge boulder. The instant the weapon hit the king, the magic repulsed against Owen. The surge of magic would have killed another man. But while his arm went numb, it was the soldiers rushing up behind him who were flattened by the blast. His entire body and arm hurt, and suddenly the king's dagger plunged into his ribs. He felt the steel slide into his flesh, and his legs turned to water.

Firebos fell from his numb fingers into the snow, where it was instantly covered in hoarfrost.

Owen slumped forward against the king's body, pain traveling through him in spasms. He saw the fury and hatred melt away from the king's face as he collapsed into the bloody snow. The world spun recklessly.

The king knelt by his body, staring at him with a strange look of grief and surprise.

"It worked," Severn said with awe. "The magic worked! I'll not fail after all!"

Owen lay still, his strength in tatters.

The king picked up Firebos and held it aloft. A clap of thunder broke in the sky. "Victory!" he shouted. "Victory!"

A cry of triumph came from the soldiers wearing the White Boar.

The sickening realization of defeat washed through Owen. He saw the dagger pommel sticking out from his armor. No blood came from it. The scabbard on his belt was the only thing keeping him alive.

The king turned and looked down at Owen with pity. "Take him to my tent," the king said. "Have my surgeon tend him."

"My lord!" one of them uttered, aghast. "He's a traitor! Slay him!"

"He'll meet a traitor's death," Severn said grimly, "*after* we've buried this rebellion."

# CHAPTER
# THIRTY-SIX

## *The Black King*

"Well, my lord," the surgeon said, drying his hands on a bloodied rag. "I can't account for the duke surviving. These wounds would have killed another man. I've done all I could."

The king sat on a wooden camp chair, brooding over the Wizr board and its arrangement of pieces. There were four braziers in the tent, sending up plumes of purplish smoke and warding away the deep winter chill.

"He's no *ordinary* man," Severn said with an edge of jealousy in his voice. "And he's no longer my duke."

"Forgive me," the surgeon said in apology, "but I have other wounded I must attend to, my lord. If you'll dismiss me."

"Go," Severn said with a wave of his hand.

Owen had been treated on the king's own pallet. He slowly sat up, feeling the stitches groan in protest. The empty scabbard, still strapped snugly to his waist, continued its secret work of healing.

"Would you like some wine, my lord?" Lady Kathryn asked, bringing Severn a flagon. He nodded gratefully and took it from her, their fingers grazing. The king's mouth softened slightly as he looked up into her hazel eyes. Then she returned to the chest where she had been sitting and lowered herself next to Drew, who was staring helplessly at Owen. The boy looked frightened, confused, and miserable. It was the look of a boy whose hopes were being dashed before his eyes. Little did he realize what the king was capable of.

Owen felt the same way, but at least the boy was still hale. Along with the pain of his wounds, his heart throbbed with the torment of failure. He had tried twice to bring down Severn, and he'd failed in both attempts. He'd felt sure the Fountain would grant him its favor, and yet his plans lay dashed to pieces like so much broken crockery.

"Tell me if I have this right," Severn said musingly, staring at the Wizr board. "I'm the black king here. I just took the white knight. That was you." His eyes glanced up at Owen and a mocking smile twitched on his lips. "The tower . . . this is Elysabeth *Victoria*. It's Dundrennan." He paused, stroking his clean-shaven cheeks. He still wore his battered armor. His knuckles were bruised, but Owen could see his coronation ring on the fist near his nose as he tapped his mouth, deep in thought. "This piece . . . this is Iago. Another white. And down here . . . the Wizr piece. This one has been moving slowly up the board. The white Wizr. That is the Duchess of Brythonica. See the row the piece moves across? If this board represents the kingdom, then these pawns are at Kingfountain, and she came from Ploemeur over here." He gave Owen a shrewd look. "This isn't a game. There is real magic here. My brother never told me how it worked or that it was more than just a game. I think I saw him use it only twice. It was a great secret. Now I know it."

"You are correct, my lord," Owen said, rubbing his hand along the fur blankets on the pallet. "The magic is real. And the warning I gave you is also real. You've broken the rules of the game, and your kingdom will be buried in snow because of it."

"*Chah*," the king grunted. A dark look came over his countenance. "You say that because you *lost*."

"I fought against you because I *knew* it was going to happen."

The king scowled. "Then why not tell me, Owen? Why the duplicity? You're like every other person who's betrayed me. This crown is a curse to whoever wears it."

Owen shook his head. "It's a curse because it was never *yours* to wear. There are patterns in history, events that repeat over and over. It began with the death of the first Argentine king, if not before. The king's nephew, Andrew, was the rightful heir to the throne, but his uncle captured him and had him killed so he could claim the throne for himself. He was the one who started the pattern, but my lord, it must be broken. You *must* relinquish the crown to the rightful heir!"

"And who is that?" Severn asked with a look of utter incredulity. He glanced at the boy cowering by his mother. "Some whelp you've *chosen* to supplant me? The only Argentine left is my niece and her brats. I don't believe in superstition. It will take more than a little snow to convince me."

Owen clenched his teeth, trying to subdue his frustration. After a moment, he was calmer. Should he reveal Drew's identity? Or would that risk the boy's life unnecessarily? He felt nothing from the Fountain to encourage him. "Then what will it take, my lord? The death of every man, woman, and *child* in Ceredigion? I tell you, this storm will not relent until you do. It will bury every one of us."

"I don't believe you."

"What do I have to lose, my lord?" Owen pleaded. "You've beaten me. I'm a condemned man. But do not let your stubbornness destroy everyone. Forsake the crown. It's a burden you've not wanted."

Severn rose from the chair angrily. "It's a burden that was thrust on me! My wife and child were threatened by Eredur's black-hearted queen and her poisoner."

"Ankarette never threatened you."

"And how would you know that?" Severn snapped. "She came to Beestone to murder me before Ratcliffe killed her!"

Owen shook his head. "She came to Beestone to save *me*. She was my friend. My tutor. She's the one who first taught me about my powers. My lord, I've been a traitor to you since I was eight years old, and you never knew it. But a traitor only because I kept secrets from you. The Queen's Poisoner saved my life and taught me aught I know about duty and compassion."

"She aided you!" Severn burst out in outrage. The revelation had clearly stunned him. "Ratcliffe was right? Why would she even care?"

"She gave her life so that I might survive. And for no reason other than that she cared about the life of a little boy." Owen saw Drew from the corner of his eye, but he dared not look at him directly. He hoped the lad felt the meaning behind his words. "I tell you this now so that you might know the truth. You've not beaten me, my lord. It was never about *me*. If the game continues on thusly, everyone will die. Including you. The game must go on with the true king. With Andrew's true heir." Owen felt a swell of relief in his heart. The secret had finally wriggled loose. It was no longer a burden to him.

Severn started pacing. "And you've duped me all this while," he said with growing passion. "You've tricked and manipulated me."

Owen leaned forward. "Ankarette had a great gift of discernment, and she helped me see the truth about you. She knew you were not the one who murdered your nephews, for she heard your confession to the queen dowager. She was there, my lord, though you did not know it. I've served you because you weren't like the tales everyone told. But you've changed, my lord. You've become the *very thing* people always feared you were. How can I be loyal to that? How can I stand by while you plan to butcher the children of the realm?" This was another warning to Kathryn and Drew. If Owen could not escape, perhaps they could flee. "Can't you see you've broken every rule? The king is now a law unto himself. That is the danger of the crown. It convinced you that you were above it all."

Severn shook his head as he paced with a limp. Owen risked a quick glance at Kathryn and saw the paleness in her cheeks, her look of ardent fear. "You cannot understand what it is like," he ground out. "You cannot know, you with your fair face and long stride. You are young and still not totally corrupted by the world. You do not know what it's like to be hissed at. To have your own servants mock you behind your back. You don't know what it's like to be *hated*, Owen. No one *loves* me. You want me to spare the kingdom? I don't believe all this fluff you've said is true. But even if it were, what has this kingdom ever done for *me*? If I cannot rule it, then no one shall. I'd rather leave it a graveyard."

Owen's heart was bleak. "You will go to the Deep Fathoms with this on your conscience?" he demanded.

The king chuckled. "I'd welcome it," he said snidely. Then he turned back to the board. "I know for myself that magic is real. I saw what you did with this blade," he said, patting the hilt of Firebos, which was now in his scabbard. "It has shown my mind what it is capable of doing. With this sword and this game, I cannot be defeated. Let's prove your words." He stood and gazed down at the board. "The white Wizr is still several squares away. Let me crush the tower, and then I'll face that scheming duchess from behind its walls with her betrothed as my hostage." He smiled deviously. "A hostage once again. I think you're right. This situation is very familiar, is it not? Captain!"

The tent flap opened and Severn's tall, grizzled captain entered. "My lord?"

"I want Kiskaddon bound and guards set about this tent. No one comes in." He spared a look at Kathryn and Drew. A pitiless look. "No one leaves until I return. When the castle falls, bring him over to watch it."

"Aye, my lord," the captain said gruffly. He produced some irons and quickly shackled Owen's wrists together. But Owen had meant what he'd said—he did not care about his personal well-being, only about the fate of Ceredigion. His eyes were fixed on the board as Severn hovered over it and then reached down and moved the black king against the white tower.

Owen felt something shift in his mind, the strange magical sensation that accompanied the movement of one of the pieces on the Wizr board. He wanted to rush against the king and stop it from happening, but he could only stare helplessly as the king lowered the lid on the board and locked it in its case.

Stuffing the key into his pocket, he turned to Kathryn. "Wait for me here, Kathryn." Then he turned to Owen once more. "I'll give your regards to the Mortimer brat," Severn said viciously as he left the tent.

Owen hung his head, seething and twisting his wrists against the iron cuffs. The tent was surrounded by soldiers wearing the symbol of the white boar. He could see them through the flaps as the king left.

What could he do but wait for Evie's army to be destroyed? He felt impotent, furious, and filled with despair. His eyes found Kathryn, still sitting on the edge of the chest, stroking the boy's flaxen hair with a feverish, protective air, her other arm wrapped around him. "You must set me free," he whispered.

"To what purpose?" she answered pathetically. "You're in the midst of Severn's army, and you're a known traitor. It is over, Owen. It is all undone." Her eyes filled with tears as she stared at her son's face.

She was right, he knew. And it was a torture worse than death to have to listen to Severn's army attack the walls of the castle of his childhood, knowing all along that he was fated to win. But it frightened him even more to think of what would happen to the children of the realm after he achieved his victory.

And it was in that moment of utter despair that he heard the sound of lapping waters from the distance. His heart began to quicken with hope. It was a familiar sound, a comforting one. *Sinia.*

The tent flap rustled and a woman cloaked in mist entered. The mist dissolved away, revealing Sinia, a determined look on her face. Not a single snowflake stuck to her.

"Who are you?" Lady Kathryn asked, coming quickly to her feet. Drew stood as well, gazing at her in wonder.

"I am here to help you," she answered with a knowing smile. She looked at Owen, her eyes full of emotion. "I came as quickly as I could."

"How did you travel without a fountain?" Owen asked eagerly. He'd nearly given up hope.

"The fountains are the anchor points," she said, "but I can travel anywhere along the line. We do not have time for explanations. First, you won't need those anymore," she said, gesturing at the chains securing his wrists. "*Anoichto*," she whispered. The locks on the cuffs unfastened, and the chains dropped to the fur blanket with a rattling noise.

Owen rose, and she rushed into his arms. He hugged her fiercely, his heart swelling with relief. He looked down at her upturned face.

"I'm sorry, my love," she whispered to him. "The agony you've felt. I can feel it keenly myself. You're injured, and in pain." She took his hands and squeezed them hard. "You must go. You must leave the camp immediately. I'm going to call down a storm to end this battle. Take Kathryn and Andrew and flee back to your army. I've magicked the guards outside. Get these two far away. Bring them to Brythonica. If you leave now, you should make it before the blizzard overwhelms you. My soldiers will help you escape."

Owen looked at her in confusion. "I don't understand."

"The game is ending," she said. "Severn won't relinquish the crown, and now he knows too much. He will invoke the curse deliberately."

"Have you seen this in a vision?" Owen said in despair. "Is there nothing we can do to save the people?"

Sinia was so distraught, it looked like she was in physical pain. "I saw, in a vision, a field of white, with dead soldiers in the snow. There were ravens flying overhead. Owen, I cannot change what I saw. I don't know what it means, but I know that to prevent the blizzard from destroying the kingdom, I must summon a storm to this place."

She looked agitated, but it was clear she was determined to do her duty despite the cost.

Something wasn't right, and it nagged at Owen. "Hold a moment," he said, breaking her clasp and beginning to pace.

"Owen, there isn't time," Sinia pleaded. "We must get away! The move was made. The board is acting on it."

Something snicked inside Owen's mind. He straightened, his eyes widening. "Then we *unmake* the move. We change the pattern." He went to the small table with the Wizr board. Moments before, he had despaired of opening it, but Sinia had just taught him another word of power.

"*Anoichto*," he said to the board, and heard the lock release. When he opened the board, the black king was moving to occupy the space of the white tower. He reached for the piece, but he felt a jolt shoot up his arm that nearly stopped his heart from beating.

"Drew," he gasped, gesturing for the boy. "Move the piece away. Move the tower back to Atabyrion, over there." He pointed to the space on the board.

The boy looked at him warily, trembling. He sidled closer to his mother, shaking his head no. Her arms were clinging around his body, holding on to him as if he'd blow away in a storm.

"Please!" Owen said. "You're the only one of us who *can* use the board right now! It will protect Genevieve's parents. It will keep them alive."

Upon hearing those words, Drew nodded with firm commitment. He struggled free of his mother's clasp, hurried to the board, and reached in to drag the white tower across the board to the spot Owen had directed. He did it as easily as if it were a normal Wizr piece. As soon as his fingers released, Owen felt the shifting happen again. A spark of hope caught fire in his heart. He saw the pieces fitting together in his mind, and he knew why the Fountain had chosen *him* to be here at this moment. His own gift would work with Drew's to save them. Looking down at the board, he saw the strategy unfold.

"What are you thinking?" Sinia asked Owen, her eyes wide with curiosity and approval.

"I think I understand the meaning of your vision," Owen said, feeling a smile creep across his face. "He has a childhood fear of ravens," Owen said. "Go back to your army. Each of your soldiers has a badge or a flag with the raven symbol. Use your magic, Sinia. Breathe life into the ravens and send them to attack the king's army. There is something powerful about fear. I think it will help me turn the king. He needs to know that he murdered his true nephew. That this boy is the true heir, not an imposter." He looked at Drew. "The king is your great-uncle, lad. You are an Argentine. Remember when I took you to see the funeral boats? That was your father!"

The boy started with surprise, his eyes riveted on Owen. Slowly, he let out his breath and gave a short nod.

"The king didn't understand what he was doing, lad. What he needs is forgiveness. Not because he is good. But because *you* are good. If we do not break this cycle, it will keep happening over and over again. Pity him. Or all is lost."

Sinia shook her head. "I can't leave you here with him. You or the child! No, my love. Don't ask me to do that!"

He put his hands on her shoulders. "Trust me. This is why we are both here. Fill the sky with ravens. Send them to attack us. Now."

Sinia looked worried, an expression he wasn't accustomed to from her. She went up on her tiptoes and kissed his cheek. Then she vanished in a plume of white mist.

# CHAPTER
# THIRTY-SEVEN

*Ravens*

A cheer of triumph came from the camp, the noise rousing Owen from his pondering and pacing. Kathryn clutched Drew to her bosom, her eyes full of fear and dread. Owen halted and cocked his head at the sound. Then he turned and stared at the Wizr board. The pieces had shifted again. The black king was still poised next to where the tower had been, its progress halted. The knight representing Iago was now in a position to threaten the king.

"What is happening out there?" Owen said in confusion. He saw that the white Wizr was back where it had been previously, indicating Sinia had returned to her army. How long would it take for the ravens to arrive?

"Did Severn win?" Kathryn asked nervously.

"Go outside the tent. Find one of Severn's captains. Ask him."

Pausing only to cast a worried look at the young boy, Kathryn stole outside the tent, her black, jeweled gown sparkling in contrast to the pale snow-light outside.

Drew stared up into Owen's eyes, unflinching. "I didn't know that man was my father."

Owen dropped down onto one knee near him. He put his hand on the boy's shoulder. "I tried everything I could to spare his life. Your mother and he, they used to write to each other in the margins of books. I was their messenger."

The lad looked more uncomfortable. "When did we first meet? Were you the one who brought me to Dundrennan?"

"I was there when you were born. From the moment I held you in my arms," Owen said in a hushed tone, "the Fountain told me it was you. It told me to resurrect you. It told me to protect you. I've done the best I could do, lad, under very difficult circumstances."

Drew nodded, his lips quavering, his eyes widening at the confession. "I know you have, my lord. If I don't forgive him, will I become the black king?"

"When you become King of Ceredigion, this piece will turn white, I think. The game will change, but it will continue as it should. The blizzard will end. You will already start with many loyal to you. You won't be alone."

He looked a little greensick. "I never dreamed of becoming king," he said in a choked voice, "but I think a king should show mercy." He took a steadying breath. "I think I can forgive him. It won't be easy."

Owen laughed softly, feeling his heart ache for the lad. "It will not." He gave the lad a pat on the back and stood and started pacing again. Kathryn reappeared a short time later, fresh flakes of snow scattered across her shoulders and bodice.

"The king has breached the outer wall of Dundrennan," she said, her voice shaking with fear and the chill of winter. "They're fighting

Iago's men in the bailey yard, but the keep is holding. The Atabyrions show no sign of retreating."

Owen frowned at the news. Was Evie still there? The position on the board told him that she was not, and his instincts confirmed it. Iago wouldn't run from a fight.

Kathryn approached Owen, her face full of conflicting emotions. "What will happen to the king if he's defeated? Will you put him to death?"

Owen gave her a hard look. "Only if he won't surrender. I don't seek his blood, Kathryn. While I see the cruel man he's become, I can understand how he came to be this person through the choices he's made." He paused for a moment, then said, "I told Drew about Eyric. He knows about his father."

Kathryn clasped her hands together and started to pace back and forth, mimicking Owen's anxiety from moments before. Then she went to her son and hugged him close. She had tears in her eyes. "What will you do if the king surrenders? Will you spare his life?"

Owen looked at her, his brow furrowing. "You're pleading for him?"

Kathryn bit her lip, looking up at Owen. "I . . . I don't know what to think. I should be happy to be free of him. Yet, it would pain me to see him suffer in a dungeon. To see him treated as my lord husband was treated. To be deprived of so much, if he *gave* up the crown." She shook her head and returned her attention to Drew. "I don't know, my son. I'm torn."

"Kathryn, he used his magic on you," Owen said. "You know this."

She did. He could see it in her eyes. But there was a part of her that cared for him regardless. The magic hadn't worked on empty feelings. All his kindnesses, all his gifts, all his adoration had impacted her over the years.

Drew's face was twisted with confusion and concern. The boy was too young to be dealing with such adult conflicts!

The sound of approaching boots was the only warning before the tent flap flung open and Severn Argentine strode inside, his armor encrusted with ice and frozen blood. He had a ferocious look, and he was limping severely, his armored hand pressing a wound at his side. He hobbled to the camp chair and flopped himself down onto it, breathing in ragged gasps.

"Fetch my surgeon," the king said to Kathryn. Then his eyes found Owen, and he glanced around until his gaze found the chains that lay in a heap on the pallet.

Owen sensed the king was going to reach for his dagger to defend himself, and before it could happen, he raised his hands. "I'm not waiting to ambush you, my lord. Your guards patrol the tent."

"How did you get free?" the king snarled, his nostrils flaring with fury.

"The same way I opened the board," Owen said, gesturing to the table. "You are defeated, my lord. Threat and mate."

"But how?" Severn demanded, stifling a groan as he shuffled to his feet. He limped to the board, breathing hard and fast, and stared in astonishment at the change in the pieces. "How did the tower . . . ? I've not touched . . . how did this happen?" His face was twisted with confusion and a budding sense of fear. "Only an heir can move the pieces! How did you manage it?"

"Because the heir is in this tent. Lord Bletchley didn't murder Eyric. You arranged that yourself. The boy is Eyric's son! Kathryn is his mother. Don't you see why she never gave in to you? She knew the truth, as did I. This is the last truth, Severn Argentine. This is the last secret. And it is your *last* chance! Look at the board. Do you see the army of Brythonica? The white Wizr is coming to defeat you."

The king's lips quivered. His eyes were wide with shock, and his skin had gone chalk-gray. He stared at Kathryn, then at the boy who was looking up at him with something like defiance. "You want to play games with me, Owen? Another trick? Another vision?"

Owen shook his head. "What is the most powerful piece on the board, my lord? Even the king is powerless against the Wizr. I've tried to warn you. I've given you every chance to end this madness. But I will not let you destroy your kingdom out of spite."

Kathryn stood near the tent door, her eyes full of fear and awe. She was edging toward the tent door with Drew, as if she intended to flee with him in case the king turned violent.

"You have nothing!" Severn shouted. "This is a trick! It's one of your ploys. I put your army to flight. Your life is in my hands. I could kill you this very moment."

Owen stepped closer. "And why haven't you, my lord? What prevents you from destroying me? Because you remember the shivering little boy I used to be? The one you used to taunt at breakfast? Your special child. Because I'm Fountain-blessed, as are you. Because I'm the only other person who understands you. Even if I grieve at what you've become."

The king's face contorted. He began to draw the dagger from his belt, and Owen worried he'd said too much—a worry that only heightened when Kathryn cried out in alarm—but the king slammed the weapon back into its scabbard in the nervous gesture Owen remembered from his youth. He repeated the motion and started to pace the tent, his eyes haunting and desperate.

And that was the moment the ravens began their attack.

The sound of flapping wings, the bark-like croaking, filled the sky over the army. Shouts of fear started up in the camp. And then the shouts became cries of pain and terror.

"What is happening?" Severn exclaimed.

Lady Kathryn and Drew were nearly knocked to the ground as one of the king's captains burst inside the tent. "My lord! Ravens! They're falling on us from the sky!"

"Speak sense, man!" the king roared. "It's winter. There are no ravens!"

"They're huge! These are no beasts of nature, sire, and they're swooping down on us. They're killing your soldiers!"

Suddenly there was a heavy thump on the king's tent and several black shapes began clawing and shredding at the pavilion fabric with beaks and talons. The cry of the ravens was primal and fierce, and Owen felt his own heart quail. Drew pulled his mother over to one of the braziers, where she maneuvered herself in front of him, protecting his body with her own.

The look of fear and uncertainty on Severn's face showed Owen that his plan had worked. When he reached out to the king with his magic, he saw that all the man's sense and reason had fled beneath the onslaught and the guilt of what he had done to his own flesh and blood.

"Get them away! Keep them away from me!" the king gibbered.

The captain took one look at the utter fear and helplessness in Severn's eyes and turned and fled for his own life. Moments later, Owen watched as the captain was obscured by a pair of jet-black wings and a set of claws raking his face. The camp was full of commotion as the men tried to escape and were hunted down by the cawing, merciless beaks and razor-sharp talons. Owen's heart began to thrill.

Severn hunkered down on his knees and stared up at the shredding fabric of the tent. Black beaks poked through the holes, screaming down at them. Kathryn shrieked with terror, turning away her face and pulling Drew closer to her. The boy wasn't afraid. He was staring at the display of magical birds with rapture. Owen felt the magic of the Fountain whirling around him. These were magical creatures, and he knew through experience that his particular set of abilities would protect him from them.

"No! *No!*" the king groaned in terror, his face white, his lips quivering.

"Yield," Owen implored, standing before him, his hand outstretched.

One of the ravens was nearly inside the tent, its beak snapping viciously. The cacophony of noise from the terrified camp filled the air, but Owen's eyes were riveted to the king's face.

Severn shrank from the threat, scrabbling backward on his arms and leg, exposing the wound in his side, which seemed to drive the birds into a frenzy.

"Stop! Stop!" the king cried in terror.

"Yield!" Owen shouted back, pinning the king with his gaze. There was nowhere else to flee. The guards surrounding the tent had been plucked away. Wails of pain and fear resounded all around them.

"I yield! I *yield*!" Severn bellowed. He frantically unbelted the scabbard around his waist and thrust the blade Firebos into Owen's outstretched hand. As soon as Owen touched it, he felt the magic's strength surge through him.

"Yield your crown!" Owen said passionately, holding out his other hand.

The crown was fixed onto the king's helmet as part of the design. Owen could feel the magic of the Fountain exuding from it, summoning the winter storm that was about to annihilate the realm. The metal was tarnished and ancient, the fleur-de-lis patterns rising above the steel dome of the helmet like decayed flowers.

The two men locked eyes. Severn stared at Owen with fear and hate. But being confronted with his own sins and fears had completely unmanned him. He hesitated only a moment before wrenching the helmet off his head and hurling it away from him. Owen caught it in one hand.

"I yield!" Severn said, flinching and quavering.

Owen stood over him, sword in one hand, helmet-crown in the other.

"They're *yours*," the king snarled. "You win again, Kiskaddon!"

Owen stared down at the king, using his magic to sense any further threat from him. But there was none. The king had been defeated at last.

"It is enough," Owen said. He lifted his left hand toward the roof of the tent. The ring's magic flared to life, repelling the ravens that had finally broken through that barrier.

The rioting in the camp began to ebb.

Owen saw Kathryn lift her tear-streaked face, looking worriedly at the shredded gaps in the tent and the snow coming down on them from outside. Drew continually gazed at Owen with wonder—not fear—as Owen lowered his arm and the light extinguished. Bending her head to kiss her son's fair hair, Kathryn nuzzled her nose against his neck, breathing a sigh of relief.

"You've wrenched everything from me," Severn whispered in a strangled voice. Owen turned and looked down at him, prostrate on the ground, sniveling. "What is to be my fate? You owe me the truth of it, at least. I'm . . . I'm broken now. All is broken. I've nothing left. What will you do with me?" he finished, his voice breaking at the end.

Owen stared down at him and felt the throb of compassion. "Your fate will be decided by the new king," Owen said in a wearied tone.

The king's face blackened. "But aren't *you* truly the new king? Isn't that what this is all about? You hold the sword. You have the crown in the crook of your arm. It's yours to claim, Owen. Take it! No one can stop you now."

A part of Owen was still tempted by the thought. Laying down the power that he had wrested from Severn would put him at risk too. What if Drew ultimately felt threatened by having such a powerful subject? Might the boy not try and strip him of his rights and privileges? He listened to the insidious thoughts in his mind . . . and then crushed them beneath his heel like a roach.

"It is as I've told you. I'm not the true king of Ceredigion," Owen said in a steady voice. Then he turned and nodded respectfully to the boy. "I am only his knight."

Severn had a queer look on his face. One that could almost be called admiration. "But what is to become of me? Where will I go? How will I live? You've taken away everything. Must I beg for my bread? Even the dogs will snarl and howl at me. There are those who would be revenged. I am defenseless. Cursed. What will become of me?"

Owen stared down at the fallen king, his pity increasing. The man's concerns were real and valid. "My lord—" he started, but Severn interrupted him.

"I'm no man's lord!" he spat out.

Owen closed his eyes, feeling the prick of pain in his heart. "You were once a great lord of the realm," he continued. "I know your story. Not the lies that were whispered about you. You were guided by a motto. *Loyalty Binds Me.* You've always sought that kind of loyalty, but when you failed your brother's children, you lost the right to demand that kind of obedience from others. If *I* were the king . . ." He paused, then turned back to Drew once more. Their eyes met for a moment and he saw the bud of forgiveness in the boy. "If it were my decision, I would reinstate you as the Duke of Glosstyr, yours by right since you were a child. I would make you lord in your own domain, much like the Duchess of Brythonica is in hers. You would owe obedience to the king and to the king only. That is what I would advise. We have too many enemies, and your presence along one of the borders would help secure the realm."

Owen felt a flutter in his heart, a gesture of approval from the Fountain—or Sinia?—he couldn't tell.

The king's demeanor softened as the spark of hope began to light within him. "I tried to execute you, lad. How . . . how can you show me such compassion?"

"Because you are the closest thing I've had to a father," Owen answered, his throat becoming thick. "I've feared you. I've hated you sometimes. But I have also admired your courage and determination. You embody the aspect of the Fountain's rigor. Use your gifts for good, my lord. I implore you." He set aside the scabbard and reached out to take Severn's hand to help him up.

The king wrested the gauntlets from his own hands, revealing the nicks and battle scars. He clasped hands with Owen and was helped to his feet, wincing. The two men stared at each other, and then Severn clasped Owen's hand harder.

"I couldn't have endured losing," the king said sincerely, "to anyone else but you." His shoulders fell. Then he gave the boy a sulking look. "Mayhap the new king will do as you say. Mayhap not. Regardless, I will submit. I will swear fealty to the new king. But I would give up Glosstyr castle and every sheaf of wheat thereon to not be alone. It is loneliness that I dread the most, my boy. It is a demon that torments me."

"It torments us all," Owen said, understanding the sentiment from his own heartbreak.

He saw movement from the corner of his eye, and Lady Kathryn was suddenly standing by them, her face streaked with tears.

"If it be within my power," she said with a sad look, "then let me dispel that demon for a season or two each year. I made you a promise, my lord. And I do not break my promises."

The king looked at her with such wild hope it was like a burst of sunlight through the fog. He wrapped his arms around her neck and sobbed into her shoulder like a child.

# CHAPTER THIRTY-EIGHT

## Our Lady

The victors of the Battle of Dundrennan had gathered in the spacious solar in the castle while a blizzard spilled snow from the skies. Owen stared out the large window, feeling the heat from the fires on his back as well as the cold air seeping into the room from the glass. Many of the dead were still buried in snow, and the soldiers were hard at work trying to find survivors. His heart clenched with grief at the thought of the many casualties. A soft hand touched his elbow.

He hadn't noticed Sinia approach, but he was comforted by her presence in the castle of his boyhood. She gave him a knowing look, always sensitive to his moods and expressions.

"Everyone is here now," she said in a low voice.

Owen reached for her hand and squeezed it, summoning his courage once again. Sinia remained by his side, her warm hand linked with his, and he felt the buds of hope poking through the snowy debris.

They had been waiting for Iago, and he strode into the solar flanked by several nobles from Atabyrion in their strange battle garb. Their looks turned wary and fierce when they saw Severn Argentine and Catsby seated at the long table in the center of the chamber. Owen wished Evie were there. He would have valued her wisdom. Kevan Amrein was present as well, representing the Espion. With Sinia, they formed a royal council of sorts. Lady Kathryn was seated nearby, next to her son, who looked intimidated by all of the gathered men with storm clouds on their faces.

Iago folded his arms, refusing to take a seat at the table. "My queen's ship left just before we arrived," he said, his voice curt. "She's halfway back to Edonburick by now. I'd like to go after her and bring her back to Kingfountain for the ceremony. I think she should be there when the new king is chosen."

Owen felt a subtle tightening on his hand, a flinch. He glanced at Sinia, who was staring at Iago, her expression grave and anxious. "Do you have a concern?" he whispered to her. She quickly shook her head no, but did not meet his eyes.

"I don't think that's a problem, my lord," Owen answered. "This must be done in the presence of the people. The one who draws the sword Firebos from the fountain of Our Lady will become the new king."

Severn's gaze was stony and a slight curl to his mouth showed his resentment. But he said nothing.

"What I want to know," Iago said, letting his anger boil up, "is why you have promised Severn such an important position. Giving him power will only weaken the new king."

"And what would you suggest? A longboat in the river?" Severn shot back immediately.

Iago was about to counter him, but Owen let go of Sinia's hand and stepped forward. "Iago, please. I think we all recognize the fragile nature of this peace. We have enemies enough laying plunder to our kingdom while we dither here. I made no promises to Severn. It is a decision that needs to be made by the new king. Severn recognizes and accepts that."

Iago's eyes narrowed. "So you aren't guaranteeing that I'll be the duke of the North either?"

"*I'm* the duke of the North," Catsby said under his breath.

Severn shot Owen a cynical look. "Thus is the nature and disposition of most men," he drawled.

Sensing the tension building in the room, Owen stepped forward. "None of us is entitled to anything," he said in a steady, deliberate voice. "Myself included. It will be the king's decision whether *any* of us continues serving. Myself included."

"Are you serious?" Catsby said in a withering tone. "You're willing to give up Westmarch?"

Owen put his hands on the table, flinching slightly when the stitches in his waist tugged. Every hour he was feeling better as the magic of the scabbard continued to heal him, but he had to move cautiously for fear of pain. "I was given Westmarch by the king. It can be taken away by the king. Instead of squabbling, I think it best that we prove our usefulness to the new sovereign." Owen sighed and turned to Kevan. "What is the latest report on our enemies' movement?"

Kevan had a calm, unflappable manner even when bearing bad news. "Word is traveling slowly because of the weather, but that's understandable. Chatriyon's army is ravaging Westmarch. His men are marching into Brythonica, and are only two days from Ploemeur."

Owen glanced at Sinia, whose face was twisted in a worried look. "I know," she answered. "I cannot remain here. I must go back to Brythonica or risk Ceredigion's fate."

Owen frowned, but he understood the need. "What else?"

Kevan cleared his throat. "Brugia has taken Callait. They're preparing a fleet to strike at Kingfountain. Duke Maxwell wants the throne. An army from Legault is ransacking Blackpool. In other words, it's a bloody mess. The people are fleeing to the palace in terror. The good news is we'll have plenty of people to celebrate the coronation," he added dryly.

Owen smiled at the comment. "Thank you, Kevan. As you can see, if we do not band together, we won't be fighting each other for our lands. They'll be stripped away from us by force. And this storm won't end until the new king is crowned. That must happen first of all. I suggest that we all make our way to Kingfountain."

"Even Severn?" Iago pressed.

"Of course me, you dolt," Severn snarled.

"I want to go to Edonburick first," Iago said. "I have ships near the coast, and can probably get to Kingfountain before all of you, if you ride there."

Owen nodded. "Then we will meet you there. You've all been told the truth of our situation. You know my intentions. I am not the Dreadful Deadman, nor did I ever want to be. And I meant what I said; I will gladly yield my duchy if the new king wishes it." He glanced back at Sinia, who was giving him a proud smile. "But I will not be losing what is most important to me," he added, giving her a wink.

He turned back to those assembled. "We meet again at the sanctuary in Kingfountain."

◆　◆　◆

Owen caught up with Iago as the regent mounted an enormous horse— only the behemoth steeds of the North could make it through the snow-clogged roads to the port. The flurries were growing thicker and thicker, another reminder that the boy needed to be crowned as soon as possible. Iago was covered in thick jackets, two cloaks, and fur-lined boots that went up past his knees. Hardly any of his face was visible past the hood.

"You're a good man, Kiskaddon," the Atabyrion said with a snort. "Although technically, *I* should be the one to see *you* off from

Dundrennan. I think my wife will be disappointed if we don't get to keep the place." He smiled wryly, looking down at Owen.

"I don't think it'll come to that," Owen said, putting his hand out to the king. They clasped each other's hands and exchanged respectful nods. "I think your children would enjoy being a part of both worlds. I hope I'm welcome to visit Edonburick someday."

Iago laughed openly. "You're a rascal, lad. We like those in Atabyrion. I might spare some time to go hunting with you. We have moose as big as a farmer's hut. Not the same as hunting *boar*, though." He winked at Owen.

"I think I could manage that," Owen said with a smile. "My best to your wife and your children. Tell Genevieve I miss her."

"Aye, I'll do that." He adjusted his grip on the reins and then gave Owen a penetrating look. "Well, you're welcome to come as oft as you like. But I do insist on one thing. I'd like to watch you play a round of Wizr with the queen. She beats me every time. Someone ought to humble her now and then."

◆ ◆ ◆

There was a private chapel in the castle that contained a fountain people visited for moments of solitude or prayer. Owen entered it hand in hand with Sinia, and the only sounds were the licking flames from the torches and the echo of their footfalls on the stone. She was looking down at her feet as they walked, brooding silently, her expression guarded.

"Are you fretting about your people?" he asked her, squeezing her hand.

She nodded without answering and then squeezed his hand in return before releasing it. The chapel was small and honeycomb-shaped with small inlets on three of the sides. She walked to the edge of the fountain and then slowly sat down, folding her hands in her lap.

"It's not just your people," Owen said cautiously, trying to meet her eyes. "Something *else* is bothering you."

She remained still, staring down at the stone tiles. She wouldn't meet his gaze.

"What's wrong?" he pressed.

"I can't tell you," she answered softly. She reached her hand into the water, and he watched as the surface rippled and flinched from her, repelled by her touch. He did not see any evidence of a ring or some other relic invoking the magic.

Owen folded his arms and leaned back against the stone pillar at the doorway of the chapel. He knew she needed to leave, but a nagging feeling inside him wanted to forestall their separation. How long would it be before he saw her again?

"If I ask you a question, will you answer me truthfully?" He gave her a pointed look as he asked.

Her eyes lifted to meet his face, and suddenly she was full of suffering, as if something deep inside her bones were causing her pain. "If I can," she whispered.

"Why can't you share all of your visions?" he asked her. "If you knew something terrible was going to happen, wouldn't you try to prevent it? Shouldn't you?"

"It's not that simple, Owen," she answered, but he could tell the limitations wounded her. "What if preventing an immediate evil only caused a worse one in the future? If we always knew what would happen to us, would we ever have the courage to act?"

"Can you change the future?" he asked her guardedly.

"Should I even try?" she asked. "Sometimes meddling only makes things worse. I do what I *can*, Owen. You must believe that." She gave him a pleading look, as if begging him not to ask any more. The distress in her eyes, on her mouth, made his stomach tighten with dread.

"Did I do wrong to save Severn's life?" Owen asked her.

Sinia sighed and smoothed her dress over her knees. "Many of your choices over the last few days will have . . . consequences. I've seen what some of them are."

Owen rubbed the bristles on his chin thoughtfully. "You didn't warn me against them."

She blinked. "I tried to, Owen. As best as I could. I don't think you were *wrong* to make the choices you did. But some of them will cause you pain later. That's why I'm upset, you see. I foresaw this moment long ago." She rose to her feet. "I must go."

"Wait," he said. "When will I see you again? Can you tell me that?"

She looked heartbroken. "It's up to you, Owen. It always has been. I will hide the sword in the waters of the sanctuary of Our Lady of Kingfountain, as we agreed. It will exist in a state between our mortal world and the Deep Fathoms. When you are ready for Andrew to claim it, just summon it as you would for yourself, and he'll draw it from the waters."

Owen frowned. "Will someone else who is Fountain-blessed be able to draw it out? I don't want Dragan to steal it like he stole the Wizr board."

She pursed her lips. "No one will know it is there, Owen. It will be waiting for you."

"Will you be there to see the boy draw the sword?" he asked.

She shook her head. "I can't. I've been away from Brythonica for too long. I must defend my people."

Owen walked up to her and took her hands. "I will come for you, Sinia. I gave you my word."

Her forlorn look softened a bit. "I know. I hope you will keep it."

He started to bend down to kiss her, but she pulled away. "Not now," she whispered. "Not like this."

It was painful to see her so vulnerable, so dejected, when he did not know the reason. He sighed in frustration and then caressed her cheek with the edge of his finger. "In the legends, the Lady of the Fountain was a water sprite. An Ondine. I've intended to ask you about that."

She flinched when he said the word, her cheeks blushing furiously.

"You are not the natural child of the Montforts, are you?" he asked.

She wrung her hands together, twisting her fingers and entwining them. "I was a gift," she whispered. Then she gave him a pleading look. "A gift from the Fountain to save the kingdoms. A gift to grieving parents whose children were all stillborn. We must all make sacrifices, Owen. I willingly made mine."

Owen sensed the layered meaning in her words. He started to unbuckle the belted scabbard, but she covered his hands with hers. "Just the sword," she prompted.

Grasping it by the hilt, he withdrew it and handed the blade to her. As soon as he set it on her palms, it started to glow. She started to glow as well as she backed away from him and stepped over the lip of the fountain into the low pool of water. The ripples moved away from her, leaving even the hem of her gown and her shoes perfectly dry.

As she stood in the Fountain, clutching the sword, a sheen of mist began to form around her. His heart nearly burst at the sadness in her eyes, the unspoken plea there: *Don't betray me.*

The mist enclosed her, and the surge of the Fountain's magic came and left like a tide embracing the shore.

She was gone.

# CHAPTER
# THIRTY-NINE

## *Misfortune*

Owen had anticipated that Elysabeth might already be in the beleaguered capital by the time he reached it, for a boat journey from
Atabyrion took only a day or two, depending on the weather. But when
he reached the palace, he learned that no one from Iago's kingdom had
yet arrived. The storm clouds in the North had likely caused the delays.
The city was pristine in a veil of white, except for the roads they had
trampled to get there.

Owen found himself at the center of everything. He was the protector, though no law or decree had given him that right. The other
dukes had gathered together to fret over the events unfolding throughout Ceredigion. The Duke of Brugia had landed troops in East Stowe.
Towns throughout Westmarch had evacuated under the onslaught of
Occitania's army, which was marching unmolested through that land,
seizing territory. It was as if every lord and commoner looked to Owen
as their new king.

That first sleepless night back in Kingfountain was spent dispatching orders to his own troops and requesting assistance from any who would help. Owen was decisive by nature, and he felt the magic of the Fountain coming to his aid with suggestions and ideas to stave off the impending disaster. The Genevese traders offered loans to hire mercenaries at exorbitant interest, but Owen would not defend the kingdom with hirelings. If the people did not rally under the new king, all would be lost anyway.

The throne room was full of chaos the next day as people clamored for direction. Owen felt the weight of the duties on his shoulders. He had guards posted at the docks to alert him the moment Evie's ship arrived. His trust in her was complete, and he would welcome her counsel.

Around noon, with still no word from Atabyrion, he called Lady Kathryn to meet with him in the solar. She arrived, Drew in tow, and bowed to him.

"There is no need for that," Owen chuckled with a dismissive wave. "Thank you for coming so quickly."

"There are so many troubles facing the kingdom," Kathryn said, her hands resting on the boy's shoulders. Owen had done his best to keep her informed, knowing that the new king would look to his mother for counsel and advice. She would be a powerful woman in the realm, but he thought she'd fill the role well. He'd always been impressed by her strength and sense of duty and faithfulness.

"I'll admit I'm overwhelmed," Owen said, pacing to dissipate his nervous energy. "I've seen the storm clouds approaching. They are following the crown. Without a king, we will face annihilation. I wanted to forestall the ceremony until the Atabyrions—your people—arrived. But I fear we cannot delay any longer. I think it's time. Do you agree?"

He looked into Kathryn's hazel eyes—the look there told him she too was experiencing the burdens that would shortly fall on her shoulders. Drew was just a child. While he would grow to become a king, he was too young to lead soldiers into battle. Too inexperienced to pass laws or choose his councilors. Drew would look to his mother in all things. Owen had known that, so over the past years, he had done what he could to ensure she was prepared to assume her place, even though it would not be as the queen of the realm. That role would fall to another. Genevieve, perhaps, if the Fountain had told him true.

"I agree, Owen," Kathryn said, squeezing Drew's shoulders. Then she turned the boy and knelt down in front of him, her black gown shimmering with small pearls and gems. She stroked his hair tenderly. "Are you ready, my son? Everything will change once you become the king."

The boy looked greensick. "I don't really want this," he said, frowning with concern. "Will you . . . stay by me? Will you always be near?" He looked both at his mother and at Owen.

Kathryn's face saddened a little at the words. "If you wish it, my son," she said, cupping his hands in hers. "I will be near you as long as you wish me to be."

He nodded energetically. Then he turned to face Owen. "Will I still learn how to be a knight? I . . . was rather looking forward to it."

Owen grinned and approached. "The King of Ceredigion doesn't sit on thrones all day long," he answered and then mussed the boy's hair. "Your grandfather rode from one end of the realm to the other regularly. You can't defend land you don't know. Every river, every grove, every *waterfall* will be yours."

Drew smiled at the thought. "I can go anywhere?"

"It is your right, lad. And I will serve you through the best of my days as Duke Horwath served the Argentines. Loyalty binds me to you. If you will have me."

Drew smiled again. "I should like you to serve me, my lord."

Owen shook his head. "It is *I* who will be calling *you* by that title shortly." He stared down at Kathryn and offered a hopeful smile. "We will go to Our Lady."

◆　◆　◆

The proclamation went out from the palace that every boy near the age of eight should be brought to the sanctuary of Our Lady by their parents to be presented to the deconeus. The prophecy of the Dreadful Deadman would be fulfilled, it was said. The new king of Ceredigion would draw a blade from the fountain, just like King Andrew had done, according to myth.

Owen, of course, had told Kevan to secure the sanctuary with his most trusted Espion. He walked the entire grounds himself, using his magic to seek for threats such as Dragan. He had summoned the blade to the fountain once, to test it. It had appeared, shimmering in the waters. Then he had let it vanish. As he walked around, overhearing parents whisper and boast that *their* child was the special descendant who would pull the sword from the waters, he suppressed a smile. Perhaps this smug feeling was how the Wizr Myrddin had felt in the days of old.

Guards wearing Owen's badge were positioned strategically at every doorway and throughout the crowd. No one wearing the White Boar had come, which did not surprise Owen. Severn was confined to the castle, watched day and night by the Espion. He had chosen to brood in his private chambers, which he would relinquish after the new king was named. Severn actually seemed relieved to have given up command. Owen had requested his input on some matters, only to be snappily reminded that the responsibilities were now his.

A mass of children had gathered outside the gates, and Owen gave the sexton the signal to begin. The lower classes had been allowed to come first, and each child was brought forward to stand before the water, state his name, toss in a coin, and look for the sword. The sexton had a private smile as he watched the fountain being filled with coins.

From the corner of his eye, Owen saw a man approach Kevan and whisper in his ear. A fretful feeling bloomed in Owen's stomach as he watched Kevan walk briskly to his side, and then waited for him to share the tidings.

"Trouble?" Owen whispered as Kevan sidled up to him.

"A ship from Atabyrion was spotted approaching the harbor."

Owen felt a burst of relief. "Slow the line down. We're nearly to the noble families. I want to save the surprise for the end, after they've all had a chance. That should give Iago and Elysabeth some time to get here."

"I'll see to it," Kevan replied. He slipped off to do Owen's bidding.

The endless procession of children wore down Owen's patience, and he began to pace by the edge of the fountain, his heart pounding in his chest.

Hours passed as the children of the realm continued to visit the shrine, each leaving the fountain without experiencing a glimpse of the blade. No one else in the vicinity used Fountain magic. As the day wore on, Owen felt his tension begin to fall away.

One by one, the noble children came and went. One impetuous lad actually tried to slip a dagger into the fountain, undoubtedly at his parents' behest. Owen sent the boy on his way, sparing a scolding look for his parents.

The tension in the room grew more and more acute as each successive child came away swordless. Would the prophecy go unfulfilled after all? Was someone missing? Lady Kathryn stood off to the side with some of the other nobles. Drew was behind her, watching the crowd warily and rocking from foot to foot. There were only a few supplicants left when Kevan walked swiftly through one of the doors with an older gentleman, dressed in the ceremonial trappings of Atabyrion. He was a grandfatherly man with long white hair that was balding halfway across the dome of his head. He was followed by several warriors. The steward at the old man's elbow looked familiar, and after a moment, Owen placed him as the man Owen had met at Eyric and Kathryn's manor in Atabyrion.

The old man was Lady Kathryn's father, Earl of Huntley, who had not seen his daughter in years.

Owen heard Kathryn gasp, and then she rushed to her father, tears spilling from her eyes as she embraced him. Their reunion tugged at his heart, but where was Iago? Where was Evie? Kevan rushed over to him, hopefully to give him answers.

"The Earl of Huntley came alone," Kevan whispered in his ear. "There was only his ship."

That did not make sense to Owen. Why would Elysabeth and Iago have missed this opportunity to witness the young king's coronation and to claim the right to North Cumbria? The anxiety in his stomach grew keener.

The last child of the nobles sulked away from the edge of the Fountain. Owen was filled with unease, but the time had come to act.

The deconeus lifted his voice to be heard above the murmuring. "Is there another child who would like to approach? A foundling perhaps? Someone who has not been given a chance? The Fountain will choose a king for this people. Please, come forth!"

Owen licked his lips and scanned the crowd. A few ragamuffin lads who were clearly thieves stepped forward at the invitation, some shoving at the others. They each walked away empty-handed. A solemn quiet descended on the room and then people began to chitter and talk anxiously. They began to *doubt*.

Owen glanced and saw Kathryn standing next to her father, one of her hands on his chest, her other on his back. She was looking at Owen for the signal. He nodded once.

With a subtle gesture, she motioned for Drew to approach the fountain.

The boy hesitated, all nerves and jumbling emotion, and then stepped away from the adults who had been shielding him. The entire room fell quiet as he made his way forward, wringing his hands. His golden hair shone in the torchlight as he moved down the row of white and black squares leading to the fountain. Suddenly Owen was overcome with the memory of when he had sought sanctuary in this place as a boy, only to be tricked into leaving by the king's power. He swallowed the memory, feeling his heart nearly burst from the rush of emotion it summoned.

Drew stood by the edge of the fountain, staring into the water. He had been given a coin for the occasion, and he dug into his pocket for it. Cupping it in his hand, he closed his eyes, and Owen saw his lips move in a silent prayer. Then, opening his eyes, he flung the coin into the fountain.

Owen summoned the blade Firebos into the water. It was there in an instant, gleaming and majestic in the waters. A hushed groan came from the deconeus as he watched the blade appear.

Drew looked in fascination at the water, then hiked up his sleeve to his elbow. Bending close, he reached into the water. Owen felt a shudder of magic as the boy's hand touched the hilt of the sword—the Wizr board was moving, transforming. Ancient stone grating on ancient stone. The hush in the sanctuary was absolute.

There was a whisper from the Fountain, a sound that penetrated every heart and sent shudders through all of them, Owen included.

*The White King has come*, it said.

Drew pulled the dripping blade from the fountain. It seemed to rise in the air of its own power, until everyone saw the young boy quivering by the edge of the fountain, holding the sun-white blade aloft.

It was too solemn of a moment to cheer. Owen watched as people fell to their knees, and he joined them. Water dripped down the boy's skinny arm. The look he gave Owen was one that said, *Now what do I do?*

A warm breeze began to blow outside.

And the snow began to melt.

♦   ♦   ♦

Owen leaned against a pillar in the sanctuary. The people were celebrating in the streets, the noise rising above the sound of the waterfall crashing beneath them. He felt he had done the right thing, but his heart was full of knives as he watched Kevan speak with the Earl of Huntley. Then the Espion escorted the man over to him.

"Lord Huntley, I don't believe we've met," Owen said formally, bowing in greeting. "Welcome to Kingfountain."

The man's voice was heavily accented with the brogue of his country. "I've supped at Tatton Hall, my dear boy. When your older brothur was a wee one. I saw you when you visited Edonburick in disguise. Clever lad, as always."

"What news from Edonburick?" Owen said, dropping his voice low. The earl did not look comfortable. In fact, despite the happy reunion with his daughter, he looked to be grieving.

"There is news. Aye, there is news," Huntley said. "I came on embassy from the queen to fetch my daughter back in the commotion. But I arrived to find the situation much less bleak than we had feared. And my queen bid me to entrust this letter with you and no one else. Secrets have a way of being found, I've learned in my old age. Best if you be the first to know of it."

He withdrew a sealed letter.

"Where is Iago?" Owen asked, his mouth suddenly dry.

"Read for yourself," Huntley said, but Owen already knew from his puffy eyes and desolate expression that Iago was dead.

♦ ♦ ♦

*My dearest Owen,*

*I know this secret cannot be kept for long. I apologize for the tearstains on the page. My lord husband died crossing back to Atabyrion. His ship was wrecked in a storm. There were no survivors. I would have come to Kingfountain to witness the coronation, but now I am to be the queen dowager, and I cannot leave. My son is too young. Genevieve is as heartbroken as I was when I lost my father at her age. I need your friendship more than ever, Owen. I need your comfort. Can you please come to Edonburick? My heart is broken.*

*Evie*

♦ ♦ ♦

# CHAPTER FORTY

*Cruelty*

Many sought refuge at the sanctuary of Our Lady when their hearts were torn in half. But Owen knew he wouldn't find the comfort he needed there. Evie's desperate plea for comfort had wrung him down to his deepest core. Yet equally demanding and ferocious was his resolve that to go to her would likely destroy his promise to Sinia. He knew Evie wasn't trying to persuade him of anything rash. But their feelings for each other would make them vulnerable. The mere act of reading her letter had made him vulnerable.

He had chosen the poisoner's tower as his sanctuary. It was a place where he could be alone with his thoughts, alone with his demons, but not truly alone—for there were ghosts there.

The room had been made over after Etayne's tastes, and the lingering smell of the chamber reminded him so vividly of the thief's daughter that he nearly fled back down to the stairs. He sat on a small chest with his back against the wall and looked up at the rafters, letting the weight of his dilemma rock on his shoulders a bit. He had not felt this terrible since the day of Evie's wedding. Memories had painful edges that could still cut.

Over the years, Owen had secretly hoped the King of Atabyrion would somehow die, giving him another chance with Evie. Such had happened to Severn and his first love. But he had long ago given up that hope. Now the impossible had happened. If only he had known . . . if only he had known!

He'd gone down to Brythonica with a sneer on his mouth and spite in his heart, sent to woo a duchess with curses and disdain. Despite his ill treatment of her, Sinia had patiently endured his sarcasm and discourtesy. She had accepted him because she saw something in him that made her care for him. *Love* him.

Could he truly break his promise to her? Did he even want to?

He kept thinking about how heartbroken she had looked before leaving Ceredigion. It was clear to him now that she had known about the cruel choice he would be forced to make. *This* was why she'd been so on edge.

Owen rubbed his mouth and closed his eyes. Drew had already named him the lord protector of Ceredigion. He could not fulfill his duties to the king from so far away. The boy needed someone at hand, someone who would help him learn how to take the reins of state. Yet how could he not go to Evie when she most needed him? When he could feel her pain as if it were his own? How could he make a choice that was sure to devastate one of the people he cared about?

In time, he grew accustomed to the smells of the tower. The pain of Etayne's death made his chest throb, but he had not only come here to connect with her. Feeling each ridge of the stones pressing into his back, he shrunk inside himself, willing the years to fade away, returning him to the terrified little boy he'd been. The boy who had been nurtured and protected by Ankarette Tryneowy. How he wished he could see her again. To whisper his fears and doubts to her. To receive her comfort and succor. He would have given all of his wealth to make it happen.

Sadness and longing filled him, and tears warmed his eyes, building up on his lashes without quite falling.

"What would you advise me to do?" Owen whispered into the stillness. Up in the tower, he could hear a gentle night wind. The thin candles he'd brought up were the only source of light, and shadows smothered the room. Owen rose from the chest and pulled open the curtain, standing before his reflection on the glass. If anyone in the dark city below was looking up at the castle, they might see a pinprick of light coming from the tower and mistake it for a star.

He saw the frown on his mouth in his reflection. The dilemma was truly awful. This was the kind of fateful choice Severn had been forced to make after the death of his brother Eredur—a choice that had yielded years of fateful consequences. Owen was not wise enough to see the future. He had no mantic gifts.

But he did have Sinia's warning. Someone like Owen had existed before. Someone like him had been faced with a terrible choice. And he had chosen to forsake his wife. How many times would the story be repeated until the cycle was broken? The heart was such a powerful force. Owen could see why his predecessors had chosen as they did.

Owen stared at the glass, unable to see the city beyond it in the darkness. The future was just as dark. He could not see it. No matter how much he wanted to. He had to make a decision without knowing the repercussions of it.

Well, he did know some things that would happen.

Owen knew himself well enough to know that if he *did* go to Edonburick to comfort Evie, he might never leave. He would not be able to see her pain without trying to comfort her. It would likely scandalize the people in that kingdom, which could have repercussions for young Iago's leadership.

He'd made no promise to Evie. But he had promised his troth to Sinia Montfort, a pledge nearly as strong as the marriage oath. He wore a ring. There was something *wrong* about forsaking it, something that made him squirm inside. Before he could go to Evie, he would need to be released from his engagement. But the thought of ending his connection with Sinia made him tremble with dread. She was a powerful Wizr, yet she was so vulnerable, like the butterfly she was named after. He had no doubt that she would release him from his promise. She was kindhearted and forgiving. But she had silently and secretly helped him for years. She'd given his parents and siblings a home. She'd saved his life and his army with her powers. And she had saved Ceredigion from an eternal winter.

That was not all, though. Since getting to know her, he had grown fond of her. He had begun imagining his life with her at his side—a thought he quite liked. Sinia was not as talkative as Evie, but she was a better listener. She was Fountain-blessed, like Owen, so they could relate to each other on a special level. Together, they had saved the kingdom from destruction. With her help, he was confident they could restore the ancient court and the principles of Virtus that had once held sway in this land.

"Ankarette, what should I do?" Owen moaned softly, wrestling with his feelings.

He imagined her sitting by the bed, one arm gripping her stomach to stifle the pain. She'd been sick the entire time he'd known her. Some disease had made her suffer, yet she had always tried to appear cheerful and comforting.

Ankarette had always known his heart. Which of the two women was more like her? The answer came to him unbidden: *Sinia*.

Owen heard soft steps coming up the tower. His sense of hearing had always been keen. He listened to the sound and imagined, with a sudden spasm of hope, that it was Ankarette climbing the steps. He turned away from the window, blinking with growing surprise. Who was coming to see him in the dead of the night? Despite all logic and sense, he wanted so desperately for it to be Ankarette.

It was Kevan Amrein, newly appointed as the head of the Espion. Owen sighed with disappointment.

"I'm surprised I even found you," Kevan said, eyeing the room warily. "We've been searching the entire palace for you."

"Sorry to alarm you," Owen said. "I needed some time to think."

The man smiled sympathetically. "I was sorry to hear about Iago. When the earl told me . . ." As they both brooded on the implications of the news, the room fell quiet except for their breathing.

Owen realized it was time to leave the ghosts of the tower behind. These were decisions that could only be made by the living.

# CHAPTER
# FORTY-ONE

*Ploemeur*

It amazed Owen how quickly the frost melted away after the sun pierced the clouds. Patches of snow still clung to the shadows, but the roads were clear again, and the army of Ceredigion was on the move. The bulk of the riders were hard pressed to keep up with the Duke of Westmarch, who swept through his domain like a farmer's scythe at harvest time. He flanked the Occitanian army, preventing it from retreating back across the border. Owen's new captain had them penned in at Rougemont castle, which Chatriyon's forces had taken during their advance. Owen kept them there and moved forward, charging hard to cross the border to relieve the siege at Averanche. He arrived just in time to surprise the besieging army before the city was forced to formally surrender.

It may have helped that the king's banner flew beside his.

Soldiers had flocked to Eredur's standard—the Sun and Rose—and joining with Owen's bedraggled force, they had won a series of quick victories in just a few days, while war continued to rage.

Owen and Drew took over the pavilion that had been occupied by the lord marshal of Pree, who had been caught while napping. The man hadn't even been wearing armor when his camp was overrun. The palisade was broken down, and Owen's captains had secured the roads, preventing anyone from escaping to warn King Chatriyon, whose army was infesting Brythonica, according to the latest reports. Of course, Owen did not need to rely on the latest reports anymore. The Wizr set provided him with more information than the Espion ever could.

The pavilion, constructed of a cream-colored fabric embellished with hand-stitched frills, was furnished with beautiful rugs and ornate braziers. The marshal's pallet was stuffed with feathers, and bottles of expensive wine were chilling in chests brought from distant castles. Owen and the young king sat on the camp stools overlooking the Wizr board that sat open on a round table in front of them.

Drew's face was alight with eagerness and anticipation. He no longer wore the drab colors of a knight in training, but was bedecked in garments befitting his new rank. The coronation ring glistened on his finger and a coronet pressed against his flax-colored hair. Severn's crown traveled with them. The sword Firebos was in a brand-new ornate scabbard, propped against Drew's chair. He never let it out of his sight. Owen continued to wear the battered raven-marked scabbard for his own weapon.

"What make you of the pieces?" Owen asked thoughtfully, his shoulders slightly hunched as he stroked his bottom lip.

The boy's grin was infectious. "I think we're winning."

"No doubt we're winning," Owen said with a laugh. "Show me the positions. Who is where?"

Drew put his finger on the white Wizr. "This is the Duchess of Brythonica, Sinia Montfort. The black king is Chatriyon. He's right next to her. That's a foolish move because a Wizr is more powerful than a king."

"Indeed," Owen said, admiring the boy's sagacity. "Go on."

"We are here," he said, indicating the white king and the white knight. "This piece is the Duke of Glosstyr. He's a tower now."

"You're right," Owen said. "And where is his piece moving?"

"Against Legault. They outnumber him. Should we send reinforcements?"

Owen shook his head. "I don't think you should worry about him being outnumbered, my lord. Even with a third of their number, he'll still win."

He saw the king's face darken a bit. "Do you think he will serve me well, Lord Owen?"

Owen tightened his folded arms a bit and frowned. "I hope so. It would be best to keep an eye on him, though."

Drew nodded. "Have Lord Amrein see to it."

Owen had already done so. He'd also ordered Kevan to assign a man to hunt down Dragan. He would not let the thief off easily. "As you will, my lord. And who is this?"

"The Duke of Brugia. His piece is black."

Owen nodded. "And this?"

"The Queen of Atabyrion. She's white. I like this game, Lord Owen. The pieces are constantly shifting, but the consequences are real. It's more exciting than just playing Wizr. Do pieces only come off the board, or can they come back on?"

Owen grinned, pleased by the boy's quick mind. "I've seen both happen. Not only do the pieces affect the board, but the board is affected by our decisions. It helps very much, lad, that *you* can move the pieces. Why are we going *here* and not to Ploemeur?" he asked, indicating their destination.

Drew rubbed his mouth thoughtfully. "Because you ordered our navy sent to Ploemeur instead?"

The boy was bright. Owen was grateful he was trying so hard. Remembering how Ankarette used to praise him for following her teachings, he reached out and touched Drew's shoulder. "I'm glad you remembered. And what will Chatriyon do once the fleet arrives in the harbor to defend Brythonica?"

Drew looked at the board studiously. He was quiet for a moment, pondering deeply. Then he cocked his head. "Flee?"

Owen smiled smugly and leaned back. "Yes. That's what he always does. And when you capture the king, a new king will rise. As long as there is an heir, the game goes on."

◆　◆　◆

The first time Owen had ridden into Brythonica, it was to do the bidding of Severn Argentine and provoke the duchess into defying him. He could hardly believe how much things had changed in the short span of weeks since he'd left. He could still sense the magic hidden in the woods as he approached, the constant jostling in the saddle a normal, comforting feel. King Drew rode beside him, along with a retinue of knights from the king's household. The boy stared into the woods, his eyes narrowing.

"What are you looking at, my lord?" Owen asked him.

Drew turned back, frowning. "There is something in the woods."

"Can you feel it?"

The boy nodded slowly. "What is there?"

Owen wondered if the lad was beginning to show the first signs of being Fountain-blessed. In the legends, King Andrew had not possessed that ability, but he had surrounded himself by those who did. Curious.

As they rode into the lush lands of Brythonica, Owen's heart skittered with anticipation. He'd had much time to think as he'd battled his way here from Kingfountain. He was fretting about seeing Sinia again, but despite his nervousness, he was at peace with his decision.

As they came down the road, he saw two riders approaching from ahead. He recognized both men as heralds. One was his own, Farnes, and the other was Anjers, herald to the King of Occitania. Anjers looked miserable, his hair was askew instead of combed forward in the Occitanian style, and his armor was dashed in mud and grime.

As Owen and Drew reined in, they met the two heralds.

"My lord king," Farnes said with a beaming smile. "We have captured Chatriyon Vertus in the woods as he attempted to escape back to Pree. There were only twenty knights with him, and he was quickly apprehended. What is my lord's pleasure to do with him?"

Drew smiled at being addressed so formally.

"My lord," Anjers said with a desperate voice. "I am authorized to negotiate the ransom for my master. If you will release him immediately that he may return to his wife and child in Pree, he will grant you most generous terms. Please, my lord." Anjer's face twitched with emotion. "He is quite frightened. He fears being alone with this . . . butcher." He stared at Owen with hatred.

Drew looked to Owen for guidance. "It's your decision, my lord," Owen said softly. "I'm here to pay my respects to a far more important person than the King of Occitania."

Drew was silent for a moment, then he turned to Farnes. "Take him to Beestone castle under guard. I will deal with him when I return."

Anjer's expression crumpled and tears began to trickle down his cheeks as the humiliation of defeat closed in on him. Owen could feel the grating sensation of the Wizr board in his mind. The game would shift now. But it would not end.

◆　◆　◆

The crash of the surf on the sandy beach was a pleasant noise. The air held a salty tang, and a few seabirds squawked overhead as Owen climbed down the stone steps leading to Glass Beach. He had expected he would find Sinia there. It hadn't surprised him in the least when they'd arrived at the castle of Ploemeur only to find that she wasn't there. Owen had left Drew in the care of his own parents and sister, who had greeted the boy king warmly and kindly. They'd offered to provide him with a tour of the castle that would—Owen had insisted—last for several hours. Owen had not assigned anyone to look after the king. He didn't imagine it was even necessary.

The castle had graciously received the King of Ceredigion and thanked him effusively for the ships that had been sent to relieve the blockade. Drew had insisted on giving Owen credit for the strategy that had so effortlessly captured Chatriyon. In addition to soldiers, the ships had brought cattle and food to replenish what had been taken by the Occitanians during their invasion. Perhaps this was a first step toward a better understanding between Owen and the people of this duchy.

As Owen left the steps and his boots crunched into the sand, he spied a pair of sandals. Smiling to himself, he squatted to pick them up, arranging them in the crook of his finger. The breeze was warm and sunny and ruffled his hair pleasantly. There were two knights guarding the top of the steps, but no one else was on the beach. As he trudged through the sand, trying to see her, the sun shone off the water, blindingly bright.

As he came closer to the water's edge, the sand changed to the small beads of smooth glass. He stopped to scoop up a handful and toyed with them with his thumb before dumping the pile back down. Then he looked up and saw her. Sinia was circling a hulking boulder, but she came to a sudden stop at the sight of him crouching there. Her hand went to her breast and she started to tremble.

Owen felt a throb of love inside his chest that was almost painful. He rose and sauntered toward her, dangling the sandals out before him.

"You left these behind," he said with a light tone. A wave crashed nearby, creating a spume as it spread along the flat beach. It was about to reach her bare feet before it lost energy and began to recede.

Sinia approached, her eyes alight with hope, her mouth on the verge of a smile.

Owen tossed the sandals aside, walked up to her, and took her hands, holding them before him. "Sinia Montfort," he said softly, breathing her name like a prayer. "Will you be mine still? Will you let me kiss you as a husband should? Will you walk with me along this beach and teach me how to please you, how to woo you? Will you be mine from this day forth? My friend and my confidante, my lover and my wife, my companion and my solace. I'm so weary of being alone." He felt his confidence rattling, his heart nearly bursting. "Can you forgive my imperfections? My sharp words when we first met? Can you forgive me for being *tempted* to betray you? But I did not. Will you let me give you a soul so that you may be one with me, so that we may have children who are as beautiful as you are?" Owen sighed. "You are truly a blessing from the Fountain, and I feel *unworthy* to claim your affection. But may I claim it all the same? Will you consent to be my wife?"

Tears ran down her cheeks, and the smile she gave him was so radiant he thought he would break inside.

"Yes," she answered, then flung herself into his arms, hugging him so tightly it amazed him how her little fingers could inflict pain. He held her to him, stroking the softness of her hair, feeling her body so near.

He tipped up her chin and looked down at her face, at the longing in her sunshine eyes. He lowered his head, his mouth just barely above hers.

"*Nesh-ama*," he whispered before he kissed her mouth. The magic of the Fountain began to swell inside him. It rose like thunder, swelling and building and exploding inside him as his magic imbued her with a mortal soul, the breath of life.

He felt the next wave engulf their ankles, the sucking of the sand beneath their feet as it receded. She gasped with delight at the sensation, digging her fingers into his unruly hair. The magic filled her completely, and Owen felt his energy drain as it always did after giving the breath of life. He was falling, spent and helpless as a babe, but Sinia held him against her as he blacked out.

# CHAPTER
# FORTY-TWO

*Confession*

He awoke to the sensation of Sinia kissing his eyelids. He felt as exhausted as if he'd swum around the world. His head was in her lap, and he was stretched out on the beads of glass, soaking in the warmth of the sun and feeling quite drowsy and content.

Energy began to fill him as well as the magic of the Fountain. He had been drained completely, but he felt her sharing her reserves, uniting their magic together. To his amazement, he was quickly restored to his full strength, though hers was hardly diminished.

He blinked his eyes open, seeing the wind teasing golden strands of hair across her face. She brushed them aside and looked down at him with so much love and tenderness he felt unequal to it.

"You are beautiful," he murmured, reaching up and touching her lips. She kissed his fingertip.

"I've always loved you, Owen Kiskaddon," she confessed. "I saw this moment so many times in my visions. You loving me, *truly* loving me. When you first came to Ploemeur, I'll admit it was a disappointment." She smiled wryly at him. "But it was worth waiting for."

Owen smiled. He had rarely felt so languid and relaxed, and he utterly enjoyed being cradled against her. He lifted himself slowly and then pressed his ear to her bosom, listening against the sound of the surf for her heartbeat. There it was. She looked shyly at him, smiling, and then nodded.

"I am mortal now," she said. "Not every Ondine gets her wish. Few do, actually. But I'm one of the fortunate." She smoothed his hair over his ear.

Owen sat up higher and kissed her again, taking it slowly, enjoying it much more than their rushed, awkward kiss at the betrothal. He started to pull away, and he felt flush with pleasure when he realized she didn't want him to. "I'm embarrassed by my memory of our first kiss at St. Penryn. My apologies for not being more practiced."

She smiled knowingly. "You don't have to apologize for *that*."

Owen grinned. "I can imagine it was different for you as well," he added with a chuckle. "This was our *true* first kiss—the one you saw in your visions. That must have been very confusing for you, to know what would happen but not always how. Or when."

She nodded in agreement. "I fell in love with the possibility of you, Owen. How many men would jump into a river to save a child about to be pulled over the falls? How many men would forsake their first love?" Her eyes were suddenly wise and tender. She touched the side of his face. "It was painful to watch you go through it, Owen. Please know that."

He nodded and took her fingers and kissed her knuckles. "You've been quite aware of my pain, Sinia. In a way, you've borne it alongside me." He rubbed his thumb across her fingers. "I'm heartbroken still. Not because I chose you, but because I'm sorry for Evie." He sighed. "This will be so painful for her. She's still my friend, and I want her to be happy, but it didn't feel right. I knew it was my choice to make." He looked in her eyes. "I chose *you*."

Sinia threw her arms around his neck, hugging him to her. They held each other for a long while, and it was soothing to Owen's heart and his wounds to be close to her. There were tears on her lashes when she released him. An encroaching wave came near but not near enough to soak them.

"You're not immune to the water anymore, should we move farther up?" he suggested.

She shook her head. "No, I love the feel of it. I want to take a long, warm bath. I want to swim in a river. Now that you've made me complete, I can enjoy the things that have been denied me for too long." She smoothed some hair behind her ear. "I have something else to confess, my love. If you'll let me."

"Of course," Owen said, looking into her eyes.

"We learn much through suffering," she said. "But I think what we learn most is who we really are. I've known the true you for some time, Owen. But you were like a chick struggling to escape its shell. Now you're free to grow and become what the Fountain intended you to become. You may have thought what the Fountain forced you to endure was unpleasant, even cruel. But now you know yourself. Now you know what you would have chosen without any foreknowledge of the consequences. That's why I *couldn't* tell you, Owen. I knew what would happen when you intervened in the Wizr game. I knew it would trigger the events leading to Iago's shipwreck." She looked almost apologetic. "But I had to let it happen so that you would know yourself. And the other outcomes would have been much worse. But the story isn't over." She looked down at her lap, and Owen felt a little uneasiness creep over him.

"What?" he pressed.

She looked up at him. "I saw the shipwreck in my vision. All the crew were killed. Only Iago survived. In the vision, he was wearing a brooch on his cloak. A brooch with the raven symbol. It was a sign to me that I needed to *give* it to him. And so I did, ere he departed. He did not drown, Owen. The brooch is a talisman against it. He was washed up on shore days later and discovered by a fisherman and his wife. They're tending his injuries, for he was buffeted against the rocks. He can't remember his name right now, but he will. And then he will return to Edonburick, and he will find his wife and children waiting for him."

Owen stared at her, his eyes widening. His first reaction was shock, followed by an all-encompassing sense of relief. "Thank the Fountain!" He could not fathom how he would have felt if he'd gone to Evie right away. He clenched his fist and pressed it against his mouth, feeling as if he had narrowly escaped a horrible fate. For both of them.

Sinia stroked his hair. "You can't tell her," she whispered. "She will find out in due course."

"And you've always known?" he gasped out.

She nodded, and the heaviness of the gesture revealed the burden of the secret.

"I'm so grateful I chose as I did," Owen said.

"Not more grateful than *I* am," she said, taking his hand and squeezing it. "Owen, I've seen her reunion with Iago. I've seen her joy when she learns the news. I wouldn't rob her of that moment for all the world." She paused, and a small smile tipped up her lips. "I've seen friendship between our families too. Between our children and theirs. But I cannot reveal all that I've seen. There are troubles ahead as well as behind."

"I hate to think of how she's suffering. She lost her father when she was Genevieve's age." He looked at her. "As you did yourself. I will trust in your judgment, in your gifts. If you feel it is better that she learns the truth in its due time."

Sinia sighed. "I do. Her influence will be strongly felt in Ceredigion for generations. The past has a way of coming back, you know." She smiled at him lovingly and smoothed his hair. Then she ran her finger along his smooth cheek. "Thank you for shaving before you came to me."

Owen shrugged. "That's another thing about you I figured out on my own without you telling me," he said. "I can be quick to observe when I put my mind to it."

She nodded and kissed the edge of his jaw. "I like it much better this way."

"If my lady wishes it," he replied gallantly. "But I do have a question for you, Sinia. One that I cannot figure out on my own. I *think* I'm right. I am right every now and then."

"Indeed," she replied, putting her hands in her lap. "What would you ask me?"

He leaned back on his elbows, feeling them sink a little into the glass beads, and crossed his boots. "It has to do with the Wizr Myrddin."

"Very well, what would you ask me?"

"According to the legends, he fell in love with a Lady of the Fountain. She did not requite his love. He taught her all his tricks, the words of *power*, and then she imprisoned him in a cave of stone. It was after that that King Andrew was defeated and the Wizr set went missing."

"What is your question?" she asked, tilting her head and giving him an encouraging smile.

"Well, my question is whether Myrddin is still alive. I think he's trapped in the grove in the forest, with the silver dish that makes it rain. Now that King Andrew has returned, does it not coincide that Myrddin must return as well?"

Sinia seemed to have anticipated his question. She did not look surprised by it at all. "He is trapped beneath the stones. Some of my father's ancestors tried to move the stones, but no team of horses was strong enough. The boulders are too massive. Even the Fountain's magic is not strong enough to lift them."

Owen looked at her with a smirk of self-confidence.

"What are you thinking?" she asked him.

"You mean you cannot read my mind?" he teased.

She shook her head. "I've never had that talent."

"I think I know a way it can be opened," he replied. "It's one of the reasons I brought the king with me to Ploemeur. Have you had any visions that say we *shouldn't* release Myrddin?"

She looked curious and interested. "None at all."

Owen sat up. "Do you think he'll be angry for being imprisoned so long? If he's even alive?"

"Oh, I know he's alive," Sinia said. "He's trapped between the mortal world and the Deep Fathoms. He does not age where he lives. If we succeed in saving him, he could bring back knowledge that was lost long ago."

Owen had been considering it. "I'm hoping he would be grateful to those who freed him."

"Wizrs have been known to be generous," Sinia said.

He took her hand in his and helped her to her feet. They stood at the edge of the beach, staring at the crashing waves, hand in hand.

"Shall we?" he asked eagerly, nodding toward the rush of waves.

Sinia's smile was all the coaxing he needed.

# EPILOGUE

The day was cool and mild, the air thick with the fragrance of trees. A few ravens croaked overhead from the branches as Owen, Sinia, and Drew carefully made their way through the maze toward the sound of trickling water.

After passing the gorse, they reached the stone plinth to which the silver bowl was fixed with a chain. Memories clashed inside Owen's mind—a battle had raged in this place where he had defeated Marshal Roux and become the protector of these woods. This time he felt safe and confident as he walked into the hallowed grove. He was welcome here—the forest recognized him as its new master.

"What is this place?" Drew asked, staring at the massive boulders lodged together against the backdrop of a stony hill. The oak tree's haggard branches were twisted at crooked angles. The leaves had grown back, and were draped with clumps of mistletoe that caught Owen's eye. He sensed magic in the tree. Just as before, water was coming from its roots, trickling down the lichen-speckled boulders.

"A place of ancient magic," Sinia answered, her voice hushed to match the solemnity of the place. "The Montforts have been its guardians for centuries."

Drew gazed up at the tree in awe, his expression wise beyond his years. "It feels familiar. Have I been here before?"

"There are many memories in this place," Sinia answered, setting a gentle hand on his shoulder.

Owen hefted the large shield and slung his arm through the strap. The shield was emblazoned with the sigil he had seen throughout the palace. It was of two faces, opposing each other. It was a mark of the Wizr board, Sinia had explained to him—a sign that Brythonica was one of the places set on the board to hold in balance the barrier between water and land.

"When I pour the water on the table," Owen said, taking a few steps forward before looking back. "There will be a loud peal of thunder. Be ready for it. Then a storm will rage around us. It cannot hurt you while we are near. Don't be afraid."

Drew's eyes were deep and serious, and a little afraid, but he nodded with the encouragement. Owen glanced at Sinia, meeting her gaze to see if there was any look of warning. She said nothing to encourage or discourage him.

Owen hiked up to the edge of the table and then picked up the bowl. He felt the power of the Fountain flow through him. It was like trudging through a river, feeling the force of its current push him from behind. He was not trying to walk crosswise against the current, but with it. The magic swelled and strained inside him.

Reaching down, Owen carried the bowl to the small waterfall streaming down the face of the boulder beneath the tree. He placed it under the flow and watched it fill and then brought it carefully back down onto the plinth, the chain rattling as it scraped along the rocks. Excitement churned inside of Owen. His plan would work. He was certain of it.

Standing over the plinth, he turned the bowl over and splashed the water onto it. Then he set the bowl down and retrieved the shield just as the sky cracked open with thunder, sending a percussive boom that made Drew flinch and cover his ears. Just as Owen reached his betrothed and his king, the rain began to pound down on them, coming in fat, heavy drops that immediately turned into a torrent. Owen held up the shield and Sinia and Drew sheltered beneath it. The boy's eyes were wide with fear as the storm slammed into them, the rain turning into sleet and then rock-sized hail.

Sinia lifted her arm and helped Owen support the weight of the shield, her eyes widening with excitement at the ferocity of the storm. The shield took a battering and Owen's arm throbbed under the weight of it, but the magic of the storm was parting around him. After a few terrible moments passed, Drew's frown of fear turned into a grin of ease.

The storm stopped as quickly as it had come.

Owen remembered what happened next, and it followed that same order. The leaves of the oak tree, which had been torn unceremoniously from the branches in the storm, swirled eddies down the hill and away from the plinth. Then birds appeared in the branches and began to sing, and their song was so full, so rich, so heartbreakingly lovely that Owen lowered the shield, and the three of them listened to the music. The final notes were a cry of loveliness that made Owen swallow the rising thickness in his throat. Tears danced on Sinia's lashes. It was a familiar song to her, yet it moved her still.

Owen turned to Drew.

"Now it is your turn," he told the boy. "Take out the crown."

The boy quickly unfastened the buckles and opened the flap of the leather satchel he wore around his neck. Wedged inside was the hollow crown, the symbol of office for the King of Ceredigion.

"Do you remember what I told you?" Owen asked the boy.

Drew nodded and removed the crown from the satchel. Owen's heart was beating faster now, his mouth suddenly dry.

"Bring the winter," Owen said softly, gazing at the tree and then at the stone.

The boy held the crown before him and then lifted it onto his head. There was magic in it, and the crown adjusted its size to fit the boy's head. The tines along the fringe were battered and ancient. Owen felt the magic throb and swell as the boy settled it onto his head.

Drew stared at the boulders, his eyes suddenly fierce with determination.

A cold wind swept through the grove, rattling the branches. Puffs of steam came from their mouths. Sinia started to shiver, and Owen pulled her close, his arm around her shoulder. His other hand rested on Drew's. Little crackling, tinkling sounds started as the water in the grove began to freeze. Frost appeared on the boulders, glistening in the sunlight. The cold pervaded the grove so deeply it turned the limbs of the trees rigid. The birds flapped away, seeking shelter.

Staring at the boulders, Owen watched the designs of frost zigzag across the faces. His ears and nose began to tingle with the chill. The boy's gaze was transfixed on the boulders in front of him. He did not tremble or close his eyes. He was mesmerized by the magic flowing through him. Creaks and groans began to rumble.

Owen held his breath. He felt Sinia reach up and rest her hand atop his.

"Colder," Owen breathed softly. The hairs on the back of his neck stiffened.

The boy stared at the rocks, his mouth turning down into a little frown as he concentrated. The air was so cold it was like breathing knives.

Then there was a cracking sound.

The main boulder behind the tree split in half and tumbled to the side. A jagged series of seams and splits showed where the water had been carving inside it for ages. Owen jolted when the boulder broke away, moving backward involuntarily in case it tumbled toward them.

Beyond the rock, a black cave lay open. There was a sigh as the breeze found it and began to explore the edges.

Drew stepped forward, drawn to the gap in the stone. His eyes were narrowing, his expression grave and intense.

"Do you hear it?" the boy asked in a hushed tone.

Owen did not. He looked at Sinia in confusion. She shook her head no.

"What do you hear?" Owen asked.

"Whispers," the boy replied. He stepped cautiously toward the riven boulder.

"You can hear them, boy?" said a gruff voice with a strange accent from within the cave. "Bless me if you can. Bless me indeed. It's still daylight out?" There was a grunt and a stifled groan, and then the shape of an older man with a crooked staff was silhouetted against the darkness. "And who are these *pethets* you brought with you, eh?"

# AUTHOR'S NOTE

I still remember sitting on my bed, talking with my oldest daughter about the plot of the Kingfountain series. I told her that Owen and Evie weren't going to get together in the end and I explained why and told her about Sinia. I told her some of my readers were going to hate me for doing it. I suspected she might be one of them, though as her father, I knew she'd eventually forgive me. "Go for it," she advised. "If that's the story you need to tell. Go for it. But please give Evie a happy ending."

This is the story I've been wanting to tell for many years. It was inspired by a dream I had long ago. The dream was about a man in his early twenties who was sarcastic and ill-tempered and really good at insulting people. He was sent by his father, the king, to a neighboring realm to demand the princess there marry him or it would spell war between their kingdoms. In my dream, the princess sacrificed herself to save her country and willingly married the nobleman. Because of her goodness, she had the power to change him and make him something better. As a result, this young man fought against his father the king.

That's the inspiration for *The King's Traitor*. I also want to give credit for the shipwreck idea to one of my early readers Robin, who predicted after *The Thief's Daughter* that Iago and Evie would be shipwrecked and he would die, leaving Owen and Evie the chance to get together. This isn't exactly what she had in mind, but I really liked how it played into the story.

I love reading biographies. I read one once about the first American president, George Washington, and learned that he had a first love whom he did not end up marrying. So did Abraham Lincoln. If you look through the nooks and crannies of history, you'll find plenty of instances of this. While I prefer stories where the main characters do get together in the end, sometimes things just don't work out that way. So if you are one of those readers who were disappointed by Owen's choice of partner, I beg your pardon. This was the story that has been metamorphosing inside me for years.

And it's not over. As I wrote this novel, I saw more light farther down the tunnel. The setting was obviously inspired by the Arthurian legends. As I read many of the classic older texts, I kept seeing recurring themes, even though the details often differed. The whole mythology around Our Lady was inspired by the myths of the Lady of the Lake. The prophecy of the Dreadful Deadman wasn't invented. Europeans in the late-fifteenth and early-sixteenth centuries believed that King Arthur would return someday and defend England. Henry VII named his firstborn son Arthur to invoke that legend. He claimed to be Arthur incarnated himself when he fought Richard III at Bosworth Field. The legend of the Dreadful Deadman is a fascinating historical tidbit. I based my version of the Arthurian plot on the writings contained in the Mabinogion. That's where I learned about Sir Owain who betrayed the Lady of the Fountain. That's where the silver bowl and the magic hailstorm had their source. And it's also the origin of the magic chess set that belonged to King Arthur.

I hope you've enjoyed this new world. I have a few more stories to tell before I'm done with it. I think the children of these main characters need a turn on stage.

And if a movie is ever made about this series, I politely request Richard Armitage to play King Severn.

# ACKNOWLEDGMENTS

I would like to thank many who helped this series in numerous ways. First, to my sister Emily who gets to read my chapters each week and provide feedback. It must be sweet torture having to read my writing in spurts. Also, thanks to my wonderful early readers: Robin, Shannon, Karen, and Sunil. To my amazing editorial team for their enthusiasm and influence! That would be Jason Kirk, Courtney Miller, Angela Polidoro, and Wanda Zimba. We make a good team, and I appreciate you all!

# ABOUT THE AUTHOR

Photo © Kim Bills

Jeff Wheeler took an early retirement from his career at Intel in 2014 to become a full-time author. He is, most importantly, a husband and father, and a devout member of his church. He is occasionally spotted roaming among the oak trees and granite boulders in the hills of California or in any number of the state's majestic redwood groves. He is the author of The Covenant of Muirwood Trilogy, The Legends of Muirwood Trilogy, the Whispers from Mirrowen Trilogy, and the Landmoor Series. He is also the founder of *Deep Magic: the E-zine of Clean Fantasy and Science Fiction* (www.deepmagic.co).